AMELIA

Jenn LeBlanc

THE DUKE AND THE BARON

BOOK TWO IN THE LORDS OF TIME SERIES

Dedication

This book is dedicated to every person who
ever thought they were less because their brain
didn't quite work the same as those around them.

You are not broken.
You are not damaged.
You are amazing, and you are unique.

It is also dedicated to all of those who loved Rox and Perry, and
who have waited very patiently for my ever-elusive Twitchy to
surface.

Finally it is dedicated to all of my lovely daughters, each of
whom is on a grand adventure and will hopefully go far.
I love you all.

my thanks :

Assistant for allll the things: Kati Rodriguez (you can't have her)

Hair and makeup: Monika Graf, Cloud 9 Boulder (stunning work)

Copy editor: Joyce Lamb

Delilah Marvelle: one set of beautiful brass balls... in my pocket

Derek Hutchins: very important insight into a touchy subject.

Vertical assist: Elizabeth Haysmont's scaffolding (many thanks)

Early critique: Kristin Anders, The Romantic Editor

Becky Stine: You bestowed my hero with a beautiful name,
                    (even if copyedits were annoying)

Pamela Clare, Melinda Piñon, Tammy Myers-Clarke, Kati Rodriguez, Elise Rome, Maíre Claremont, Delilah Marvelle, Rita Jett, Tina Dowds, Tilly Greene; your feedback, proofreading, nudging and love for #Twitchy was invaluable.

My lunch ladies (yeah, we need a better nickname for that) Pamela Clare, Thea Harrison, Courtney Milan, Elise Rome, Hillary Seidl, Libby Rice (Maíre we miss you!) for so much support and spirit.

Ann S. Brady, LPC, your willingness to read my novel and diagnose my lovely Twitchy was of paramount importance to my ensuring I respected her illness (for lack of a better term) and her beauty. Thank you.

credits:

Amelia:
Britt Cormack

Charles:
Tristan Edwards

Hugh:
Alex Kirkland

Louisa:
Stephanie Klinger

Maitland:
Ava Dalgaard

a note about the illustrations:

These illustrations are meant to be
a work unto themselves.

They aren't meant to depict the scenes with perfect accuracy in setting, costuming or design. They're meant to accompany the text and evoke the emotions of the scenes in the same way the words do.

More of a companion than a direct visual translation.

Certainly you will notice discrepancies between the scene and details in the images, but that's the nature of creation, some things don't work visually when they do work literally.

Thank you for understanding and I hope you enjoy this illustrated version of Amelia.

Hugs n' smooches,

Jenn

ONE

It always started with a twitch, because that meant her mind was racing,
like a child caught in a flood, swirling, hands flung out to catch anything solid
with which to stop the rush.

What followed was a darkness that closed in from the edges
until she was blind and in a panic.
He'd seen her rage in fear during that closing in.
It terrified her and, truth be told, him as well.

If the edges descended, it was too late—she was lost.
So he always attempted to bring her back from that edge before she fell…
for he was always afraid that the next time would be the last time,
the one from which she never returned.

1881

London, England

Amelia stood. It was the simplest explanation, really. She did nothing else. Her back straight, her hands held gently—not too tight—just below her waist. Her reticule dangled from one wrist, resting just behind her hands. Her skirt did not sway—as she did not twitch.

She blinked.

The room was full.

Nobody looked her way.

She corrected the angle of her chin because it had been too severe. She lowered her chin slightly and tilted her head gently to the left to balance the flowers in her hair because her girl had angled them to the right.

She smiled gently—*there's that word again*—and shook her head. *Gently,* she thought. *Gentlygentlygently.* Amelia's shoulders drooped at the thought, so she lifted and rolled them back gently—*no, unnoticeably. Yes, I rolled them unnoticeably, not gently. Well…gently as well, but more unnoticeably than gently. Or perhaps so gently as to be unnoticed? Perhaps that's it.*

She twitched.

Amelia wished she knew what was wrong with her. If she could give a name to this malady, perhaps it would lose its power over her.

That's a ridiculous thought. The fact was, to give it a name would be to give it more power—to the people who would diagnose her, to those who would judge her, to the doctors, physicians and others who would determine she was unhealthy, unworthy…unwell. Power to those who would then control her future, and that of her entire family with her. Giving a name to her illness was an impossibility. She had to remain hidden.

"Amelia." Her name rolled across her senses like a heavy fog. *He should not be using my common name. I am not common. He is not common. It is not done. What if…what if someone hears?*

"You," she whispered, and Amelia's eyes darted to and fro to ensure their conversation was private as he reached for her hand. "Endsleigh," she said just a bit louder to deflect any complaints that she'd not responded to his greeting. *That would be improper, unheard of. A terrible cut.*

Amelia looked down. Hugh had her hand, and her heart skipped a beat as her breath increased as if to make up for it. It was her right hand that he held, *as is proper,* and her reticule hung straight down. It did not catch on her gloved hand or her gown. She'd chosen this particular reticule because once she'd chosen one with cute little baubles and shiny beads and the beads and baubles had snagged her gown and—

"Might I have the honor of this dance, my lady?" Hugh interrupted the train wreck of her thoughts.

Amelia's eyes widened as she shook her head quickly to bring herself back to the ballroom, to the man, to the hand on her hand—certainly for an inappropriate amount of time by now. But his hand was warm and as he tightened his grip...she could breathe.

Hugh waited more patiently than he ought. He was regal in his black and white, his broad shoulders enhanced by the stark lines. Amelia took another breath. It was a concerted effort until—*cinnamon and rich cigar, perhaps a hint of brandy*—the knot in her belly loosened just a touch. She looked up to the all-too-familiar whiskey-colored eyes and forced a smile. "Yes, my lord, yes. The honor."

Amelia's hand slipped from his, and her breath caught. Her eyes drifted as she checked the ballroom to see who was watching, but the answer was more simple than "who." The answer was everyone, and she knew it before she looked, as well as she knew the chill on her skin was caused by the trickle of sweat rolling slowly down her spine, pausing every so often like a tease as the bead of sweat rounded a small bone then continued on its merry way.

She looked past him to see that the eyes of the *ton* were on her, but were not yet narrowed.

Hugh took her hand, this time her left, which was good, because her left hand was rather cold and the other was a bit warm now. The warmth of his hand on her hand—*or rather my hand in his warm hand*—called her back to the ballroom.

"Bollocks." Amelia's eyes went wide as she heard the word come from her mouth so softly she could only hope it made it just as far as her own ears. But when she heard Hugh clear his throat—*more loudly than was seemly*—she knew that was not to be.

He smiled at her gently—*yes, gently, it had to be gently*—as he turned her and rested his hand, his other hand—*that first warm hand*—on her back. Very *low* on her back. The heat sank through the layers of her gown and stays and underthings and straight through her skin to her soul.

Breathe.

As much as her pulse raced, her body softened, sinking into the safety of his embrace. Warmth. Security. It rankled at times that her body calmed to him even when her mind wished to revolt. If she could have been constrained beyond the boundaries of her corset, she might have been okay—but that was not within the realm of possibility here in this room.

Amelia shivered. Logically, she knew she wasn't cold, because the room was brimming with bodies. *Bodies with eyes and opinions and all of them on me. Breathe. Damn you,* she thought, then twitched and sent the thought from her head. She glanced up from below her eyelashes to see if he'd noticed, and he had—*of course he had. How could he not, after all? His hands are on me—they are ON me. Breathe. Damn me!*

She twitched again and his fingers tensed as his hands relaxed. *Odd that—that his hand could attempt to let go as his fingers tensed to...to what?* She knew she shouldn't be seen dancing with him. Not tonight, of all nights, because Charles was here. Somewhere.

She needed to get away, before Charles saw her dancing with Hugh. She looked up again, and her eyes went wide as they caught Hugh's. Then his eyes narrowed. *Oh...oh no.*

Hugh knew without doubt she was preparing to bolt like a spring lamb—awkwardly and without proper balance—and yet he was not prepared to let her get out of this as easily as with an inopportune and well-placed twitch. She was not going to run from the room. For one, he was bigger than she.

Hugh relaxed incrementally, lulling her, letting her believe he was unaware of her intention.

Damn me. His grip tightened, and he pulled her toward him through the corner—a warning of sorts.

"Amelia..." he managed through a clenched jaw. What he wished to say was, *Do not make me regret this.* But that would have been too harsh, too much for her delicate state to handle at the moment.

They sailed down the far side of the ballroom, his arms so tense he knew they would cramp that night. Hugh worked toward relaxing his features—at the very least. Because were this to be effective, he had to appear happy to be pulling her through the turns. Hugh had to give her the restraint she required, without providing a show for the *ton* gossips to flourish on.

Damn me twice. Why? Hugh watched the emotions fade and pulse across her features like so many birds flocking from a predator.

She twitched.

Damn me twofold.

He stumbled.

God in heaven.

The song ended.

Praise be.

Hugh tightened his hand on hers—*we are not yet finished here*—then turned them toward the balcony bordering the ballroom over the gardens. Hugh shook his head to stay her and moved her hand to his elbow but did not release his grip.

"You've no idea the effect you have, do you?" Amelia said nearly *sotto voce*, her smile solidly in place. "You've no idea the power you wield so easily."

Hugh grunted, then checked to make sure the sound was not so loud as to draw more attention, and politely raised his hand to clear his throat. Again. Certainly tomorrow he would receive all manner of gifts and cards to usher a speedy recovery from whatever malady they believed him to have—*if they only knew.*

In fact, he *was* aware of his "power," as she chose to call it. But his heart rent to see her in these situations, where she could so easily be ruined for all the world. It was a very precarious position. In the wrong hands, she could easily end up in Bedlam, never to return to the world. Her mother didn't understand, and her father…well. He believed the duke was either entirely too ill to notice much beyond himself, or much too calculating to care what would happen to his daughter, who was currently charged with securing her own future and that of her mother. Hugh thought it terribly cruel, but it was the way of the world. There was nothing to be done about it. Her illness was not compatible with the pressure of the *ton*.

If only to satisfy her, he kicked up a smile on one side and knew the minute she saw it—because she twitched.

The strange thing was that no thought had come before the twitch, as was common. Hugh's hand tightened on hers as he handed her through the narrow doorway to the balcony, then followed without letting go. If she could just breathe.

Damn me twice. But his hands are on me. On me, touching me, on me.

Her arm jerked and managed to dislodge him, and she turned, her eyes wide. This was her chance to run. She shifted left, only to find the outside wall of the ballroom, and when she looked right, the high balustrade blocked her, the rest of the space taken by that giant ominous beast of a man who insisted on rescuing her.

Damn him again. She huffed and stomped her foot. "Must you be so pervasive? Must you be so insistent? And why?" she whispered viciously to the floor before he could answer, as her eyes shifted around the balcony.

She knew he smiled.

Damn him twice.

She turned away from him toward the gardens, watching the moonlight paint the ground with patterns from the oldest trees in the county. She'd no idea how long she stood there before the air shifted behind her, and his hand brushed her neck.

"Amelia."

The anger left her then like a muddied body diving into a clear blue lake—a cleansing. She closed her eyes. "Hugh." But his name sounded more like "you" on a breath. She absorbed the calming effect of his very presence. *Why do I fight this?*

"Yes, Amelia mine, none other than I. I only wish to help. You can put an end to my incessant pestering with one word. Should you choose to."

Amelia could feel the words as he spoke against her neck, then the absence of heat when he stepped back. When she turned, he was gone, as though he'd never been there.

Perhaps just a memory.

You.

A powerful sob threatened to rend her stays, and she squeezed herself tightly as though to prevent herself from falling into a million tiny pieces on the balcony. The truth was, she couldn't give him the word he wanted. She loved him, true, but her father would never agree to a match with a mere baron, particularly a baron with no income to speak of—no matter her dire circumstance.

"Ma Belle!" her mother shrilled. "You should not be out here alone."

Amelia turned to see her overbright mother traipsing toward her with the air of grace and the intent of mastery. No wonder Hugh had disappeared so quickly.

"Yes, Mother." *Improper, improper, improper. How many noticed, how many wondered, how many remarked that he left me here?*

"Back inside now," her mother singsonged with saccharine sweetness in her fading French accent. "They're waiting for you to return. Where is that smile?"

Amelia looked down and pulled from the depths of her toes the most brilliant smile possible, then strode lightly back toward the ballroom.

Hugh watched as Amelia stepped through the narrow door, and her very skin reacted, tightening as though she'd walked through a cloud. He saw her joints stiffen slightly, her fingers curl around her reticule, her chin rise just a touch. His head moved back and forth, not enough for a shake but plenty enough to show discontent.

Hugh could see her awareness of him ease her, relax the muscles between the blades of her shoulders. She dropped them slightly and allowed herself to float across the room, away from him and toward the man who would be her husband.

Damn me forever.

He turned to leave and nearly ran down a young lady.

"Pardon me—"

"No, my lord, I'm entirely at fault," the girl said. She couldn't have been more than eighteen and in her first, possibly second, season. He noticed a woman watching them to his left. The Countess Rigsby. Hugh was never one for the young chits put out every year because he preferred women with some experience, some…*seasoning*. He closed his eyes and groaned inwardly so as not to further fluster the child before him. He took her hand, as she'd been placed in his path, and bowed over it.

"The Lord Endsleigh, at your service."

She curtsied. "Thank you, my lord, I am Miss Rigsby," she replied with a shy smile.

He released her hand and took a step back. He considered her. As the charge of the Countess Rigsby, this could be nothing but trouble, particularly as it seemed she wasn't merely a charge, but a relation. Lady Rigsby was a gossip of the worst sort and tended to trap gentlemen into marriages for her daughters, nieces—anyone put in her charge. And many girls had been placed in her care for the season, because she was ever so successful. Hugh found it the worst sort of irony that her family tended to produce naught but girls, and by the lot of them as well.

"Miss…*Maitland* Rigsby?" he asked carefully. Her eyes widened, and she nodded stiffly. He closed his eyes momentarily to consider his next step, because he knew, now, who she was—and just how delicate. He determined the best course of action was to remove himself, as expediently as possible.

"It has been delightful to make your acquaintance. However, I was just on my way—"

"Why, Lord Endsleigh, I wasn't aware you'd been made known to my niece," Lady Rigsby said from behind him. Her tenor rankled, and he squared his shoulders.

"We had not, previously, been introduced, no, but we managed well enough after I nearly tripped over her," he said, perhaps not as politely as he should have, as Lady Rigsby rounded him to stand next to the girl. She shied, and his heart sank. Hugh wasn't sure whether it was a game meant to pull at his honor, or whether the girl was as much a victim of her aunt as the lady obviously hoped he would be. "She's a delightful *young* lady, however. You should be proud," Hugh said more politely. *He* was rather proud at just how politely, considering.

"Well, perhaps a dance? Miss Rigsby is quite popular this evening, but I'm sure she has one dance available…for you." Lady Rigsby's smile was toxic as it sank past his guard.

Hugh was not about to be trapped, but he didn't wish to damage this girl in public with a refusal. He also knew the kind of gossip this woman could start, and he certainly didn't need an enemy in her, particularly with Amelia in such a precarious position. A fact he was certain the lady was full aware of.

Hugh nodded stiffly as he watched Amelia remove from the ballroom on the arm of her duke. If only he'd been paying more attention, he could easily have avoided this and been gone by now. Instead, he took Miss Rigsby's hand and led her to the dance floor.

Amelia knew the moment Hugh quit watching because her skin tightened. *This is not going to end well.* She closed her eyes but for a moment, then lifted her chin defiantly to greet her intended. She could not give a thought to her friend, the boy she grew up with, the man who would forever hold her secrets. The sole light in her darkness.

It was wholly inappropriate, a man other than her husband privy to her innermost thoughts. Her body—*no, but that's not what theirs was about, was it? Was it? Was it?* Amelia closed her eyes. She needed to concentrate and, as if to remind her, she received a sharp jab to the rib.

"Amelia Marie!" her mother whispered. The woman's face did not shift, as though no word had been spoken. Her mother didn't seem to understand that her idea of handling the "situation" was about the least helpful thing of all.

Amelia widened her eyes to fend off the tears, and when they glistened, she hoped Charles would think it from happiness. She saw him then, through the crowd, speaking with the inimitable Duke of Pembroke-by-the-Sea. Her father.

If he'd not been born a duke, we might have been happy, Amelia thought.

Amelia shook off that thought as her mother clucked her tongue. She'd not seen Charles in nearly a year, but it seemed that this had been the year when everything had changed about him. He was more than recognizable, even though he was no longer the shy boy she remembered from their youth.

Charles turned toward her, his blue eyes searching the room, she knew for her. When he found her, his eyes smiled. Remarkable, that, as his mouth never moved. A full head taller than the whole of the ballroom, Charles was not merely a presence now, but a reckoning.

He'd grown into the gangly limbs that seemed to be more of a hindrance than help when trying to keep up with her and Hugh at Pembroke. Charles's appearance seemed at odds with the overly agreeable personality she remembered, and yet she could tell by the look in his eyes now that to misjudge him would mean a quick end.

Jackson and Endsleigh. Jacks and Ender. Charles and Hugh. Hugh had always been the light to her darkness, even outwardly, Hugh was the light and Charles the dark. Charles's liquid brown eyes, Hugh's bright as the sea. Charles's deep, thick hair, and Hugh's longer sun-kissed blonde. It was nearly humorous, the differences between the two.

She always wanted to reach first for Charles's smooth hair, but she simply could not, of course. She felt the want in the tingle in her fingers, an itch she could not quite scratch. She wanted to touch, to feel, to explore Charles. Whereas Hugh, she wanted to laugh with, chase, sink into.

Her father took her hand, and the contact startled her. She hadn't realized she was already here in the circle, because her mind, as it did, had wandered. She looked down to her father and softened instantly. He seemed so small in his wheelchair, a rug across his knees to prevent a chill to his worn bones.

His eyebrows pinched ever so slightly. "My dear, might I present the Duke of Castleberry. Of course you know of him." He turned to Charles, eyebrows raised with a smile.

And of course she did, of course she knew him. Or, more specifically, knew *of* him, because she didn't know this Charles, the one who now towered over her, the one who seemed to look straight through her. But she wanted to. This night had been planned, set up and determined for years now, and all that time she had done nothing but look forward to the reality of it. Now that it was upon her, she was frightened.

Charles nodded easily, his eyes never shifting from her. "My lady, it's an honor."

Amelia's heart trembled at the deep baritone of his voice—something she didn't remember—and she brought her hand to him slowly. Charles took that hand and bowed over it quickly. Her other hand pressed to her belly, attempting to constrain the loose feeling that once again threatened to spill.

"Your Grace." She smiled when the title sounded strange on her tongue. He'd grown into, and inherited, his title, but all she could see was Jacks, the awkward boy who'd followed her around during those young summers. "I'm certain the honor is mine," she added as joyfully and as full of smiles as she could muster, curtsying slowly, gracefully, carefully. "I was sorry to hear of your mother." From the corner of her eye, she saw her own mother's eyes widen and her smile freeze.

Charles released Amelia's hand and stepped back. As was proper. Not because of her statement, she was sure. He could not be seen to be standing too closely, that was all. Charles was nothing if not full of graciousness and propriety.

"Thank you." His voice was nearly a whisper.

The strain of music picked up yet again, and her mother bumped her elbow. "Your Grace, I believe my daughter has been saving this next dance for you." Amelia thought her mother's smile was bound to cleave her face clean in two, rather saw it happening, and Amelia's eyes strained as she stared, expectantly, for the first crack.

Charles turned to her mother quickly, drawing all attention with him, as Earth to the sun, his smile tight. If for no other reason, Amelia decided then, she could love him because he measured the intent of her mother rather quickly.

"Perhaps some refreshment and a turn around the room, my lady?" Charles turned back to her, bringing her gaze with him. "I find I'm not much for dancing this evening."

"By all means, Your Grace, as you please." She smiled as she hazarded a glance at her mother—who was actively suppressing a frown.

Because, of course, a dance with a duke—and not just *any* duke but the Duke of Castleberry—would solidify her position. Not a soul would dare speak out about her after that—but a turn around the ballroom would have to do...for now.

A

Beyond being taken with his future bride—if he could call her that—he was absolutely intrigued. Charles knew beyond reason that if he were to wed her, his life would be more interesting.

Charles remembered all too well the girl he first met so many years ago. Full of spit and vinegar and laughter. He could not quite reconcile that with the woman she'd grown into, the one the ladies of the *ton* whispered of behind their fans. But that was of little concern to him. *Ton* gossip was old hat, something he'd never bothered with. Charles could see the movements, the odd-placed tics, and could not quite figure why she shivered often, but her actions called to an extreme sense of protection.

Stunning as she was, he knew she believed herself to be unworthy of the attentions paid and, in some sense, she was. The only true attention received from the *ton* was a great disdain for her awkwardness and a jealousy that, due to her position, they could not, under any circumstance, call attention to it. Instead, they waited, they stared, they laughed privately, and they said to themselves what not a single one of them dared to utter aloud—not even to their closest confidants—but they all knew: She was strange.

Odd.

Different.

Regardless of her delicate nose, her bow-shaped mouth, and her viridescent eyes. Irrelevant that she had the most vibrant smile and impossibly bright and luminescent hair that he wanted spilling across his hands. Inconsequential that he had been in want of her since the first moment he'd drawn breath in her presence more than ten years past—beautiful, exciting, laughing and playful.

Pointless that he saw these things above all else. Because he knew that she could not yet trust him. Not a stone's throw, not a toe. She trusted Ender. That much was obvious from the dance they'd already shared tonight. That much was obvious from the summers he'd spent attempting to keep pace with them. That much was obvious from the times Ender had been allowed in her presence—and Charles had not.

That much was obvious from the paste smile she had carefully set upon her lips now. Charles shifted uncomfortably.

"Your Grace, are you well?" she asked quietly, so no one would hear. She might make the perfect duchess at that. She was so very aware of her surroundings and propriety, always watching, always aware, always a paradigm. Charles frowned, and her hand tensed against his arm, and he wondered what all this caution cost her.

"I have always been well when with you. It's been so very long since we've had a chance to speak, and this is not the time nor place for great discussions, is it? Yet there are so many great discussions I wish to have with you," Charles said.

They passed the Duke and Duchess of Roxleigh, and he nodded in deference and received a welcoming smile from Her Grace. They were so different from the general *ton,* it gave him hope for the possibilities it presented. Roxleigh answered to no one but the queen.

Amelia shivered, recapturing his attention instantly, and he schooled his reaction. Ever wary in public he must be with this masterful beauty. Ever concerned that his reaction would call her out.

Charles's position being what it was, if he were to respond badly, the *ton* would follow without heed. He would be the gate to which the flood would flow, and he felt that certain pressure keenly on his shoulders. He didn't wish to ruin her, regardless the outcome of their suit. He cared for her, whatever that meant. Well, if he was being honest with himself, what it was was an insuppressible want of her…but that he'd wanted for so long, he believed he might have a genuine care for her as well. Charles turned for the balcony. "Perhaps some air."

"As you please," she said.

Charles followed, properly keeping well in sight of the ballroom, then stayed himself when she released him, walking toward the balustrade.

"Endsleigh," was all he said. Charles couldn't help himself. He watched as she controlled her reactions incrementally, like a sudden freeze, starting with her ears and traveling down. He saw every muscle stop, coming to attention. It was a rather beautiful dance beneath her skin and caused his fingers to itch, the physical manifestation of a wish to touch.

"Endsleigh," she replied with a catch in her voice. "My oldest friend."

"Dearest?" he asked, wanting to know, truly.

"Perhaps." She turned toward the sleeping gardens, resting her gloved hands on the marble barrier. "Out there, at the far side of England, away from society, the only friends we have are those born to us." She smiled back at him, over her shoulder.

"I imagine. And beyond that?" he replied, perhaps hopefully, needing to know how close they truly were. He had a deep need to posses her body, certainly, though more than that he wasn't sure he was capable of. Regardless, if she were his, he would expect every bit of her to belong to him, without exception. Body and soul.

"Beyond that, there can be nothing," she said simply. She lifted one shoulder, a concession, yet not enough to allay his fears.

"He's always been allowed in your life, while I have not been. Until now," Charles said.

"All true, and yet—"

"And yet?" he asked.

"And yet…" Amelia's voice faded as she turned, and he saw in her eyes the request…no, the defiant demand that he quit this line.

For a man to sigh called thoughts of weakness, for men were never to question their thoughts, their wishes. But sigh he did, and he put his whole heart into it.

"As you please," he responded.

Her perfect smile returned. Charles was taken away at how well she did that, effected that persona. Created that incredible wash of calm while he could feel, even at this distance, that she was falling apart from the inside.

Now that he looked closely he could see those little shivers, jerks, and ticks that never quite went away, were never quite hidden.

They both looked out over the gardens. Shoulder to shoulder— she with her hands held perfectly in front of her, he with his clasped tightly behind his back—as the moonlight drifted down upon them like a spotlight in the vast darkness.

Charles was not quite as good at schooling his physical features. But then he never had cause to be. He was not nearly as practiced with controlling something so seemingly uncontrollable as she. His control at this point was simply his nature. All emotion had been schooled out of him as unacceptable, and truth be told, he'd never been witness to, or

party to, anything like love. Though he thought it must be kin to joy… and that he *had* witnessed. In her. Charles shook his head and wished… what did he wish? He wished he knew what it was she needed to keep herself together.

"Amelia, I love…I love—"

Charles stopped abruptly when her eyes widened. His father had always told him that women wanted to hear they were loved, that he should wield those three words like a weapon.

"I love…pudding." *What the hell?*

But when she laughed in answer to the statement…he realized he would have done it again for that moment. *Pudding, for fuck's sake.* He wished he knew what it would take to bring that joyful girl from the sea back to him in a more permanent fashion.

Endsleigh.

Like an unwelcome voice in his head, the name intruded.

Endsleigh.

To banish Ender from thought would be his greatest wish, but Ender's effect on her could not be banished. Charles had watched that dance. He'd seen her standing. Just standing. Attempting to simply stand. Then Ender was there, and she had spiraled up and then back, like a top would. Tightened then released, all that difficulty gone. There was something more between them. Charles had always known that, but what he could not understand was why. When they were younger, Ender had been allowed to be there with her, no matter what. Whenever it seemed she was acting out of sorts, they had removed Charles and let Ender stay.

This was without a doubt a level of jealousy he had no wish to control. And yet…*and yet,* to have that same power for her—but he feared that level of concern came from a level of connection that was beyond his ability. Charles shifted again, looked at the leather toe of his shoe as he tapped it quietly, once, twice, a third time. Once they wed, her friendship with Ender would be officially at an end, and all this maundering would have no consequence. She would be forced to *his* confidence. What would have consequence was if she were unsuitable.

Charles knew she had this magic inside her. To find that again… *no.* He wanted her. She was the only person he'd met in his life who had been so open, so free. Everyone else in his life spoke to the Duke of Castleberry, but she always spoke to Jacks, and he wanted her to speak to Charles. She was never put off by his title, didn't want him for it. Somehow, she saw the boy and the man. That intrigued him.

"It is odd, is it not? The last time we spoke, you were merely Amelia, and I was merely Jacks," he said wistfully.

She smiled then, and it was genuine, and he could not help but return it with the knowledge that that girl, the one from before, was still in there. Charles took her hand and smoothed a circle into her palm with his thumb, dropping her mouth open slightly until he could see the pink of her tongue.

"Mon Dieu," he whispered on a breath. Her jaw snapped shut. "Malheureusement." he said. Charles swallowed, his mouth suddenly dry, his tongue swollen inside. "Pardon me." He cleared his throat and dropped her hand. "I believe I've had quite enough of this function. I shall return you to...to your—" Charles coughed in an attempt to vanquish the image of that perfect pink tongue from his mind. It didn't work, so he closed his eyes as he continued. "Your family. Perhaps I could call on the morrow to take you for a ride in my carriage? I hear the Royal Gardens are beautiful at the moment," he said distractedly. "Something to be seen. Perhaps then we could attempt the first of many great discussions."

"As you please," she whispered.

*If only...*he thought. Charles reached for her hand carefully, then, quite without his permission, his hand landed gently on her shoulder and dragged slowly down her bare skin to the top of her glove, catching on the edge, then continuing until he had her hand.

"And what would *you* wish, Amelia?" He was rewarded with another perfect view of that pink tongue as her mouth dropped open to answer him, but all he was given was a quick breath. He placed her hand on his arm, and her other hand pushed at her belly, as though she would be ill.

"Do you need a moment?"

Amelia shook her head. "No, thank you, I simply need to..." She looked up into his eyes and seemed to press that hand harder into her stomach. Her eyes showed pain, and he was truly at a loss as how to proceed.

"Amelia, if I have offended—"

She shook her head adamantly. "Please do call on the morrow. For tonight, I feel I'm overtired. The trip from Pembroke..." She waved her free hand in a circle, as if to say *etc....*

Charles nodded, but knew an excuse when he heard one. Tonight was merely a beginning, the first opening of the window. He held her hand to his arm and brought her through the crowd, willing some of his strength to her. He thought she needed it much more than he at the moment.

All too aware of her physical proximity, he led her through the jostling throng to her waiting mother. He handed her off and turned to the duke. This man he needed to watch. Charles's own father had told him to be wary of Pembroke but never did elaborate as to why. Charles knew peers used different tactics to attempt to control those around them—it was one of the most important lessons from his father. Control was important, lack of such could destroy a dynasty. As such, whatever control Pembroke had, whatever tactics he used to maintain it Charles would need to determine as they moved forward.

"Pembroke, with your leave I would very much like to call upon Lady Amelia on the morrow."

"By all means, sir. By all means. We shall arrange to have a chaperone availed to you," her father replied.

Charles turned to Amelia and took her hand once again. He bowed over it stiffly, nodded to her mother and took his leave.

It was then she breathed.

"I do hope you did not ruin this," her mother mumbled through a stiff grin.

Amelia's hands tensed, one on the other.

"I'm quite sure nothing is ruined, Your Grace. You heard yourself he's to call tomorrow. As for now, I'm to Pembroke House. I see no further *use* for me here."

"Now, my dear," her father started, "you should not manage your mother so. You know she only wishes the best for you."

"By all means necessary, only the very best," Amelia said a bit too loudly and with an irrepressible smile.

Amelia turned and made her way to the front of the house. So very close now, within reach, a stone's throw, so simple. Her arms snaked around her middle. Safety beyond those two great doors and then home to peace, within and without. Amelia's heart raced her feet to the threshold.

Away from here, away from these people, away from everything she hated—everything she was born to be. Everything. This was everything to everyone. Everyone but her. Her everything had already quit the ball, as she did now.

TWO

If Hugh had thought he could delay leaving the ball and not be hurt, he'd been wrong. He had needed to leave before he saw them together, but when Miss Rigsby had been placed in his path, that wasn't to be. Because as much as he wasn't interested in the machinations of Lady Rigsby, he was even more disinterested in creating another generation of angry matrons bent on revenge by ensuring their own daughters' successes, and that particular miss he knew to be delicate to begin with. As a gentleman, there had been no refusing the dance.

Hugh felt the prickle on the backs of his arms first. Like a numbness was coming, or perhaps an awakening. He should have quit before he'd seen them together. He should have quit sooner than he had. It was not cold in the manor, but he shivered, then his stomach lurched. He groaned, and the swift beat in his head signaled the coming pain, and he winced.

Hugh turned toward the front of the house to collect his mount. There was nothing to be done. *Damn him and damn me, and whilst I'm at it, damn her as well. Damn her for…damn her for being simply the most extravagant, kind, incredible woman to ever walk the face of this earth.* Even in his own mind he could not endeavor to make himself hate her.

Hugh's gut tightened as he turned away. Never again. Never again could he lay eyes on her without this pain. To suffer the pain was to be alive, to feel, to be real, here and now. The pain would serve as a reminder that she was not his and could never be his. She was unreachable.

The pain was equal measure to the joy he'd always felt when near her. No, that wasn't quite correct. The pain was equal measure to the joy he'd always felt for her until the summer they'd both realized their lives would be forever severed. The summer *he* first came to Pembroke-by-the-Sea. *Jackson.*

Hugh felt the sob like a vice in his chest before he heard the sound, and his hand clenched. He tried to steady himself as it tore through him, made its way from his gut through his chest then burst like an explosion in his head. It was all he could do to stifle the screams.

Hugh lurched toward his horse, which shifted uncomfortably with wide, nervous eyes, and he schooled his demeanor. Tried desperately to control his unhinged passion so as not to lose his mount when he took it from the boy. He breathed slowly, closing his eyes and thinking of their childhood together. The last time he was truly happy. The time before the guillotine was placed securely above their heads. Hugh thought of her smile, then he vaulted to his mount and turned away from the ball, and this time, he didn't stop. This entire situation was something that was beyond him.

Hugh rode like the beat of his heart depended on the sound of the hooves to continue its own rhythm. He bolted down the lane with no regard for those around him.

Amelia was his closest friend. Truth be told, she was his only friend. They just managed with each other so well. Her father had always allowed Hugh's presence because he'd lived nearby, and what would the harm have been? For whatever reason, she'd always trusted Hugh. Perhaps because he'd always been a steady influence in her life? He wasn't sure, but he knew he was able to help her. Whenever she had an episode, whenever she'd come close to falling apart, whenever she lost control, he was there to help. And her mother had relied upon him after a time, because *she* couldn't do anything to help her.

Of course, if her mother had truly cared about Amelia, and not simply about her worth as a ducal asset, she may have been able to help her as well. Hugh knew that was part of the problem, that her mother saw only that her behavior was going to inhibit her ability to make a suitable match, to secure their future beyond her father. It angered him that she was merely seen as a means to an end. Amelia's mother should have been the one to care about her, the one to know her, the one to help her. But she wasn't—he was. And what now? He wasn't sure anyone else could take the place of him in her mind. He was sure he didn't *want* anyone else to take his place.

Sure, Jacks seemed like a decent man. What Hugh knew of him. But Jackson was far removed from Amelia, and because she was promised to him, Amelia's mother had ensured that Jackson had never seen her behavior when they were younger. Jackson would then have had a reason to cry off. Whenever they'd visited during school breaks, her mother had made sure that Hugh had been there as a buffer. To help control her. But the animosity between Hugh and Jackson had only grown, because Jacks had seen that Hugh was allowed to spend time with her, while Jackson was sent away under the guise of propriety...or because she was not yet "out" in society...or a host of other excuses used to prevent Jackson seeing one of her episodes.

Hugh knew, however, that Jackson was no simpleton. The man would be looking for answers now. Hugh knew that Jacks had the patience of a saint. He'd learned this when they were much younger, and Jacks had never called Hugh out for the tricks he'd played on him. Hugh should have been called out for them. He had wanted to be called out. But Jackson was bred to lead, trained up to control, and nothing Hugh could do had ever broken that.

Hugh arrived at Endsleigh Hall within the hour, pushing past his stable man in favor of rubbing down the horse himself. He needed the methodical sweep across the horse's flesh to calm his ragged nerves. He wasn't entirely sure why the day had ended in such a shock to him. When Jacks had arrived at the ball, Hugh should have known it was the end of his bid for her hand. Truly, he should have accepted that fact long before then. If he were to be honest with himself, he would admit to knowing long ago that he was chasing an impossible dream.

Stubborn? Perhaps. Stubborn...yes, all right, stubborn. he thought. But it was Amelia, and she was perfect. So incredibly perfect. It was terribly unfortunate, that.

Hugh shook his head and stripped the saddle, throwing it across the stand heavy enough to startle his overwrought horse.

Hugh paused, his hands still on the stiff, polished leather. *Calm,* he thought. *Calm yourself or call for the man to handle the steed.*

He turned back to Termagant and rose his hands in apology as he pulled the brush from the wall. The horse stepped back, his eyes bright and wary, but Hugh spoke gently, reassuring him. As Hugh calmed, Termagant followed suit.

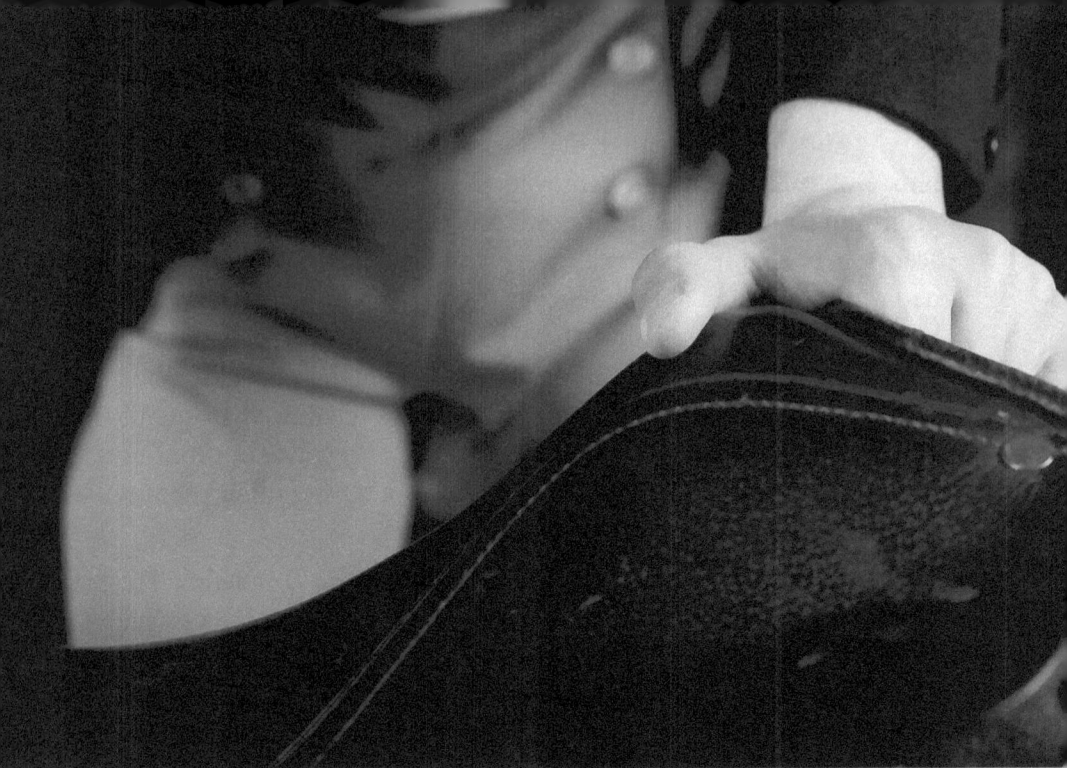

Hugh brushed his withers, unbraided his mane and worked his way down the rich coppery legs, then moved on to his back. Hugh smoothed and soothed and calmed himself with every stroke of the beast.

Hugh's sore muscles pulled and swayed as Termagant shifted into his movements, finally reassured. Hugh pulled a fresh bale from the gateway and spread a thick mat of hay around the stable. He then vaulted to the bare back of the steed to brush and rebraid his mane. Braiding was a talent Hugh had picked up from the daughter of one of the kitchen maids in his father's house. He'd used it on Amelia's long tresses and taught her to braid her horses' manes as well. They'd had competitions, figuring out more and more intricate weaves, adding ribbons, wildflowers, and bells to the patterns.

Hugh smiled at the quiet peace of sitting atop a great hunter in the small stable, braiding his thick mane. *Such an odd thing for a baron,* he thought suddenly. An odd thing for any peer, any man, really, not of a stable. Yet he knew he'd never felt part of the peerage as it was, living so far from London and not trained up like Jackson was. Hugh hadn't been raised with such strict beliefs in the hand of God in who he was. His father simply hadn't had enough interest in it, or him. Hugh left off the end of the braid and slid from the horse. He watched Termagant's eyes blink slowly, and the drowsiness washed over him as well, his head clearer, the pulsing pain subsiding.

Hugh shook his head and walked out of the stable toward the stable master's quarters at the end.

"I'm off, Duncan. Termagant is stabled. There's no need to bother with him. I handled him."

Duncan shifted on the small crate he used as a stool and nodded stoutly.

"Lucky ye didna get squashed in there the way ye had that steed worked up, sir," Duncan said gruffly.

Hugh nodded and looked away. Perhaps he was of a mind to get brained. He swept the back of his fist across his sweaty brow as he shifted.

"Yes. To be sure, I was…terribly irresponsible," Hugh said.

Duncan grunted then looked back to his card game, and Hugh turned and strode to the town home, sufficiently chastised by a man he'd grown up worshiping for his mastery of animals. The only man in his life to ever show him much interest.

Hugh marched through the main hall and went straight to his study. The place was large and empty, lonely, abandoned. He supposed it was time to find a wife to fill the nursery. He would speak to Amelia in the morning. Tell her good-bye—as was best—and move on with his own life.

Charles entered his carriage and directed the coachman to his town house before he settled against the squabs. He closed his eyes and thought back on his childhood. He remembered chasing after the other two children, drawn to her as a moth to flame, wishing for the burn.

It was the summers he looked forward to the most through the long wait of winter. His mother often dragged him along to the house parties when she visited her lifelong friend, the Duchess of Pembroke-by-the-Sea. The closest estate was that of the Baron Endsleigh, and his son, Hugh Garrison, was often found at Pembroke-by-the-Sea as well, playing with the girl.

It was *that girl* with whom he'd fallen irretrievably in love the moment he'd set eyes on her. For a young boy, perhaps love was a strong word. And he knew now that what he had for her was a far cry from love, if that could even exist in him. What he'd felt for her was a deep yearning, an undeniable want of her that he had no wish to quell, and what pulled at him now was the thread of that feeling that lingered still, the want of her. He wanted her so badly he'd asked his father to arrange for it, and his father had. The one thing Charles had ever asked from his sire and received.

Amelia was sweet like sunshine and sugar on a lemon, so many flavors at once you wished to smile and pucker and lick your lips all at the same time. What struck Charles most was her laughter, so vivid, so pure and full of truth. Her laughter stopped his breath every time it rang through the countryside, and he waited, as a prisoner in a dank, dusty gaol, for that bit of joy to return—even for just a few stolen moments. It was something he'd never felt for himself. Something he wished to somehow capture by being in her presence.

Amelia had been allowed to run the estate without a keeper, which he'd thought odd, as she was young, and female. But perhaps at that age a chaperone wasn't as necessary. *His* father would have thought so, however.

"Charles, hurry! You've no one here to do your running for you! You must keep up on your own." She'd turn and smile at him over her shoulder, and he'd marvel that she never tripped and fell when she chased after *him*, with Charles in tow.

So run the estate they had, the girl, the boy, and Charles.

That boy, her boy, her best friend, had always been by her side, and this her father had taken no exception to either—which had been shocking to Charles as well.

"Amelia! Amelia! Here, look."

"What is it now, Hugh?"

"Look, Amelia, you'll see. There in the thicket." The boy pointed.

"Hugh, I don't have time for your trickery. If you—" The girl's hand flew to her dropped-open lips, her eyes wide and searching. "Oh, Hugh, don't disturb them—look! I can see three—no, four! But where's the mother?"

"I see nothing." Charles strained on his toes to try to see over the two crouched in front of him.

"Charles, look closer," Hugh said as he shifted to the side. "Look, there..." He pointed deeper into the brambles.

"I still see nothing. It's too dark." Charles frowned. He always felt left out of their fun, by nature of the third-wheel principle. Though he often wondered that, if a third wheel might actually help to balance the other two on a bicycle, why it would be considered so terribly inconvenient.

Amelia took his hand, and he jumped—staring at the point of contact. "See the trunk of the tree just there to the left?" she asked, and he nodded, but his eyes were on her mouth as it moved. "Now follow the right side of the trunk down...down...down—"

And his gaze did travel down, down and down, to the pulse in her neck.

"Let your eyes adjust. Now, when you can see the base of the tree and the ground, look just beside it, just there."

As she released his hand, he was bereft of the warmth of it, and his eyes followed that hand to where she pointed.

Charles sucked in a breath. Her finger, her lips, her throat all but forgotten in his sudden fear. "Will they bite us?"

"No, silly! They're just fox cubs. I imagine their mother is off looking for lunch," Amelia said.

Charles righted himself suddenly, his gaze darting around the shadows in the wood for the slightest movement. "Are we lunch? We should go...should we go? I think we should go. I think we should leave, in case—" A raucous peal of laughter cut him off.

"Hugh, don't! Damn you twice. He's unused to the wild," Amelia said softly.

"Twice already? We'll see about that. Besides, that's ridiculous. He lives in the country, just as we do. Why wouldn't he know about animals?" Hugh replied stiffly.

"My father, he doesn't let me run about the estate without a governess," Charles said, annoyed that they played games around him, the secret messages he wasn't privy to. *Damn them both,* he thought, knowing it made no difference, that it didn't count in *their* game and never would matter.

"A governess?" Hugh replied in haughty disbelief. "What on earth do you do with a governess? Take tea?"

"Hugh! Damn you three times." Amelia smacked his arm, and Hugh looked to her. "You will cease this instant. If Charles isn't comfortable in the forest, we shall return to the manor. I'm sure there are plenty of adventures we can have in the attics. They've been storing things up there for centuries. We shall have a treasure hunt." She turned to Charles with a grand smile, and he grimaced.

"Dust," he returned quietly.

Her smile faded. "Well, then, we shall...we shall...find something to do on the way back to the manor house. Charles, would you lead the way?"

Charles was all too happy to lead them from the forest, across the moors and back to some semblance of civilization. Even if it meant an afternoon of dust. He could feel his skin itching already.

"Amelia," Hugh whispered, but Charles heard anyway. He didn't dare turn back, though, knowing that Hugh hadn't wanted him to hear, so he wouldn't be the one to give himself away.

"Hugh, what are you going to do with those?" she replied in just as much of a whisper.

Silence. The fine hairs on the back of his neck stood on end. His heart sped. He knew there was to be a prank in his future.

"I forbid it," Amelia said vehemently.

Charles turned at that, in time to see her eyes dart back to Hugh.

Then her voice became softer, more insistent. "You will leave them here on the moors where they belong, Hugh, or I'll not speak with you again."

"Amelia, please? It's merely for fun," the boy replied.

"No, absolutely not. Leave them now, or damn you forever."

Charles realized abruptly that their voices had dimmed more from distance than control and stopped to turn around. He saw Hugh pull several lumpy forms from his pockets, letting them drop to the soft earth, only to have them spring to life, scattering in all directions.

Charles knew his mouth was gaping. He could feel the breeze on his tongue. He snapped his mouth shut.

Frogs. Or toads. Did it matter which? Hugh had been planning yet another prank, this one involving those slimy creatures from the pond. And she—*she*—had saved him.

In that moment, he knew that he cared for her for this, for if he'd stepped into a shoe to discover a wet snapping mouth and a long sticky tongue, he was quite sure the prank would have been his end.

It was then that Hugh looked up at him and scowled. *Damn him forever is right,* Charles thought. Charles hoped it was merely the fact that Amelia had thwarted his recalcitrant efforts, but it was entirely possible that Charles had been looking on Amelia with rather a different sort of gleam in his eye, one that Hugh had not appreciated.

Well, Amelia may have foiled Hugh this time, but Charles was rather certain it wouldn't be the last. No matter what Charles hoped for... with that one look from Hugh, the game was afoot. Such as the game was, one-sided and all.

It would be a long summer, he knew then, obsessing over his shoes and socks, the placement of things in his wardrobe, checking his sheets and his hats. It would be a tedious—but necessary—fact of it.

Charles didn't understand what Amelia saw in Hugh. Hugh was a mean-spirited prankster, always getting her into trouble with her family. But Charles knew, in the smile she gave Hugh as forgiveness now, that she adored him. And in the quick wink Hugh returned, Charles understood that feeling to be mutual.

The following summers had been more difficult for Charles as his mother changed. The tincture of laudanum had become her dearest companion, first fending off the night terrors she'd always had. Then once his father died, any hint of emotion and the laudanum was in her hand, ready to calm her nerves.

Amelia and Hugh treated him carefully. He became the Castleberry, and Hugh became the Endsleigh, but Amelia was still, forever, Amelia. Strange that, that the young men grew into titles and presence, whilst the girls were commended for staying young...innocent.

Amelia and Hugh spent their summers avoiding his mother and attempting to avoid him. Even as children, they seemed to know just how horrid it all was. Hugh…*Ender* played no pranks, and Amelia didn't defend him. In truth, Charles was unsure which he preferred. At least the pranks had been normal, the defense heartfelt. The care they took with him after—that was painful. A constant reminder that life had forever changed, that he was now something more. And possibly something less.

There wasn't anything to be done about it, and the pain of the fact had faded, even though the truth of it was still shrouded in shades of gray.

Charles opened his eyes and leaned forward on his knees, considering the current predicament, which was…well, truth be told, *he* was the problem for Amelia and Ender. It didn't have to be so. He didn't have to pursue the marriage claim discussed over brandy by two men twenty years prior. But he knew he still wanted this. Charles wasn't sure if his motivation was because of the frogs…or because of the frogs. That's to say, he wasn't sure if he wanted *her* or hated *him*.

Charles also wondered if her acceptance of his pledge was more pity-laced with necessity than want. As well, he wasn't sure he cared either way on that front, but there were certain things that bothered him still.

Things he hoped to resolve.

Charles had watched as Ender and Amelia, now Lord Endsleigh and Lady Pembroke, returned to the ballroom from the balcony. He knew the *ton* talked about her. He knew they suppressed the rumors because her father was still a powerful duke—regardless of his illness—and he also knew the minute the duke wasn't there to guard her she would be fodder for the masses. Unless Charles stepped into the fray.

Whether the rumors were true, Charles knew not. He didn't remember anything terribly odd or different about her, but that was many years ago. Any visits he'd had once he and Ender had gone off to school were often cut short, citing propriety or her need of rest. It bothered him that Hugh had often been allowed to stay while he had been turned out, but he'd believed it was because Hugh was a friend to the family, and Charles, the Castleberry…well, nobody needed a duke hanging about even if that duke was somewhat betrothed. Charles had been more like a mouse in duke's clothing at that point, and simply had done their bidding, afraid to have all permissions revoked. Of course, that wasn't who he was now, and if anyone came between them, between Charles and what he wanted…well, woe to them.

A childhood crush could mask many things about a person, irreconcilable behaviors being the least of his worries when met with the face of an angel and the laugh of a siren. But there wasn't anything to the rumors that bothered Charles in truth. He could see what they whispered about and found no merit in any of it, because if she were his wife, the rumors would simply cease to exist.

The single thing he was concerned of at this point—and, truth be told, at all points—was Ender. He needed to deal with the issue immediately, and if there was one thing he'd learned in taking over the business of the duchy, it was to go to the source when there was discord. He hit the roof of the carriage to call his driver.

THREE

Amelia descended the carriage in front of Pembroke House and twitched her skirts straight, thinking how she hated Hugh. She dislodged a stubborn wrinkle at the hem as she walked briskly into the house, nodding politely at the servants as she passed.

Hate is a rather strong word, she thought. Perhaps she only disliked him a great deal. *Or perhaps it's quite the opposite. Must he always appear so? Like a rescuer just when he's needed, as though I cannot handle myself. Which I cannot. But that's neither here nor there, now is it?*

She followed the long hallways and turns and finally entered her rooms.

It's quite unfair of him to continue with this savior knight persona. We're not children anymore, for goodness sakes. Really. I'm to marry another. As he's aware. A tear fell as she collapsed into her old worn chair by the fire, pulling her feet up and holding herself as tightly as possible. She'd insisted the chair come with her from Pembroke-by-the-Sea, much to her mother's disdain.

Hugh was her oldest friend. *Dearest. There Jacks had it. Dear, he was dear, quite dear,* she thought, and Charles was none too happy about that fact, it seemed.

She and Hugh had shared so much, but when Hugh had left to pursue his education, her life had spiraled beyond tether. Social situations had become difficult, small, independent trials of her patience and sanity. Her parents had slowly closed their beautiful, powerful seat of the dukedom in favor of a quiet, secluded life. One, where their prized daughter, their sole heir, would not be discovered for what they believed she was: *a freak.*

Amelia remembered her first true episode, when Hugh had told her he was leaving… She shook off the thought as she yanked the pins from her hair, letting them pull the tendrils at her scalp, feeling the pinch and the burn, wishing anything could take this other pain from her.

Hugh. Ender. Endsleigh. Hubert Percival Alexander Garrison, the Right Honorable Baron Endsleigh. Hugh. Dearest Hugh. She shook her head. He must be Endsleigh to her. Only Endsleigh. *Nothing more. Never more. Never, never again more.*

She looked down to find her hands mussing the silk of her ball gown terribly, and they unclenched, the fingers stiffening in their straightness. The tendons stretched then eased through her knuckles as she relaxed and feebly attempted to brush the wrinkles from the skirt.

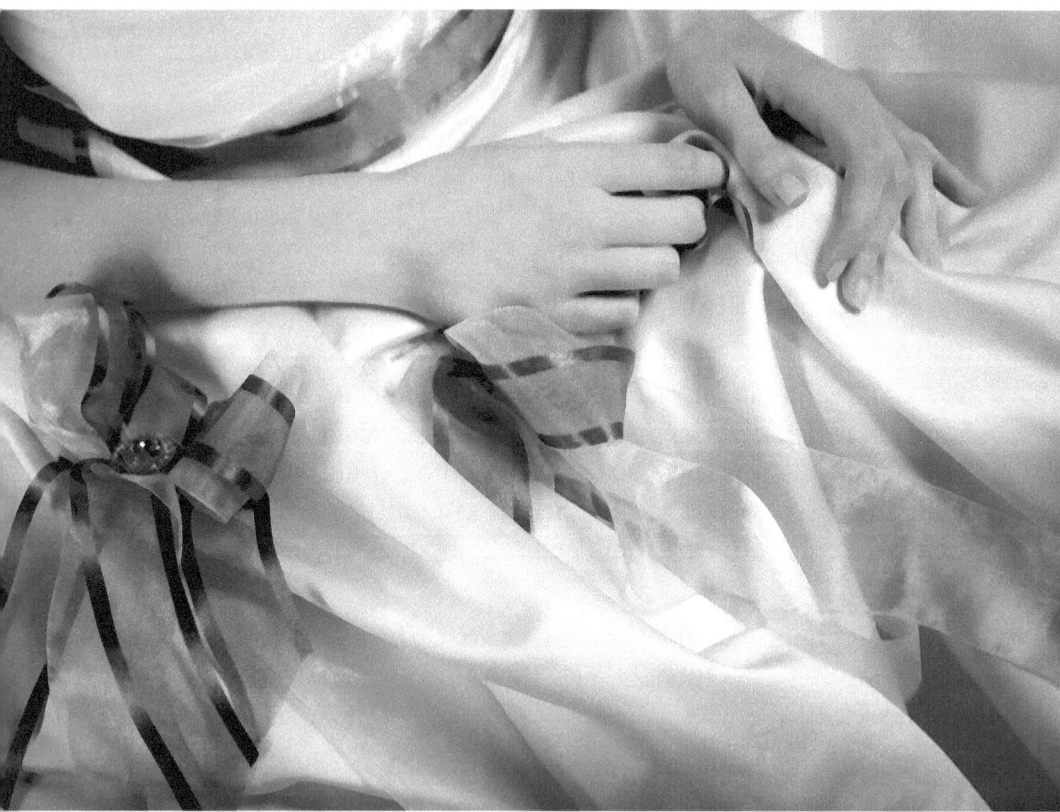

Damn me. Damn me…what? Where was she? Had she actually lost count? *Certainly Hugh had made it to at least thrice during the ball alone.* Amelia's smile eased her tension as she tangled her fingers together and pulled her feet up under her skirts. She and Hugh still played the games they'd made up when they were children. The rules were simple: If they reached four, Hugh had to go home. Neither of them had wished for that, so they'd worked together to prevent his departure from happening. That had been a goal to be avoided, and for whatever reason, it worked.

What was she to do about this man? And he was a man, no longer the boy of her youth. The entire situation was all too far beyond her control. He was ingrained in her life, too much an integral part of her happiness. Yet as much as she would be happy to spend her life with a man who could calm her in a heartbeat, she was promised to, taken by, and terribly in want of another. One she had known as a child then watched from a distance only as allowed. One who'd been turned out every time she'd begun to act out. One she'd begun to be reacquainted with tonight, truly acquainted, really, for the first time in so very many years. One who made her very skin ache to be touched. One she hoped had no idea she was on the verge of being an outcast.

Amelia's cheeks burned from all the forced smiles and politesse, and she pressed them in to ease the muscles, then caught a glimpse of herself in the mirror and chuckled. Her mouth was pursed like that of a fish.

Truly she was frightened at the prospect of being near him again. She'd thought perhaps her crush was merely that, and seeing him again those feelings would have been gone, but they hadn't been. His very presence called to her.

Jacks. Charles Henry Tristan Jackson, Duke of Castleberry, Marquess of Braverton, Viscount Melbrey, certainly many other lesser titles she wasn't aware of—she would have to look in Debrett's for that information—but his friends still called him Jacks, she was sure.

If he had friends. Did he have friends? Surely there would be friends.

Amelia poked at her cheeks, in and out. She had been the first to call him Jacks, when they were young and allowed such frivolities. She hoped he would allow her to call him Jacks again. Perhaps even Charles. Charles, such a simple name for a man who was not nearly so simple.

Now why would her lips puckered like a fish call his nickname to mind? She dropped her hands and fidgeted with a loose thread on her skirt. *Presenting His Grace, Charles Jackson, Duke of Castleberry and his wife, Amelia Jackson,* she thought with a smile, then shook her head. *They would not use his Christian name—*

"Your mother is the very devil's undergarments!" grumbled her girl as she burst into the room.

Amelia's attention jerked up, and with it the thread she was fidgeting with pulled loose, making a hole in her dress. She attempted to smooth the fabric, and when that didn't work, she folded the skirt over the hole to hide it.

"Louisa, dearest, my mother is as she is, as you should be aware by now."

"Promise me you'll not leave me to her when you are well and married. Please, take me with you."

Amelia giggled and stood as the irreverent girl pulled and twisted and shed her of her clothes. "I would never do such a thing as leave you here, you know that," Amelia said as she suffered Louisa's ministrations like a fish caught in the tide.

Louisa had been with Amelia for what seemed forever, and Louisa knew Amelia nearly as well as Hugh did. Louisa was able to help Amelia, but her presence wasn't as calming as Hugh's always had been— but Louisa could manage her, and that was usually enough.

"Viper, she is. You'd think the world was at an end simply because you left the ball."

"Ah, well. Is my mother home or did she send a footman to check on me?"

"Send a footman?" Louisa squealed. "Send a footman! Why the very—and leave the ball with only three liveried men to accompany the coach? You cannot be serious, Amelia. The very idea, I mean, *really.*"

Amelia collapsed back in her chair with a smile. "Goodness me, the coachmen must be dizzy from circling London this night. Mother must have been waiting for their return."

"Hush now," Louisa said. "She'll hear you, and then where will we be? In the stocks in the grand courtyard, that's where." Louisa lifted the skirt to the light, prodding at the hole Amelia had just made, and Amelia winced.

"Louisa, the stocks were removed to the attics decades ago," Amelia said, trying to distract Louisa from the damage.

Louisa tossed the dress aside. "Oh, my lady, don't think for a minute that she'll not pull them out simply for this transgression. Truly, you sound like a schoolgirl in this fit of giggles. She'll think you've become much too far gone and have you off to Bedlam by morning."

Amelia calmed then, rather suddenly, and she felt the sting at the backs of her eyes as Louisa's shocked face turned to her. "Oh there, milady, I've gone too far. I always do. Come, come, never fear. If she had off with you, I'd be at your side to take the brunt of it."

Amelia tried to smile, and it cut her tension as she heard Louisa sigh. "All right now, up with you. Here's a great soft bed calling to you," Louisa said.

"Louisa, don't leave me," Amelia said quietly as she leaned in to hug her maid. *Her maid.* What on earth would her mother think of this? For shame, beyond all things, to embrace a servant girl.

"Don't start now, milady. You know no good will come of this. Just simply take me with you."

Amelia smiled and nodded profusely, then crawled into the bed as Louisa fussed. She remembered the first time she'd heard her maid speak ill of her mother. Shock. *It was most shocking!* Servants were to be seen and unheard, but this particular servant—she shook her head—this servant was not meant to be in the position she was in. Of that, Amelia was certain. Wherever she'd come from, she'd been a blessing, but born into the service of a blue blood she was not.

Louisa flung the heavy counterpane up over Amelia and proceeded to shove the edges around her, tight and secure. Amelia finally relaxed, like a violin string let loose after a long concert.

"I will," Amelia said quietly, already so relaxed she was nearly asleep.

Louisa prodded the fire and dimmed the gas lamp left in the far corner of her room to chase the shadows.

"I know," Louisa replied. She put out the remaining gaslights as she left, the heavy door clicking shut behind her.

Amelia drifted off on a thought, and that thought was not about the maid or her dearest friend. She smiled, her jaw slackened, and sleep took her.

A

"My lord." Hugh waved his butler into his study and took the card from the tray.

Damn me thrice. Hugh grunted and waved his hand as though to say, *Send him in.*

"Yes, my lord. Do you require your jacket?"

"Not at all. If a duke is to call in the dead of night, he will find me as I am, decency be damned."

"Yes, my lord."

Hugh stood and poured a finger of whiskey, then another and another. *Damn it all.* Hugh stopped counting and filled the tumbler. The whiskey burned his throat as he poured it down then nearly doubled over. He wiped his chin with his shirtsleeve and leaned on his desk.

"For the love of all that's holy, Endsleigh, do you mean to stand at the end of the night?" Charles asked as he entered.

"Stand? No, I'll not be standing for this," Hugh said quietly then sat and leaned back in his heavy leather desk chair. He pointed at the decanter on his desk, but Charles shook his head. "What have you then? My mood is none for the House, I'll have you know."

"I imagine not, but this has naught to do with the House. I need a moment."

Charles's voice was gruff, and Hugh looked at the man in front of his desk and raised his eyebrows a measure. Tall, broad—like him—not afraid to work. Not afraid of his own strength. "Pugilist?"

Charles shook his head. "You?"

"If the need arises," Hugh said, narrowing his eyes a bit.

Good God, he'd need to school himself if he was to survive this chat. "Sit."

That wasn't any better, but he wasn't interested in niceties. Though he and this man had only a passing acquaintance as of late, they knew very well who the other was, and there was nothing for it. All that these men had between them was the woman they both loved. *Amelia.* "Get on then."

"I…as you know, I'm to be…well, I plan to request her hand, and everyone's aware that—"

"Yes, you are. I'm aware. Everyone's aware. We are understood. Will that be all then?" Hugh bit out.

Charles's eyes narrowed on him, and he shifted in his seat.

Damn me, Hugh thought. *Keep your wits, man.* It wasn't like him to behave in such a repugnant manner, but he wanted none of this. As a gentleman, this duke should have known to simply steer clear of him as Hugh would his wife—*when* she became so. It was unspoken, unnecessary, uncalled for—*this.*

This—what are we about here? Charles needn't come to threaten, needn't come at all. I understand. I'm a baron, she the daughter of a duke, their lifetime together irrelevant. Stolen. Didn't Charles know that had been drilled in to him from the start?

"No. Not by measure," Charles said, interrupting his train of thought. "Amelia…What is it about her that you're so familiar with?"

Hugh felt his jaw slacken, and he traced a leather-pressed curl at the edge of his desktop with a fingertip as he snapped his mouth shut. Fancy that, a series of delicate curls pressed into the leather of his desk. Handed down generations only to be first useful tonight.

"I'm not entirely sure I understand you. Perhaps you could elaborate," Hugh said.

"Enough. We both know, as does the majority of the *ton*, that there's something about her, and of all people…she trusts only you." Charles paused. Twisted his hands. Looked up and caught Hugh's eyes. "I want that."

As if what he was already taking wasn't enough. As if Charles merely decided, and it was so. Hugh closed his eyes and listened to the whiskey whispering in his head. He should have stopped at the one finger.

"You want…so you take everything. Then what of me?" Hugh said quietly.

"You…I…I know not, but I *am* asking for your help. For her sake. Can you see past yourself to see that this is for her?"

Hugh's eyes snapped to his. This duke was infiltrating his home, his study, now his heart. Hugh's gut clenched, then his stomach twisted. Who knew the leather would cut so easily with a fingernail?

The duke continued.

"I see I should not have come, but I only wanted to make arrangements before…well. I plan to speak with Pembroke on the morrow, and I want her to know she'll be safe."

"There is nothing *I* could do to ensure her safety outside the realm of *my* possibility. Which at present is an impossibility. She trusts me. There's nothing…I can do…for *you*," Hugh bit out.

"That understanding of her is something you have to give."

"Not. To you," Hugh said. He could tell Charles was attempting to remain calm against the tension radiating across his desk.

Charles leaned forward. "Perhaps I do need a bit of whiskey."

"By all means," Hugh replied with a wave at the tantalus. Charles presumed too much. Hugh was not going to serve this man. This was his study, he was…*what was he? Good God, even two fingers would have sufficed.* Hugh pushed the decanter toward the duke, who took it and reached for a clean glass.

"I wish to know how to gain her trust," Charles said. "What it is about her that sets her apart? I know there's something, and I know that you know what that something is. I believe if *I* know as well, she will see that she can trust me."

"And by default would no longer trust in me. I cannot help you. You must understand. She's my…she is my friend."

"She appears to be more than that," Charles said with a strong tone of warning.

"*That* is none of your concern."

"She will be my wife. That makes it my concern. Expressly," Charles said stiffly.

"She has always been *mine*." Hugh roared that last bit, coming out of his chair as he prodded his desk, perhaps a little too strongly. His head swam.

Charles dropped the glass back into the tantalus. "You intend to come between us." It was not a question.

"My intentions are none of your concern," Hugh replied as he straightened what he could, then dropped back to his seat.

"Again, everything about her is of my concern, as *we* are to be wed," Charles replied.

"Then perhaps...you should rethink that." Hugh saw the words leave his mouth as though a gauntlet had launched itself from the cavern of his mouth, and yet he was not of a mind to stop them. Hugh held the other man's gaze. Charles's eyes were such a light color Hugh felt as though he could see through them to the man's very soul, and what he saw there was disconcerting for the fact that everything about him was honest and true.

Hugh's head pounded.

Charles shook his head. "This is not how this conversation should have gone."

"Oh? And how should the conversation have gone? 'I want to know your deepest secrets.' 'By all means! Take them!' Would that have been more to your liking?"

"No. Well, perhaps it would have, but that's not what I expected. However, I did believe you to be a reasonable man," Charles said.

"Where Amelia is concerned, there is no reason. Tell me, Your Grace, you do not seem to have considered her in your actions tonight. Is she aware you're here requesting this of me? Have you even considered that her secrets are not mine to give?"

Hugh saw Charles stiffen on the realization. "I understand. I had hoped...well, I had hoped. I should go. Perhaps we can discuss matters again, when you're better able to reason."

"Again with the reason. Take this to heart, Castleberry, there will be nothing from me, without the wishes of *my* lady. I'll not be one to bandy her secrets about as if they are nothing. There's more between us than that."

"I am to be her husband. There should be nothing between *you* and everything between *us*," Charles said.

"There is not yet an 'us.'" Hugh met Charles's eyes across the desk and held them.

Charles watched him for a moment, seemed to consider his thoughts, then turned to leave. "This is not finished."

Hugh chose to hold his retort. Apparently, the whiskey had not yet gotten the best of him.

FOUR

Amelia faced the mirror, waiting for the twitch. Scanning every bit of her face, looking for the signs and practicing her response. Jacks would be calling on her within the hour. All she need do was survive one trip in his carriage, then he would meet with her father. Charles would obtain a license within a sennight, and she would be married. There would be very little contact between them once today was finished. Very little reason for him to see through her and cry off.

This man she'd wanted to love from the age of ten. She remembered his visits to Pembroke, long before her condition seemed to spiral out of control. Long before her joy was wrapped up in whether or not Hugh was there.

It was something she could not admit to her future husband, though she believed he knew. He'd been there during the summers, *of course he knew*. She and Hugh had been the only two children on that remote shoreline. They had grown up with only each other.

Hugh would inherit his land, but Amelia would not. She needed a match to preserve her safety and that of her mother—should she outlive her father, which was a distinct possibility.

There was only her.

It was a tragedy, really, the end of a line, the successor a distant cousin. But she was still the daughter of this powerful duke for as long as he lived—and therein lay the catch. She must secure their future, before the future was upon them.

It was pure luck that the boy who had visited with her family had been the future Duke of Castleberry. Then again, the possibility that it had been less chance and more orchestration was also entirely within reason.

Particularly considering that his mother had been terribly difficult to be close to after his father died.

She could feel the twitch coming before she saw it, the tiny pulse of the muscles in her cheek. She would avoid talk of his father, his mother—as propriety would dictate—but she had to remind herself. Her mouth tended to precede her brain when she felt things passionately. She must remind her brain to stay itself.

If she'd known back then that she would now prefer to *not* like him, she might have let Hugh put the toads in his shoes. She was terribly rambunctious, and when Hugh was there—which was always—there was no reckoning.

But there had been something about that boy, and she'd wanted to know more. She had not allowed the toads, and Hugh had not liked that, not a whit. Then Hugh had left, and she'd been heartbroken. That was when she had first noticed the tremors. Apparently, the people around her had known of them all along, but she'd been distracted.

When she entered a room of people, she would tremble. Her knees would go weak, and her heart would race. She felt as though her insides were attempting to turn themselves out. She became inconsolable. Said things she shouldn't. Without Hugh as a buffer, someone to take the blame, she was noticed entirely too much.

Her mother only ever told her to gather her wits. Well, not so. There were the jabs to the ribs, a convenient elbow, the twist of the thin skin on the back of her hand.

She looked in the mirror. "Gather your wits, Amelia Marie!" She twitched. There, at the very corner of her eye, the smallest of movements, but she saw it. She thought of her mother again, the dinner parties, the invitations, the balls, and finally her father's decision to find her a husband before her coming out. They believed it to be the only way. Keep her hidden. Keep her a precious mystery. It had been blessed happenstance that the then Duke of Castleberry was amenable to presenting a future to his son.

The parlor door opened, and she turned.

"The Right Honorable Lord Endsleigh," Smythe said.

She'd been expecting the duke, so when Hugh was announced instead, an instant relief passed through her system, a great betrayal by her body. Her mind determined to counter the effects, and she was once again tense, the relief from his presence only momentary. She frowned but managed to control the shock in her eyes as Hugh skirted the butler and walked toward her. Her heart seemed to slow, though the sound of her pulse seemed to increase. *Strange, that.*

Amelia's face was void of emotion, then the suppressed smile fought for purchase and gained on her as she met him halfway. "Hugh."

"My lady," he said as he took both of her hands and kissed the backs of each in turn.

"Hugh, I—"

"No. Please." He pulled her to the settee, and they fell, knees together, her hands still bound to his. It was more of a knot, really, his fingers twined with the one hand, the other wrapped up around her wrist. Her pulse beat against his fingertips. "Last night. I want to apologize. Quite profusely, really," he said.

She shook her head. "No, I'll not allow it." She sighed heavily, and then, "I wish to return to Pembroke. So very desperately. The need to return exceeds every other wish I have. The sooner I'm betrothed, the sooner I'm to quit London."

His head bowed, and she saw the errant bit of curl that he'd never been able to tame. That curl made her smile, and she untangled her fingers from his and reached up to it with a giggle. This errant curl was the cause of so many chases through the wood near their homes. She, always teasing him.

He looked up to her without raising his head as she twirled the curl round her finger. Then she caught his eyes. Her smile faded, and her hand dropped.

"How will I ever…how will I ever live without you? I cannot bear it. You've been…you are—"

He took her hand again as her tears fell. "Do not muss your beautiful face. You know Jacks will be here soon," Hugh said quietly, skimming a tear from her cheek with his thumb.

She shook her head. "I want him here. I want him to ask, do I not? I want to be with him…yet I do not. Ever since we met, I've wondered if I merely believed him to be my salvation, or something more. Now, after last night I believe…I believe he might be more."

Why did her heart beat harder at that realization? Hugh breathed, and it was as though the air had stolen from the room as she waited for the words to follow. Willed her heart to slow.

"I understand," was all he said. He released her and shifted away. "I need to say something. Please do not interrupt, because there will be no way for me to finish this, should you do so." Hugh glanced back as his eyes narrowed, and she nodded slightly. Any words she had stayed at the edge of her tongue.

"Jacks came to me last night." His eyes crinkled as he gave her another unspoken warning then stood and turned away. "He wishes to know what it is about you that makes you so different from the rest."

"He knows." Amelia's heart skipped as she spoke on an inhale.

"How could he not? Amelia, he's no imbecile. If you wish it…if you wish for me to…I would teach him."

She stood, and he turned to her.

"You cannot. You…no, I could not bear it for you. It's not something to be learned, at any rate. It's simply me—and you with me."

Hugh raised his eyes as hers widened. She felt her pulse again and saw him tense, then he took her outstretched hand, seemed to engulf her hand with his larger one and pressed as he held her eyes, and her breathing slowed.

"Amelia mine. There are things he can do. I've taught others before him, and I shall give all my secrets away if you wish it. Because I know you love—"

"I love you," she cut in. *Others? Louisa,* she thought. But her thoughts were immediately interrupted by Hugh speaking.

"Do you? If that were but true, I would be the happiest man alive. But you may love him as well, and you simply cannot have me." Her heartbeat paced again, and he pulled her closer. "Amelia, my dear sweet Amelia, look at me. You will always have a piece of me. I'll remain with you forever in some form. One cannot spend a veritable lifetime with another person and not carry them within for all eternity."

Her hands wrapped around his lapels as she buried her face in his shirt.

Surely he will be in need of a new neckcloth.

It was true. There was no time in her memory in which he did not exist. As though they were born to each other.

This man, this man, this man. This strength, this heat, this heart that beats against my skin. This hardness, this body, this soul, these eyes.

Amelia's insides tensed in preparation for the spiral, and as though he knew, his arms went around her, held her together, then slowly released. She looked up and—*when had his hands moved?*—he wrapped them around her cheeks, his fingertips sinking into the hair at her nape. He looked into her eyes, paused for an insurmountable amount of time as she watched. He seemed to be considering her, waiting, looking for something. She drew a slow breath, then her eyes dropped to his mouth when his lips opened slightly, and then she felt him on her.

His lips, so heavy, so soft, so gentle...*gentle, oh, could anything ever be so gentle as this?* She sighed, and he took advantage, and her mouth betrayed her, allowing him the intrusion. It was the most sincere of first kisses. This kiss was truth and it was pain.

Her hands reached up to his wrists, holding them, holding her.

She knew this—this kiss, her first, their last, their one kiss—was her forever. How could she ever recover from this man? He was her rock. Her hands smoothed up his arms then attempted to cover his face.

"Amelia."

When had the kissing stopped?

She opened her eyes to see the bright, terrified gaze of her friend, closer than he had any right to be.

"You've ruined me," she breathed. "There is no choice now."

His gentle chuckle bid a smile from her unwilling mouth. *So very unwilling.* She swayed toward him, but he held her steady.

"Should I speak with your father? Throw open the door to the parlor and call upon your mother to witness your ruination?"

She shook her head. "It could not possibly be this simple. No, it would not be. Would it?" Her eyes fluttered, then snapped to his. "Oh, was that aloud? I did not mean to say—"

"Of course you didn't, and therein lies the difficulty. You're still bound to him."

Amelia's head fell, and every muscle in her body pulled her down as though weighted to sink to the depths of the ocean, his strength the only thing holding her up.

"Amelia, I'll not give up this easy. I'll have you as my wife, but not with a doubt in your mind."

"I thought you came here to…to…"

"I did, and then I saw you, and I could not, and now I find it's not as simple as even that. I do not believe him to be the better man for you. I thought—I don't know what I thought. After last night, I believed what you believe. That perhaps this was not meant to be. But here, in your arms, with that kiss, I find I'm unable to simply give you up."

"Yet you must. He's coming. We are to go to the park. He's to speak with Father. You know what that means."

He looked at her then in a way that she could feel his eyes within and without and knew to the toes of her boots he meant what he said next.

"I'm bound by no man's wishes. And neither are you—yet." Hugh turned and walked out.

Wait was on the edge of her tongue. *Do not go* tried its level best to free itself from her mind. "Please," was all that came out, on a breath, and that—much too late.

She raised her hand to her lips, whether to feel the softness, pliant and warmed by his kiss, or to attempt to expunge the memory, she was unsure.

Hugh strode from the house without a backward glance. He'd no idea what he was to do next. He stopped beside Termagant and leaned over, resting his hands on his knees, attempting to catch his breath. He felt as though his soul had been torn from his chest and what was left but the empty, angry, shell of a man. If it had been up to him, he'd quit London this very moment and return to his estate. But he would not, could not simply give her up.

Damn me.

Hugh looked down the street to see the carriage with the ducal crest of Castleberry emblazoned on the side, and a roar boiled in his gut. He straightened, took his mount from the waiting groom, and jumped to his seat. He would be damned to be standing on the same footing with Jacks when he arrived.

The carriage slowed, and the outriders jumped down, securing the horses and opening the carriage door.

Hugh waited, though he knew he shouldn't.

Charles sat in the coach, his mind twisting around the possibilities of why Ender was here. Ender had made it clear to him last evening that he'd no intention of helping. Charles knew that Ender was a part of Amelia's life, and he was prepared to be tolerant until their marriage was final, but he didn't feel quite so prepared today.

Charles tapped his cane on the floorboards as he glanced out the door. He could see Endsleigh sitting his horse in an arrogant fashion. Ender should have dismounted if his intention was to greet him.

They both knew it.

Charles tapped his cane again and looked to the house to see Amelia in the window of the parlor. He could see her hand pressed to the glass as she watched Ender. She lifted a delicate white cloth to her eyes, and he knew she cried.

He looked back to Ender, the tension rippling through the man, his mount restless under it.

Charles moved to the door and stepped out and saw the curtain in the window swing in his periphery as Amelia stepped away. He took a deep breath and turned toward Ender. Charles looked up, then bent at the waist in the most respectful bow he could pull from his ducal training. Perhaps this bit of regard would prove his worth. When he straightened, he found Ender's angry gaze boring into him. Ender gave a stiff nod and kicked his mount, who reared and took to the street in a dead run.

Had Ender done it? Had he broken with her? Was she to be his? Charles looked back to Pembroke House. Why did he not feel as though this were a victory?

He shook the thoughts off and walked slowly to the door as Smythe opened it wide. Charles stepped in line behind him as he was led to the parlor.

"His Grace." The butler's voice cracked. "The Duke of Castleberry." *Was the entire household affected badly by this turn?*

Amelia turned toward him, and it was as though the sun had risen for him in this room.

Charles moved to her as another woman entered the room behind him, pulling him up short. The chaperone, of course.

"Your Grace, how wonderful to see you again. This is my aunt, Lady Mathorpe."

"My lady," he said as he took Amelia's hand, only to feel the tremble within. He paused, considered, and then, "If you're not well enough for an outing today, I would—"

"No, Your Grace, nothing would please me more." But her voice had caught on the word please.

Her smile was the brilliance of a thousand daffodils opening at once to him. *When did I become so maudlin?* Charles thought. He shook his head.

If he managed to get her out to the park, they might have a moment to speak on these things that were so very important. He smiled to reassure her as he saw the edges of her lips waver.

"My lady, shall we?" He proffered his arm, and she took it so gently, it was almost a whisper of a touch. He had to look to see that her hand was actually touching his sleeve, she was so cautious. He turned for the door, nodding to her chaperone. "Lady Mathorpe, an honor."

Lady Mathorpe nodded but seemed a bit annoyed. Charles knew Amelia was aware of her aunt's annoyance by the grip of her fingers, no longer delicate.

He placed his other hand over hers, stroking her fingers gently through the dual layers of gloves, and felt them ease a bit. His smile widened, and he led her to the carriage.

Lady Mathorpe took the seat next to Amelia, leaving him to ride facing the rear. He shuffled past their hems, careful not to step on the delicate fabrics that seemed to fill the carriage floor, then shifted his knees as he sat so as not to bump either lady. Once carefully seated, he smiled at both in turn and nodded to his outrider, who shut the door soundly, and they were off.

A

Amelia turned her head toward the carriage window. She closed her eyes and took a deep breath, then relaxed her features and opened her eyes slowly. She marveled at how the duke filled the carriage, and it was not a mere conveyance, by any means. The carriage was impressive, and this man's presence was formidable. And he was watching her.

Charles did not appear frightened or nervous—she hated nervous—and he definitely did not watch her with any pity, but he was cautious and perhaps concerned. That was acceptable after this morning. She would be silly to think he was not aware something had transpired in her parlor.

The fact is, if it had been anyone else, if it had been her mother— God save her—she would have already faced the inquisition for simply being a bit out of sorts.

But Charles—he simply watched.

He had held her hands, not the duke, *him*. Hugh had held her hands and taken her mouth and effectively declared war on her future, and Charles merely waited for her to be ready to inform him. She turned her face to hide the shock of pain, revisited so suddenly.

Amelia concentrated on the sounds of the horses, the pounding hooves, the turn of the wheels on the cobbles, the creak of the outrider on the rear step. She heard more hooves at the rear, not from the team at the front. Those hooves, just to her right just beyond the carriage, those hooves…belonged to him. *Him*. She knew Hugh followed.

She felt a gentle sweep at her hand and saw his hand there, the duke's, with a handkerchief, and she reached up to find a tear on her cheek. Charles's offer was so very personal, so very thoughtful, not condemning, not judging, but concerned. And given with caution.

She should take it.

She could feel her aunt's gaze on the handkerchief. The heavy weight of tension doubled.

Take the handkerchief. Take it. Take the cloth from his hand, she thought.

Her hand twitched as she willed herself to move, then nodded toward him when she did. "Thank you, I seem to have something…" She waved her hand and let herself trail off for the benefit of Lady Mathorpe. As well as for the duke. She hid behind the cloth momentarily, breathing. Feeling his warmth invade her, his personal scent—leather and polish— masculine and strong. She breathed deeper, attempting to catch more of him in her senses. There was something else below those scents, but she could not manage past her aunt's cloying odor. It seemed to cling and hang from everything inside the carriage. Like the Spanish moss draped across the trees in paintings she'd seen of the American South.

She dabbed at her eyes then held the warm, scented cloth just below her nose and breathed again. There it was. Below the leather—or perhaps buffering it—strength, fresh cotton, and man. Time slowed, it stood, it waited.

Time would wait for Hugh no longer—

STOP.

She breathed again, then looked to the window, as she did not trust herself to look at him. Not *him*, the duke him. *Was he now him?* Another tear fell.

Get yourself together. Her hands shook.

The carriage made its way along the street to the park then pulled into an open spot on the walk. The carriage lurched from the jerk of the reins. She heard the boots hit the ground. One set, two, a third, then Hugh's.

They were last—they were cautious. His boots were whispering his discomfort to her. Not commanding, not demanding, not jumping from the carriage to purpose. His boots were silently stepping down

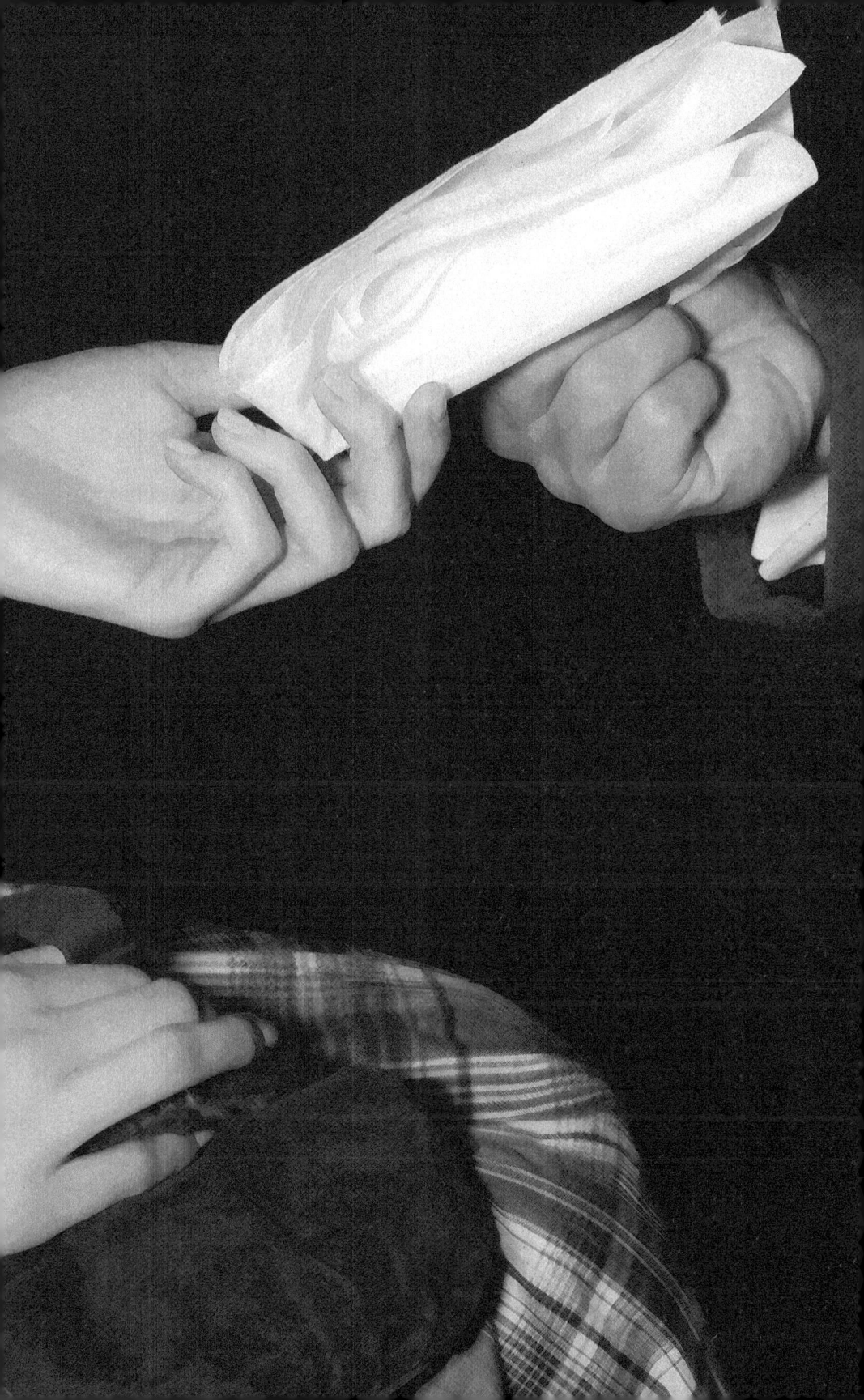

from his mount, quietly shuffling aside the carriage as he tied his horse to the bar at the back.

Amelia's eyes dried. She tested her smile and pushed Hugh to the back of her mind for the moment. *But only for a moment,* she promised, as though he could hear her. Only a moment. She turned to Charles to return the handkerchief, but he raised his hand.

"It would honor me if you would keep it." The deep rumble of his voice soothed as it spoke of his want for intimacy. *With her.*

Amelia froze when she heard her aunt huff in the seat next to her. She saw Charles's indifference to the woman's opinion and smiled. "The honor is mine, Your Grace." It was a revelation presented in a sentence. She'd always been nervous that he'd been chosen for her because he could be controlled by her family—so this was a mollification of sorts.

The door opened quickly, pulling the air from the carriage with it, and she startled. Charles stepped down, then handed her out to the green of the park, the laughter of children, the singing of birds and rushing of water. She inhaled the gardens and sighed heavily, her very being relaxing incrementally.

She felt Jacks place her hand on his arm, keeping his hand, his warm, warm hand, upon hers as they strolled away from the carriage. She glanced around, expecting to see Hugh, but he was nowhere to be seen.

Another trick of my addled brain. Was it because she'd wanted him here with her so desperately that her brain had attempted to conjure him for her? She inhaled the scenery again, trying her level best to school her features, to control her thoughts, and to prevent them from running away with her. Hugh was not here. Charles was here. Charles, her future husband, her…future.

Perhaps this could be a good place for a beginning, she thought. *It's not too crowded*—crowds made her nervousness infinitely worse—*if only I can maintain a certain presence.*

Charles turned back to the carriage as his outrider stepped up and helped Lady Mathorpe down the steps. He was starting to believe that she was of her sister's ilk, holding the belief that Amelia brought everything on herself, that she behaved as she did merely to vex her mother. But he could see that it was so much more. It seemed to him that the more they openly disapproved of her, the more difficulty she had.

Charles narrowed his eyes on Lady Mathorpe, and she shifted uncomfortably. Good. Let her writhe within her own distaste. She had merely been sent as a minion, required to report back a successful outing.

He moved to turn back to Amelia. He stopped her, placed her hand on his arm, allowing her aunt to catch up with them. He heard the lady take a breath to say something, and he knew Amelia's gaze was on him, waiting to see his action, so he turned—recalling Lady Mathorpe's full attention to him. His eyes narrowed further on her as if to say, *You have nothing to say.* And, lo, she did not.

What Charles needed was for Amelia to speak with him. Perhaps he should leave the chaperone behind, forget convention, take Amelia down to the lake, to rest and chat without this woman to overhear. He simply wanted to be truthful. He wanted to know. He was a man of action, and all this dancing about was making him as disturbed as it appeared to be disturbing Amelia.

Charles could see the tension course through her. He had seen her relax at the surroundings, but the nearer her aunt drew, the more he attempted simple conversation, the more her muscles drew tight. The words between them were inane, mundane, simple and easy, not at all what they should have been discussing. Nowhere near the lightness he wished to see in her.

And he could tell she knew that as well as he did.

Amelia stretched her fingers, wishing she could know what they would discuss. Discussion was always easier for her were she able to prepare. She expected questions of Hugh. Perhaps she could move him to reminisce. She would have been quite comfortable talking of the past.

She smiled to herself, thinking of the three of them on the moors, then she felt him turn, the muscles of his forearm tense and, like water on steel, it spread to her.

Tension. Like a bow, drawn so tight the wood bent backward. The first time she'd ever seen an unstrung bow she was mesmerized, amazed that the bow was bent the wrong direction. It made perfect sense, suddenly. The extreme amount of tension—*yes, there was no other word unfortunately*—required to string a bow, to turn that piece of yew inside out and hold it taut was understandable to her.

No. Not understandable...familiar.

She felt as an unstrung bow at her best moments. Home, on her father's land at Pembroke-by-the-Sea. Running amok with Hugh as children.

Unfortunately, right now she was strung. Tight. Waiting to be fired from...*upon, without? From. Simply from.* Knowing even once the arrow was loosed, the bow simply returned to well strung. Not retired, not loose, not comfortable. She was uncomfortable in her own skin. As if all that skin were not hers.

"My lady." That was all he said, but her shoulders relaxed slightly, her neck returned to a decent length, her fingers calmed. Had she been grasping her reticule? *Oh dear.* It seemed she'd knocked some of the beads off.

Unfortunate.

"I beg your pardon for my inattention," Charles said with an easy smile.

Had he been inattentive?

She returned the smile, not as easily, then a twinge threatened a searing pain, and she looked away, but not before she knew he'd seen it. She glanced around the park, expecting to still see *him* here. *Hugh.* Her shoulder blades spread, like angel wings, and she concentrated on that, willing the rest of her body to follow suit.

When she felt a pull, she moved with Charles again, and they walked, the two of them. As it should be. She watched her toes peek out from under her skirts as they strolled in tandem. His black shoes brushed her skirts, sending them to sway. Perhaps she should have worn the blue. The color would have matched his eyes.

She smiled, and his hand squeezed over hers.

"I would very much like to know what you're thinking," he said, quiet enough to not be overheard.

"That I should have worn the brown to match your eyes." The second she said it, she realized she shouldn't have. *What have I done? That was much too forward.*

"Oh—I...well, I very much like the blue. If that makes a difference. The color matches *your* eyes. Rather seems to make them shine." He was watching her too closely, and she felt a flush creep over her skin. "You have beautiful eyes, Amelia."

Her breath lodged somewhere in her throat.

I did not give him leave to use my name. Should I give him leave to use my name? She turned to look out over the gardens, willing her breath to return. "I did not give you leave..." She cleared her throat when the words were barely audible, and he leaned toward her incrementally. The heat of him, the warmth...it begged her to melt against him.

She inhaled suddenly. "I feel as though I cannot lie to you," she croaked.

He stopped and took both of her hands in his.

"This is a good thing. 'Tis the basis for a strong relationship. I certainly do not want to hear anything untrue from you, as I'm confident you're not interested in lies from me." His hand traveled slowly up her arm, the right one, the one without the reticule—and the pace of her heart, and the breath from her lungs, sped with his advance.

Charles circled the side of her bare elbow with his thumb, just above her glove, and Amelia watched as his eyes darkened. She leaned toward him to get a better look, and he stopped, then turned and led her to a small bench under a willow just beside the water.

Amelia took a seat and saw her aunt had stopped several feet away, then Amelia looked up at him as he paced. Now he seemed nervous.

"Society dictates that a man be delicate when dealing with a woman. This simple dictate would prevent me asking every question I have of you," Charles said as he stopped and looked at her.

Amelia's hands tightened on her reticule, and she felt a bead pop off, bouncing to the ground in front of her. Her eyes followed as the bead rolled across the dirt and into the blades of grass. This reticule was a particularly bad idea, too many baubles and beads. It simply wasn't compatible with her. It was a nice reticule, pink and beaded, though it was a bit large. She shouldn't blame the reticule for being a reticule.

"Amelia?"

She shook her head and looked back up to him. "Your Grace, yes, I do beg your pardon. I was..." She waved her hand around, his handkerchief floating behind it. She watched the linen drift then dropped her hand to her lap rather suddenly. "I was trying to be delicate. I've learned from the best, you see." She set her reticule on the bench next to her, fearing it would be completely denuded should she continue to handle it. She stared at the reticule, as though it would castigate her for being reckless. The reticule seemed to stare back.

A reticule. The very idea...

She heard him moving slowly toward her, much like a hunter, to avoid startling his prey, then he took a seat, the reticule between them. The bench wasn't made for him. His knees were at a strange angle, she realized, because the bench was a bit short and he was a bit long. She worried whether this would bother him.

"I'm not like other women," she said distractedly. *Damn me.*

Charles waited for more, and she felt that wait in every single hair of her nape as each one took its turn in coming to attention, spreading a shiver across her skin. "I...prefer to be frank. That often comes across as indelicacy," she said as her body drifted toward him, as though a magnet.

"Is that all there is to it? A preference?" he asked quietly. "There is nothing more than that?" Charles drifted slowly toward her as well. Or perhaps the movement was all in her imagination. She dearly wished her mind would quiet so she could concentrate on him. The offending reticule continued to stare up at her.

Amelia looked out over the water, hoping that if she broke the tenuous bond between them—she and the duke, not she and the reticule—that her mind would set to rights. She knew there was so much more, but also knew that there was no way to explain to him everything that she was.

"Well, I dislike crowds and..." She turned back toward him. "I *hate* this reticule—" She caught herself before saying more. They both stared down at the offending bag.

"That's easily rectified. Is there anything within the reticule that you need? I have a pocket to spare." Charles shifted on the bench and showed her the pocket in his coat, right next to his chest. She thought she'd like to curl into that pocket, it looked so cozy and warm, and now she was suddenly jealous of the contents of her reticule—such as they were.

She found herself looking at the duke's handkerchief in her hand, then slowly opened the reticule and pulled hers from it, handing the handkerchief to him. Her eyes were trapped by the movement of his hand, on her handkerchief, moving toward that pocket. She could feel the safety wash over her bones as the linen square disappeared in there, cozy and secure. Then he closed his coat and patted it from the outside, and she could feel it bodily, as though he'd patted her, and that feeling broke the connection. She looked up to him.

"I shall return this to you before we leave the park or whenever you may have need of it."

Amelia felt the nod but couldn't pull her eyes from him.

He stood and reached for the reticule, picking it up carefully, his eyes never leaving hers, as though to be sure she weren't a snake preparing to strike. When he had full possession of it, he turned swiftly and launched the reticule into the lake. Water fowl burst from the surface and spread in all directions, regathering to land on the far banks.

They didn't like that reticule, either, it seemed.

She laughed, and he turned back to her, basking in the sound that raised goose bumps across his forearms, traveled his body and rested somewhere deep inside. Her laugh was beautiful, whole and hearty, and he loved it. He felt quite rewarded.

"Problem solved," he said with a shrug.

He saw her demeanor shift slightly, saw her regather her composure as though it was made of marbles spilled across the lawn. Amelia then lifted his handkerchief to her lips, to cover her mouth discreetly, and he realized the show had begun again in earnest.

Disappointing, that.

"Amelia, if ever there's a reticule that offends, please call on me. I will not hesitate to come to your rescue." The smile, though covered, was genuine, and he relaxed a bit into the bench.

"Your Grace," she said after a time.

"My lady," he responded, willing her to continue.

"Why ever would you toss my reticule into a pond?"

"Well, you said you hated it. And you were looking at the reticule as though it might attack. I determined the danger and rectified the situation. It's…what I do."

"My mother—"

"Was it your mother's reticule?"

"No, Your Grace, the reticule was mine, but my mother will wonder what happened to it. She will be quite disappointed in me."

"You didn't throw the reticule in the lake. I did. In fact"— and here he turned to check, then took her eyes with his as though a physical possibility—"Lady Mathorpe can attest to that. Can you not, lady?" he said a bit louder, knowing full well the chaperone had heard every word between them. He then winked at Amelia, pulling her into the conspiracy. She giggled. Another reward—this one he felt a bit lower. He wished to do it again and again, until his entire body was awash with her laughter. Someone should take up a study of this. He rather believed her laughter was willing him to misbehave.

They sat peacefully for a time, then the air shifted, as though a heavy blanket was, very slowly, being lowered over them.

"I thought you had grand things you wished to discuss with me," she said quietly.

"Was saving you from your offending accessory not grand enough?"

She smiled…but the blanket remained. The moment had passed.

Charles nodded and leaned forward. "Amelia, there are many things I wish to discuss with you, a lifetime of things, in truth. Where shall we start?" He absolutely had questions for her, but did not want to break what jovial mood was left in her.

"Should we start with the difficult and work our way to the mundane? That only seems logical," she said quietly. Hurriedly. Worriedly.

He tensed slightly and knew she was aware of it. "You said you dislike crowds, but here we are…the only crowds the fowl, which have removed to the far edge of the lake, and I still sense a wariness about you." He paused and watched her smooth his handkerchief across her knee. "Is there more to it than that?" he asked quietly, hoping that Lady Mathorpe had found enough of a distraction off by the edge of the water. He watched Amelia as she considered his words, then saw her flinch.

There is something so very wrong with you!

Her mother's voice in her head prevented her saying what she truly wished to. "That is the simple of it. Beyond that, I believe you would require a certain knowledge of me to understand." With that, she looked directly at him, something that *had* been carefully trained out of her. "We are not that familiar, you and I." The hairs on her neck revolted at her frank speech and wilted, a shiver coursing her flesh, her mind reeling, attempting to pull the words back even as it was much too late.

"I understand that there are things that require a certain familiarity, one which we do not *yet* have. But isn't that what this courting is for? An attempt to discover if we would suit?"

She nodded once, then words burst from her, escaping much against her will. "I would think if you knew me better you would not consider me the least bit suitable." Her hand flew to her mouth then, as if to trap the words, but this, much too late. She bit her lip as punishment.

"Amelia, I—"

"I did not yet give you leave—"

"Yes, I—I beg your pardon. I feel as though I know you. Perhaps I feel that bond between us from childhood yet and wish to hold on to it." He shook his head. "My lady, I do not know how to make you understand my feelings on this matter. I appreciate..." Charles paused, and she considered how well *his* mouth was being controlled by *his* will. Marveled in it, was terribly jealous of it. "I appreciate that you are different, but I believe it is that difference that has always held my sway. When I was a young boy, nobody ever spoke so frankly to me as you. Your forwardness was quite...refreshing."

She giggled, then politely covered her mouth. "Refreshing? Is that what you choose to call it? My mother would call that impertinence, an attribute frowned upon by future husbands the world over."

"Impertinence." He grunted. "I rather like your sort of impertinence. It kept me in line."

Amelia couldn't help but smile. She had rather spoken her mind at him as a child, pulled him from his cushy womb of dukedom and forced him out into the viscid wilderness of the world.

"Well, I will endeavor to be as impertinent as possible. Though I'm unsure what that will look like as I am ever attempting to be not so impertinent, and the result is truly blatant impertinence and..." He started to laugh. "Oh goodness..."

"Yes, well. I think you lost me on the second impertinent, but we'll just have to see how it goes, won't we?" He reached out and took her hand again, and she realized at that moment—she wasn't shivering or overconcerned with details.

But then he touched her, and her mind homed in on the contact, like a single burst of energy between them. The shock of the heat of his hand through the layers of gloves was nearly too much, and her heart stuttered. She jerked away.

"I beg your pardon," he whispered.

No no no no no! she nearly cried, surprised when her mouth didn't actually make the sound, but stayed silent, vigilant, though a sob rendered her sadness with stunning clarity.

"I...Your Grace, I didn't mean to…I didn't mean to offend. I would have liked to hold your hand. I don't understand why that happened." She closed her eyes, saw Hugh, then looked up to see Charles.

A

Charles reached for her slowly this time. Much more slowly. Made sure her eyes were on his hand. This time, her hand nearly melted into his, and it verily took his breath. Never had he felt such synergy with another person. It was more than the sum of their two worlds.

He knew, in the way her lip trembled, that she felt that connection as well. A peace seemed to rend her motionless, while the whole of her self appeared to relax. All those muscles, retreating into a whole, like melting butter in the sun.

She looked up to him with glazed eyes.

"Would you please call me Amelia?"

"I would be honored, beyond measure, to call you Amelia." He heard her aunt huff from the shore, not a far enough distance away, and her control snapped back into place instantaneously, the feel of her hand whipping away nearly leaving him dizzy.

Every defense she had fell into place like the heavy gates at Castleberry Keep, and that pained him. *What now?* he thought. He had to bring her back.

His father had told him that every woman wanted to hear that she was loved. Charles had no idea what that meant—love. He knew he felt for her like he felt for no one in the world, but he assumed that if he'd felt love, for anything or anyone, he would have known it. He did feel something…and he was happy to call it love, if it were to make her happy, but using with her the tactic his father had taught him—it would have felt more than wrong. He did not want to taint this…whatever this was.

FIVE

Hugh walked into his study, poured two fingers of whiskey from the tantalus on his desk, then paused with the tumbler at his lips, allowing the scent to burn through his nose and reach his lungs. He slammed the glass to the desktop, shaking off the splash of liquor that hit his palm.

He sat heavily in the chair, then turned the chair toward the windows at his back, putting his boots up on the sill and leaning against the worn leather. He'd kissed her. He'd promised himself, long ago, that he wouldn't kiss her unless she was truly his. He'd known, to the depths of his soul, that if he kissed her, he simply would not release her. And he had, most definitely, kissed her.

Truly, it had been so much more than just a kiss, as he'd known it would be. He'd poured every promise he had into that simple touch of lips. And what did promises mean now? He probably wouldn't have thought so harshly of himself, of his own broken promise, if that damned duke hadn't been so damnably honorable.

He closed his eyes and threw his arm over his face, his nose resting solidly in the crook of his elbow. He breathed deep. His jacket smelled of her where they had been melded together. Where they had touched.

The sweet, wholesome scent of her.

'He breathed of it slowly for a while.

Castleberry should not be so patient. He should not have offered that bit of respect. So much had been spoken in that bow. As Hugh had meant to convey as much by ascending to his seat and staying himself, looking down upon the man who was so much more than he ever would be.

This was inconceivable. He could not, would not, allow this man an honorable character. That quite made him impossible to hate, and Hugh wanted so desperately to hate Charles.

Castleberry was forcing him to rethink everything he knew to be true. That she was taken from Hugh. That she belonged to Hugh. That this duke was the enemy. That she could never be happy with Charles. That Charles was not at all what she needed. That the only man in the world for her was Hugh. That she was meant for Hugh, meant to be his, meant to spend her days with him, the rest of her life in the comfortable seat of his barony.

Hugh groaned and swung his legs down, leaning forward on his elbows, his hands steepled between them. Could he—he closed his eyes and forced his mind around the thought—could he allow this duke to care for her? Could he let her go? He felt the pain of it so suddenly, so keenly, that the entirety of him shuddered. To separate her from him, to push her out of this soft place inside where she had so completely invaded the very breath of him. To turn, and to walk away.

Hugh realized then that he'd not truly prepared himself to break with her that morning. In fact, he knew then that he'd gone to do exactly what it was that he did do. Hugh had been a fool to think otherwise, and now…Hugh turned back to the whiskey and downed it, hoping to dull a bit of that raw, gaping wound that had torn through his very core at the thought of sending her off.

He'd always seen Jackson as a rival, and thus the pranks, the childish games to push him away, to keep Jackson from Amelia. Hugh's actions had been cruel, and he'd known it, even though he'd been just a boy. But Amelia's father had told him that she was meant for Castleberry, had asked Hugh to help foster a relationship between the two. Even then, the division from her had affected Hugh in a tangible way, and thus began the assault, keeping Castleberry from coming between them in those early years. Quite opposed to what her father had asked of Hugh.

Hugh didn't seem to be the honorable man that he'd always wished for Amelia when he considered these things. Hugh's head fell to the desk with a mighty , and he groaned yet again. What had he done? He'd been selfish, single-minded in his belief. All this time, telling himself he knew what was best for her, that was what was best for her, and with a single bow to his cocky, overbearing, improper self, Castleberry had shattered everything Hugh believed to be true.

How terribly unfair.

Charles stood. Looked at the woman. Might have growled at her. Lady Mathorpe backed away slowly, and Charles turned back to Amelia, pulling her up from the bench and walking her farther down the crystal water's edge. Amelia looked to make sure Lady Mathorpe did not follow closely before she spoke.

"I believe we would suit, if you're willing to take me on. I do understand that I would be a chore. However, your suit would make my father and mother quite happy should you agree." Amelia offered this statement to him as an apology, though it did sound terribly clinical to her ears.

Charles shook his head slowly. "It would not at all be a chore. Marriage to you would be an honor." His feet stopped, and she nearly tripped on the sway of her skirts. "Did you just offer for me?" he asked as he steadied her. "You amaze me. I have—" He looked down in concentration, and she focused on the feel of his thumbs circling the backs of her hands.

"I believe I've cared deeply for you, in some form, since the moment I first saw you." Charles cleared his throat then as he looked a bit confused, and she felt her jaw relax a bit too much. "I could only hope that you would also be terribly happy, and perhaps even one day you would come to care for me as well."

That echoed in her head for a bit of time, along with: . She tried to breathe through the realization of it all. He had said "as well." Which meant—to her mind—that he already did. Care for her.

It was then, after an insurmountable pause, that he caught her gaze again, and she was locked to his. If she had wished with all her might, she would not have been able to turn away.

"There is no chore considered when I think of spending my life with you. There is no place I would rather be. There is no woman I would rather share my every simple day with." Charles squeezed her hands, and when he blinked, she was able to look down—and breathe. She desperately needed to breathe.

"I...I thought you were merely following the wishes of your father," she said. "I knew he had words with my father. I knew they'd arranged this when you were there that summer."

"No, Amelia, that was merely the door that gave me access. And won't you please call me Charles?"

Her mouth dropped open, as if to say it. To breathe the very life into him on the sound of his name on her lips, but she paused and scanned the park—

Charles dropped his gaze to her hands. "Perhaps soon you'll be as familiar with me as you are with Endsleigh." He said the words quietly. Purposefully. His gaze traveled slowly up her figure. The dress really was quite pretty. It reminded him of the broad sweeping meadows near Castleberry Keep, the soft turn of her hips, the pinch of her waist, and the beautiful curve of her—he forced his gaze to her eyes. The dress did, truly, match her eyes. His own eyes betrayed him and fell to her lips.

"There are things we should discuss, prior to our betrothal," Charles said. A tremble rippled through her, and he knew she worried. He desperately wanted to allay her fears, but he also required a bit of reassurance himself. "Amelia. I would be honored to spend my life with you, but not if it isn't what you truly wish, and at this moment, I don't believe that it is.

"I believe you need to discover what it is you desire. Whether it be me..." He smoothed both hands up her gloved arms and stroked the bared skin at the very edge of the fabric. He felt her tension ebb, her body sway. "Or Ender." With that name, Charles pulled his hands away, clasping them behind his back. Perhaps removing his touch had been a cruel move, but he needed her to realize that if her heart were engaged elsewhere, his could not be availed to her.

She swayed, and Charles wished to steady her, but he forced himself not to. He clenched his hands together and sent up a prayer for the will to keep a certain distance between them. It seemed an age before he knew she was ready to speak.

"I understand," was all she said.

Charles turned and glanced at their chaperone, standing at a mere twenty paces, yet between them nonetheless. Amelia lifted her hand to her lips, holding his handkerchief, and inhaled deeply as she looked around. He followed her gaze.

"Amelia, I cannot help but feel our marriage bed would be crowded."

Her eyes widened, and she looked away yet again. "I cannot promise more than I know, and I know this—he and I cannot be together. It is as simple as that."

"So not simple at all, really."

"I can only wish...I do not know. I cannot know. Please understand that when I think of him, I consider him a dear friend, whom I will miss terribly."

"But certainly your friendship has grown over the years." His eyes traveled her figure again. "You have grown into a woman, and he...a man. Undoubtedly, your friendship has grown as well, perhaps changed as much as you have?" Charles was truly worried now.

"No, I…I don't think so, at least not from my perspective, though I know not about Hugh. I have a feeling he isn't of the same mind. In truth, I cannot tell you. He's all I've ever known of love, beyond that of my father. So judging these feelings…I know what I feel for you is different. This I know for certain. I also know that I would like to experience more of it. To better understand it, because my feelings carry a great deal of confusion with them…" She gazed into his eyes, nearly bored through them to the back of his skull as if to attempt to read his very intent. After a moment, her gaze settled into a confused countenance. "You threw my reticule in the pond."

He grinned, then nodded. "I did, yes. That was me." He relaxed incrementally. This is what he'd hoped for, in a manner at any rate. That she had no idea was entirely better than if she had believed she loved Ender as more than a friend.

"I should get you back to your mother. I will speak with your father today, Amelia, because I told him I would, but I must tell you I will ask for permission only to court you formally. Is that agreeable to you?"

"Yes, I—yes." She sounded resigned, as though she had been prepared for more…or even less.

His heart stuttered. Something inside him tried to force him to his knees to beg her forgiveness, but, alas, whatever it was, it was not powerful enough to do so yet. Charles took her hand, then gained her attention and smiled.

"Amelia, can we call this a beginning?"

"I would very much like to," she whispered.

"As would I. May I call on you tomorrow? Perhaps we could attend the opera later this week as well?"

She nodded, and Charles finally saw what he believed to be a very genuine smile.

They turned together for the carriage. Lady Mathorpe followed.

SIX

The return in the carriage was fraught with confusion. She had prepared herself. Truly, she had. Practiced endlessly, not only for the hopeful conclusion, but as well for the inevitable rejection. She had not prepared herself for maybe.

She had never prepared herself for maybe. Most people knew in a moment whether they wished to be near her, but this man...how could he not know? This confused her greatly. She twisted the handkerchief until some of the stitches popped, then frowned when she realized what she'd done.

She had planned to place the handkerchief in her jewelry box. Carefully protecting the square of linen from damage, able to pull it out at any moment and remember his kindness, and the way he smelled. She smoothed the linen and reached for her reticule, so as to protect it from herself. When her hand met the soft cushion of the carriage, the empty space where she knew her reticule should be, she winced. Not because he had thrown her reticule in the lake, but because he had thrown it in the lake *for her*. Amelia wished she still had that reticule, to remember this day by, even though in having it…it wouldn't have happened. There she was caught between the memory and the memento.

She cut a glance to her aunt, who was looking out the other window, then pushed the handkerchief carefully into her bodice, for safety.

She looked up to find Jacks watching her, closely, and realized she hadn't checked to be sure his attention was elsewhere before placing his handkerchief, *his handkerchief,* in her bodice so close to her bosom. His eyes seemed to darken again—surely, a trick of the light—and he reached into his jacket, never taking those dark eyes from hers. She watched as his hand searched, then he finally pulled her own handkerchief out of the elusive pocket and handed the linen to her.

"I believe this is yours," he said, so quietly she thought she'd imagined it.

She endeavored to paste on a genuine smile—which only meant her face was most likely twisted and pained into some semblance of propriety, so she closed her eyes and attempted to calm her now-racing heart. She lifted the handkerchief partly to hide her face and partly to breathe of him. She sank into the scent that was now all his. That fresh cotton smell. The smell reminded her of the laundry on the moors. She longed to see cotton plants. She'd seen drawings of them, and they seemed magical, somehow familiar, something so sweetly soft erupting from such a harsh and inhospitable shell.

Even deeper than the scent of cotton was the very essence of him, that bit of man that had invaded this square of fresh linen the moment he'd placed it in the inside pocket of his coat. The scent was warm, like heat, like safety. She felt her heart steady and swell to take it all in, and she sank into the feeling. She imagined him on the moors with her, the fresh linen carried in the breeze, pinned to the lines, making the sunlight around them dance…

The carriage stopped abruptly, and her eyes popped open to find him contemplating her. A chill coursed her spine as she had the sudden fear that she'd done something inappropriate while daydreaming. She looked from the corner of her eye to her aunt, whose eyes were wide with shock— and so she had.

Damn me twice. What have I done? Her mind ramped up the spiral that would end with an inevitable episode—like a runaway carousel. She clenched her fist around the handkerchief as if to hold on…but then Charles smiled, and her heart paused in her chest. The smile merely quirked the left side of his face, as though there were two of him. This drew her full attention. She could see the smile before she'd even looked at him fully, then this grand, wicked smile broke across his face, left to right, as though awakening her very soul like a sunrise. It finally alighted in his blue eyes, which narrowed. As she watched, the smile seemed to go deeper, darker. This concerned her, and her heart answered with a violent knock, a warning.

What have I done?

In a flash, the safety she held so dear was gone. Her blood thundered in her ears. The door to the carriage jerked open, and the steps clanked as they dropped, startling her. Jacks moved stiffly to the door, and she thought she heard a stifled laugh.

What have I done?

Charles stood with his back to the carriage, shifting and adjusting his coat as she waited, more patiently than her being wished to allow, for him to bring her out.

What have I done?

Charles turned, and she attempted a smile, but the smile quite glanced off his now serious visage. He reached for her, and she paused, was quite unable to move her hand to his. Wasn't sure if his hand would be warm salvation, or the harsh, sharp exterior of the cotton plant.

What have I done?

Charles finally reached in and took that hand that hovered just above her lap in indecision, and the tension broke and flooded her. She breathed then, not a small feat, but a great inhalation of London air. She filled her lungs as much as she was able, bent as she was, corseted as she was, confused as she was, then stepped down.

"What have I done?" Her hand flew to her mouth but couldn't stay the comment, and she pinched her eyes closed, hiding behind her handkerchief.

Charles led her up the stairs. She felt as though he dragged her behind him rather unceremoniously. Charles's head swung around, and his gaze fell to her. She could feel it. Hot, and heavy, and intense. She was thankful for that one great breath of air, as she decided that breath would be her last.

Charles laughed, and the laugh traveled through his broad chest down his arm and into her ribs, where he pressed against her. He pulled her through the front door and into the parlor.

The room was empty, and he blocked the door to entry by pressing her up against it.

Amelia panicked, was truly out of breath, decided begging was her only recourse. She watched the top button on his waistcoat, as she couldn't bring her eyes to his. "What happened in the carriage?" Silence. "Jackson, there's nothing that can come between us if we refuse to allow it. Yet…I'm truly frightened. I only wish that you could understand. Please…tell me what happened in the carriage. Please allow me to explain." She was breathless. Truly, inarguably, without breath.

He grumbled.

"Charles, please, the carriage?" she begged again, desperately wishing to know what had changed his demeanor.

He let out a breath, then advanced, backing her against the door, crowding her. Her breath stopped altogether when that top button became so large in her field of vision she could see little else.

He seemed to be indecisive, this man of decision. His hands floated from her elbows to her shoulders, then they moved to the door, effectively trapping her as his body pressed into hers. As though the touch of his hands required permission, but the rest, the rest he would simply take. She shivered.

"What happened in the carriage?" she sobbed.

He leaned into her, and she closed her eyes tight. "You wish to know what you did?" He groaned the words next to her chin, his breath ruffling the loose hair at her ear.

She nodded, overwhelmed by his proximity, his grand presence, every bit of him surrounding every bit of her. This must be the reckoning. She could feel all of him, the restraint of his hands, the force of the rest.

"Amelia." He breathed in through his nose as he ran the tip of it up the soft skin behind her ear. A wild surge coursed her veins, hitting all of her most intimate areas.

He continued, the words hot on her neck. "Amelia…if you wish to fill your senses with me, there are more direct ways for you to accomplish it. This, for example." He pressed even closer, fitted himself to her, then one hand, his right hand, skimmed down her shoulder to her elbow, spinning tiny circles into the bare skin there.

"I…don't understand. Please, I beg you tell me now."

"Amelia, what you did in the carriage was make quite an unladylike sound while breathing the scent of that handkerchief. I can only assume by the…sensual groan you uttered, that my scent *pleased*

you." The way he said *scent* was so powerful, so strong in tone, that she almost felt the word.

Her eyes snapped open in shock, possibly shame, still trained on that button, and she attempted to explain herself.

"I must beg your forgiveness, Your Grace. I know not what I did, please..." She brought her arms up between them, her hands balled into fists at her chest. She controlled the want to rub her nipples, which had become tight peaks of sensation against her corset.

"Amelia, I feel you may have misconstrued my...reaction. I'm not the least bit appalled, disappointed, or upset by this. There are things running through me, Amelia, that are much more powerful than any displeasure I may have felt."

She had yet to breathe, and she would certainly swoon at any moment, but his weight against her held her steady. "You're angry with me," she said.

Charles's hand tightened on her arm.

No, this is the reckoning, she thought.

"I am *not* angry." Charles's hand loosened, but only just.

"Then what—"

Charles hips pressed against her again, and she concentrated on the connection, attempting to discern what he was trying so boldly to tell her, and she felt a certain hardness that bespoke his ardor. The world stopped. She gasped. Willed the air to her lungs. She grasped his coat and held on as the world spun the other way 'round, and heat flooded that emptiness low in her belly.

"Your Grace."

"Say my name, Amelia. I gave you leave. Now say my name." The sound of his voice was like boulders tumbling in the ocean, angry for being disturbed.

"Charles." She breathed it, then hazarded a glance to his eyes.

As her eyes fluttered to his, her mouth dropped into the shape of a breath, an inhale on the wind, as though to continue on. Waiting. Her lips were the perfect shape for a kiss, which occurred to him so suddenly his own breath was stolen.

"It will not be your first," Charles said simply.

She inhaled as he examined her mouth in detail. The soft pink had darkened, blood rushing to all those intimate points of contact, certainly without her leave. His mind traveled to all the other places she would be flushed. Her nipples would draw tight. Her sex would dampen. This she could not control, even though he could tell she wished to control it.

Charles knew he should back away. He should leave off. He shouldn't be handling her so roughly. He shouldn't be handling her at all. But Charles couldn't effort to turn away as her mouth began to move.

"No." Her breath hitched. "But I am recently determined that yours be my last."

Charles watched her mouth form the words. The sound floated toward him on her breath, and he could not stop his advance. There were warnings in the back of his mind, his conscience throwing him a line to catch—he rather slammed the door on it.

Charles's hand left the door and took her neck, bracing her jaw as he tilted her slowly to him, holding her steady as he descended, watchful, then kissed the very edge of her upturned mouth. He saw her close her eyes, and she relaxed into him, all of her tension concentrated in those two small hands clutching his coat. He traced her lips with his tongue, decided she'd had honey with her toast at breakfast, reined in everything in him that screamed *TAKE*, then kissed her sweetly, gently.

A promise.

She leaned further into him, and he wrapped his arm around her waist, holding her against his body, attempting to be ever so gentle, ever so sweet. An apology for his untoward behavior. He ministered to those lips, left no crease untouched, and she relaxed incrementally. His hand expanded at the small of her back, as though to hold as much of her as possible, and he noticed a new sort of movement—the tension like a living thing traveling her spine as he held on to her. He opened his eyes.

Amelia's very life breathed into him as he tasted her, the fresh honey with an underlying flavor of lilac. He broke away when he heard voices outside.

Good God, what have I done?

Charles's breathing was unsteady, a prelude to what his body wished to come next. His eyes shot to the door of the parlor, and he backed up a pace, with much difficulty. She nearly fell to the floor, her body left without his support, and he reached for her, but her hand shot out and caught the edge of a table. As the table shook, a vase fell to the floor, certainly alerting the household.

"I beg your pardon, Amelia. That was entirely uncalled for. I—" He needed to beg forgiveness. He should have been on his knees. Damn the consequences, the audience that made its way to them now.

She held up a hand to stay him. "No, please don't apologize for something so...something." Her hand moved to hover at her chin, as if she debated whether to touch her lips or retreat. "Thank you."

Charles winced at the formality of the phrase, then spoke when her lips reminded him again that he was second. "I understand you have the very best intentions. I'm just not entirely sure that *he* has those same intentions." He wasn't sure why he was talking about this. He had just kissed her. Thoroughly. In the parlor. Why had he brought to mind the man who was still between them?

"No, that he does not." Her admission was unexpected.

Charles looked at her, shocked she'd followed his line of conversation, or chose to continue it. "Did he tell you as much?" he asked.

He saw her falter, her eyes sweep the room, the way her lids fell but didn't rise as quickly as a blink. The way her hands shook. His soul called to hold her. To take all that force and fission into himself, to will her to calm. Instead, his hands held at the ready, not at his sides, but prepared, staid.

"He did. Hugh intended to say good-bye this morning, but then he didn't, and then he did and then—" She lifted her hand to her lips again, and he knew.

"Just this morning then. I was a mere hour late to being your first."

Her nod was so small it was nearly imperceptible. She shook her head and closed her eyes. "Of course I understand completely should you decide I'm not worthy." she whispered.

"Your worth, Amelia, was decided years ago. The decision to be made now is whether our life together can survive a man who may be determined to ruin us." When she gazed upon him again, he saw the shine in her eyes and knew he had possibly gone too far.

"Amelia, I must go."

She felt herself nod.

"Do you need me to stay?"

"You mustn't stay. My mother is undoubtedly coming. You must go."

Please stay…

Charles took her shivering hand as the footsteps neared, gazed at it, held her hand as though it were the entirety of her, then kissed it, the soothing heat of his mouth a tonic that rushed her veins. Then he turned and left.

She nearly melted into a puddle there by the door, but it creaked wider, and she turned swiftly for the windows.

Amelia attempted to gather her wits. Because they were scattered, possibly shattered. Her wits were undoubtedly, irreconcilably and irretrievably bestrewn about her.

She plopped down on the window seat and attempted to untangle from her mind the previous hour or so. Truly it was the last little bit that had her in a dither. She held on to the cushions, to anything that would help to anchor her. Hold her to the earth.

Charles had been hard in places he shouldn't have been hard. Not if he were upset. She pressed a hand to her chest. In truth, she was hard in places she shouldn't have been as well. She rubbed in a feeble attempt to relieve the sensation of her taught nipples against the barrier of her corset.

She had drilled Hugh about it once, while they were watching her father's men work with the cattle. Hugh had been very patient about it, because he knew she didn't like surprises. Of any kind. He also knew her mother would never say a word to her. So Hugh had patiently—*ever so patiently*—attempted to explain what happened to a man when he liked a woman. In very brief, and vague, terms.

A man could be hard—*there*—while upset, but being upset wouldn't make him hard. He was made to be hard only because he was interested. *In her.* Charles had said she'd groaned in a sensual manner. *Sensual* meant sex. Amelia knew this as well. But she didn't know what sex sounded like. At least, not when humans were involved.

She dearly hoped it sounded nothing like the cattle. That certainly wouldn't be sensual, would it? To a human? That lowing and pitching? Or the goats, or the horses, or—

"Amelia." She jerked her hand to her lap, and the flush rose from her corset to her face. "His Grace has asked to speak with your father. I take it the outing was successful?"

Amelia clenched her eyes.

What the devil? Her mind spun, then caught on the last word from her mother.

Successful. Charles was speaking with her father.

The cushion leaned when her mother sat next to her, and Amelia straightened. Let loose the fabric, attempted to relax her fingers on the handkerchief.

"I…expect it's entirely possible that in the future he may decide to opt for me," Amelia said to her mother in the easiest voice she could muster. Amelia turned in time to see her mother's features pass from excited to confused to appeased—with an underlying bit of annoyance.

"Mother, I am…terribly weary. I believe I should rest." She attempted a smile and waited for permission to leave. She could see that her mother wanted more from her, but more she wasn't able to give. First off, she hadn't even had a chance to remember the morning as it was, to consider every word, every hand gesture, every movement that might need examination.

Amelia truly had no idea whether the outing had been successful. The outing had been a production, as any courting experience would have been.

We are not that familiar, you and I. Goodness, she had said that to him.

She stood rather abruptly. "I will see you for tea, perhaps, if I feel up to it."

"Amelia."

She smiled down at her mother, feeling her nerves coil, attempt to regather, prepare to bolt. She shook her head. Hopefully, her mother knew better than to push her at this point. Her mother had what she wanted. Now, Amelia wanted to be left alone.

Amelia didn't wait. She turned for the door to the parlor and left as quickly as she could. She watched the door to her father's study as she traversed the entry, knew Charles was in there, *knew* he was asking her father to court her, *knew* he was neither here, nor there. Knew not what to think of the situation.

It wasn't *good* or *bad*. It wasn't *yes* or *no*. It wasn't an *answer*. It left her hanging, and she hated that more than anything, the *not* knowing. She would prefer that he decline and walk away. This...this nothingness of unknowing would be her undoing.

She heard the shoes hit the hardwood at the edge of the rug and realized much too late that the door was about to open.

When Charles emerged, he caught her eye, smiled easily and nodded. As though he had no idea what he had done to her—and he didn't, did he? She turned and ran up the stairs as if that smile had teeth and planned to nip at her ankles like a shepherd. She had to get away from him before she ruined everything. She could feel the pull of her composure, did not have the strength to hold herself together any longer. The morning had quite thoroughly exhausted her. When she hit the landing, she lifted her skirts and she ran.

She flung herself through the door to her sitting room, so brimming with colorful boxes there wasn't anywhere to sit. The reticule would have lived here, in one of these boxes, waiting for her attention. The handkerchief would live here. She would need a new box, one specifically for Charles. Until then, she needed someplace safe to keep it. Amelia knew she whimpered at the thought, and she tugged at her shirtwaist and moved through the boxes.

Finally, she flung herself into her room and tore at her clothes. She needed…what did she need? She needed more air. She needed to be free from the constraints of her clothes at the very least. She needed her blasted nipples to be away from this corset. After that, she wasn't sure. She *was* sure that she would know precisely what it was she needed as soon as she was free from these stays. She screamed, and Louisa ran through the connecting door to her bath.

"Oh, milady, please, let me help ye."

Amelia sobbed and pulled at her gown, even as Louisa batted her hands away. Amelia knew she was hindering the process but couldn't seem to keep her hands out of the way. Her head spun. Her heart beat a tattoo strong enough to send a battalion to war. "Louisa…Louisa!"

"Yes, yes, milady, here we go, here now!"

The dress fell away, and the stays followed, and Louisa threw a large blanket around her. Amelia pressed her forearms against her chest as Louisa guided her to the bed, stretching her out and tucking her in.

Why did she have to suffer so? He'd still spoken with her father, hadn't he? But perhaps he had spoken with him to cry off. Perhaps it hadn't been to ask to court her. Perhaps he'd said that only to distract her so he could take his leave peacefully. Perhaps he'd finally seen through everything she attempted to be and could now see what she truly was. Unworthy. A mess.

But he threw my reticule into the pond.

Yes, but he also kissed me then spoke of Hugh.

Yes, but he also made me laugh, at great difficulty.

Yes, but he did not offer for me.

Yes, but he did speak with my father, regardless of what happened in the carriage.

Or…possibly because of it? But I behaved terribly.

Yes, but he didn't seem to mind that as much as wish to discover it.

Yes, but he left…

Yes, but he threw my reticule into the pond.

He threw my reticule into the pond.

She closed her eyes tightly as her mind spun around the events.

Louisa's hands were on her back, kneading and rolling, attempting to soothe.

"Tell me, sweet child, tell me what has you in a bind," Louisa begged.

"He said possibly," she croaked, and then it was all crystal clear, and she was up from the confines of her blanket and her bed in an instant. "He said maybe! Who says that?" She turned on Louisa, screaming, "Who holds your heart and then tells you that your wishes might be possible…we'll see? Who says that? Oh, Louisa, and then I…oh, I—oh dear. I was quite unladylike." The room spun, and she grabbed the back of her chair and let the darkness come down over her like a whirlwind, carrying her voice into the ether.

Charles wasn't clear whether it was the hastiness of her retreat or the sway of her bottom as she ran up the stairs that gave him pause. But pause he did, to consider her retreating form and perhaps the hastiness with which it did so.

Charles knew two things for certain: He was treading in difficult waters, and he was very nearly to the point at which there would be no retreat. He knew he had to ascertain her suitability as quickly as possible. His want be damned. But he did want her. Oh, how he did *want*.

Charles watched her go, disconcerted by her reaction to his smile. He must have scared the wits from her. Hopefully, he would still be welcome when he called tomorrow. Had he really pressed into her in the parlor? Had he truly treated her in such a low manner? He pressed a palm to his forehead as if to stave off an ache as his body screamed at him to follow her. *Protect her.*

Charles saw her mother speaking with Lady Mathorpe in the entry and cringed when they both turned toward him.

"Is aught amiss?" her mother asked. Her slight French accent skimmed his awareness, momentarily softening him, reminding him of his own mother.

Was aught amiss? Charles wasn't sure. Amelia had bolted at the sight of him. Was her mother looking for a confession, or was she concerned for her daughter's behavior in the carriage above all?

"Ma'am, I'm to call on Amelia tomorrow."

She gave him a smile. Albeit warily.

"Is she well?" he asked. "She seemed to be in a bit of a rush."

Her mother stiffened, as if frozen from the ground up. He could see the freeze travel up her skirts and her spine until her head tilted back, and she looked up her nose at him. "Whatever do you mean?" She very nearly screeched it.

"I only mean that she was upset in the carriage, and I attempted to speak with her in the parlor, but may have…" He rubbed his chin. "I only meant to let her know that I was not offended by…what happened."

Her mother cut a glance to Lady Mathorpe, who shook her head derisively. "What *did* happen?" Amelia's mother asked, now quite concerned.

Charles looked to Lady Mathorpe and her haughty demeanor, then back to Amelia's mother.

"We spoke," was all he said. She studied him.

The shriek that rent the hall was so piercing, so fully realized, that everyone within earshot was rendered momentarily incapacitated. He imagined most of London, in fact, to be sure. As one, they looked up toward the origination of the sound, somewhere high above them. Charles, Lady Pembroke, and Lady Mathorpe. Possibly a butler and a housemaid or two. Certainly, the house cats and mice.

Then everyone moved at once, scattering. Lady Mathorpe turned to the parlor, shaking her head. The servants disappeared behind doorways, and the cats and mice faded into the shadows. Her mother bolted for the stair, and he followed.

They went up, then up some more, then through a series of turns. He was sure she was leading him into a trap. He would never find his way out again. At any moment, the lights would dim, Lady Pembroke would disappear in a gale of laughter, and he would be lost forever in the series of winding hallways.

Where do they keep her, for God's sake?

Finally, a door swung open, and her mother ran into a room. This room was well lit, unlike the many hallways they'd traversed. He peered in and saw the smallest of figures in a heap on the floor. There was a lady's maid next to her, comforting, whispering, and then her mother's hellish voice broke the sad symphony. His body jerked in attempt to get to her, but her mother was there first.

"Amelia, Amelia! Get up and get dressed. It isn't the thing to be half-made at this time of day." The shriek made him cringe. Any softness he'd previously felt vanished with those words. If he'd grown up with that voice, he might have been insane by now as well.

Insane... No, he couldn't think that of her...or should he? *No.*

Charles needed to speak with her parents, with Ender again, with doctors, physicians, people who...people who would take his tale and spread it to the world—effectively ruining her in the eyes of society. And now Charles understood why there were so many stairs, and halls, and turns. He understood the delicacy of the situation. He understood how easily she could land in Bedlam. One wrong word. One misplaced comment, and she would be taken away and never heard from again. Bedlam was nothing but a hold for lost souls. For those who couldn't be found, didn't want to be found. Or for those who someone else didn't want coming back.

Charles watched again. Amelia, his beautiful Amelia, was now sitting in a chair by the fire, curled in a ball, and her maid was trying to persuade her mother to let her be. To whit, the mother was adamantly opposed.

Was this *his* doing?

The blood drained from his head, and Charles steadied himself with a hand on the doorjamb.

"You act as if I don't know my own daughter!" Another shriek, another cringe, and the maid shrank.

If you could sway while sitting, that was what Amelia did. She swayed, toward her maid and away from her mother.

He straightened his spine and his clothes and tried to convince himself—in this straightening—that he was strong enough to take on this woman. "Lady Pembroke. A word?" Charles's voice was shakier than he wished it to be, and he cleared his throat. "Now." *Better.* Much more commanding.

Silence. Stillness. The woman rose quietly, then turned as a well-oiled machine, without so much as a ruffle from her skirts. "Your Grace, I had no idea you—" She pasted on a smile. Charming, that.

"If we might speak. With Pembroke as well. I believe I have some questions."

"Of course, Your Grace, I…well, I should see to my—" Her hand fell gently open toward Amelia.

"Now would be best. I'm quite certain she'll be fine, yes? There isn't anything terribly *wrong* with her…is there?" Charles asked innocently— and there he had her.

Lady Pembroke could not admit to any sort of true malady, not to him, and he knew this. He smiled, charmingly.

Her smile faltered as she nodded and moved from the room. As she swept past him, the maid rushed to Amelia and pulled her into a tight embrace, and Amelia seemed to melt. She seemed to not realize the scene about her, either— just the touch of this maid.

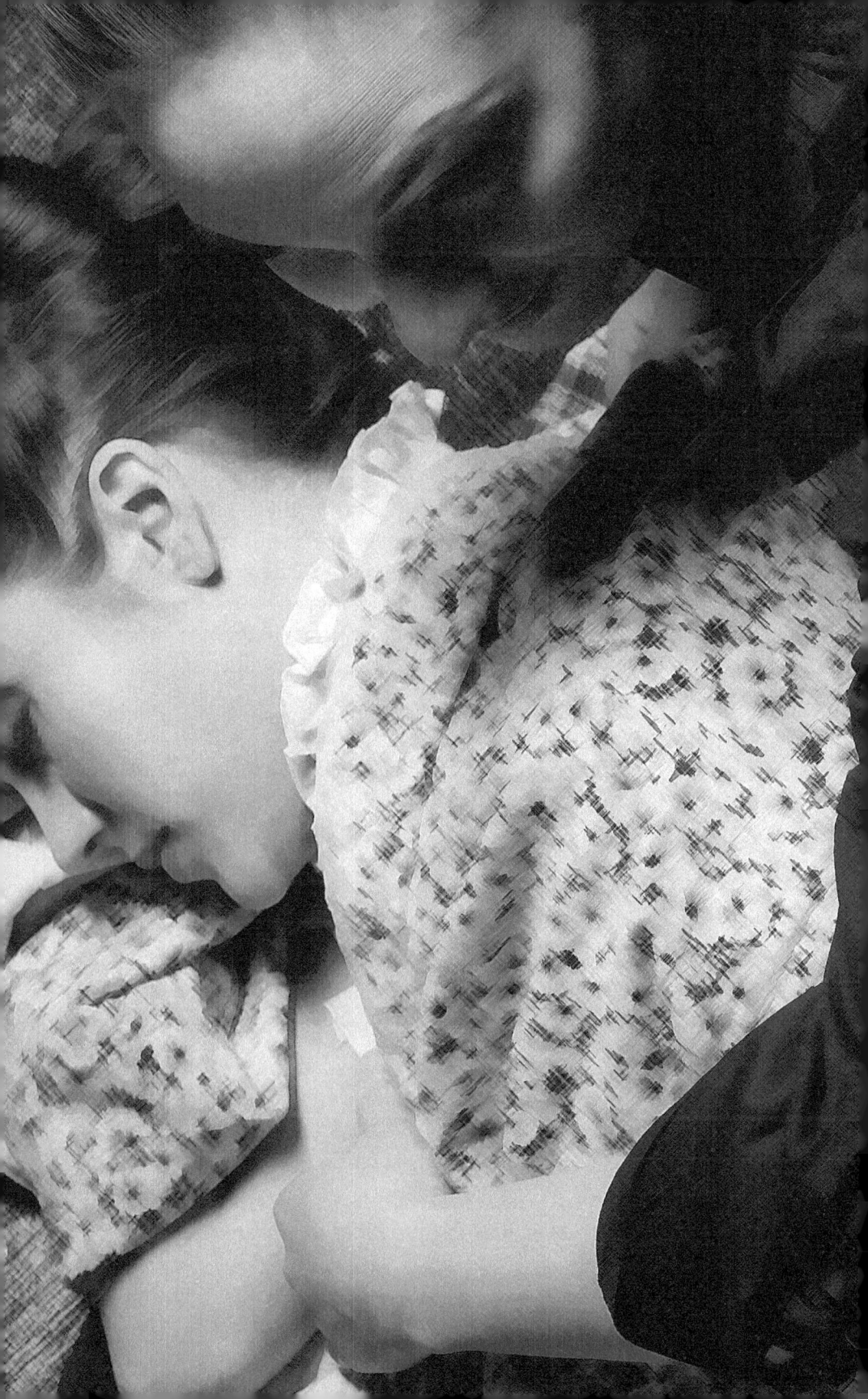

Charles watched as one tiny hand found its way out of the blankets surrounding her and held on to the maid's arm. He felt that touch on his own arm, and his want returned. To be that person for her. This.

This was his most basic desire.

He pulled the door shut quietly, but not before he caught the maid's eye, and the words from her mouth. "Thank you," she said, *sotto voce*.

Charles followed Lady Pembroke back through the many halls and corners and down the stairs to the duke's study. His mind raced, attempting to wrap itself around the events that had led him here. What could he have done differently? What should he have done differently? Kept his distance? But so much had been learned today…so much displayed. Dependent on a favorable outcome, he wouldn't change a thing.

They entered the duke's study, where they all stood and stared at each other. Well, Pembroke remained in his wheeled chair, but Charles and Lady Pembroke stood, though Pembroke did share in the staring bit.

Pembroke finally cleared his throat and looked to his wife. "My dear, is aught amiss?" he asked carefully.

This household, Charles was finding, was quite careful. In all things.

Be cautious when working with Pembroke, his father had said.

Lady Pembroke looked at Charles and merely continued to stare.

So Charles looked to Pembroke and decided to lay all the facts of the matter out. "Your daughter seems to have an issue." Charles then joined the careful dance with them. "What have you done for her in the past? Has she seen any professionals? Any at all?"

Something crossed Pembroke's features so briefly that Charles would ordinarily have brushed it aside, but under the circumstances, he took note.

Pembroke sputtered, "Well, I...my wife handles all *delicate* matters of the household. If she were in need of a physician or some such..." His voice trailed off, and they were back to looking at Lady Pembroke. And she them. In turn.

Quite the contest, in truth.

Charles tried again. "We have an agreement, you and I," he said simply to her father, as if the agreement would have been forgotten in the mere minutes since they'd entered into it.

The duke nodded. "We do." His eyes darkened, and Charles realized this man may not have been as ill as he presented. Perhaps that was how he kept his success, by keeping his adversaries on edge, by playing the illness. Perhaps that was why Charles's father had warned him.

Charles realized he needed to tread lightly to play this game. He looked back to the lady as he spoke to Pembroke. "Our agreement remains in full force. I will return and expect to be admitted to see Lady Amelia. Without prejudice." He felt the duke's consternation, could see his head swivel from his wife and back to him, and knew he wasn't to give any more away.

He kept his unblinking eyes on the lady. Until she nodded.

"You must understand in all things, it is my duty to find a suitable wife."

Lady Pembroke's eyes widened incrementally, and he realized then how difficult this all would be. It was his duty. His queen expected a *suitable* match. Followed by the begetting of heirs. He had to put aside the powerful emotions he'd experienced with Amelia today. He had a duty.

He was a duke. The thought was a sharp blade.

He had a duty.

To his queen.

His heart fell a bit within his chest at that moment. But he knew one thing without a doubt: He would do right by Amelia, regardless of whether he could take her to wife. And he knew another thing quite certainly: Ender held the key.

"Your Grace," he said by way of farewell, then bowed to the woman and moved to the door. Which may or may not be barred to his entrance the next day. That fact was dependent on so many things. Amelia could refuse him…and would she? He certainly deserved it. But he knew she had been with him in the parlor, regardless that he should never have treated her in such a fashion. She'd been with him. It had been one of the first moments of his life that he had known, *known*, that she returned his regard in more ways than the simple marriage contract.

The door to the town house closed behind him, and he breathed for what seemed the first time in years. He was overwhelmed by the entire day. He wondered how Amelia was. Then his mind wandered back to Ender. Again, with this man. Their discussion last night had been disconcerting and quite unsettling.

Charles wasn't sure what to think and wanted to speak with him again, but he knew that wasn't his best idea. The last time they'd spoken, Ender had rushed into Amelia's arms and stolen her first kiss from him. Or had he? Had that kiss always belonged to Ender? Was this *Charles's* penance? Charles had been raised to believe that if he wanted something, he simply made it his.

Charles hadn't truly considered Ender in all of this—beyond him being an old acquaintance. Quite obviously, Ender was much more than that to Amelia and, at this point in time, he believed Ender held the key to helping her, whether Charles pursued his suit or not.

Perhaps he should help them to be together. Ender held a barony. He could provide for her, perhaps not in the fashion to which she'd become accustomed, but in truth Charles didn't believe she cared all that much for that. As well, a baroness, while important, was not a duchess. There would be much less required of her. Perhaps the duchy was too much to expect of her. Then again, she had been able to traverse the ballroom last night without incident.

He shook off his thoughts and entered his carriage. He did need to speak with Ender again. Because he was beginning to understand that at the moment all that mattered was Amelia.

SEVEN

ouisa?" Her voice was smaller than a mouse's, but at least she'd found it. She had no idea what time it was, though judging from the long shadows, it was nearing supper.

"My lady." Louisa came to the side of the bed. "Well, 'tis good to see you at rights again." Her smile was warm and genuine, and Amelia returned it as she moved to sit up.

Louisa helped her, stacking pillows behind her back and fluffing them incessantly until Amelia waved her off. There were too many pillows now. Too many. She pulled one out and tossed it to the floor, giving her tongue to the offending bag of fluff.

"Have I missed supper? Tell me I've missed supper."

"Oh yes, quite," Louisa said with a nod and a grin. "But not to worry. I requested a tray sent up. I'm rather surprised your mother hasn't—"

"Oh, my mother." Her head fell to her hands. Then she looked at Louisa. "Castleberry?" *The duke the duke the duke.* What had she done?

"He's gone, but not for long. I believe he hasn't been entirely frightened off. Not to worry."

"Oh, Louisa, I truly thought I'd destroyed any hope of—"

"Tsch tsch tsch, now, don't be so cruel to yourself. You know if he were frightened off, as you say, he wasn't so worthy of you to begin with. And there's always Lord Endsleigh."

"Yes, he and I can retire as spinsters together, taking my mother and living in his modest estate on his moderate income. He would just *adore* that. No doubt, he'd take up knitting. Or needlepoint."

"He would, because he loves you. And you know he'd create beautiful pillows that all the ladies would be jealous of."

"But he deserves so much more than me." *More. He deserves an easy wife, who'll not work him so...and Charles, doesn't he deserve the same?* Her head spun.

"Now here we go again. Must we always go round-and-round like this? Must we? If Ender were to spend the balance of his days with you, not only would he be the luckiest man alive, but to have you in his life would be more than he deserves. And you as well. The two of you are well suited. Except for that one, small issue."

"That issue being that he's not good enough for me in my father's eyes? A baron only? For shame. I should only be so lucky."

"Your dear father has only your interests at heart. He wants the very best life for you. He doesn't know—"

"That I'm impaired? Oh, but he does, Louisa. He does. Don't let him make a fool of you as well. I think this to be his greatest farce—to marry his unacceptable daughter to one of the most powerful of the peers. As for Castleberry, he certainly understands that I'm not well at this point." Certainly. *Of a certainty.* She could only hope that Charles would return. Even if she waited for her father to die then married the man he'd disallowed so many years ago, there would be no true happiness. She knew this. She pulled another pillow and tossed it across the room. Better. Not fully comfortable, but better. *Betterbetterbetter.*

It was only ever better, never perfect, just like her future, for her mother would be with her, reminding her how she could have done so much *better* if only she'd behaved herself. If only she'd persuaded the duke to marry. If only she'd controlled herself long enough to complete the license and consummate the marriage.

Consummate.

Dear Lord, if she believed Ender's stories of the farm animals, Charles had been ready to consummate the marriage in the parlor this morning. Perhaps she should have allowed him, taken the ruination, married him by default. But that he would always then resent her for it.

She slumped in the bed. It simply wasn't in her to be so dishonest. Her fingers picked at the loose threads on the counterpane. She needed to speak with Charles again. She had to make sure he understood. Though, in truth, after today he most likely understood the worst of it. He most likely had questions he needed answered. As did she.

For example, why were her nipples sore? Why were her drawers wet? She sneaked a look at Louisa, who was bustling about the room straightening, no doubt cleaning up the mess left from her fit. She could

ask Louisa about these things, couldn't she? She'd seen Amelia at her most dreadful and stayed with her. Amelia was truly lucky in that regard. So many people had abandoned her to her oddish behaviors. Her mother would have abandoned her, surely, but had had no choice. So now what her mother held was merely a great disdain.

Amelia looked through her lashes to see Louisa leave the room, closing the door quietly behind her. She sank into the bed and crept her hand toward her chest. She grazed one finger over one sore nipple, and it straightened to attention as though looking for something. Expectant.

Charles.

She truly believed he could ease this new ache she had, but she was frightened. So very frightened. She'd never had this sort of physical response to anyone, not ever. She loved Hugh, though, so why was this different? When she thought of Hugh, she felt warm, safe, as though she could control nearly everything. She desperately needed that, the safety of that.

Charles made her feel wildly unrestrained. Fully beyond control. Dangerously unbound. The feeling was both exhilarating and terrifying. She moved her hand to her mouth, skimmed lightly over her lips, closed her eyes to remember his kiss.

Charles had been so deep inside her mind, and all he'd possessed was her mouth. The feel of his wet tongue sliding across her swollen lips gave her chills, and she shivered. Her nipples rose again to tight peaks, and she pressed a finger to one, tried to persuade it to retreat—to no avail.

Amelia closed her eyes and thought on the darkness in Charles's eyes. The way they'd bored into her, bypassed her flesh and muscle, sank straight into her blood and traversed the whole of her from the inside. She let her hands follow the feel of him in her blood. Across her chest, up her neck, down her shoulders, across her belly, then lower…and lower… The heat spread wickedly, the pulse beat between her thighs like a second heart, calling to him, singing his name.

She stopped, hovered there, feeling the warmth emanating from her very core. Tears coursed her cheeks, hot and fast. She simply didn't understand any of this. She didn't know how she was supposed to feel about either of these men. They were so entirely different, and while her brain called out to the safety of Hugh, her body seemed to scream the name of the other. Her body screamed for Charles in the gooseflesh that rose across her skin, the sheen of perspiration that broke out, the heartbeat she could feel everywhere, like a primal call to war.

Charles.

She twisted and curled into herself, let the tears soak into her pillow quietly.

Hugh. Hugh could set her to rights with just his presence, her heart beat steadied. What was she to do? How was she to live? The Cliff House was the only property she would own once her father was gone if she didn't marry. A mere pittance on which to survive. Certainly not enough to keep her mother in the comfort to which she was accustomed.

Amelia could have been happy at the Cliff House, forever, on her own. *Alone.* She could be happy as a spinster, left to the breaking waves on the cliff. The sound the most calming she'd ever known. She could make a life for herself there. But not her mother, and Amelia had to see to her mother.

There was a gentle sweep at her temple, and she opened her eyes to find Louisa there, rubbing circles into her back, sweeping her hair from her face. She sat up and held the girl. Took her into a tight embrace and held on as though this embrace was all that held her to the earth.

"Hush now, sweet girl. I've got you. You're safe. No need to fret."

"Louisa, I…I don't understand what's happening. I feel so terribly frightened about what's to come of me."

Louisa nodded against her, felt her squeeze tighter, then release her and take her hands. Amelia was too afraid to open her eyes just yet.

"Listen to me, lady, you are one of the most incredible souls I've ever met. And there's a place for you. We just have to figure out where that is. Whether with Lord Endsleigh or the Castleberry. You've a place. Perhaps it's with neither. I'm here. I'll help you. Whatever you need of me, I'm here. We'll see to this together. I promise you."

Amelia nodded and looked at her then. "When you say things like this, I can't help but believe you. I'd be lost without you."

"But you're not lost."

Wasn't she? She twisted her hands in the sheets. "Louisa, I need to get out of the house tonight."

"Oh, miss, I'm not sure *this* is an idea worth our attentions."

Amelia pushed her away and stood. "Quit being polite. Of course it's a bloody stupid idea. But bloody stupid be damned, I need to see him."

"Which him?" Louisa asked quietly.

Amelia stopped suddenly, then smiled.

A

Charles had quit Pembroke House as quickly as possible. He went straight to the Iron Duke taproom, desperately in need of a pint and some time to think through everything that had happened. Now he was off to see Ender, hoping, possibly beyond hope, that he was there. When it was announced that he was in, Charles took it as a good sign—after all, he could easily have been placed on Ender's disallowed list. Charles was led to the library, but Ender wasn't waiting for him. The door closed stoutly behind him, somewhat like a final bell.

He moved about the library, reading the few titles on the mostly barren shelves, wondering if the man read them or simply kept them from some previous owner. The library was a chaotic assemblage of volumes, novels and periodicals. He pulled a well-worn copy from a particularly full shelf: *PUNCH*, it read in large lettering across the top of the cover. A periodical known for humor, both literary and visual. He nodded and riffled through the issue before hearing the footsteps approach. He replaced the periodical carefully on the shelf, moving to a chair in front of a large desk.

It was an all-too-familiar position, and Charles believed, once again, that he was asking permission for something he really shouldn't ought to be asking permission for. The door opened.

"So soon, Jackson? I was expecting—"

Charles stood. "I witnessed an episode. I'm at a complete loss. I understand now that I may be in entirely above my head." Well, that was putting it all out there.

"When?" Ender had stopped moving when Charles spoke, as though there was no moving forward until he had all the information.

"Today, after the outing to the park. I fear I may have been at fault. I may have—"

Ender moved closer. "Explain," he ground out.

Charles did, quickly and quite thoroughly, and swallowing much pride in the act of it. He even explained the reticule. He did not, however, go so far as to speak in detail of his advance in the parlor.

"So you tossed her reticule in the pond," Ender said finally as he moved forward, apparently appeased that immediate action on his part was unnecessary.

"Much like a javelin," Charles said.

Ender laughed. "It's not you. It's her. Quite honestly. Well, mostly. Though, to be sure, if you had the skills to help her, the episode would not have been...well, was it bad?" He turned toward him, and Charles could see the concern. Could almost feel that concern as a palpable force.

"When I saw her on the floor, her mother—yes, in my estimation, yes, the episode was bad. But I have no basis for comparison, as you must have. It occurs to me the reason I was often turned away was to keep me from being witness to this. You...were not."

"Of course not, because her mother didn't want to take the time to discern what Amelia needed, and I happened to be available. I was pushed into the position and then...well, there was only me. You were sent away to protect her future. I'm sure that's not what you wish to hear, but that's the truth of it. Amelia's position with you was to be protected at all cost."

Ender motioned to the chair, and Charles took his seat. Ender sat in the chair next to him, instead of across the great hulking ship of a desk. "I assume she is well now, since you're here," Ender said.

"As best I know, yes. I removed her mother from the room. Her maid—she seemed to be helpful." Charles had liked her maid and wondered then if she would be allowed to move with Amelia to his household. He was sure Amelia would appreciate that.

"Louisa? Yes, she is. I chose her for the position once I realized how alone Amelia would be once I left for school. Louisa wasn't born to service, and she's quite intelligent. When we met, she'd needed a friend and somewhere to go. I believed her personality was one that would suit because Louisa was protective and delicate. She needed protection herself and a place to live." Ender paused as he seemed to asses Charles. "You did well to remove Amelia's mother. The woman does naught but make Amelia's condition worse for her. As you seem to have recognized."

Charles nodded, remembering the scene. It had been difficult to watch—he'd never felt so helpless—but he'd no basis to intrude, or interfere, or help. He believed himself as much to blame as he wished to help her. So he'd retreated.

Charles thought for a second, considering his next words carefully.

"You should know I entered into an agreement with her father. This is quite possibly the only reason I'll not be barred from the household should I return. I've a feeling her father knows more than he allows about her…episodes? Is that what you call it? Her mother seemed to want to keep information from him."

Ender nodded but seemed lost in thought even as he seemed to take the news of his official suit in stride. "But she was well when you left her?" His face was tense.

Charles knew Ender felt a great deal of sadness, possibly helplessness, and he found this a disturbing kinship with the man. Was it enough that Charles could leave her to him and not look back? Just the thought shook him to the core.

"I suppose as well as could be expected, considering the circumstances." Charles paused and took stock of his adversary, such as he was. "Endsleigh."

"Castleberry." The man returned the regard, then attempted a grin. "Ender is sufficient. I've a notion we'll become much more familiar in the near future."

Charles narrowed his eyes. "Will we?"

Ender paused, then nodded. "If this is to work, we're to become very close indeed. For in truth, the things you need to learn can't be explained. They can only be shown. If you want this, if she's prepared for this, this is how it should be done."

"Truly? I'm not sure either of us is prepared for what lies before us. I have so many concerns," Charles said. He tried to list the concerns in his mind, but they were such a jumble, he could not find the beginning, nor the end of them.

"Understandable, as do I. And yet, for Amelia…you see, I simply would do anything. Tell me of your concerns. Let us see if we can alleviate at least some of them," Ender said.

Charles thought for another moment, then decided to tackle the one concern that was foremost in his mind. "My immediate concern is you," Charles said carefully.

"I understand…please believe me when I say that I also want to spend as little time in this situation as possible. I wish to be done with it. With all of it," Ender said stiffly. "I…if we are to work together, I imagine that will require a measure of trust. Though we've never been more than acquaintances, I'll trust you at your word, and hope that you'll trust me. I will do nothing to undermine what trust we build."

Charles waited a moment. He didn't want to like this man, the boy who had teased him mercilessly. "Do you truly wish to be done with it? Because Amelia led me to believe that that was not at all your intention this morning."

Ender nodded. "This morning it was not. In fact, I'm still unsure of my intentions, other than to see that *my Amelia* is safe and well cared-for." He held Charles's gaze. Quite an unspoken challenge, that.

"And something has changed that you allow me to attempt this?" Charles asked carefully.

"Yes, quite drastically, in fact. For one—" Ender paused and looked Charles in the eye. "You threw her reticule in the pond."

Charles was quite tired of discussing the reticule and was believing that action to be a grave error. Until Ender continued.

"You gained a measure of trust there."

Charles stalled. "Did I?" But that had been such a silly maneuver. So ridiculous, really. "I believe it was an action taken out of desperation. I'd no idea what to do, and she gave me a tangible foe. I simply…removed it." Charles hadn't thought much of his actions at the pond, beyond the fact that throwing her reticule had drawn out that laughter that had haunted him for so many years.

"Slayed the dragon, did you, Saint George?" Ender replied with a wicked half-grin.

"I suppose, of a fashion. Though her reticule seems to pale in comparison to her mother, as far as dragons go."

Ender laughed at this. "I believe you just may understand. You've met the desperate feeling with which I've come to be so familiar."

"Desperate?" Charles considered this. "I suppose it is, of a fashion. For at the moment we both want desperately to help Amelia, and thus… well, here we are." *Throwing reticules into ponds* was left unspoken. He may have been convinced that this man was not at all bad.

Damn.

Ender wagged a finger toward him. "Yet she'll not have us out of desperation. She is…she's quite true to herself, and her feelings. I cannot express enough how strongly her soul plays into this. She's not one for games. She's not one for lies. She'll know, beyond doubt, if one of us is false. She has a keen sense of justice, ethics. In fact, she does know, beyond doubt, that I'm *not* false. It's merely you that has to be proven."

Charles leaned back at that, seemed to take stock of Ender for a moment as he considered the words. "And you? What do you believe? Do you believe my intentions to be false? Uncaring? Filtered somehow?" Charles asked, attempting to hide his annoyance at being labeled shallow.

"I know not. At this point, I only know the situation on its face." Ender held up a hand. Apparently, Charles hadn't hid his annoyance enough. "She cannot marry me, but she *can* marry you. Her father disallowed me decades ago. It's the reason we were so close…in part. Because there was none of *that* allowed between us. It's so much more difficult when there's another level of threatened intimacy between a man and woman," Ender said quietly.

Charles nodded. "And this intimacy you speak of…is that what frightens her?" He thought back to her response in the carriage, then the parlor. She'd seemed frightened at first, but he knew when she'd relaxed. He could feel her supplication. She'd responded to him, and that response had been truly lovely. "Is that what keeps her from trusting me? Because I am happy to—"

Ender let out a great peal of laughter then, cutting Charles off. "Happy to…what? Remove sex from the equation? We all know *that* isn't possible, as you're required an heir. Or am I now mistaking the requirements of your duties to Her Royal Highness?"

Charles shook his head. "No, there are certain requirements of the peerage, certain expectations, the begetting of heirs being one of them. I meant only to belay the action of it…should that be necessary." He cringed. That was an untruth. He wasn't sure he could keep himself from her, considering the feel of her against him. He believed they could be well suited in bed. It was the rest of their life together that concerned him.

Charles rubbed his temples with one hand stretched across his eyes. Tried to hide his reaction to the realization that he wanted her so baldly.

"And for how long? I'm a man, as you are, and then what? Because I know Amelia would come to believe you are satisfying *those* urges outside the marriage bed, if not with her. And do you realize? This is possibly one of the reasons she's terrified."

"And what of the duchy? I need to know she can manage it, not merely for me, but for her sake. I do *not* want to put her in a position that would hurt her. As much as I wish for her to be my duchess, I also wish for her to be comfortable. In your estimation, with whatever it is that she has to deal with on a daily basis, can she handle the management of a duchy? The societal requirements of it?"

"I wholeheartedly believe she can, if she knows that whomever she is with will support her without fail, no matter what were to happen. Yes, if she has your unwavering support and trust, yes, she can manage a duchy—and quite brilliantly at that, for sure.

"That being said, at the moment our Amelia is in a situation quite beyond her control, and this"—Ender motioned between the two of them—"in and of itself is enough to cut her tethers, but that there is so much more here…Amelia's mind is very much at the brink of complete and total destruction because of the situation. There's so much pressure on her. I know her as I know myself, and though I don't wish to pursue this, for her sake, I will. I understand that she thinks…*overthinks* every situation to the detriment of her health, and therein lies your conundrum. You cannot be responsible for this, because in her mind…*I will be hurt.* This is something that must be dealt with. But for you to tell her that I am *not* hurt will not suffice. She's much too smart for that. This fact must come from me."

"And are you…hurt?" Charles asked quietly, dropping his hand to rest on his thigh.

"Am I? That has yet to be determined, I suppose. At the moment, I'm undecided."

"As you are undecided in other areas." This time, *pursuing the woman promised me* was left unspoken.

"My suit, you mean? Well, that was decided long ago. It's only wrapping it through my brain that must be done. You see, the heart wants what the heart wants. Getting it to believe otherwise is the difficult task."

"How easily you speak of hearts," Charles said quietly. Men tended to shy from speak of hearts, love, anything of softness and lacking an edge. Not this man. It was unexpected. Charles had assumed him much colder, more distant.

Ender grinned as if he knew he'd just shattered a misplaced opinion.

Charles continued, "And how can I ask you to help me, if you are here for you?"

"Oh, but you misunderstand. I'm here for Amelia. I always have been. That's the simple truth of it. My bearing on the matter is inconsequential to me, and therein lies another catch. As inconsequential as this is to me, it's *not* to Amelia."

"Were it that simple," Charles said.

"Does this all sound simple to you? I wish you would explain it to me then, for I'm having difficulty understanding why it is I'm here. This morning I went to break with her, but found I simply could not. Then to see you…*very well played*, sir, I might add. Had you called me out this morning, I would have been none too happy to fight your suit. But as it happens, between that and the reticule, you've now shown me a genuineness of character I find I quite like for *my Amelia*. In truth…I believe you."

"That's unfortunate," Charles said distractedly. He bounced a fist on his thigh, debating whether to truly be honest with Ender, or hold back his—possibly misguided—intentions.

Ender studied him. "Meaning?"

"Upon leaving Pembroke House, I was determined…to pursue… what was best for Amelia. Whether that be my suit or yours." Charles watched from the corner of his eye as Ender's jaw dropped.

"You can't be serious," Ender said finally.

"Quite, in fact. The thing of it is…I have that specific duty to the crown, as do you. But in my determination today, I found my concern for Amelia far outweighs my…*want* of her. Though 'want' seems a tawdry and unacceptable description for what I have, mind you. I do want her, in every way. But if the duties of duchess are more than she can take on, I would wish to see her happy…with you. A baroness is no simple chore, either, but not so much as a duchess—as *my* duchess. The expectations of such are…"

"Extensive."

"Quite. So, you see, I cannot make this decision for her, not by measure. She has to be ready, prepared, able to perform the duties to the crown required of her. After today, I'm not sure these are duties she's interested in taking on." Charles paused, working up to what he decided he must say next, and when he did, he spoke so quietly, he wasn't sure the air before him could even hear it. "I'm not sure these are duties she's *capable* of taking on, even though you say she is. Though I wish it. I do. I want for it."

Silence.

"So where do we go from here?" Charles asked quietly.

"I…am unsure. We must determine that Amelia is truly up to the challenge of a duchy, I suppose."

"That seems unfair, that we should be the ones to determine it. She wants this. That should be enough," Charles said determinedly.

"But it isn't. No offense to you, but she has quite a bit of pressure from her mother to pursue your suit. She may not be seeing what will be required of her…after."

"So my suit comes down to the technical of the position. How perfectly terrific." Charles leaned forward, elbows on his knees. He let his head drop into his hands, his fingers sinking into his hair, pulling, requiring some tangible source of feeling.

"I sincerely hope not. You and I, we'll work together. We'll determine what's best for her, where she'll be safe, cared for...loved." He said this last bit as though it wasn't a possibility. That rankled a bit.

"I believe wherever she ends, she'll be cared for. Deeply," Charles countered.

Ender nodded. "Love is blindness. I cannot allow for my feelings toward her to color this decision, and yet—"

"And yet, how do we not? Truly, I don't believe I can be objective in this. When I hold her..." Charles shook off the thought, unable to discuss this much with Ender as yet. "This is not how I wished for this to progress," Charles said, holding both hands up between them as if to physically push Ender away.

"Well, had you chosen a simple chit, you'd be well and truly wedded and bedded by now," Ender said with a grin, a poor attempt to lighten the mood.

Charles merely shook his head then leaned back in the chair, smoothing his disarrayed locks as he did. He was desperately in need of more ale.

"I will help. I believe the first impediment is her...condition," Ender said.

"And how will you help me with this?"

"I'll observe. Simply think of me as...another sort of chaperone. One who may have helpful suggestions."

"You are going to teach me how to manage her?"

Ender visibly cringed. "That's not how I wish to see it. I...you must understand it isn't management she needs. It's something more."

"But I *don't* understand. That's precisely the problem."

"And that's what I'm here to rectify. But if you're unable, you're to cry off. I won't have her in a marriage that's unsuitable." Ender was leaning toward him, pointing rather menacingly. "Are we in agreement?"

Charles considered him for a moment. He saw no reason why he couldn't learn to manage—*to help*—Amelia to the point that their marriage on face would be successful. Perhaps if he had this knowledge, the ability to calm her... Quite the opposite of what he'd done today. Charles nodded once, then stood, pulling Ender from his seat with him.

Charles put his hand out to Ender. They had a common goal. Even if they were on opposite sides of it.

Ender raised his hands, shook his head, and spoke softly, "You must understand. We are not friends. Someday, perhaps, but for now I simply cannot…"

Charles nodded, pulling his hand back and waving the statement off. "I understand. I do *hope*, for Amelia's sake…but I also understand."

"Do you? Truly?" Ender asked.

"Do I…hope? Every moment of every day. I wish I could explain to you…but then—" Charles nodded. "Can we simply agree that I will call you Ender, and you will call me Jacks?"

Ender then lifted his hand with a smile, and Charles took it. "Yes, Jacks, this we can agree on."

A tiny gasp came to him then from the doorway. "Well, isn't this…interesting."

Charles and Ender turned together toward the entry to see Amelia. Watching…listening.

EIGHT

"So very…interesting." Amelia paused, not sure whether to run or go deeper into the web they were, quite obviously, attempting to weave for her. *Charles and Hugh. Hugh and Charles. Charles and—*

"Amelia—"

She jerked toward them, unsure which of them had spoken, closed as her eyes were, every bit of her attempting to remain standing.

I won't have her in a marriage that is unsuitable.

If you're unable, you are to cry off.

We'll determine what is best for her, where she'll be safe, cared for… loved.

She opened her eyes on the hand that held the doorjamb. Her fingers too numb to feel. She concentrated on that connection, willed her hand to feel the hardness, the smooth wood beneath her fingers. Had she gone to see Charles, which had been her first inclination, she would have been met with an empty house. As it happened, she was here, privy to a conversation that, quite obviously, she hadn't been meant to be privy to.

She swooned and was caught up by strong hands on her, too many to count, carrying her, arguing over her, moving her, then releasing her to a soft bed of cushions.

Amazing how hands can argue.

She felt the safety of Hugh surrounding her, calming her, even as the insistent touch of Charles wound her to the core. She kept her eyes closed and merely attempted to feel.

"Amelia." This was Charles. *Charles*… Her heart raced at the whisper of his name in her mind.

CharlesCharlesCharles.

"Amelia mine?" And this was Hugh. To effect a calm so completely with that phrase—only he could do that. She felt Charles bristle at the endearment.

She opened her eyes slowly. They'd placed her on a chaise near the fireplace. Charles on the floor at her shoulder and Hugh at her knee, both with the most concerned faces she'd ever seen on either of them.

"You mean to manage me," she whispered.

Manage. Not love, but manage.

She'd thought they both loved her, of a fashion anyway. For she knew she was so desperately oddish that she was truly unlovable. The realization was a true pain to her gut. She shrugged off their hands. *All of their hands.* She watched as they withdrew in unison, as if properly choreographed. All those big hands, hovering above her as if they feared that final step to retreat. As though once committed, they could never return.

Amelia could feel their fear as a palpable, graspable, touchable thing. A heavy fog in the air around her, weighing her down. She moved to sit up, and they were back, but she stayed them all with a glance.

So many hands. Four, to be sure, but it had felt like thousands.

She straightened her skirts as she righted herself. This was an interesting position. This, between them. They were both crouched low, now on either side of her knees, their hands still hovering a bit, not knowing where to alight, as though to find a resting place anywhere but on *her* would be a terrible concession neither could live with. "You mean to manage me. You both believe I cannot make up my own mind about what I can or cannot do."

You do not mean to love me. She closed her eyes, quickly.

They do not love me. She stared forward, between their silences. There was more hovering, a bit of discomfited shifting, eye dodging and throat clearing. She could feel them both, the serene care to her right, that wild caution to her left.

"You think me weak." She nearly dissolved from the inside out with these words, she felt them so keenly. A sob rent her countenance, and her hand flew to her temple to stave off an impending pain there.

"No. No, Amelia, we do not think you weak," Charles said quietly, as though afraid of startling her. Causing her to bolt. Charles's mouth dropped open, but this time no sound came out. He looked to Hugh, as though for guidance, and she became truly enraged then.

"I cannot abide this!" She motioned to them both, "This… whatever this is. You think me *weak*." She held up one hand as they both began to shake their heads. The thaw had come, and they both seemed to realize they could, in fact, move. Speak. "What else would you be plotting here together? And you cannot lie, because I heard you. *I heard you.* Do not try to rationalize this with me. Do. Not. I—" They moved then in unison, and their movements did startle her, the two of them, hands out, placating. Cautiously.

She wanted to scream. To rend the very air with her frustration. Hugh had always been her safe place, someone she could be herself with, to rant, scream, love, and share her innermost thoughts. Charles…she adored him. She hoped he didn't know her well enough to hate her, to believe that he *had* to come to Hugh, to believe that he didn't think he was enough for her. Or worse, that she was unsuitable for him.

She'd always been able to relax with Hugh. She was herself. She did not have to control herself, her oddities, her wild thoughts. His very presence calmed the thoughts in her mind, made them irrelevant, more like whispers than the insistent screams they usually were.

But here, between the two, she couldn't rest. Her mind tangled to decide where to lean, to control her mind and her body in that usual fashion, because Charles was here, and she didn't want him to know… but he did know. *He'd seen. He was there.* She remembered.

She felt something like a seam come loose, straight up her middle, like a dress split for being too tightly sewn. She pressed her hand to her belly to hold back whatever was to spill forth as they moved to her sides. Hugh on her right, Charles on her left. A modicum of space between them all. Nearly immeasurable. She held very still, the heat emanating from the two of them tangible, and she knew if she came into contact with either—the conflagration of her soul would light London for a fortnight.

She breathed. Attempted to, at any rate. Endeavored to steady her nerves. She swayed toward Hugh, then stayed herself…knowing. She could not cut Charles in such a fashion. Would not. Regardless of whatever had transpired here tonight. She closed her eyes to stay at least that much of her senses. Her hands smoothed down her skirts to her knees, then tangled there, and she allowed it. Did not attempt to control that outward sign of tension. At least she knew where they were, what they were doing.

"I need to…I need to know what your intentions are where I'm concerned. I need to speak with both of you…separately. I need to know, precisely, what's to come of me." She waited patiently. Neither man moved. "I'll not choose between you. The two of you must determine which of you is to be first. I will not. I cannot." She waited.

After a time, the cushion on her left shifted, and she leaned to her right, nearly imperceptibly, as she steadied herself. She heard the door to the library close, and she melted into Hugh, latching on to his lapels.

"Damn you," she said to his cravat.

"Amelia mine, it's not as you think." She shivered and burrowed into him a bit. "Or perhaps it is, but not…not without the very best of intentions." She knew his hands hovered at her shoulders, not quite sure yet whether he would be welcome.

"And these intentions—that don't take my wishes into account— are they like my mother's *very best* intentions? Or are they more like my father's *very best* intentions?" She pushed back and took his eyes with hers. "Tell me true, because I love you at this moment as I always have. Tell me what these *very best intentions* have to do with me."

"Jacks came here, because he witnessed the episode this afternoon. After he offered for you."

"He did not, in fact, offer for me. He left me wondering. He left me without a toehold. Hugh, I'm lost, and I came to find myself, and instead, I found that I'm not entirely sure I can trust you. Or him…" She glanced back at the door to the library. "He witnessed my—how much did he witness?" She shook her head, her eyes unfocused for a moment on the thought, then she looked back up at Hugh and concentrated. "I cannot feel my fingers." She stared at them, sank her thoughts into the blinding numbness, willed that numbness to overtake the whole of her.

Perhaps she could vanish there, somewhere, without feeling, without care.

Hugh took her hands then, unlatched them from his lapels as she watched, straightened each finger, and gave them each a bit of attention through her gloves, until the pins and needles started, and she wiggled free of his grasp. She shouldn't touch him again. Somehow, it felt a disregard for Charles to do such.

"Hugh, I need for you to explain."

"I understand. This conversation between Jacks and I should never have taken place, not without your leave. I will tell you this: We have come to an understanding, one that I never thought to see from the two of us."

"What is that?"

"That our sole purpose, both of us, is to see you happy. Regardless of your family, your mother, your current situation, either of our suits. That's our intent. That is the driving force behind our *very best intentions.*"

She looked to him and read the truth of it in his eyes. She could always read the truth of him so easily that he couldn't hide from her. He had the truest eyes, and she understood him at his very base. She supposed this was why he was safe. There was never any question. Charles, however, she didn't know that well. She'd only hoped to. The wildness in him, the wildness he brought out in her, that wildness terrified and, at the same time, was exhilarating.

"And?" she pressed for more.

"That's all. The exact method of our intent had yet to be devised. Though I know we intended to be with you, together."

Her breath stopped, most likely following the example of her heart. Her eyes widened. *Together* seemed terribly untoward. All those hands. All that strength. That overwhelming hardness, doubled. "Together..." She wasn't entirely sure the word had been audible until he answered her.

"Yes, though not like this. We had hoped to come to you...I had hoped to speak with you about this. As I'm sure Jacks did. Neither of us intended for this...mess."

She realized he hadn't meant the images that her mind had called forth. He'd simply meant at the same time. *Which is the same as together...but not the same.*

She shook her head. "Together?"

"I...yes. Together. I'm not sure it's my place to tell you of Jackson's thoughts on this. I—"

"I'm quite sure that this involves me, and you'll tell me everything you know, as will he. When I speak with him. *Do* continue."

"Jacks came here out of concern, because of the episode today. He was concerned, as he should be, as to whether the position of duchess would be suitable to your...temperament."

"My *temperament*. Damn you twice, Hubert Garrison! If you tiptoe around me I shall take you on and you'll be sorry for it."

"Apologies, Amelia, I...I'm simply feeling more cautious than normal."

"Well, stop. Just...stop. Now explain. In no uncertain terms."

"Yes...yes, Jacks was concerned that the responsibility of the duchy would be too great for you after witnessing the episode today. He doesn't want to force something on you that you're unable to do, that would somehow damage you further. He has a great responsibility to the crown and...well, that's the plain of it." Hugh looked away from her, scrubbed one hand through his hair before studying his shoes. "I'm sorry."

Damage me further. Charles saw her as damaged. *They* saw her as damaged.

"Don't be," she whispered. "It's what I asked for. Thank you." She sat for a moment to consider. He was right, Charles was. He was absolutely right to take her behavior into consideration. His duchy was a powerful one, close to the queen. The title required much of him, as her title would require much of her, were she his duchess. She'd considered this in the past, of *course* she had. But she'd hoped *he* would never have need to consider it. She wasn't sure whether she could manage a dukedom. The simple of it, of course, the households, the staff, all the simple necessaries required of her, absolutely. It was the extended requirements, the parties, the celebrations, the requirements to London, the presentations, the official—and quite formal—productions that would be required of her.

It was too much to ask that she be a silent partner. A duchess was required to support her duke, to take on the tasks considered more menial, so he would be free to deal with the much more difficult tasks required by his queen.

As well, there must be children. This fact weighed heavy on her mind. Not that she didn't want children. She did. And she knew to her toes that she wanted his. But carrying a child within, when even she wasn't comfortable in her own skin, to share that space with another being? This confounded and frightened her.

She turned to Hugh. "He has every right to be concerned. These are my concerns as well. I had hoped that in courting, we would discover if my difficulties would be an issue. I had hoped, in attending functions of the *ton* at his side, that I would be able to discern whether this could be done. I had such great hopes, Hugh…" Her tears fell then, poured from her like water from a sieve. "Such great hopes."

He wrapped himself around her like a blanket and took her into the safety of himself. She soaked in that safety she was so fond of. "What's to become of my mother?" she whispered.

Hugh bristled at that, but he breathed through the anger, then waited a very patient moment before responding. "Amelia, your mother is not of our concern. You are."

"I…what? What did I say?" she asked quietly as she pulled the handkerchief from his pocket, the one that was always there, and wiped her eyes and nose.

"You asked what would become of your mother, Amelia. Your mother. Not you—her. She's not our concern, beyond the pressure she places squarely on your shoulders. This"—he motioned between them and the door, where Charles waited on the other side—"this is between the three of us. This is about you and nobody else. Your mother is not a concern."

"But she must be. She'll have nowhere and no one."

"If she has no one, that's her own doing, not yours. And if she has nowhere to go, it will be because she drove everyone away from her."

"I can't *not* consider her in my actions, Hugh. You must understand."

"I of all people understand how heavily this weighs on you. You know this. We'll deal with your mother somehow. We will…" Hugh shifted, considering a decision that was quite monumental. "*I* will ensure she is cared for, regardless of what happens next. This, I vow to you."

Her eyes crept to his, and a weight transferred. Her lightening was nearly visible in the consignation of responsibility, and he knew the decision had been the right one. "I'll see to her personally, if need be."

He held her for a time, let her take in everything he'd promised to her. Time to consider everything that had passed between them. He knew she needed quiet moments like this, time between, to rethink, re-examine, reconsider all that had come before. When she straightened, he knew she'd come to her decision.

"If I allow you to do this for me, there is one other thing you must do."

He nodded, acceded, regardless that he was nervous.

"You mustn't hold back."

His breath left him, and then she moved. Her hand curled around his neck, pulled him toward her, brought his lips within a breath of hers, until he closed his eyes, and they met. A coming together. Not one or the other, but an agreement, and then the blaze. She whimpered, and he drove, pulling her flush to his chest. Allowing her hands to rove where they might. Allowing her tongue to rove where it would. And rove her tongue did, sliding against his, tasting him, tasting his lips, tasting the tears that slid down his cheeks before he'd a chance to hide them.

He did as she asked. He did not hold back.

Charles waited. More patiently than he ever had. He thought as much anyway. He could not remember a time more difficult than this.

He knew he'd been right to stand first and leave them, to allow Ender to explain to Amelia what had happened. He didn't yet feel strong enough to be able to confront her, to explain himself…without stumbling over himself somehow. Particularly after this afternoon in her parlor. Just the thought of Amelia touching him—it had tied him in knots that he wanted her to unwind.

Charles paced, the soft murmur of their conversation coming through the door lulling him somewhat. Then the murmur of conversation stopped, bringing him to a halt as well. He watched the door, but it didn't open to him. He closed his eyes and swore he would trust in Hugh. Charles would trust Hugh to be the man he now believed him to be. Charles would trust him to explain their decision to Amelia in a way that didn't paint him badly. Charles's eyes opened on the realization that no matter what Hugh said, he was bound to look the fool in this situation.

Charles shook his head and paced again. Glanced back at the door…it was so quiet. *Why is it so quiet?* Charles stopped and turned. Perhaps Hugh had used this opportunity to his advantage. Perhaps Charles had had the wrong of it from the start. Perhaps—

The door opened, and Hugh was there, looking quite sheepish and somewhat guilty. Charles's temper snapped.

"Wait!" Hugh shouted and raised his hands, but Charles didn't wait. He lunged for Hugh, taking him by the jacket and shoving him into the wall.

"Wait," Hugh said again, this time a bit more feebly, the wind knocked from him.

Charles heard Amelia running toward the door and knew a moment of terror that she would see him like this, angry as he was.

Charles glanced to the doorway, telling his hands to release Hugh, but they weren't cooperating. They pushed harder. Charles saw her emerge, like a wraith, her hand resting on his forearm, pulling him away. Charles was helpless in her presence. His body bent to her bidding without so much as an acquiescence from his mind.

He released Hugh and followed her into the library. Charles heard Hugh coughing, then the sturdy click of the door closing behind them as she pulled him to that chaise. Not the two chairs, which is what

he would have assumed at this point. Two chairs, a specific barrier, the easier to keep space between them. The easier to break with him. Blood thundered in his head as she gently guided him then sat, patting the space next to her. Awaiting his decision.

Charles stared at it, attempted to discern the meaning, then looked at her. Her lips were that rosy flush again, but this time that flush wasn't his fault.

She placed her hand on the space next to her, then pulled gently on his hand, silently coaxed him to sit with her, while his eyes never left her.

Betrayed.

It was the only word that came to Charles's mind, like a whisper. He'd lost her, and he'd never even been given the chance for a proper fight. Charles tensed to stand again, to take Hugh on, but her hands wrapped around his wrist to stay him.

Charles eased and looked back to her. "Please…" Please what? He wasn't even sure what he wanted with that plea. To turn back time perhaps.

"Charles." His gaze turned to hers, and she had him. "I'm quite unsure of what happens next. I imagine one, or all of us, will come away quite damaged from this. However, if you will endeavor to try, I believe in my heart that what you want will come to pass."

I want you for my wife

I want nothing more than your happiness.

I want…you.

Ah…there it was, the promise he and Hugh had made to each other. Nothing but her happiness—yet overshadowed by the truth of his want. Apparently, he hadn't convinced his body that whatever made her happy might not include him—and that would be acceptable. Apparently, because it *wasn't* acceptable. Charles looked away momentarily but was drawn back to her.

"I have loved you…"

His heart stalled when Amelia said it, and he took a deep breath. "There's nothing I wouldn't do…to make you feel this—what I have inside me. There's so much. Enough, I believe, for both of us. I've dreamed of you all my life. There's nothing, *nothing* I wouldn't do. I need you to understand this. I need—"

Charles felt the tremble then and looked at her hands. "Amelia, are you well? He hasn't—"

"No...no, nothing like that. Charles, I need you to listen, because I'm trying so very hard to hold myself together. There's no other way to explain, really, except that I feel like so many pieces of a whole and, at my best, my bones are merely stuck together with glue. Funny, that, because glue is made from the bones of—" She stopped awkwardly, shifting her gaze.

Charles didn't laugh, though she'd attempted to lighten the mood. He felt terrible for that, because he knew she was trying. But he couldn't even smile at the moment.

"Charles, Hugh explained what the two of you discussed."

Charles shook his head. How could he trust that Hugh had been true to their agreement now? His head stopped when her hand rose to his cheek, the cool of her touch sinking into his heated, angry skin. "He did, Charles, I'm asking you to trust him, as you agreed to before I arrived."

Charles felt himself nod, though he didn't truly want to.

"I appreciate that you came to him. I know how difficult coming to him must have been for you. I understand, because I'm part of the past that drove a wedge between the two of you. I was there for all the trickery. So believe me when I say I understand the level of bravery—"

"Why did you come here tonight?" Charles said, suddenly needing to know. Had he been played the fool from the start?

She shook her head. "I should have come to you first. I intended to, in fact. But something told me I needed to speak with Hugh. I needed to talk to him about you and me. You must understand how close he is to me. That he holds all my secrets? He does, and were he a woman, you would think nothing of it, would you?"

"No, but he's not a woman, he's...*him*." Charles hadn't meant for the statement to be humorous, but apparently it was, because her eyes lit like a fire burned in them. That fire was beautiful, and he meant to make it happen again.

"Charles—"

He felt her hands trembling more and suddenly understood how difficult this all was for her. He'd witnessed, firsthand, how her emotions could carry her away, to that other place.

"Say it again, with that light in your eyes, say my name again. When you say my name with that light in your eyes, I believe anything to be possible, and I truly need something to believe in right at this moment."

She shied, then lifted her lashes and looked him square in the eye. "Charles."

His name rolled from her tongue like the silk shift off the shoulders of a lover. Charles groaned. Then he suddenly knew what he'd said please for.

"I need to kiss you, then whatever you tell me, anything you say, you can have the world, with me or without me. It's yours, but first… *Please*, let me kiss you." If he hadn't been watching her so intently, he would have missed the acquiescence in her nod, because the nod was very nearly imperceptible.

Charles's gaze dropped to her mouth, and his hands moved ever so slowly up her arms, chasing the blush that rose with them. Gently, he placed them both on her neck, his thumbs tracing the edges of her jaw. He felt her hands reach into his jacket and pull at the fabric of his shirt, but he meant to take his time with this. This was his one chance, his one plea. This was possibly the only time he would be able to show her how *much* he wanted her.

Her lashes fell, cutting a dark line across her pale cheeks. They lay there, fluttering like the wings of a butterfly not sure whether it was safe to alight.

Charles pushed his fingers into the hair at her nape, tangling them, holding her as he closed the distance between them. He felt her breath on his cheek, then his chin, then his neck, as he sprinkled kisses across her face. Attempting to calm every nerve in her, in him. Charles's mouth brushed hers once, twice, then waited, feeling the soft puffs of her breath across his lips like that same indecisive butterfly. He took one lip between his and pulled gently, then pressed kisses to the other. When she gasped, he touched the tip of that soft pink tongue with his own. Something he'd wanted to do since the ball.

Mon Dieu. Had that been just last night? *It was*, he thought, though it seemed ages ago now. As if they'd lived a lifetime together in this moment.

Her hands clenched on his shirt, became more insistent, expectant, and he covered her mouth, delving in and drinking her sweetness. Charles moved one hand down her back, tracing her spine, then rested it on the small of her back and brought her to him.

She broke then, like a wild mustang untethered. He felt the spasm in her muscles that warned of a revolt, and he held on to her for dear life, because he was not about to relent. Not yet. Her hands tore at his shirt, nearly destroyed it then searched beneath.

"Amelia," he tried amidst their lips. "Amelia, don't—"

"Charles…more."

The feel of his name spoken against him was his undoing, *TAKE*, his body screamed. No amount of reasoning from his brain would stop him. "Oh God, Charles, please! The ache, please…touch me here." She took his hand and pressed it to her breast through the corset, and his fingers wrapped around the edge of dress and corset and tugged, freeing one rosy-peaked nipple.

"God, yes, *please*, Charles, please."

Charles closed his mouth on that nipple and drew, and she arched so hard into him they crashed against the foot of the chaise, she now on top of him, her knee firmly on his groin.

The moment, though inopportune, gave his brain the foothold it needed to bring him back to reason. Charles took her by the shoulders and pushed them both to sitting.

"Amelia, I—" *Oh God…oh God, what have I done?*

Charles took the edge of her dress and gave it a careful yank to cover that beautiful rosy bud from his sight, then he stood. She looked terrified. By him. By what he'd done. "No, I…I beg you, I'm so desperately sorry for my behavior. I just can't seem to keep my hands from you. I—"

Charles watched as she appeared to hold herself. "Charles, it's not you…or it is, but not how you think. I just—" She sobbed, and he took her up in a warm embrace, attempting to hold all of her pieces together. Attempting to calm her as she seemed to spiral away, like a whirling dervish.

"Amelia, come back to me. Please, come back," he begged. She pushed at him, but Charles wouldn't release her. He held tighter. He wanted to be that glue for her. Charles wanted so much. His arms wrapped her up in him. He tucked his face into the crook of her neck. He tried, so desperately, to surround her with everything he was. But it just wasn't meant to be.

His head fell back, and he yelled. "Ender!"

His voice boomed through the library, and the resounding slam of the opening door was his response. "Help me, help her, I cannot…she can't hear me. She won't hear me."

"What happened?" Hugh asked as he approached. He walked slowly. He was too calm, and Charles wanted to grab him and shake him, make him see…

"I just…I did as she asked. Then I stopped her. I…I'm not good for her," Charles said, the words a knife to his gut.

"Rubbish. She's quite taken with you. It's something else altogether. You just need to learn."

Hugh took Amelia from Charles, and she steadied against him almost instantly. He sat at the edge of the chaise, against the arm, and pulled her close. Holding her tight—tighter than Charles thought acceptable—and speaking to her softly.

"Hugh…Hugh. I think—I love him." Her voice was so small. So lost in her trappings. Charles's heart tripped to hear her declare this affection. More so because he wasn't entirely sure of whom she spoke, considering she was so terribly distraught.

"Quit looming and take a seat." Hugh spoke so quietly, so gently, his words starkly contrasting Charles's tenor and demeanor.

Charles sat at the foot of the chaise, Amelia nearly on top of Hugh but between them, her skirts spread everywhere like a fan. He watched as she calmed in Hugh's embrace. Her breathing slowed and with it time. The tick of the clock on the mantel seemed to resonate throughout the room, his heartbeat the seconds, the clock sounding off minutes. So impossibly slow.

Charles closed his eyes and concentrated on the sound of his own heartbeat, knew it wasn't racing as fast as he thought. He slowed the tick of the clock in his mind, then opened his eyes to look on them. He felt like an intruder. "I should…go," he said.

"Jacks," Hugh said.

She practically launched herself at Charles then, taking his rumpled shirt in one fist as she reached back to grab Hugh as well. "Don't you leave me. Don't you dare leave me."

Charles nodded, placed his large warm hand over her small shivering one, tried to ease the tension in her fingers, tried to tell her with his touch that he wouldn't leave.

Amelia leaned back then, into Hugh, and Hugh shifted, giving her the pillow of his chest as he sank into the large arm of the chaise, simply holding her. Like a magnet, Charles followed as both of her hands came to his one, pulling his hand with hers, placing it square on her chest. Charles felt her heart race, so disconcertingly fast.

"Mon Dieu, Amelia, your heart…" His voice shook.

He let his hand open wide there, pressing into her chest between her breasts, as though to encompass the whole of her heartbeat. To will the beat to calm for him. He concentrated on the connection and felt his own heart slow. Amelia shifted slowly beneath him, turning her face up into the hollow underneath Hugh's chin, but Charles's hand never left her. Charles forced himself to ignore the other man who held her. Put all of his effort into the tenuous connection Charles held with her.

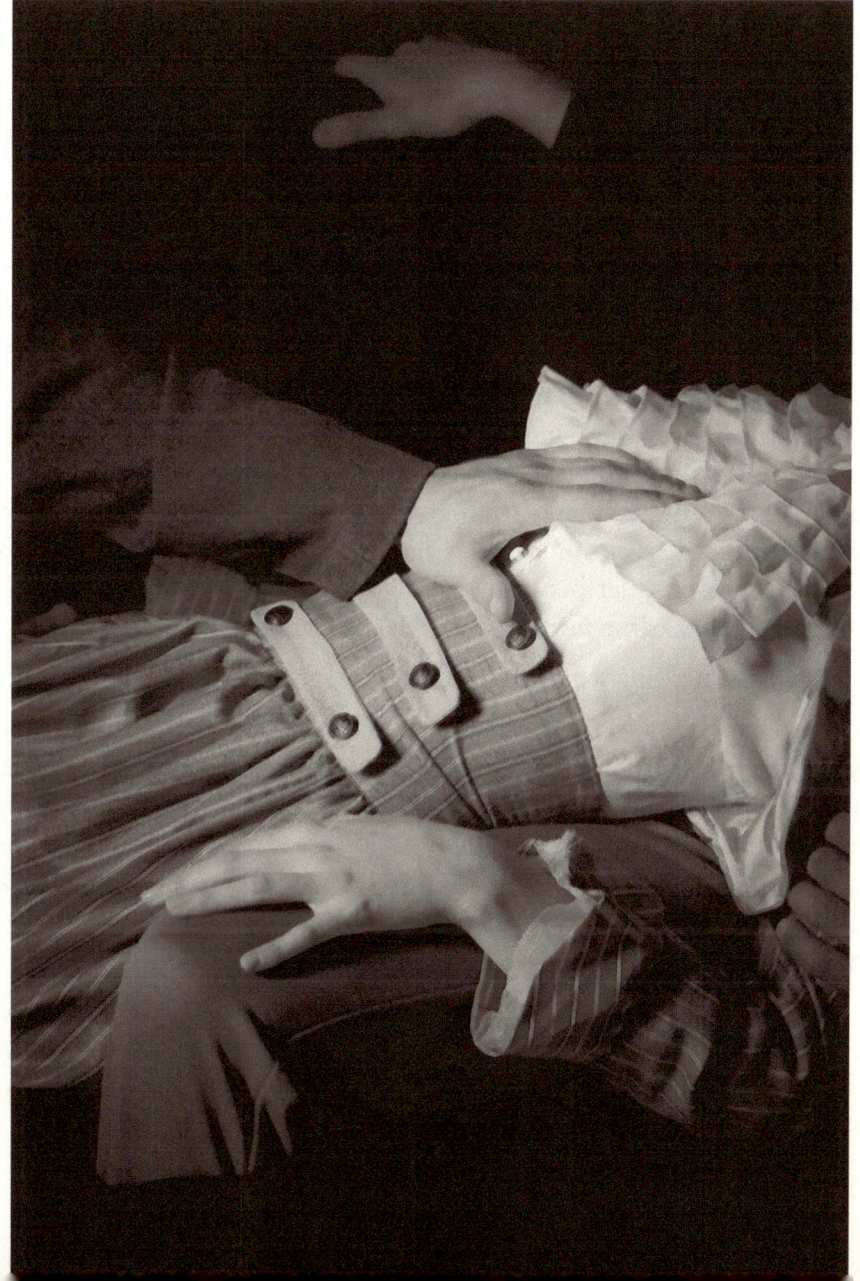

Amelia's hands softened slowly, stroking the back of his hand, delving into the cuff on his wrist, shooting sparks into Charles's bloodstream from the tips of her fingers.

He looked up to find Hugh watching him carefully, his eyes concerned but calm. How could Hugh be so calm? It was as though he knew to his very soul that she would recover from this. Was that the key? The knowing? Would this pass, too?

This was terrifying to Charles. He wasn't sure he had it in him to be so calm when she seemed so out of sorts. Charles saw Hugh nod to him, as though he'd heard his thoughts, then Charles's gaze fell to the hands on her chest. Charles's hand. On her chest. As she lay across *his* chest. This was too much to wrap his brain around.

Charles tensed a bit under her hands, knowing Hugh watched them, this connection between their hands so seemingly intimate. How could Hugh be so calm to watch this? Charles moved his other hand to her rib cage, just below her breast, held her there. Charles felt her deep breath in the expansion of her ribs between his hands. Felt her ease and her heart slow, falling into a steadier rhythm.

Amelia's eyes opened, and she placed a gentle kiss on the underside of Hugh's jaw. It took everything in Charles to remain relaxed on her, to prevent his fingers from giving away the difficulty with which he watched her kiss another man. Charles's gaze darted to Hugh, who'd closed his eyes and let his head fall back on the arm of the chaise, as though whatever came next was entirely acceptable.

"Kiss me," she whispered softly.

. Charles knew then that his hands had betrayed him, and he turned his face into his shoulder, closed his eyes. He shouldn't be here. Charles shouldn't be party to this…whatever this was. Hugh obviously had her in hand. Charles knew Hugh could care for her, knew that it was right to leave them be. Charles would find a wife. That's all he needed, a wife in name and deed. Nothing more. Charles knew no one could ever replace Amelia in his heart.

"She means you." Hugh's voice was gruff, and Charles opened his eyes to find them both looking at him. Waiting. Legs shifted beneath her skirts, between them, closer to the rest of her and allowing him to follow—to get closer to her—to them.

Charles clenched his eyes, and when he opened them, Hugh let his head fall back again. That made this easier. Whatever she asked of him, he would do. Charles knew he could not deny her. Charles also knew he could not pull her away to kiss her. He must come to her, here, while she lay on *another man's chest.*

"Charles." She breathed it, not even a sound on her lips, just the air that carried his name to her, and he was mesmerized, concentrated on those pink lips, that pink tongue between them. Her tongue darted out, licked across the top carefully, then retreated. He followed. His hand left her ribs to press into the cushion of the chaise next to them, to steady himself. He leaned in as her eyelids fell, and she reached toward him, the fingertips of one hand guiding his chin toward her. So slowly, so peacefully.

Charles's body screamed, *TAKE,* as his mind set blinders to the presence of that other warm body beneath them. The first touch of their lips was not even a touch, more of an impression, or the suggestion of a touch. Though Charles could feel her mouth, he knew this kiss wasn't yet fully realized. The kiss waited. For what, he didn't know.

Charles's eyes closed, and her tongue darted out, deliberately, inviting him in.

He pressed against her slowly, the conversation beginning, the words coming slowly at first, then rising to paragraphs, pages, music, a symphony. The hand still on her chest felt her heart pick up tempo, and he receded, painstakingly slowly, their eyes meeting beneath lashes not fully lifted. He kissed the edge of her smile, her cheek, the tear at the corner of her eye. Then his gaze caught on the movement of the chest she rested on, breaking the tenuous connection they held.

Charles paused a moment, knowing he had to progress slowly because she was calm. They were together, and she was calm. Charles couldn't be the one to panic now. He pushed away from her, from them, replaced his hand on her chest as he turned on the chaise, gazing into the fire.

She pulled her legs up onto the chaise, her skirts sliding with them as she curled lazily into Hugh. Only then did Charles see the length of leg against his was Hugh's, not Amelia's.

And reality began to sink back in.

NINE

"It's not impossible," Hugh said to Charles, watching as he stared into the smoldering embers of the banked fire.

Charles looked like a man back from war. One who'd seen and experienced too much. He looked like Amelia when she was lost in herself.

Charles's hand was still on her chest, and hers stroked it, from the fingertips to the edge of his cuff, ducking underneath the fabric occasionally. Hugh watched her movements and felt them on his own flesh as though she stroked Hugh's wrist and not Charles's.

Hugh lifted his hands, one resting against her temple, the other arm wrapped around her middle. He knew it was time to bring Amelia back to the world. They hadn't the time to discuss this tonight. She needed to be taken home before her family discovered her missing. She'd a difficult enough time in the *ton* without being labeled for inappropriate behavior.

"Jacks..." Hugh waited a moment, then, "Jackson, we must see her home somehow."

Charles turned to him, some sort of consciousness coming back to his eyes as he looked at her lying so peacefully there. Charles nodded.

"I'll see to her. I'll make some sort of excuse to her mother should she stop us. I've an agreement with her father. It should be me to see her home. My carriage is ready as well. It—"

Hugh waved off his maundering. "Yes, Jackson, of course." Hugh turned toward Amelia and spoke softly into her ear. "My sweet, we must get you home now. Before you're missed." Hugh kissed the shell of her ear, couldn't help but taste it, smell her hair, nudge her a bit with his nose as she came back to them from wherever it was she went.

Hugh saw Charles's eyes dart to his hand, still on her chest, and knew Amelia's heartbeat picked up. Hugh tapped that wrist with one finger to get Charles's attention, then gave a small shake of his head. *Stay calm.* Hugh saw Charles's nod of understanding, then watched as the rise and fall of his hand steadied on her chest.

Amelia's breathing slowed as she stopped trailing her fingers on Charles's wrist, then she took their hands, one of his, one of Charles's, and moved to sitting on the chaise between them.

"Well, I—" She left their hands in her lap, then lifted hers to her mouth, the edge of her dress, her temple, as though to retrace their steps…to make sure all these pieces of her were still in attendance.

They sat for a moment, one of Hugh's legs trapped behind her, in quite an awkward silence. Then Amelia stood, and they both followed. She wrapped her arms around her middle and took a few steps forward, then turned toward them, attempting a smile. When it failed, she looked down to the floor.

"I can't speak to you together. I…Hugh, might you call on me tomorrow?"

Charles spoke then. "I'm set to call on you tomorrow as well, Amelia."

"Yes, well, I'm sure tomorrow will feel quite different from tonight? Perhaps we can all be together…I mean, perhaps we can picnic to…together, or some such?" Her hands went to her mouth to cover a sob, and they both stepped forward, pushing her back toward the fire grate. Her other hand came up before her to stay them as her skirts swayed dangerously close to the embers. "No, please—" She looked up then. Hugh could tell she attempted to keep herself calm, and she took his hand. "Until tomorrow, Hugh." Then she walked out of the library.

Charles turned to him. "I don't know—"

"That makes two of us." Hugh held his hand out, and they shook, both staring at the sudden warm, strong contact—and, like they'd been burned, severed it.

Charles walked past him, following Amelia from the house. Hugh heard the sturdy click of the front entry door and fell into the chaise. What an…interesting turn of events.

To watch Amelia with another man was inconceivable, yet here it was. Hugh had lain still as she'd lain upon him, and another man had kissed her. Touched her. Accidentally touched him. At some point, he would need to tell Charles to mind his cock and where he pressed it.

Or would he? Was this to happen again? That would mean sharing her, and he was strangely at peace with this. Charles had called him to help, and help he had. Hugh had done for her what he always did for her. He'd calmed her. Allowed her to take in the world without fear. Allowed her to be herself, and when she'd asked for Charles to kiss her—

Hugh rubbed his face in his hands. Had someone said to him this was a possibility, he would have laughed heartily. A mere hour past, in truth. He stared into the dying embers in the grate. Hugh preferred the light of the fire to the gas lamps in his town house, but they required tending to be strong enough. Much like his Amelia.

Everything in his life seemed to need a great deal of tending to.

Hugh pulled a candlestick from a nearby table and lit the wick on a red-hot ember. The candle flared to life as he stood watching it strive to burn. The flame flickered and danced, waiting for direction from its keeper. Hugh held a hand in front of it to keep the air from putting out the fire and went to the desk, where he placed the candle amidst a great pile of wax. Decades of wax. Some sort of strange mountain of history in the pile of wax that had been left to build on this one corner of the desk.

Hugh sat in one of the leather chairs, crossed one ankle over his knee and rested an elbow on the arm of the chair, rubbing one finger over his lip as he watched the flame. The way it moved reminded him more of Amelia, how happy she could be, but with the stiff wind of some discomfort, she shied, melted into herself. He'd spend the whole of his life endeavoring to prevent that flame from being extinguished. If that happened, he knew he couldn't bear it.

But now this—and he'd always bent to her will. What of this? Charles's hand had been pressed against his thigh. The man had leaned across his leg to kiss her. Charles had pressed into him, albeit unwittingly. Hugh had seen the other man's discomfort in his proximity, so he knew

that if there was one thing they shared, it wasn't a tendre of any sort for each other. It was for Amelia. It was all for Amelia and only for Amelia.

Charles simply needed to learn to calm himself. He didn't understand that his own discomfort drove hers. If he remained calm, so would she. Well, to a point anyway. At least, Hugh thought as much.

Hugh wondered then if she'd ever pleasured herself. Hugh knew she was a virgin. This wasn't merely obvious by her carriage and demeanor toward men, but also that she never kept anything from him. Hugh would know if something had happened in that regard.

It had seemed to Hugh that when Charles touched her she'd been driven more by desire than whatever the malevolent force was in her head that usually caused her to spiral beyond restraint.

Could a deeper level of passion be something she could handle? If she were driven to the brink—admittedly most women lost themselves a bit during that crisis—but Amelia, his smart, brave, ever-controlling Amelia…could she even reach a crisis?

She wound herself so tightly, controlled her emotions so fully, the level of release required of an orgasm might be well beyond her capabilities. As though in sad agreement, the candlewick waned and flickered, nearly guttered. Hugh's forehead tensed, and he leaned forward, resting his elbows on his knees.

Amelia could be taught. He'd taught a few women to find their own release. Not every woman even knew pleasure was a possibility with a man. Pleasure was oft times something that had to be learned, or showed—coaxed out. Requiring a level of intimacy not always readily available to newly met couples.

The candle flared, and he looked back to the flame, Hugh was absolutely getting ahead of himself. As important as this was, it wasn't necessarily something he would be charged with. As it happened, Charles might be the man lucky enough to lead Amelia through the discovery of pleasure. The thought rankled, but Hugh steeled himself. This was for Amelia. Everything he'd done always had been. He could see his way through this, for her sake. Whatever need she had. Whether that need be learning to hold a man's hand or his cock.

Hugh leaned back in the chair and scrubbed his hands across his face again then stood. He needed to get some sleep. Even his brain was working against him now, and the only release he had to look forward to was the hand in his pocket.

Hugh took the candle and stormed off to bed, attempting his level best to put Amelia from his thoughts.

The carriage rocked over the cobblestones, and Charles felt every last bump and sway to the core. He seemed to drive her in ways he couldn't truly comprehend. While Hugh grounded her, kept her tethered to herself, kept her from falling apart. And Hugh did it so handily.

Charles feared the way he, himself, made her feel, but he also marveled at it. She was wild, passionate. Something he'd never seen in her had taken over and nearly destroyed his shirt.

He straightened that shirt, along with his waistcoat and jacket, then stared out the window, the tension in his thoughts most likely evident in the way he carried himself. She looked up at him then, sitting cautiously across the carriage.

Amelia reached out and smoothed the creases at his temple, shocking them both. Quite literally, a spark caught his temple from her hand, and Charles turned to her, took her hand in his and kissed it.

"Amelia, tonight requires much thought. I must admit I wasn't prepared for what happened between us. Between…all of us." Charles watched her closely.

Amelia nodded and appeared to concentrate on the feel of his thumb making circles in her palm, even as the pace of her heart kicked.

"I…I also don't know what to think of tonight. I can't. Please don't think I had any idea…or Hugh, please don't think this was some sort of trap or—"

Charles shook his head. "No, of course not. I could see that he was just as much uncomfortable with me as I him. But for you, there is no doubt in my mind now. There isn't anything either of us wouldn't do."

And this truth was a bold one, wasn't it? Charles thought.

She watched him, her mind obviously racing. She blushed and Charles knew where her mind had gone.

There isn't anything we wouldn't do…

"Within reason," Charles finished quietly, before turning again to the window.

So I do have limits. How could he not?

"I'm frightened," she said quietly.

That was the second time he'd heard that word from her tonight. Charles nodded. "As am I."

He hoped his agreement helped to alleviate some of her fear. If she knew that she wasn't alone in her feelings… "It seems this mating dance, or courting, as it's so formally called, has come to be much more than a mere inspection to determine if we would suit. It's become a determination of whether we *can* suit. Amelia, I must be blunt, and hope that this doesn't overtax you. You understand that isn't my intention, do you not? I don't mean to disturb you or cause an…an episode. I want nothing more than to prevent such, in fact."

She nodded again. "I'll endeavor to keep myself together, perhaps concentrate on the facts, as opposed to the emotions. I'll attempt to think on the discussion as though it were a scholarly example as opposed to my personal life."

"Do you think you're able to?" *I'm not so sure* was left unsaid. *Hugh isn't here to save you* was also unspoken. The thought disturbed him.

"I'll attempt it, for you. I've become quite practiced at keeping myself together. The episodes come on under certain circumstances, certain situations, or around you at times. You seem to be a circumstance unto yourself…but I'll attempt to put another barrier between us."

Charles cringed. "This isn't at all what I want for us. I don't want for you to have need to construct barriers in order to merely converse with me. Those barriers take much more effort to bring down. I… perhaps we should leave off for now." Charles was exhausted, and he wasn't sure what he would do should she have an episode. Though if something did happen, perhaps his newfound knowledge could be put to the test. Perhaps he could help her, at least somewhat. And hadn't that been the whole point of the endeavor with Hugh? To learn how to help her?

No time like the present, Charles thought.

"No, please, just, go slowly. I'll let you know if we need to stop."

Charles gave a single, stout nod, then looked at her, leaned forward on his knees and took her other hand and massaged it as well. "Amelia. *Intimacy* is of the utmost concern to me." He held her gaze and waited. He watched her chest rise and fall as she breathed slowly. He ignored the way her breasts pressed up from the confines of her corset… well, not so. He took note of them, then forced himself to continue. "It isn't merely my duty to the crown, but that I do, quite desperately, want to be *with* you." So his thoughts were to color his words then. Quite vibrantly.

Charles watched as her pupils dilated, and she swayed in her seat toward him. Her hands melted a bit into his, and he wondered if these signs led to an acquiescence or an episode.

He leaned in, whispering, deepening the connection between them. "I want to touch you, kiss you, to make love with you."

He swallowed, wishing he could leave off at that but needing to be heard. He dropped his voice as low as he could and still be sure she could hear him. "Without the fear that I am somehow causing you great harm or distress."

His mouth grazed her jaw, and he spoke softly against her ear. "This is of paramount importance to me."

Her breath stopped against his cheek, and he looked back into her eyes, saw a tear escape, which he caught on the pad of his thumb. "There is *nothing* I wouldn't do to make you feel my want of you."

And now Charles cradled her face in his giant hand, at the perfect angle for a kiss.

"I want this, as well," she whispered, letting him support her weight. "Please, just hold me for a moment. I don't think I can bear much more from your mouth."

Well, then.

Charles laughed a bit, then wrapped her up in his arms and held on. Listened to her breathing, felt her pulse as he fit her neck against his, resting her head on his shoulder. She was okay. He had been frank, bold, straightforward—and she was okay. He marveled at the thought. Hopefully, tomorrow they could try again.

Amelia breathed of Charles.

Strong.

The word resonated. She could rely on Charles. Trust in him to support her. There was just something about him that wound her up like nobody ever had before. True, she lost control of herself on occasion. Said things she shouldn't, did things she shouldn't. But with Charles she felt different. He forced her control to slip with just a look, and she allowed it. As though he wanted to be so deeply inside her as to be part of her…and she wanted this as well.

She had some semblance of this with Hugh.

Hugh.

Hugh was so much a part of her that she was often shocked to find him a separate being, not merely her internal conscience or guard. But standing next to her, lending her his safety and control. She wanted him as well, that sereneness. That extreme sense of peace that washed over her whenever he was close. She coveted the space between them as they'd lain together tonight, Hugh providing his safety, his support, while Charles had driven her to the brink of insanity.

Amelia knew that to be the destination with Charles. That was her fear. That letting go with him would ultimately drive her insane. She wasn't capable of pulling back from such freedom of mind, of body—without Hugh. She'd never been able to.

And being with them together? That was an impossibility. She wasn't sure how their predicament had come about tonight. Possibly they had all been so frightened of losing each other that all propriety had gone to the wayside. But that couldn't happen again. She breathed deeply of Charles, the cotton and man, shifted deeper into the crook of his neck.

Even being close to Hugh tonight, kissing him, she had still been very well controlled, comforted, safe. But kissing Charles?

Kissing Charles. Kissing. I kissed him, and he me. His mouth was on me, everywhere.

The thought overwhelmed her. She opened her mouth on the pulse in his neck, licked, then laid a wet, open kiss there. Twisted her hand in his rumpled shirt. God, he tasted good. She filled her mind with Hugh to calm herself as Charles pulled back to look in her face.

This way lies insanity, she thought, then she closed her eyes, once again overwhelmed. She couldn't think of Hugh and look on Charles. It wasn't right.

"I'm sorry, I shouldn't have," she said quietly. Wishing that wasn't the truth.

"Amelia, it takes everything in me to keep myself from you. But I will, for as long as you need this of me. Because I can see, very readily, that in our joining you aren't able to be with me. You become so lost. So frightened. I don't want you frightened. I want you with me. So please don't take any of my future actions as cold, or heartless, but I feel I should warn you. I cannot be so forward with you, physically, because I fear damaging you."

And then something Hugh had said whispered in the back of her mind.

He doesn't want to force something on you that you are unable to do, that would somehow damage you further.

Damaged.

She pushed herself away from him. "You see me as damaged."

"No, I see you as...I'm not sure how to put this into words, Amelia. I don't believe there are yet words with which to describe what it is you are. I don't see anything about you in a negative fashion, and yet every word that has been used to describe your actions *is* negative. Therein lies my greatest challenge.

"How do I speak with you or Ender, about your behaviors without being demeaning, without being insulting? Because that's not at all what I intend in these discussions. I hold such esteem for you, such high regard. Amelia, I care for you. I have cared for you since the first time I met you. Long before I knew you were to be mine. Long before I knew what it meant, and these feelings have only grown with time."

He cares for me. Cares for me. Not love, but care.

She couldn't look at him. Held on to the tenuous reality of the carriage. The wheels turned, creaked over the rutted roads, the cobblestones, the occasional garbage left behind. She heard the leather creak and the brass on the horses' hardware clank, the occasional clucking of the driver. She wanted desperately to hear what Charles had to say, but could feel her mind attempting to close her off. Spinning, spinning with the wheels of the carriage. She stared at her knees, attempting to ground herself to this moment, this time.

Charles slid from the seat and crouched in the carriage, his sturdy thighs surrounding her legs as he placed his hands over hers. So warm, so strong, so...pervasive.

"Amelia, I can feel you hiding from me, and perhaps following you in is the wrong thing to do. I understand I may start an episode. But I want you to stay here with me. I want for you to hear me out. To understand. There is not a negative thought in my head where you are concerned. Do you hear me? Tell me what I said."

She choked, then closed her eyes and concentrated against the part of her mind that wanted her to let go of the moment. "There is not a negative thought—"

"In my head...keep going," Charles whispered.

"In your head where I—"

"Where you are concerned. Say it."

"Where *I* am concerned. There is not a negative thought in your head where I'm concerned."

"Do you believe me?" She did, but could not effort her head to move or her mouth to open. Charles's hand was gentle on her chin, turning her toward his voice. "Amelia, open your eyes and look on me, please."

Amelia did. Then she breathed, and with that breath came the words she knew Charles longed for. "I believe you."

She could tell by the jerk of his muscles that what he wanted was to take her up in an embrace, but he stayed himself. At great expense, Charles stayed himself. So she reached forward, slowly, wrapped her arms around his neck, and pulled him to her. "I believe you."

There were tears, hot on her neck, and she was unsure who they belonged to.

"I will take care of you." And with those words, Charles's hands came around her, clenching in the fabric of her gown. Holding on to her as though she were the last remaining tie to earth and he were being pulled away. Her gown tightened around her, and she wished for the fabric to rend, separate, set her free.

"Amelia." Charles's voice was strained, and she knew he was attempting to control everything he was and everything he wanted of her. She didn't want him to. She wanted him to be free to act on his want, on his need. For this, she hated herself. Her control had now extended beyond herself to this man, this amazing man, who wanted for nothing more than to be with her.

I changed him. I changed him.

She was suddenly overwhelmed by the thought, and her head leaned as though the spin would start. It was then the carriage came to a halt, and he backed away to his side, leaving her cold and bereft of his heat and strength.

When the door pulled open and Charles stepped down, she was truly alone. Even the air had followed him from the carriage. The solitude was piercing, sitting in this dark, small space, an overwhelming loneliness that she knew she would suffer for the balance of her life if she could not find a way to let Charles in.

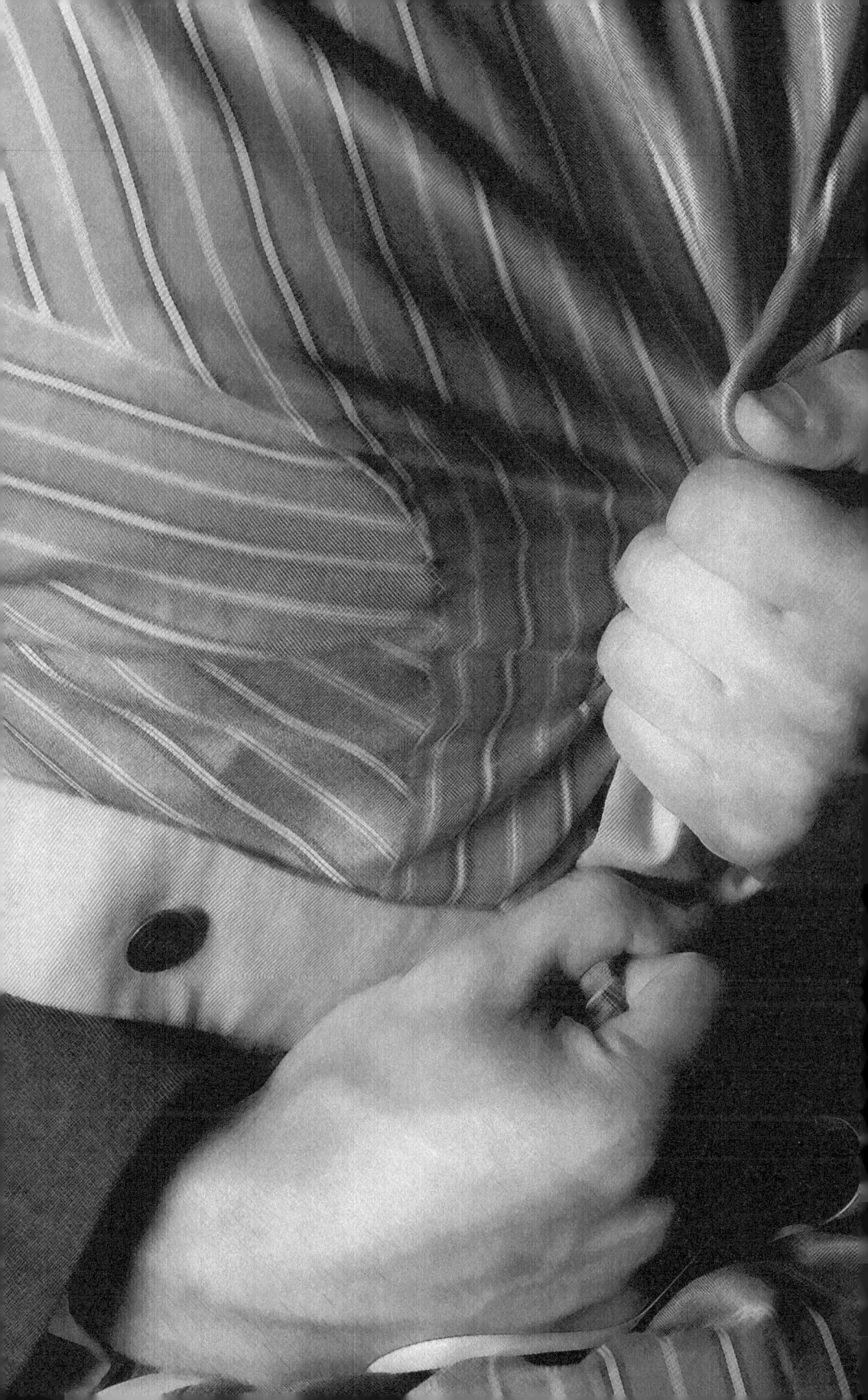

Amelia closed her eyes and let the silence sink into her bones, so as not to forget the feeling, to persuade herself to reach for what she wanted, to be strong. Amelia felt it, she owned it, she carried it. She let that loneliness weigh upon her…then Charles's warm hand reached into that darkened door, grasped hers, and pulled her out to him.

TEN

Amelia faced the mirror, waiting for the twitch. Scanning every bit of her face, looking for the signs and practicing her response. She'd received a missive from Charles that morning. He and Hugh would be calling on her within the hour. All Amelia need do was survive this day. At least, that's what she kept telling herself.

When Amelia thought on the much larger goals involved in this meeting—*there it was…*the twitch, and so she was determined to survive this meeting, this one outing. With both of them. Hopefully, by the end of today there would be some definitive plan for her future. The future they seemed to be plotting without her.

Both of them.

Twitch.

There at the corner of her eye. She breathed deeply.

They both cared for her. They both wanted what was best for her. Yet they both wanted…her. Something they both could not have.

Twitch.

This time, just at the edge of her jaw. She breathed again, attempted to calm her nerves. Attempted to relax all the muscles that gave away her discomfort. She could do this. She could see them both. *Together.*

She believed that she and Charles had come so far in the mere span of one day. So much had happened. As though they endeavored to rewrite history with their present. Charles and Hugh had come to an agreement of sorts. Granted, she had believed herself to be quite left out of their decision at the time, but she had been quite truly wedged in the middle of that decision in the end. Literally.

A tremor coursed her spine, raising the hair at the back of her neck and casting a chill across her skin. Being with both of them had been…simply amazing. As well, it was simply impossible.

They were all known in the *ton*. It wasn't like the three of them could disappear together and live happily where nobody would know about them As well, it just wasn't the thing. How selfish of her to want for both of them, yet she wanted for both of them in entirely different ways, because somehow they managed to complement each other so easily—a fact of which she wasn't entirely sure even they were aware.

Did they know they'd breathed the very life into her last night? That moment, lying upon Hugh's safe haven, while Charles kissed her. Caught between a friend and forever, between strength and safety. That moment had been the best, truest, calmest in her life. To think something like that would never happen again left her truly insecure, bereft, and… *twitchy.*

Damn.

She smoothed her fingertips across the skin at her temple, attempting to relax the muscles beneath, trying to convince them that this action was completely unnecessary. Hugh would see it—he saw everything—and he would know that all was not right. Somehow, Hugh would know before any outward signs showed themselves.

That thought calmed her a bit. The knowledge that she truly couldn't hide from Hugh. This man she'd loved from childhood. She remembered everything about Hugh, from the moment they met. How his smile canted to the left when he was truly happy and how his smile leaned to the right when he was annoyed. Funny, that.

How she could see with just a glance that Hugh knew she was upset and would help her, however he was able. How was it that she'd become so reliant upon him? Hugh had been part of her life, long before her condition seemed to spiral out of control. And her joy had always been wrapped up in whether he was there—until Charles had arrived.

Charles was a completely different sort. Charles wound her up, as opposed to Hugh's gentle release. They conflicted, not merely in personality and opinion, but their very beings seemed to be such that they could not be in the same vicinity without quarrel—and that quarrel, as it was now, was coming to tea.

She marveled at their frank speech with each other, how they had easily discussed her. As if the frogs had happened in an entirely different lifetime, or to entirely different people. They were men now, had the responsibilities that came with such. And they both believed themselves responsible for her.

There now, several minutes had passed and nary a twitch.

The door to the parlor opened, and the butler announced them, both of them.

Twitch.

She closed her eyes and sighed. So she wasn't truly as controlled as she would like.

She nodded to Smythe but remained in the mirror. Perhaps the first glance through the glass would be easier for her than the overwhelming reality that was to come through her parlor door in mere moments. Through the reflection she could see shuffling in the entryway as hats were removed and handed off, a great blur of black and white. So severe of tone, so easily reassuring.

She loved that neither of these men were fussy. No fancy waistcoats. No shiny, slippery satins. They were both of a serene fashion.

The beauty had to be searched out in the patterns and textures of the fabrics they chose. Thick, textured fabrics, beautiful more to the hands than the eyes. Their respective clothing wasn't gaudy and intense, but a much more close and intimate experience.

A throat cleared behind her, and she realized they were there, behind her, watching. She reduced them both to their beautiful brocade waistcoats, one in dove gray, the other in black, and turned to them.

Both of them.

They all stared at each other for an inordinately lengthy amount of time. Hugh knew that at any moment the tension in the room would sink into Amelia, and they would be left to deal with her state rather than her needs of them, so he spoke.

"Can Louisa attend us, or must it be your aunt?" he asked plainly.

Amelia shook her head and looked to him with a bit of confusion in her eyes, then at her aunt, who had followed him and Charles into the parlor. "I…well. I don't see why not," Amelia said.

Hugh turned to Lady Mathorpe and raised one eyebrow as though to say, *Well? What are you waiting for?* The lady returned the regard for a moment, then turned in a huff and went upstairs.

"Shall we sit?" Amelia asked quietly, motioning to the settee and chairs placed in a convenient gathering around a tray table.

Hugh and Charles moved together toward the individual chairs, then Amelia followed. Once they were settled, she sank into the center of the overstuffed settee across from them. She motioned to the tea service on the tray with a smile. Hugh noticed that she was holding herself together rather well at the moment and took this as a good sign, that the ride home the night before had gone well. That she hadn't been returned a complete wreck, as he'd feared she might be.

He and Charles both raised their gloved hands, declining the tea.

"It's Earl Grey," she said quietly, pouring a cup. As gentle as the statement was, he knew it to be more than a suggestion. He looked to

Charles, who looked back to him and shrugged. He supposed they had to wait for Louisa to prepare herself…

"On second thought, we will take tea with you," Hugh said.

She smiled so brightly he knew they both felt it across the tray, because it was magnificent.

It was tea—tea, for goodness sake. Hugh shook his head. When they had a moment together he would have to ask her why that simple acquiescence had brought her such joy. Hugh shook his head and looked at Charles. Why couldn't he ask her in front of him? Particularly after last night. Hugh looked back to her.

"Why did this simple task of tea make you happy?" he asked finally.

"In Japan, the taking of tea is a ceremony meant to put everyone on level footing. From the servant, to the warrior, to the master. It's a ceremony of peace. We thank the maker of the tea. We pardon the person drinking before us, and thank the person for allowing us to drink after. The formalities of the service are meant to remove all external forces, open our hearts and minds, to help us to find the truth."

"Japan." Charles's voice was low and gruff, as though he'd overused it the night before and had yet to warm it up today. "And we're bringing these traditions to your parlor, in Great Britain?"

"Not necessarily. The thought just occurred to me that perhaps we all needed a moment, with clear minds, to take tea together…as friends," she replied, looking up, between them, as though afraid to look to one then the other. Finally, her eyes flickered quickly over Hugh, then turned to Charles. "To forgive each other the past, to move forward in trust. To begin as friends."

Friends. The word hung in the air like a particle of dust in a shaft of light.

"I rather like the idea," Hugh replied.

"Sugar?" Amelia asked.

"No, thank you," Charles replied.

She handed the cup to Hugh, and he passed the cup to Charles with a nod.

"Thank you," Charles replied.

Amelia added a lump of sugar to the cup in her hand and passed that cup to Hugh. He smiled and thanked her as well.

"She knows how to prepare your tea," Charles stated.

"And now she knows how to prepare yours as well," Hugh replied, and from the corner of his eye, he saw Charles smile.

Amelia poured a dash of cream in the bottom of a third cup, added the tea, then two lumps of sugar. She smiled over the rim as she drank quietly.

It was the quietest tea service Hugh had ever attended. In general, tea was accompanied by many ladies with many opinions and voices each attempting to outdo one another. Though, he imagined if men took tea on a regular basis as women did, formally, in the parlor with others, tea would become more of a thing. Much like the pub. The tea room seemed the feminine version of the Iron Duke. But he wasn't willing to break the incredible peace of the silence in this room, for the silence wasn't at all uncomfortable, though he thought it should have been.

"Louisa, won't you join us?" Amelia said without shifting her gaze.

Louisa moved to the settee next to Amelia. "Milady! I'm so sorry te keep ye waiting."

Apparently, today, disruption would be Louisa's job.

"Not at all, Louisa." Amelia smiled...but Hugh could see there was strain.

He hadn't noticed the strain before and wondered whether it had come with Louisa. Perhaps it was that she was being watched? For he knew they both watched her intently. Possibly scrutinized. They needed to *not* do that. Somehow.

Hugh stood and Charles followed, placing their cups silently on the table. Then Amelia and Louisa joined them.

"Well," Amelia said, "shall we?" She straightened her skirts, then took up her gloves, but she clenched them a bit tightly. She seemed so very, very in control of herself—considering.

Hugh followed Charles to the front of the house, where Amelia stopped, examining the conveyance they'd arrived in. She turned to them, her brows raised.

"That would be my doing, my lady," Charles said with a grin.

She turned back to the midnight-blue barouche in the drive. The brass trim sparkled in the sun with a high polish, and the soft cream-colored seats awaited them. Charles had the top down and had picked Hugh up on the way to her town home, so this was the only carriage in the drive. Something he was quite sure she also noticed. Possibly the reason for her raised brow.

Amelia walked toward the carriage and Hugh held back, allowing Charles to assist her to the bench. "I hope this is acceptable. I assumed we would need a carriage for four, and with such a beautiful day, I thought you might enjoy the ride with the sunshine. If you prefer, I can have my men raise the calash."

"No, thank you. I believe this perfect," Amelia said with a smile to him.

To him. Score one, Charles, Hugh thought, then shook it off. This was no longer a competition, even though she had asked him to not hold back. This was about her. Solely.

Hugh walked down the steps and handed Louisa in to sit next to Amelia, then he and Charles ascended the steps, taking the rear-facing seat.

They drove on in silence, each looking in a different direction, Louisa awkwardly drawing their attention to a silly child, or prancing horse, or a spectacular dress. It seemed that in this particular situation, Louisa needed more comfort from Amelia than the other way around, and perhaps it helped Amelia, to be responsible.

When Amelia finally spoke, she drew all their attention. "If I were not myself, and you were someone else, I'd say so much to you both."

Hugh and Charles both continued to watch her, while Louisa turned away, quietly finding things to place her attention on.

"I would be able to tell you true that I can hardly think. I can barely breathe. I feel as though I'm sinking into both of you. So lost. So lost." Amelia shook her head and watched her hands as they tangled on her lap.

Charles tensed, in the flex of his arm as he bumped against him. Hugh nudged Charles's boot with the toe of his shoe, then saw a slight nod from the corner of his eye.

"This situation concerns me. For so many reasons. It's terribly unfair to you, Hugh, because you're simply waiting to see if I can handle being a duchess, and if not, you'll come in to sweep up what remains, take me home, put me back together."

"Amelia—" Hugh started, but she stayed him. She should know that wasn't at all how he considered this situation, though on face he could see where she would think it.

"It's equally unfair to you, Charles. As you should be free to choose from all the proper ladies of the *ton* to run your household, and yet I hold you to an agreement made by our fathers decades ago." She held her hand up to him before he could disagree as well. They all knew what he would say, because they all knew she had the wrong of it.

"In the meantime, I can tell neither of you what I wish for, because I'm so torn between the two of you. You are, quite obviously, very different men. And I believe I love both of you in equal measure. I stayed up last night in consideration of this predicament, because I could not sleep anyway after...after what happened...yesterday."

"Amelia, we're both quite aware of what happened yesterday, but perhaps we shouldn't mention it," Charles said, but Hugh knew there was no issue with Louisa. Chances were she knew more about Amelia's feelings on the matter than the two of them did…combined. Hugh had made sure Louisa understood her perfectly when he had chosen her to be Amelia's maid.

Amelia shook her head then, confirming his suspicions. "Louisa knows everything."

Hugh couldn't help but smile. He wasn't sure whether it was because he knew her so well, or because of the look of shock on Charles's face. Which quite pleased him.

"Oh look! A family of ducks is just going for a swim there. How darling."

They all looked to Louisa, who smiled.

Leave it to Louisa to break the tension, Amelia thought. Louisa did know her well. Not best, but well. Hugh knew her best, but he was dealing with much more than just her at the moment. His mind might be elsewhere. He had been rather silent.

Speaking with them had been difficult. Pulling up to the Row in the park, as it turned out, was to be worse. Everyone looked at them curiously as they passed.

She tensed and wished to tell the driver to move on, to leave, as quickly as possible, but she didn't. This trip to Hyde Park had been a terrible miscalculation on their part, while in truth it was an acceptable test of her ability to handle the *ton*.

"Drive on."

Amelia looked at Charles then. The carriage jerked and pulled back into the lane.

Charles turned to the driver behind him. "Home," Charles said quietly.

She shivered at the thought of being alone with them again.

"You've started something in doing this," Hugh said to Charles.

"I agree. However, I wish to be somewhere more comfortable. *I am uncomfortable. I don't wish to be.*" Charles looked at her then, and she knew that he was more aware of her discomfort than that he was uncomfortable himself. Though the consideration touched her. "There is enough about this outing without having to deal with these old bats and their opinions. Staying or leaving, tongues will wag. It's entirely too late to stay them, so why remain here and be miserable? What's done is done."

"Agreed," Hugh said.

Amelia was amazed at how easily Charles made these decisions. He simply decided he wanted something to be a certain way, proclaimed it as such, then waited for the world to shift beneath his feet to acquiesce. "Charles, I must beg you, forgive me for placing you in such a position. Yours should always be honorable, not associated with this." She waved her hand toward herself. *He shouldn't have to deal with this. He has enough.* The thought saddened her.

"You misunderstand if you believe that what I do now is because of my title and my responsibility. What kind of man would I be if I dishonored you? If I cut you in public and walked away from our agreement? What kind of man would that make me?" Charles asked.

"In the eyes of the *ton*? A smart one," she answered.

"And what of the eyes of Ender? For we know that my opinion would be biased. If I did this, Ender, what does that make me?" he asked without taking his gaze from hers.

"The worst sort of jackass," Hugh answered easily.

She smiled. She couldn't help it.

"Well…" Charles started, "what is it the two of you always said? *Damn me.* Yes, damn me, Ender thinks me a jackass."

"Actually, not to make too fine a point of it, but he actually does not think you a jackass. Quite the opposite. Well, in this particular instance anyway."

A warmth expanded from her chest, and she wished, quite desperately, to reach out and take their hands, but it was quite obvious that neither of them would have any of that at the moment.

They both seemed on edge there, bouncing against each other in the barouche. She couldn't possibly endeavor to make light of the situation they found themselves in, as she had quite possibly bred this situation. She knew Hugh had always loved her, but she hadn't known that Charles was in this for much more than a wife—until recently—and he had worn that fact on his sleeve for her. Had not withheld from her the truth of his want. Charles had allowed her to know his deepest thoughts on her without prejudice or bias against her relationship with Hugh. No, he wasn't a jackass. He was quite the opposite. This was possibly a thorn in Hugh's side, as it would have been much easier for Hugh to hate a jackass.

They turned onto Grosvenor, and Charles gave instructions to the driver to pull around to the mews.

Amelia watched Hugh for a moment, knowing he didn't appreciate Charles mentioning their childhood game, the one they still often played out of habit. Their game was beyond irreverent, terribly uncouth. Charles hadn't been privy to those games of heart. He had been disallowed any participation in any of the true games she and Hugh had played as children.

It saddened her suddenly. They might have had more time together to be friends, and the thought occurred to her as well that Hugh and Charles might have been quite good friends had she not been a factor in it all. They both had this terribly strong sense of ethics and morals. Something that was well used in the House.

The carriage turned onto Charles Street, then Adam's Mews and entered a small pull-through surrounded by walls of stone.

Hugh descended first and brought Louisa down. Then Charles descended and reached for Amelia's hand. When she looked back up, Hugh had entered the property through a large iron gate, seemingly deep in thought, his eyes on the great expanse of this refuge in the city. It seemed Charles had a park all his own behind his town home.

Charles took her hand, carefully, very carefully, and placed it on his arm. She watched, the heat of his touch sinking through layers of gloves, the warmth spreading through to her bones. Amelia attempted to allow the heat to work on her the way Hugh's touch always did.

"It's peaceful here," Charles said.

Peaceful. Yes. Something she'd always adored about Pembroke-by-the-Sea was the great expanse of the moors and the comfort that expanse brought. London always seemed to close in on her and made her more nervous than usual. Interesting, that. That when she felt the most freedom from herself was when she was unbound, a great expanse outside herself to reach into—*that* held her together.

They followed Hugh through the gate, and she took in the green. The back of Charles's town home was primarily a massive lawn surrounded by flowering bushes and trees that hid the great stone walls encompassing them. The effect was lovely and much more peaceful than most fashionable gardens, landscaped with fountains and small labyrinthine hedges meant to move people with the illusion of space. She often believed them pretentious and more confined.

"Is he well?" Charles asked.

Amelia looked to Hugh, who was inspecting the back of the town house. "I imagine the last days have quite tried his patience, finding that you were unworthy of his trickery in particular. It has been a difficult few days, for all of us."

Charles nodded to the coachman, and the rear gate closed them in, giving her heart a momentary squeeze with that solid and final-sounding clank. Charles handed her down to the earth beneath a large willow, then followed, resting a safe enough distance from her skirts, and her person. Safe in distance, when all she truly wanted was to be held closely so as not to fall apart.

"By your leave, my lord, shall I ask to have a luncheon made up?"

"Of course, Louisa, that would be lovely. There's a side garden with tables that leads directly to the kitchens. Just let Mrs. Harrington know I sent you and that we are not to be disturbed here."

Louisa curtsied, and Amelia watched her walk to the back of the house, speak with Hugh, then round the corner.

"Yesterday"—Charles cleared his throat—"I must apologize. This all came as a bit of a shock to me, you understand. I never expected that when I asked for his help that it would come in quite such a fashion. Not that I believe he expected to be aiding in such a way, either."

"No, I imagine not," Amelia said. Hugh walked toward them then. "Please sit with us," she said quietly.

Hugh laid himself out, watching the sun through the heavy branches of the tree, his head on his hands.

"You've been quiet," she said.

"I've much to consider, Amelia, and I'm not at all sure you'll be accepting of what it is I have to say. As well, I'm concerned about speaking with you in front of Charles. No offense."

"None taken. If you prefer, I can oversee luncheon, give you time—"

Amelia cut him off. "No, Charles, thank you for that consideration, but I believe whatever's to be said should involve all of us. We've seen what happens when it is but two of us involved in the conversation."

Hugh looked at her then. "Are you quite sure, Amelia? The things I wish to say are of an extremely personal nature. I mean only to give you the chance to properly consider your choice. I've no issue with involving Charles after we've spoken, should you wish it."

"No, I wish for us all to be open, and it seems in this matter, for expediency's sake, possibly or perhaps because I won't be of a mind to suffer your words twice…I'm not sure why. I just believe we should have it out here, now."

Hugh looked to Charles. "Whatever comes next, I'm requesting you be patient with my line of discussion and not haul off and level me."

Charles looked to Amelia, and an extreme foreboding manifested in a blush that rushed her arms, speeding her heart. *Perhaps in private, perhaps private was better,* she thought. What could he possibly have to say that would call Charles to arms? Her breath stilled as she awaited Charles's response.

"I will do as Amelia wishes of me."

"Please do not level him," she answered breathlessly.

Charles nodded, Hugh nodded, then everyone watched her. She could see them as though she were a sprite on the boughs of this great willow, looking down on their strange arrangement in the grass. Then Hugh lifted on one elbow, facing them. She could see he was debating how to approach whatever subject it was he was attempting to broach. Then his gaze caught hers rather suddenly, and his mouth dropped open on words she could not have imagined.

"Amelia, have you ever *touched* yourself?" Hugh emphasized the word carefully, and she knew it was because he didn't want to explain himself in great detail.

"Well, I—" She looked to Charles, whose eyes widened as his hands clenched slightly then loosened, and she looked back to Hugh. "I touch myself often, daily, as I do now." Her voice trailed off as she raised her eyes to the limbs of the tree, refusing to look on either of them. She knew full well he meant something different but simply could not force herself to say anything else. Which was ridiculous. Because what she'd said was simply ridiculous. She'd *touched* herself just yesterday, as she'd considered Charles. *Damn me.*

"I mean—"

"I believe I understand what you mean," she said quickly, cutting him off. She simply couldn't stand to hear him attempt to explain this, and to have Charles attempt to stay calm, and to stay calm herself. Her heart was already racing. *Racing racing racing.* Like a thoroughbred. She stabbed her fingernails into her palms, snapping back to the conversation. "And, no. The answer would be no, I…I haven't truly…" This last bit trailed off into the sunshine like the breath of a butterfly.

They sat quietly as her world began that bumpy road to spinning, the one that would take her someplace else all together. The butterflies took possession of her belly now. The flutter multiplying. She breathed heavily against her corset, attempting to feel the pressure of it, to allow that pressure to contain her. Hold her.

"Come here," Hugh said quietly. "Let me help you."

She moved toward him instinctively, as she had so many times with him. He rested again on his back, and she placed her head on his chest above his heart. "I thought on this last night, after the two of you departed, and I believe some of your fears may come from the unknown. It's my assumption that you have never…*come.* I believe if you understood what all the feelings led to, what it was to suffer that crisis, you may be able to control yourself better. Because a climax can feel quite like losing yourself."

She looked to Charles then, who moved closer, hopefully not to be within arm's length of Hugh for nefarious purpose.

She held his gaze with her own as she spoke. "When Charles kissed me, I rather felt I was losing control. When he touched me…I felt my mind losing tether. I fear losing myself, most of all. I go to another place, and I don't at all like it when I return."

Hugh nodded, and she closed her eyes.

"Ender…I'm not entirely sure what you're meaning to do here—" Charles started.

"As with yesterday, neither am I. But I do know that you get our girl here worked into a passion she's yet to release. And if she found that release, perhaps it wouldn't be so frightful for her. You do understand that her fear of the unknown is what drives her more than anything?"

"I can understand that fear. But I don't know…to what end… we're discussing this," Charles said.

"She needs to be shown, Charles," Hugh said simply.

She needs to be shown, Charles.

He said it so easily, as if it was of little consequence.

She needs to wash the linens, Charles.

She needs to be shown, Charles.

She needs to see to the staff, Charles.

She needs to be shown, Charles.

It echoed in her head for a moment, until Amelia forced herself to pay attention to them discussing her as if she wasn't there, and she wasn't—she was back up in the willow, swinging from the boughs. Someplace safe, an easy distance from both of these men.

Who is to show her this? I suppose it would be you?

I don't know, as I said, I'm merely attempting to discern what could help Amelia.

And if she simply cannot let go from fear, how do you propose to get it done?

There is only one true way to discover this.

Do you not think introducing her to this would be the right of her husband?

Show me him, and we will both allow it, will we not?

The sudden tension coursed Hugh's frame, and she snapped back into place and sat up between them. "Stop, please, I…I'm frightened."

Charles's visage melted, and his concerned eyes caught hers as he reached out and took her hand. "What does it mean when you say you're frightened?"

She thought about her fear then. She hadn't ever really thought about it when she'd said she was frightened before. She merely knew what was to come. The fear was a precursor, something that must be controlled. "I…believe what I mean to say…is that I believe that if we continue at this pace of discussion on this topic, that I might have an episode."

"Might?" Charles asked quietly.

She could see that he wasn't going to let her off easily anymore. Something had changed in him yesterday, though it seemed he'd been changing ever since the ball. Trying things, watching her and learning, then coming in for more. Last night they'd managed a difficult conversation in the carriage, and she'd been frightened at times, but she'd survived it, made it to her room before she was so overwhelmed that Louisa needed to wrap her up in her blankets nice and secure to be able to sleep.

"Yes. I'm not yet too far gone, though I'm coming desperately close." She'd never discussed this. Nobody had ever wanted to know these things of her. Not even Hugh. He simply knew what to do, so even they hadn't discussed anything.

Charles took her hands and rubbed circles slowly into her palms. She breathed. "Better?" he asked.

She concentrated on the circles on her hands rather than the spiraling in her head. "Yes. Better."

"Can you look on me?" Charles said quietly. That was when she'd realized she'd closed her eyes to concentrate on the feel of him. She shook her head slowly, breathed again.

He gave her hands a quick squeeze. "It's okay."

She opened her eyes then, the sudden realization that this man wouldn't be one to rush her a heady push to her senses. But these feelings were different from before. They weren't the dizzying, terrifying fall from herself. The inevitable spiral that would land her in a shuddering mess wrapped tight in a ball. This was different. *Different.*

Amelia held his gaze, slowly leaning toward him, her eyes on his mouth. When their lips met, it was as though her heart had begun to sing.

Charles's hands traced up her arms, then pulled her closer to him, as he leaned back into the tree. "Stay with me, Amelia," Charles said quietly against her mouth.

Her hands rested on his waistcoat, her body leaning across his as he held her ever so gently, kissed her ever so softly. She heard the shift of fabric behind her and knew Hugh was leaving them. She stiffened at the realization, then Charles's hands traced down and back up to her shoulders. Her hands twisted in his waistcoat, and he pulled her closer, one of his big hands moving to her neck, the other finding her waist through her skirts and pulling her even closer to him, practically on top of him.

The full hardness of his man's body was against her, beneath her, the muscles tensing and rolling as she lay upon him. She concentrated on that…the feel of his muscles, the roll, the sway of his body with every breath, as though she were the ship on the ocean of his chest. Rising and falling, rising and falling. She broke away from him, looking up into the dizzying heights of the willow branches above her, determined to stay with him as he kissed down her neck, seemed to lick the very pulse of it.

"Charles. I can't. I—"

His hands came up, and he held her face, stroking her jaw as she pushed away from him. "I just—"

He shook his head, cutting her off. "Hugh." Charles called him, and she heard the footsteps across the grass grow close again. What did he mean to do? "She needs you. You can't leave."

Inappropriate! She gasped and pushed away. This was so very inappropriate. "You can't mean to do this again. You make a wanton of me."

ELEVEN

"And who is here to judge us?" Charles asked, attempting to remain calm, willing himself to be strong. He tried to consider options, but what he saw, the only thing he saw when they were close was her slipping away. They'd gotten so close last night…because of Hugh. But Charles wasn't willing to give her up yet. Whatever happened at this point, he knew one thing for certain: He was determined to fight for her. From his perspective, she belonged to Hugh, and he had to prove she could be safe with him. Vexed. He was vexed.

"Ender."

"Jackson."

They watched each other as if to measure their very content of character. The fact was, neither of them wanted this, but what they wanted and what was necessary were possibly two very different things.

"I believe luncheon may be ready," Charles said.

Amelia's head whipped around, and her eyes went wide on him.

Hugh stared in shock. The broken tension lifted and wisped away in the breeze.

"Shall we?" Charles asked.

He lifted Amelia's hand to Hugh, who took it and pulled her to standing. They looked at each other, shaking their heads, and Charles rose from the lawn, chuckling.

"You both look as though you've seen a fairy. This isn't all that shocking. We're simply having a meal." He clapped Hugh on the shoulder, then took Amelia's elbow, and bussed her cheek. "This way."

What the devil? Hugh could do naught but watch as Charles strode across the lawn, Amelia following with confused, jerky steps. Constantly looking back to him. Hugh shrugged and followed. He'd been sure Charles meant for him to sit with them to…to…do again what he'd done for her last evening. Hugh knew Amelia had been sure of this as well, but here they were, walking for the terrace over the gardens, sitting down to a meal together.

Louisa took Amelia's hands and led her to a seat, chatter quiet between them.

Perhaps Charles didn't believe that the solution…perhaps he intended to push her until she tipped but never let her fall. Hugh considered this, that he could teach her incrementally to suffer him. That wasn't the right word, not suffer…more, to be with him than anything.

Hugh expected her to falter at any moment. He expected her mind to spiral off into the nether, but it didn't. Perhaps it would work, this pause and retreat. He considered this as they sat in less-than-companionable silence, the void of sound reaching out between them.

Amelia needed to speak, but her head swirled. She closed her eyes and forced her concentration to stay. When she opened her eyes on Hugh, she was more steady, more sure.

"Hugh, you said that Charles…that he quite easily drives me to passion." It didn't last long. She heard Louisa cough into her tea cup.

"And so it is," Hugh said quietly.

"But you ground me, Hugh. You keep me here. I'm frightened. Have I mentioned? I have, haven't I?"

"You have," Charles said. "I'm not sure I can do what it is that Hugh has proposed. I mean to say, I know that I *can*, I want for nothing more than…this." Charles motioned between the two of them, and only the two of them, then continued. "But I'm also frightened, Amelia, perhaps more so than you."

This strong man had just acceded a point in front of his known adversary.

"I would be ruined as I understand it, as you've explained it to me in the past, Hugh."

"No. There are ways to go about this without your ruination. You would remain intact for your wedding night…for your…husband." Hugh closed his eyes then, and she could see that he was resigned that her husband be Charles.

She looked to Charles and realized that he understood the same.

"I don't see this as possible," Charles said. "Perhaps when we come to know each other better…"

She knew he was attempting to quell her, which meant that he could see she was close to an episode, but then Hugh bullied on— something he never did. *Damn him.*

"When will that be?" Hugh asked. "We've agreed to discern what is best for Amelia, for her to be married to the man who can care for her, so long as that match will suit the crown's purpose as well. I know beyond doubt I could make love to Amelia. I could teach her the ways of pleasure, and she would not only respond but blossom in the teaching of it."

Amelia shifted at the heat that flooded her breasts, then closed her eyes tight to concentrate on the words as Hugh continued to speak.

"Yet you…you're resigned to wait. Again, for how long? This is merely a lesson to be learned. If you're not a green boy."

Amelia's eyes popped open as Charles stood, and she panicked, moved to keep herself between them.

"Do you provoke him purposely?" she yelled.

"Perhaps I do!" Hugh responded. "How is he to know now whether he would ever be able to be close to you? We've determined to care for you, however that comes. I know you'll not be abandoned, no matter the outcome of his suit, because I will *never* abandon you. What exactly is he afraid of?" Hugh stood then, closed the gap between them all, Amelia holding the only space between them. Her right hand came to Hugh's chin, holding him at bay, as her left hand reached behind her, taking Charles's hand.

"Please," she whispered. "Please do not argue. Not for my sake. I would much prefer to leave off and never return, than have the two of you at odds. You are the most important people in the world to me. You must understand, this isn't something I can manage…"

She felt faint as her mind started closing in, the edges of her vision fading, retreating, and the sunshine dimmed at the edges as she looked over the green of the lawns. Then Hugh's hands were on her, supporting her.

"Charles, if you don't mind, I would borrow your carriage to return home." Amelia said.

"We'll accompany—" Charles started.

"No, that won't be necessary. Louisa?"

She turned and, with Louisa's arms wrapped around her waist, walked to the mews as Charles instructed a footman and watched her go.

"Well, I made a right bosh of this day," Charles said.

"We. We did, and quite handily, I might add." Hugh sat back in his chair and reached for a tray of meats, allowing his words to come as they would, hesitant to stop his train of thought and consideration.

"Most likely she'll go home to consider the day, and we'll be informed of her conclusions when she's ready to share," Hugh said.

"I understand. There is much to consider, considering. It's beyond me to understand why you'd be so forward with her." Hugh pointed at himself as Charles continued. "No, really, what the bloody damn hell were you thinking?"

"Has it not crossed your mind? In her behavior? You send her out of control in one, quite tangible way. It has to do with sex."

"It had crossed my mind. In fact, we discussed that very fact on the journey home yesternight. I told her how important intimacy was to me, after what had happened. I wanted her to understand that my feelings for her encompassed that part of her as well, not merely that I require a wife to do my bidding as a duke. I found it quite important she understand that facet of my interest. Particularly after you and I had discussed it."

Hugh nodded.

Charles thought for a moment, then continued. "I requested they drive past the Row on their return to Pembroke. To have her before the matrons in my carriage without both of us so soon after we left. I wanted to make a statement, however that statement may be perceived. I believe them seeing her in my carriage, now without us, might serve to allay some rumors of her behavior."

"I agree. Though controlling the talk of the *ton* is quite beyond our means. They'll think whatever they wish to think, regardless our actions or words to the contrary, but you already know this," Hugh said.

"Yes," Charles replied.

"You've changed the subject."

"Quite handily I believe." Charles grinned. He sat heavily in the chair and sighed. Hugh knew whatever came next would be the revelation. "You want to make her *come*. You think passion a threshold beyond which she may be free to understand. You believe her fear a hindrance to my being with her. Her fear of what's to happen between a man and a woman."

Hugh nodded. "You understand the basics of it. I've no doubt you've brought many women to their completion, so you must understand the thinking behind my consideration."

"I do. What I don't understand is how you intend to make this happen for her. That, and who you intend for the action of it. For while it seems you're able to control her, and bring her about in subtle or more controlled ways, it would also seem that for you to teach her of this wouldn't help the situation at all. And whilst I am more than willing to introduce Amelia to this level of passion, I fear I cannot without the ability to also control her as you do. To that end…having you anywhere near us—"

"During the act. Yes, I agree completely, as I'm not convinced I wish to be a party to such. Last night was quite an aberration. I believe we can agree on that fact," Hugh said.

"Does she even understand what happened?"

"I would think so, yet you were the last to speak with her alone, so you may know more than I at this point."

"She was rather in control last night. Considering. Though I don't believe she's truly thought through the ramifications of her actions. Of our actions. Any whisper of this could ruin her. And while I understand she believes herself destroyed in the eyes of the *ton* regardless, she should yet be mindful of them," Charles said.

"Are you asking me to stay away? Now that you've asked for my help in this matter? Do you believe I should now fade away and let you attempt to resolve this on your own?"

Charles was quiet in his consideration of what Hugh asked. Hugh appreciated that he took the time to truly consider this thought, not to simply answer as he felt.

"I am not," Charles said finally. "I only think that we must be ever wary of our position, for while men can do nearly as they wish…she cannot. I believe you're the key to my success. As selfish as that sounds. As unfortunate as it may be. But for Amelia, as you said…if you were to abandon her now, it would be detrimental."

"Last night—"

"Here we are again. Must we?" Charles asked.

"I believe we must. After all, if we fly ignorant into this situation, we'll end up in the same position again, somewhere neither of us wishes to be. Correct?"

"Are you asking?" Charles watched him closely, and Hugh shifted uncomfortably in his chair, surprising himself with the revelation he was to share.

"For my part…when I said I would do anything for her, I meant anything. She's my heart. Part and parcel. Debating this, again and again… it rather delays the inevitable. You don't believe she can be with you and are too terrified of her episodes to control your own fear, something that feeds hers. It's a bit like a whirling dervish. Once an episode starts, it only gains. I could be there. I could calm her for you. Though to be sure, we would need to agree on this together. If we aren't in agreement on the subject, the entire situation will get awkward."

"More so than before?" Charles chuckled. "Though I yet hesitate. As we discuss the hows and wheres of this, it occurs to me that the doing of it will only become much too choreographed. I wish for whatever to happen between Amelia and me to be as natural as possible, whether that involves you or not."

Both men allowed silence to reign for a time.

"Is this awkward?" Hugh asked finally.

"Shouldn't it be? We've become quite adept at discussing her. This isn't as it should be. If we function on the tenet that this is for her, and not about us, whatever happens will not only be genuine but acceptable to us all. I believe you and I are in agreement. That *this* is for Amelia, and whatever happens happens solely for her."

Charles finished just as Hugh heard the rattle of the harnesses on his carriage team, pulling in front of the house. "We agree then. We'll spend time together, doing our best to protect her from rumors of the *ton*, and whatever happens…"

"Happens," Charles finished with a strong note of finality in his voice.

As the carriage pulled away from the mews, Amelia wrapped her arms around her middle and attempted to stay the tumbling in her belly. She wasn't concerned with leaving them to discuss her. After all, it wasn't as if that had never happened before, and what had come of it then…she blanched at the thought. While she'd spent the previous night going over every word, every touch, in her mind she hadn't truly considered the situation from any perspective beyond feeling.

I lay between them.

Between them.

Between two men.

Inappropriate.

She'd also allowed them both to kiss her. She'd been steady and sure between them and had never had such a calm freedom as when there. Yet being alone with a man—with *two* men—was so very inappropriate. An impossibility. And if anyone were to discover their actions, she'd be well and truly ruined. Where would she be then? Neither of them could take her to wife with that type of rumor over her head. The three of them being together was truly beyond the realm of possibility.

And yet when the two of them surrounded me…

The feeling of them *with* her, together, had been beyond comforting. It had been an entirely new level of security.

This was terrible. What kind of woman was she to want two men? To wish to be with them both. To feel complete lying between them. Two men. As horrific as the thought was, it was yet equally comforting.

Amelia, have you ever touched *yourself?*

Her breath caught, and her hand cinched on the side of the carriage. She was suddenly much too warm. Her vision narrowed. Amelia's other hand snaked up and tugged at the edge of her dress, and she surreptitiously blew a stream of air between her breasts, cooling her skin as what perspiration had gathered there began to evaporate.

She felt the gazes before she realized where they were, and what she was doing.

Damn me. The Row.

She clenched her eyes as though to erase her actions as they pulled through Rotten Row, and all the matrons' eyes were once again on her. As they always were. Hot and heavy and judging. A bead of sweat trickled past her nape, catching on the tight edge of her dress, making her skin itch. She leaned back into the squabs of the carriage and attempted to surreptitiously rub her back against the plush seat to scratch it as she attempted to smile, meeting each questioning gaze as she passed by.

Louisa's hand patted her knee, and Amelia gravitated toward her. The small reassurance was a warm anchor as they moved. Amelia nodded, tipped her fan, smiled, watched for the end of the Row.

Five carriages. Four carriages…

She knew Charles had sent them here, an attempt to allay the talk caused by their earlier arrival.

Three carriages…

Amelia knew Charles could not have made a more powerful statement to the *ton* had he stood on the steps of St. Peter's and shouted it himself.

Two carriages…

Whether or not it worked in the fashion Charles wished would remain to be seen. At least she had been seen without the two of them.

The two of them. Together.

One carriage…

They reached the end of the Row, and the carriage turned toward her father's town house. Louisa grabbed Amelia's hands in hers, and Amelia breathed. Finally breathed.

Amelia rushed through the entry of her father's town house, hoping to get to her room before being discovered. "Amelia?" *Too late.*

Amelia stopped, took a deep breath and walked to the door of the parlor. "Good morning, Mother, ladies." She gave a small curtsy as she looked around the full parlor. So many women, and all of them turned to her, expectantly. "Was I to be at home? I do beg your pardon, but the Duke of Castleberry had planned an outing today," she said, pasting a sweet smile on her face. But she knew her neck was just a bit too stiff. Louisa stood behind her. Amelia heard louisa gasp, shuffling her feet nervously.

"Well, the ladies were just leaving, but they'd mentioned seeing you and the duke on the Row…with Endsleigh."

Amelia froze. She saw her mother watching her expectantly, and her hands tensed on the fan she held until she heard the quiet crack of the wood. She cast her eyes about the room, hoping to find at least one friendly face. They all seemed to be leaning toward her.

She tried to release the tension in her neck, and her gaze landed on one small girl, cowering behind some of the more domineering of the matrons.

Amelia smiled to her, and the girl returned it—albeit warily—her eyes darting past Amelia toward Louisa then back to the floor. The girl looked like Amelia felt, as though she simply wished for some peace, to dissolve into the very floorboards were it possible, to hide. Amelia took a moment's strength in the kinship, then she looked to her mother again.

Amelia could feel the tension in her mother from across the room, knew she was chanting orders in her head that she could never release to the world in front of witnesses.

Come on, Amelia, answer. Give them no quarter.

They're awaiting my explanation. Wash away the shame with some brilliant words. I can do this. I've been trained so very well.

Amelia dropped her mouth open, and the room seemed to hang upon her lip like a Christmas ornament.

"Yes, of course! As you know, His Grace and Lord Endsleigh are childhood friends, yet they hadn't seen each other in an age. So when His Grace and I saw Lord Endsleigh walking, of course I insisted they take some time to speak and send me home. I can stroll with Lord Castleberry at any time, of course. Yet Endsleigh and Castleberry seem to always cross paths. I thought it only decent I allow them some time." Amelia smiled.

Lady Pembroke beamed at her, then turned back to the room. "You see? Perfectly innocent explanation."

"This is why I'm home early, Mama. I should change out of my carriage dress, however. Won't you all excuse me for a moment? You aren't all leaving now, are you?" she asked respectfully.

Her mother smiled at them. "No! No, we were just standing because Lady Ambrose had to depart rather suddenly, and then you arrived. I've no doubt there's much more to discuss. Go ahead and change, then join us."

Amelia smiled and offered a quick curtsy, and her mother waved everyone back to their places. Amelia stayed her want to run for the stairs. She could feel Louisa's presence behind her and stole every bit of strength she could from her, though it seemed her maid had little to give at the moment.

Amelia walked slowly up the stairs. Perhaps too slowly. Perhaps she should go faster? *No, this was a good pace.* Amelia pulled her skirts up tight against her and reached for the banister to steady herself.

Do not trip do not trip do not trip.

The door to the parlor was yet open, and she could even now see the ladies chattering away. She didn't need to cause a scene after so narrowly defusing the same. She was sure to hear of this later when the women departed. For now, she needed to calm her nerves and attempt to put on a show. She could do this.

Amelia entered her rooms, swept her bonnet off, then sat to remove her boots. Louisa went straight to her and unhooked her skirts, though her hands shook, and it took a bit of time. Amelia turned and held her hands for a moment. "Louisa?"

"It's nothing, milady. Don't mind me. I'll be right as rain in a moment's time. Never you mind."

Louisa turned, then pulled Amelia's larger, caged petticoats from the wardrobe, tossing them over her head as the carriage skirts fell away. She followed the petticoats with her blue plaid skirt as Amelia buttoned up her high-collared blouse. Louisa straightened and smoothed the long lines, bustled the skirts over the caged petticoat and then squeezed her shoulders.

"Just remember to breathe. If you need a moment, sip your tea. You'll win them over, just as you win over everyone who knows you," Louisa said with a smile.

Amelia took her hand and squeezed it. She loved how certain Louisa always was. Amelia gathered the strength in that statement and held it close as she left the safety of her room and headed toward the fray.

A

"Ah, Amelia!" Her mother sounded extremely happy to see her, but below that, which nobody would pick out but Amelia, was a strong note of stress to her voice. Her mother introduced the room, and Amelia did her best to remember each of them. "Come sit with us," her mother said as she pulled her to the big settee and placed her in the center. "You must tell us of your day. It sounds as though you had a bit of an adventure?"

"Adventure?" Amelia wasn't sure what to say. She was certain by the earlier reception that someone had seen her at the Row, and several someones had rushed to her father's house to prattle. "It wasn't truly an adventure. We merely intended to take a stroll at Hyde and on the way met with Lord Endsleigh. He joined us, then as we pulled through the Row, I determined they needed some time to be men and discuss those things men discuss without women." This was met with giggles. Amelia was on the right track, she hoped.

"I merely suggested His Grace call on me later, and we dropped them at his town home, and he sent me off in his carriage. It was such a lovely day that Louisa and I did take a detour back through Hyde, mostly to see the ducks." They *had* seen ducks. "Castleberry was nothing but thoughtful. In fact, I had to *insist* they abandon me. He, the duke, did not want to do anything untoward. You see, he did not want anyone to think ill of me. But I *quite insisted* that nobody would dare think such." Amelia smiled brightly and saw the younger ladies sigh as the matrons nodded approvingly. This was more difficult than she'd thought.

They all continued to gaze at her as though she should continue, but she truly had naught else to say. "And that is where you join the story, when I arrived home…here." Amelia held up her hands in what she believed to be a welcoming gesture.

Her mother smiled, and Amelia eased a small bit in that. "Oh, what a gentleman, insisting he stay by your side," her mother crooned. She turned to the lady beside her, Lady Rigsby, Amelia believed, and whispered to her.

Then Amelia caught her aunt's disapproving gaze as Lady Mathorpe stood silently and left the room. Amelia's chest tightened, and she looked away, chatting with the young lady on her other side, Miss Maitland Rigsby, the shy girl from before.

Amelia had had no idea the speed with which news could travel in London. Her mother had warned her, she had, but in all honesty who would have believed the rapidity with which the gossip had happened in truth? Amelia was shocked.

She understood, now, the need to be careful. This morning had been a grave misstep. She didn't want to call Charles's respectability into question, nor Hugh's. She needed to heed this warning and behave as a young girl in her first season ought to behave, regardless she was no young girl attending a traditional season. Amelia must keep a fair distance from them both, because now…everyone would be watching them.

"A statement? In front of the *ton*? But we have only begun to court. I'm not sure—"

Amelia had tried to return to her rooms as the guests left, but she wasn't quick enough to escape her mother.

"Amelia, you diminished your choices when you pulled up to the Row with two men in tow. What were you thinking? No, do not answer that. I don't believe my heart can stand any of the excuses you would deign to give me. Your father and I should never have allowed such excesses with Lord Endsleigh. That was our mistake, but I believed you understood that relationship was a thing for childhood, not for proper company! Men and women cannot be friends. They simply cannot." Her mother emphasized this, then turned to the parlor window. "We shall attend Lady Greensborough's ball tonight. Gelema is an old friend. She'll not mind the late response."

Amelia knew her mother was hatching a plan to further attempt to rescue her tattered image. But another ball? So soon? She wasn't sure she could manage it, particularly considering how difficult it was to be around Charles at the moment. Yet this wasn't something she could discuss with her mother, who was at ends as it was.

Amelia walked to her mother, skimmed one hand down her arm, then sat on the window seat, pulling her hand gently to have her sit. Amelia was entirely too overwrought, and it was mostly her own doing. As much as she hated her mother's tactics, her mother's opinions on her behaviors, her mother's ideas for handling her…the woman was still her mother, and she had stood up for Amelia today. That had meant the world to her. If only her mother would relax enough to allow she and Amelia to be close, to work together toward a good end for the both of them… Amelia took her mother's hand in both of hers.

"If you believe that my appearance at the Greensborough fete will smooth over the injured pride of the *ton* matrons, I'll go. I should send a missive to His Grace immediately. I've no doubt he'll be thrilled to attend us."

Her mother squeezed her hand, and Amelia saw something shine in her eyes that she very rarely saw, but it was gone all too soon, and her mother's usual countenance returned.

"We're nearly there. Very nearly there. Oh, Amelia, I've no doubt this can be done, and then we'll have no further worries. I simply…I—"

Amelia patted her mother's hand. "Not to worry, Mama." She stood and moved to the secretary in the corner of the parlor. "I'll send the missive, then rest to ensure a successful evening."

TWELVE

The last thing Charles had expected after Hugh left his town house was a note from Amelia. *No*, in fact, there was one thing he'd expected even less than that: that she would request his accompaniment to the Greensborough ball this evening.

He attempted to straighten his cravat. Charles wanted the knot to be perfect, but the stick pin looked a bit long. He switched the pin in favor of his father's diamond pin and moved back to the mirror. He was happy with the knowledge that she'd recovered from their misstep that day. Perhaps the situation wasn't as bad as he was making it. He stabbed himself in the thumb, as though he knew he needed a touch of reality. So perhaps it was as bad as he remembered. Charles looked in the mirror, a spot of blood on the badly mussed cravat he'd been attempting to repair. He yanked the cravat from his collar and dropped it to the floor as he recalled his valet, who grumbled.

Amelia held on to the bedpost as Louisa yanked on the corset laces. "Are you entirely sure you wish to attend another ball?" Louisa asked.

"Not entirely. I must make this appearance in public for Charles, and for my mother. It's the right thing to do, and I wish it. I should be fine, for a time." Amelia thought for a moment then smiled. "Louisa, that's not entirely true. I wish to see Charles. I wish to make a grand statement. I wish to attend the ball."

Louisa smiled at her as she turned her around and flung the crinolines over her head, fastening stays and laces and trimmings as she moved like a tempest.

"What will you do with your evening off, Louisa?"

"I've an idea, my lady."

"Do you? Are you off to meet with your beau?" Amelia asked quietly.

Louisa frowned slightly then smiled.

"You are." Amelia considered the difference between Louisa and herself, how Louisa was free to love and do as she pleased with no true recourse. "Is he wonderful?" Amelia asked.

Louisa darted her gaze to Amelia, then away again. "I…well, a lady should never kiss and tell, you know," Louisa said, but she seemed lost in her thoughts.

"Amelia."

Amelia turned as her mother walked in. She'd wanted to ask Louisa more, but she could tell her mother was no longer in an agreeable humor. One of her dark moods had set in. "Mother," Amelia said carefully. Her hands moved to the front of her dress, shifting and adjusting the seams as Louisa fastened innumerable buttons up the back.

Amelia picked at a small thread and showed it to Louisa, who went to the dressing table for her scissors. Her mother took the scissors from Louisa, then reached toward Amelia. And she flinched.

"Really, Amelia, is that necessary?"

"Not at all. I beg your pardon." Amelia steeled herself as her mother reached for her again.

"You need to watch yourself. It's entirely possible for the duke to cry off as yet. We still await confirmation. He has yet to secure the license. It would not take much."

"Yes, Mother," Amelia said quietly, trying to calm her heart. It swirled, whirled in her breast. Was this corset too tight? Louisa did like them tight. Amelia's head joined the spin, and she reached out to the bedpost again as her mother fussed over the few loose threads on her bodice.

Charles Charles Charles, she thought.

She willed her pulse to slow, imagined it drifting on a lake, no waves, no wind, just the peaceful sound of the water lapping the shoreline and a few pipers in the sand.

"Lovely." She heard Louisa say just behind her.

"It will have to do," her mother mumbled.

Amelia closed her eyes.

A

Charles took Amelia's hand and led her to the dance floor. "Are you sure?"

Amelia looked up at him and realized that second-guessing her

served only to highlight an opinion on her weakness, which she knew was not his intent but still niggled at her consciousness.

"I beg your pardon," Charles said. "I only meant that being here, with you, should be enough of a statement. What I should have said was, '*Thank you* for the honor of this dance.'"

Amelia smiled uncontrollably at his change in tack, and Charles swept her out to the floor, pulling her briskly through the turns. She enjoyed the heady rush of the dance floor, so different from the dizziness of her disorder. She fell into it, enjoyed it, let him pull her, let her head swirl in the excitement and the motion as she ignored the *ton* that surrounded her.

She held on to Charles, feeling the heat of his arms against hers, his body holding her more tightly than he should—yet for some reason it never crossed her mind to concern herself with it.

Her pulse quickened with his steps, but it was with excitement, not fear or worry. Then she considered his hard thighs pushing against her skirts, his trim waist, his broad chest that led to the expanse of his shoulders that overshadowed her greatly, and she determined to think only on the movement, not the man, as her head threatened to swirl.

Amelia felt safe in the lee of his size. Protected within his stance, untouchable, free to enjoy herself, the rest of the room be damned.

Too soon the dance ended, and she hadn't even the time to see who watched, who looked, or who cared. She laughed as Charles took her arm and escorted her out through the doors to the garden.

There were torches lit on the grounds, lighting a walking path that meandered through the hedgerows and flower beds. Amelia wondered how any woman managed to escape the gardens without being set aflame. Some of the dresses were rather extensive in the skirts. It seemed…dangerous.

"You enjoyed that," Charles said.

Amelia turned away from the flames. "I did. So very much," she said as she glanced his way, her heart still racing in her throat. She let her breath come heavily, unconcerned for who noticed. As well, she was thrilled at her ability to control herself with him. It had been so much easier tonight than before.

"Perhaps we should rest? There's a bench just over here behind this row." Charles pulled her along, wrapping his arms around her again and waltzing her around the corner, spinning her in his arms and calling forth laughter the likes of which she'd not heard from herself in years.

"Oh, Your Grace, I…well."

Before she knew what he was about, she was wrapped up tightly against him, toes to nose, his thighs alternating with hers through her thick skirts, his breath and hers mingling before them.

Amelia could smell the punch on the air as he leaned the slightest bit closer. *The sweet tang of punch…I didn't even get a drink. I suppose now I shall have a taste of the punch, though,* she thought as she concentrated on the lips inching toward hers.

Charles seemed to hesitate, his eyes grazing her face as intimately as a touch to her skin.

"Amelia."

She thought his voice feral, deep, *nearly illegible...no, intelligible... No! Unintelligi—*Then his nose nudged hers, and Charles captured her mouth.

Sweet, sweet so sweet, Amelia thought.

Charles was gentle and slow, taking his time. This kiss was different from the others in that this kiss was quite controlled. She could feel his fetters, like tangible threads anchoring him to the earth, and she sank into the kiss. Amelia let her hands stray against the landscape of his back, for his back was a landscape...so great, it seemed. The unexplored territories, rivers and valleys, mountains and fields. Well, certainly more mountains and valleys than flat spaces on this man. *Certainly.*

"Stop thinking," he mumbled against her lips.

Stop...thinking? Stop thinking... She concentrated on stopping her thoughts. *The sky, the sky is empty, if my mind could be the sky...*

The kiss was heaven, then...it was a frenzy.

Charles held her tighter, and she could feel him everywhere— and suddenly—herself not at all. It was *his* hands on her backside, up her spine, in her hair, around her neck, upon her shoulders. It was *his* thigh between hers, pressing against her: solid, thick, searching. It was *his* body pressed full against her, pushing her against the hedgerow. Amelia gasped for air as *his* mouth moved to her neck, and her hands held on to *his* shoulders. Then Amelia felt it, when he stretched out against her once again, *his* mouth at her temple, *his* hands on her waist—*his* erection at her hip. It was like a pipe, that erection, not so out of place from the rest of him, pressing, wanting, pushing.

A virgin she may have been, but she was no true innocent. She'd learned enough from Hugh. *Here in this garden. The ton just behind this hedge, the world a hair's breadth away. How can he be everywhere at once, and how can I be nowhere?*

The heat of him drove her temperature up and up. The beads of sweat coursed her spine, saturating the edge of her dress and corset. The air in the brambles behind her caused a chill across her exposed skin.

The cool rush forced her forward into him, her breasts pushing against her trappings, his hands searching, searching. Her nipples tightened against the chemise and stays, the sensations spiraling through her before she had a chance to consider them. It was all too fast, too much...she needed time to consider, time to think, time... She pushed, she sank, her mind spun...she was lost and then...and then she felt *him*. Like a whisper across her senses, she knew Hugh was there to save her.

A

Charles had not meant to have off with her, but that laugh…it had been so free, so powerful, like a drug to him he'd no wish to control, and she'd been with him throughout that entire, magical dance. Charles took her mouth then wrapped her up tighter, and when her body relaxed in acquiescence, he'd pushed her toward the hedge wall. The new growth was soft against his hands, a cushion behind them as he moved against her.

Charles searched every inch of her, wanting to convince himself that what he'd felt for the entirety of his life was real. His hands coursed her curves, stroked her hair, held her mouth steady, then traced her neckline, wanting in—though he knew he should not. Charles knew he should stop, but she felt *so*…and in turn he believed the world was now possible because Amelia was there with him.

Charles felt her freedom like he'd felt her acquiescence. He felt it now as he tried to rein in his excitement. Perhaps this was possible, perhaps they'd reached a point at which Ender would be superfluous. Then she pushed against his chest and said *his* name. It broke the haze. Charles paused, considered, loosened his grip, and then managed to release her. *So*…he was not yet a beast.

"Charles, I—"

"Give me a moment, please." Charles turned away from her, from the way her breasts swelled against her trappings, from the way her mouth dropped open on his name, from the way her cheeks flushed with passion. He wanted nothing more than to drop her to the earth below them, stretch out above her and claim what was his, once and for all. So he turned away even as his entire being screamed, *TAKE TAKE TAKE.*

Well, perhaps he *was* yet a beast.

Charles looked back over his shoulder at her ruined countenance and pushed at his temples with the heels of his hands.

Hugh. Charles had heard the name plain as he heard his tempered breathing now.

Was Amelia calling for help? Calling out in passion? Was it like the night before in Hugh's parlor? Did Amelia truly need him to anchor her? Charles tried to school his features and looked back at her again as reassuringly as he could muster. Her hands were clenched in the branches of the hedgerow, and Charles wanted to go to her, to soothe her…but he turned away yet again because he didn't trust his hands. He shook his head.

Charles was nearly unhinged. It had been years that he'd thought of her, knew he was to be with her, and finally he'd heard the laugh that had haunted him all this time, the laugh she'd only ever bestowed on *him*. *Hugh*. The man who'd been allowed, even as Charles had been turned away. Wasn't that just the opposite of the way it should have been? But it seemed logic ended where Amelia began.

Charles's patience snapped. He did not turn around. Instead, he took the anger upon himself, to spare her. "I know not what came over me, but that I have wanted for so very long. Simply *wanted*." He knew what his voice must sound like to her. Raw, edged, untamed.

"Charles, what is it? I only…well. It's a garden, there's a ball, I'm only—"

Then he realized, whatever had happened, Hugh had come between them without her even realizing it.

"You said his name." Charles turned then, in time to see her pale. He saw the confusion in her eyes, the shock cross her features. The flush of her cheeks swept away. She truly had no idea. He reached for her, but she backed away.

"Amelia."

"No, I…no. I thought—" She choked on the words as Charles reached for her again, but she blocked him, then pushed him back. "I'm so very sorry. I don't know what to say. I could feel you, everywhere, and I started to believe myself lost. I started to…until I felt…I felt him, and I—"

"What you felt was *me*. Everything you felt—" Charles stopped. "There was no one between us, I assure you," he said in a quieter voice, if still roughened.

A shadow moved at the end of the hedge, seemed to step forward and move slowly toward Amelia.

"I beg your pardon, Your Grace, but unfortunately my lady has the right of it." Hugh straightened his jacket, pulled on his cuffs, checked the cant of his top hat, polished the toes of his boots on the backs of his trousers, obviously concentrating on his being, if only to avoid considering his position.

Ender glanced up as Charles walked toward him, and he stilled, squaring his shoulders, preparing for the worst.

"Endsleigh," Charles said through clenched teeth. Whatever it was that had held him back snapped. "What should I make of this? Have I unwittingly given you leave to join us without invitation? That's not the man I thought you to be."

"No, Your Grace, that's not the man I am. I was here long before you. I left the ballroom because a certain lady keeps throwing her niece in my path. I grew weary of dodging her, and then the two of you took to the floor, and I wished to find some space. I truly did not expect to see either of you here tonight. Particularly not like this." Hugh waved a hand between the two of them.

Charles looked at Amelia and saw the blush take her face again as she looked down and away from both of them. Charles turned his head. "*Damn you*, and *damn me* while you're at it." He could feel his anger like a third lung, breathing, inflating, attempting to gain more air.

Ender smiled, albeit abashedly.

Charles didn't feel like giving him any room for apologies, and he felt the tension then, pulling his features tight. From the edge of his sight, he saw Amelia's skirts swish as she turned away from them, most likely to attempt to set herself to rights.

"What's it to be then? I'm not to have a moment's peace with Amelia, ever? The woman who's to be my wife? Are you to be everywhere we are? Are you to join in our marriage bed as well? Because, apparently, until she felt your presence..." He heard the words, then tensed as the thought solidified in his head, creating a rather erotic vision. He shook it off and looked back to Amelia. He simply couldn't deal with this at the moment. He needed to deal with his direct actions to Amelia and setting her to rights. This night was meant to repair her image in the *ton*, not lessen it. He whispered, "Amelia, you simply cannot go back. I've been terribly, terribly inappropriate."

"You've done nothing I did not allow," she said quietly.

Charles could see her shaking and wanted badly to comfort her, but she stayed him with a look that he felt like a fist to his gut.

"And, yet, you cannot return," he said. "Let me call my coach. I'll make your apologies to the duke. We've made an appearance. I believe your original intentions for this night have been met."

Amelia nodded, as Charles left her with no choice. He had very nearly ruined his future duchess in the Greensborough Gardens.

He shook his head and approached her, slowly. He held his hands up in front of him. "I just want to help. I'll get you to the carriage." He shrugged out of his jacket and wrapped it around her shoulders.

Amelia looked up to him, and he frowned. "I'm so desperately sorry for this," he whispered, attempting to keep their conversation private. "I should never have...I let myself get carried away on your laughter."

"I'm the one who's sorry," she said.

"No, this is my fault entirely. You've spent your life doing your utmost to fit in with these people whom I so easily take for granted. I should never have put you in this position. Particularly tonight, of all nights."

"Your Grace—"

"Amelia, we are not back to this, are we?"

"Take me home."

Charles's heart broke on those words. He'd truly made a mess of this night. Why was he so unbound where she was concerned? He managed countless estates, led men through the wilds of the House, aided the queen and her counsel as needed, but this woman...she undid him at his core. He had no control.

He nodded, then turned to Hugh. "Can I trust you to look after her until I return with my carriage? There's a gatehouse there, the mews just beyond. I'll meet you there post-haste."

Hugh nodded, and he and Amelia watched as Charles ran across the lawn as dark as night. He seemed to float along like a spirit, his lithe form in the white shirt and vest separated from the dark of his trousers and the ground below.

Hugh could feel her tension and migrated closer.

"Take yourself away from here," she whispered as she turned to him.

"Amelia."

"You cannot do this to me. You cannot do this to *him*."

"I meant no harm, and yet…it seems I arrived in time to save you from—"

"From myself! He did nothing, *nothing* wrong!"

"I know, and I'm truly sorry. I only want what's best…"

"I'm not sure I understand *want* anymore. I feel I *want* for so much, and yet…whenever I start to want…"

"We can help you…or we can try." Hugh knew he was begging, but he couldn't let her walk away now.

"Stop. Simply stop. This afternoon…" Her eyes flitted around the gardens as if looking for someone to rescue her. "I cannot believe what you said this afternoon."

"Amelia, I only meant to point out to you that it's possible that you don't know what happens, that your fear may be your problem with Charles. Because you aren't afraid of me." *Please don't forget who I am to you. Please.*

"Were I to have a chance with you, we would not be here now. You cannot take my one chance at happiness from me. Please—go."

Hugh removed his hat, dropping it to the ground so he wouldn't appear so pretentious, and he knew he did, in this full dress. But he needed her comfort at the moment, to strip down to who he was, not who he attempted to be. Because that was who could help her. "I don't mean to take anything. I only mean to help you, in whatever way possible. I realize my speech this afternoon was forward. I beg your pardon for that. I only meant to attempt to open the conversation, one that would hopefully help you understand yourself more, help you understand what it is that drives these episodes. Fear...panic...if we can alleviate that at least somewhat—"

"I understand your intentions. I understood them at the time as well. I just need...I don't know what I need. A respite. I do love you, Hugh, but Charles...and he's a good man. One of the best. Even *you* cannot argue that. He must be my future. There cannot be *us* if there's to be *him*. I'll not do that to him."

"Are you asking me to walk away? After all?"

Silence.

His query was met with silence. Much too much silence. He couldn't stand it. "When just last night—" Last night she'd requested that he not hold back. His shoulders fell. "I understand..."

"No, Hugh, you don't. How can you when I don't? When none of us do?" Hugh watched as her hands started to shake, and her voice quavered. "Hugh, I—"

He stepped toward her, held her, calmed her even as she tried to fight it. "This is my doing, and for that I'm so terribly sorry."

"That's exactly the problem, Hugh. It's not your doing. If it hadn't been for you being here—" She heard the carriage at the back mews and pushed past him toward the gates.

He followed. "Amelia, I—"

"No, Hugh. Believe me now. I'm to marry Charles. I want so very much to remain friends with you. I want to be able to share my joy with you. But this we cannot do. It cannot be the three of us. I don't know how he and I will suit, but I'm determined to that end, as is he. He wants me."

"As do I...I do, I want for you, so desperately."

"Perhaps it's this desperation that's at issue. Hugh, I understand you wish to help, but for your sake, and his, this needs to end now, tonight. It simply cannot be, and we all know this. I must stop considering it. What I said last night...what I said was a mistake." She turned on him. "Do you know how I had to work to rescue all of our reputations this afternoon?" She paled, then turned and stormed through the gatehouse with him at her heels.

Hugh watched as Charles handed her into the carriage, and she turned, sitting on the seat, taking his jacket from her shoulders and giving it back to Charles so he could return to the ball, find her parents.

"I need to speak with you," Charles said, "but I should go, Amelia. It's already been too long since we've been gone. There will be talk."

"Of course there will be, and the talking will be frenzied, because I am…broken. I need to quit this place. I understand that this may change everything, but above all else, my wish is to not hurt anyone. Even so, all I ever manage to do is cause pain." Her voice was tense, erratic.

"I don't understand, I—"

Amelia slammed the carriage door and yelled to the driver. The carriage pulled away from the mews.

"Jacks," Hugh said quietly, so as not to startle him.

Charles whirled. "You're still here."

"You asked me to watch over her, did you not? Perhaps if I'd made myself known sooner, I might have prevented—"

"You could have prevented nothing," Charles spat from clenched teeth, obviously confused by Amelia's dispensation. "You have caused *so much*. She's run away…again."

Hugh turned to walk away, but Charles caught him. Hugh did not want to be a witness to this…this… What was this? What was Charles's intention?

Hugh had found his own bed two nights ago with every intention of finding a way to hers. Marry her or ruin her. It had mattered not at the time.

When Hugh awoke, his mind more clear, he had gone to see her straightaway, determined to break with her, to end their suffering. Then they'd spoken, and his mouth had betrayed his mind when he'd seen with a physical acuity the pain in her eyes. The question had been whether the cause was him, or this duke, and he'd had to know. Hugh had had to pursue her.

"I don't mean to take this out on you. You were merely a victim of my excitement, much as she," Charles said, obviously attempting to calm.

"A victim," Hugh said.

"I should know better than…I *do* know better than to be so callus with my regard for her. I have just waited for so very long, and then that dance. I…I've no right to discuss this with *you*, of all people. I beg your pardon."

"Who would you discuss these thoughts with then?" Hugh asked with a pained smile, attempting to break the tension that was as thick as London fog.

Charles watched him for a moment, then his tension seemed to ebb even as Hugh's flared.

"That was…a disaster," Charles said.

"Your Grace."

With his title tossed at him, Charles knew this discussion was not going to be easy. "Jacks…we agreed on Jacks, Ender. It would be my wish that, in the end, when all is said and done, that you can think on me as a friend. I believe if you think of me in that regard, this situation might be easier. This all may be uncomfortable now, but if we're to regard each other as friends, if you were to gain trust in me…"

Hugh nodded and shifted. "Yes, of course, Jacks and Ender." He said it like a child teasing his foe. It was quite obvious that Hugh was still a bit flustered, out of sorts. "It seems you're getting on well enough. I cannot." Hugh shifted. "I do not want—"

"To lose her," Charles finished with sudden clarity.

Ender shook his head. "It seems I've already lost her. I'd prefer to not *hurt* her, or anger her, or in any way tarnish what we've had."

"No. You still don't want to lose the possibility of a future with her," Charles said as he put his jacket back on and Hugh quietly studied him. Charles watched Hugh tense like a lion worrying a thorn in his paw.

"Damn it all, Jackson—Jacks." Hugh shook his head. "Jackson. This is not a conversation to be had between us. We are supposed to be rivals in this."

"I'm willing to change the rules. My purpose here is not to damage what you have, or had, or will have. It's merely to attempt, somehow, to lessen the shock."

"The pain," Hugh corrected offhandedly.

Charles shook his head. He could not rightfully fathom how he was to retain this man's regard for his future duchess, or why he should want to so desperately. He knew everything Hugh did was for Amelia. He knew that to lose Hugh forever would tarnish the light in her eyes, and that was not something Charles was willing to do, because it was that light that he chased. Charles was aware that he and Hugh could be friends if it weren't for this mess. He was aware, now, that Hugh was a good man through it all, and Charles truly wished to see him well.

"Ender, I don't mean to pry, and by all means, don't tell me what's happened between the two of you. I do hope to understand someday. Actually, I'm hoping I've begun that understanding somewhat already. But just what is it between the two of you? She knew you were here. She quite obviously *felt* your presence through the reality of my physical proximity."

Charles saw the stiff nod reverberate through Hugh. "I can't tell you that. We've always just…been. I should go and leave you to it. I can no longer help you in this. It was selfish of me to mislead you in that regard. But the fact is, what we have cannot be taught, cannot be explained, it just *is*. I will be leaving London shortly, until this business is over with, and you're both safely back to Castleberry Keep."

"You assume we're to live there primarily?"

"I assume nothing. If you're to make her happy, that's where you'll live."

"I'm a duke. I have a presence—"

Hugh looked at him calmly. He was always so terribly calm, and that calm always unnerved Charles.

"You misunderstand her completely then," Hugh said. "It's not merely that I help her. It's this." He waved his hand through the air. "The *ton* as it is, London society and all its dregs. This is not where she belongs. If you want her, you must understand her. She's in London for her mother, for her father. *For you*. She will suffer it, but is that what you want? For her to suffer?"

Charles considered him as he leaned over and picked up the other man's top hat. "No, I suppose not. I presumed that what you have transcends all that."

"You, again, presume too much. If we're done here—"

"Not entirely. Ender, I…I've cared so much for her from the moment I saw her. I wish to understand more."

Hugh nodded. "Then understand she will suffer it silently. This life. As she does now."

"I see," Charles said. "What is it about then? The crowds? The judgment?"

"I don't rightly know. All I know is that she can be more herself when she's away from them, and already I've said more than I ought. I must be off. This evening—"

Charles took his arm to stay him. Then handed him his hat. "Ender, do you believe we would better suit were we to leave London?"

Hugh turned the hat over in his hands. "I believe it possible. As it seems, my other postulate is not to be tested. Perhaps that one can be."

"And yet I fear progressing without you nearby. I still have fear, for her sake." Charles watched as Hugh studied him. "You realize that before she realized you were here, I believe she was close to losing her… to becoming…"

"I understand…and we have yet to decide on a course of action for her. And, again, she's not a party to the current discussion, which she's made perfectly clear she's not comfortable with," Hugh said finally.

Charles shook his head, and a sudden push of anger gripped him. "You try my patience. You do realize it would be easier for me to simply call you out than to give you leave to interfere in something you know you shouldn't. I merely ask because none of us want to be in the situation we continue to find ourselves in. *We* are to be married. I'm not certain how much of this situation I can manage. It's obvious that she cannot handle much more of it, and as for you…" Charles shook his head again. "If you were to walk away now…this has all been quite beyond me and tested every bit of patience I have."

"She loves me. She still needs me. Is that not perfectly obvious to you? This isn't simply about *you*," Hugh retorted.

"Of course it isn't, but she cannot *have* you! And she certainly cannot have *us!*" Charles yelled as he took Hugh by the lapels. "Cry off or I shall call you out and be damned for it, because she will *never* forgive me. But I'll not stand idly by and let you ruin the lot of us." Charles shoved Hugh away, and Hugh stumbled as he smoothed his jacket.

Charles was finished. He turned and stormed toward the Greensborough ballroom while he attempted to calm his erratic pulse. There was only so much his pride could allow, and he'd quite obviously already allowed for too much. That was his doing, and something he would rectify immediately.

He smoothed his hair and pasted a smile over the look of discontent he knew he carried as he approached her parents to make his apologies.

A

"Everything, Louisa, everything. I'm not returning. I've had quite enough of London to last me a lifetime. Pack it all."

Louisa's jaw dropped in shock. She'd only just walked in the door, so Amelia was quite sure that finding her packing her things had not been expected. "Milady, I cannot see as how this is good. You should speak with His Grace. I'm sure he would understand."

"Understand what? That I said Hugh's name while he was having his way?" She paused and sat suddenly at the edge of the bed, feeling the tingle rush through her limbs, toward her belly. "I said Hugh's name while in his arms, and I didn't even know I'd done it. Oh, Louisa, I believe I'm lost. I thought I knew what love was, and then he touched me, and I realized I'd no idea. None at all."

Louisa sat next to her, taking her hands. She hadn't even removed her wrap. Smythe must have told Louisa that she was upset, and Louisa had come straight to her room instead of going to her room first. "Milady, please, he'll understand."

"No. I cannot spend my life breaking his heart. It's better this way. I'm the only one who's broken. I was always broken. It seems it's to be my destiny."

Louisa's arms wrapped around her solidly, and Amelia let herself melt into her.

"Louisa, I do love him. I love them both. But the difference between them is night and day. I cannot have the one for the other, but I cannot dare to damage either. It's best if I simply go. It's best for everyone. I cannot imagine the pain I would have should either of them be injured by my choice."

"Milady, you cannot give up. You cannot run away," Louisa said.

"It's done. Please help me finish with the cases. I'd like to be off as soon as possible."

"Amelia!" The door swung wide, and Louisa released her and stood, then quickly scampered toward the wardrobe to busy herself.

"Mother," she said calmly as she stood.

"What are you about? The duke said you were not feeling well, then I come here to find the traveling carriage being loaded. Where are you off to?"

"Home. I'm leaving."

"Quitting London?" she practically squealed.

"Yes. Please make my apologies. I shall not return."

"But…but…but the duke said he would be by in the morning to check on you and finalize the arrangements."

Amelia paused at that, that he would say such a thing after tonight. She could not be swayed, however. She needed to leave them be. "Please make my apologies."

"Amelia!"

"Mother, enough. I'm old enough to make my own decisions."

Her mother…what would come of her?

Hugh had promised that regardless the outcome of his suit…but she'd not hold him to that promise. "I'll work if need be to support us once father has passed. Until then, we'll be happy at Pembroke."

Her mother stared as Amelia stood and turned, packing up her oils and powders, the glass clinking as she placed the bottles in a smaller case. Amelia heard the door shut behind her mother, then the wail as she carried off down the hallway. She shook her head as Louisa poked her head out of the wardrobe to look at her.

"Carry on, Louisa. Time is wasting."

The next morning, they waited at the station as all the furniture and trunks were unloaded from the rear car of the train and strapped to the Pembroke carriage. Amelia turned to Louisa, who seemed more distant than usual. "Are you well?" she asked.

"Oh, I am, milady. I just wasn't expecting to quit London so quickly this time." She smiled at her.

"Oh, Louisa, I'm sorry, I…I should have considered you—"

"Oh, no, milady, that's not your responsibility. The responsibility is mine. You're mine, not the other way round. It's true I'm a bit more sad this time, I just…well, it gets more and more difficult to say good-bye."

Amelia nodded. "I understand that feeling. I wish I could help you with it. Can you tell me of him? Could he come work for us at

Pembroke?" Amelia assumed he was of the working class, but by the shocked look on Louisa's face, perhaps she shouldn't have done so. "I apologize. I assumed—"

"No, milady, it's all right." Louisa was silent for a long moment as she seemed to consider the offer. Then she shook her head slowly. "There isn't a position suitable. I appreciate your thoughts, but there really isn't a position that would work in this matter."

Amelia reached out and wrapped her arms around Louisa. "You could return. I would give you the very best references, as well as settle a fair amount on you for your service."

Louisa turned and took her arms. "Absolutely not, my lady. I'll not leave you. Not for all the money at Pembroke. I trust everything will work out as it should. For now, my place is with you. I hold no grudge against that, never you think it."

Amelia smiled and hugged her, but she still wished there was aught she could do. With an estate as large as Pembroke-by-the-Sea, practically a city unto itself, there was nearly every position a man could want. She couldn't see why Louisa couldn't manage to bring hers here.

"Know that should you change your mind, Louisa, the offer stands. Both for you to quit my father's employ, or for your gentleman to take a position with our household. You just need say the word."

"What do you mean, she's gone?" Hugh attempted to control the panic that welled in his belly.

"She departed last eve after she returned from the ball."

"Damn it all," Hugh said, then turned to see the blush across her mother's face. "Begging your pardon."

"Endsleigh." The Duke of Pembroke took his attention. "She requested we make her apologies, and I must follow her wishes. I'm most disappointed, but I don't believe my daughter is thinking clearly. I blame myself. You were the only other child within a decent distance who was of acceptable breeding besides Castleberry. Perhaps I should have allowed her friendship with the kitchen girls instead, but I simply didn't believe that to be appropriate. I was terribly misguided in her friendship with you, and that friendship may have ruined her chances at a decent match."

So Hugh would be blamed. Amelia must have said something. How would they even have known he was at fault in this? What had he done? He should have known to leave well enough alone, he should have let them be, he should have refused Charles…

Charles.

"Does Castleberry know yet?" Hugh asked.

"He does not, though he's expected in two hours' time, and it falls to me to break what agreement there was. I know not what will come of my…daughter," her father said, his voice wrought with anger.

"I came to tell her. I came to apologize. Now I see I've gone too far."

"*Now* you see?" The duke stood, and Hugh backed up a pace at the shock of it. "Endsleigh, if it were not for my friendship with the former baron, I would ruin you."

"Your Grace, I believe there's already a queue," Hugh said quietly before bowing and leaving. He had to get to Charles.

TWO

Amelia hung the laundry on the moors at the Cliff House. She enjoyed the pure solitude of the act of doing the laundry for the Cliff House, hanging it in the breeze, sitting amongst the bed linens and spare clothing, and reading her favorite novels, out here at what seemed to her the edge of the world. It was a methodical peace not requiring much thought. Bringing the linens out, bringing the tub out, heating water from the well over the fire, hauling kettle after kettle to the wash tub, carefully scrubbing the linens, hanging them to dry.

Her mind was clear, it was calm, it was her own.

Amelia clipped one last chemise to the lines, removed the washing apron that helped to keep her work dress dry, then lay on the rug amidst the linen, the sun and the breeze flowing through the thin white fabrics, casting sun and shadow across her small world.

She reached into the basket she'd brought, full with fruits, cheeses, wine and books. The perfect basket, should you ask her. From it, she pulled the books, shuffled through them, and settled with one.

After carefully peering through the linens to ensure none of the servants were approaching her solitude, which they shouldn't have been. They left her alone out here until they were required to return. But because of the book, she was nervous. She took up *Fanny Hill.*

It hadn't been much of a chore to obtain once she mentioned it to Louisa, but after she'd heard Hugh joking about it, she'd determined to read it, and Louisa had made it happen. There must be something more she didn't know about sex, as Hugh had said. Perhaps it was merely fear. Perhaps if she understood.

Perhaps…

She opened the tome to a random place and began to read.

"*I had it now, I felt it now, and, beginning to drive, he soon gave nature such a powerful summons down to her favourite quarters, that she could no longer refuse repairing thither; all my animal spirits then rushed mechanically to that center of attraction, and presently, inly warmed, and stirred as I was beyond bearing, I lost all restraint…*"

I lost all restraint.

This alone disturbed her. For losing all restraint, in her mind, meant losing herself. Which is exactly what she feared most, exactly what she'd felt happening in the gardens with Charles.

As well, it was exactly what Hugh referred to, had he not?

Would that she could do this, this losing restraint, without also losing herself. She flipped through the well-worn novel to another section, for it wasn't difficult in this book to find the scenes that would explain what it was she wanted to know.

"*I saw, with wonder and surprise, what? not the play thing of a boy, not the weapon of a man, but a Maypole, of so enormous a standard, that had proportions been observed, it must have belonged to a young giant…*"

Her eyes widened in such a manner she was surprised they stayed in her skull.

"*…then the broad of blueish-casted incarnate of the head, and blue serpentines of its veins, altogether composed the most striking assemblage of figure and colours in nature. In short, it stood an object of terror and delight.*"

Terror.

Terror?

Amelia closed the book, then was immediately regretful, as she hadn't marked the place. Hugh had said nothing of the terror. In fact, when he'd explained the act in relation to the animals, he'd been quite specific that a man's…*equipage* was nothing like that of the beasts'. That didn't quite seem so now.

She had detected the steeled length of Charles through both of their trappings. His…appendage hadn't terrorized her at the time. But now—upon a bit of consideration—perhaps it should have. It was

certainly no pen, and she'd explored her own self, and when compared to the size of him… She scanned the pages, attempting to find the section where she'd left off.

"But what was yet more surprising, the owner of this natural curiosity, through the want of occasions in the strictness of his home breeding, and the little time he had been in town not having afforded him one; was hitherto an absolute stranger, in practice at least, to the use of all that manhood he was so nobly stocked with; and it now fell to my lot to stand his first trial of it, if I could resolve to run the risks of its disproportion to that tender part of me, which such an oversized machine was very fit to lay in ruins."

Lay in ruins.

That tender part of me.

Well, now, here's the terror.

Her heart stomped a beat against her ribs. Her maidenhead would certainly lay in ruins, though previously she'd thought that only figuratively. And now she truly *was* terrified. She'd meant to educate herself, possibly calm herself on the consideration of intimacy. After Hugh had suggested that she might merely be frightened. Yet now…

What now? She was quite a bit more frightened than she had been. The book had termed the penis a maypole. She held up her own hand and made a circle with her fingers. They could not circle a maypole. She held up both hands, and the blood slipped from her head. She wouldn't have used such a term with Charles, certainly, but remembered having thought his to be similar to a steel pipe. Of course, now the simple mechanics…yet Fanny was a practiced woman, so very unlike herself. Amelia was untried and—

"Well, now, what have we here?"

Amelia looked over her shoulder to find Hugh staring down at her between two of her chemises and knew she paled in the dizziness that overtook her.

Oh no…nonono…

She stood suddenly, the book falling to the rug amongst her things, the world in a bit of a spin.

"What are you doing here?" she asked Hugh. Her voice shook. She hated that.

"I came to see you. Your father informed me you quit London, and I feared that your leaving had much to do with me. With us."

Us? Which us does he refer to? Hugh and I us? Or Hugh and Charles us? Or Hugh and Charles and I... "Well, you always have been able to get to the crux of a matter," she said stiffly.

"Amelia, please, I beg you. I came to attempt to right things. Between you and—"

"Charles. Yes. Charles." She shook her head. Between her and Charles. Where, then, did the *us* come into it? She turned away from Hugh.

"Do you love him?" Hugh asked.

The words were quiet, so quiet as to be painful to her. She took the entire weight of that question into her bones. It weighed on her so heavily, she couldn't effort to vocalize a response, and her lips refused her service. She knew what this would mean. She didn't think Hugh would hear her...to know, to know that she loved him as well, as she always had...as she always would. Amelia had to at least honor Hugh by facing him, and so she did. Then her head managed a nod so stiff, it was a mere twitch.

Hugh looked down, and the world shifted beneath her feet. "Hugh," she said.

Hugh shook his head but didn't look back up to her yet. "I know you do. I know," he said quietly. This took her by surprise, and he caught her gaze.

"Why did you ask? If you know...how did you—"

"I know you, Amelia. Do you think I wouldn't see what was between the two of you? Don't you think I know you well enough by now?"

"True, and how would he react to find us here together? Had you thought on that?" she asked quietly.

"He had, which is why he brought me with him," Charles said.

Her skirts whipped about her as she turned so suddenly toward Charles's voice, she nearly lost her footing. Then there were hands, all those warm hands, holding her up. She pulled back from them, stumbled, and fell arse over teakettle into her wet laundry tub, water splaying everywhere. It shocked her to her work boots, and her mind stilled completely.

Then she laughed.

It was loud. It was hearty. It was unladylike. It filled the meadow, and it was incredible. Then she heard the bass undertones of her accompaniment, and the hands returned, carefully attempting to help her from the tub.

Amelia wiggled her way upright, her eyes on Hugh, laughter still staining her world. She was soaked throughout the middle, and the water coursed toward her feet, saturating her skirts. She took Hugh's lapels, careless of the wet of her hands, and a pair of hands wrapped about her waist. She looked down and saw Hugh's hands, heavy at his sides, and knew then that Charles truly was here with her as well.

Amelia closed her eyes on the remembrance of that heady laughter, the swinging freedom of her happiness, then leaned back until she met the solid wall of Charles's body behind her.

A beat passed. Then another. She refused to move. She tilted her head back and up until she could fill her lungs with his scent.

Maypole.

Amelia's eyes snapped open and were met with Charles's scruffy chin. She'd never seen him without a perfect shave, and she wanted to touch, to graze her palm across his chin and feel the burn of his stiff whiskers.

The weapon of a man…

She pushed her hips into him. There was no maypole here, but rising beneath the fabric of her skirts and his trousers was certainly something that may rend her, leave her in ruins, possibly in more ways than one. Her hands tightened on Hugh's lapels. It was all she could do simply to breathe. So she concentrated the whole of herself on that simple act, until the filling of her chest, the expansion, began to chafe at her nipples, which had once again perked within the confines of her corset.

Her breath became more ragged, and she concentrated still, the sharp pull from her nipples traveling deep within her, down to some secret, untouched place, not just in her body, but her soul. She closed her eyes, for she did not want to look on only one of these men when she spoke next.

"What are you doing here? What are you *both* doing here?" she asked.

"We came to help you, Amelia," Hugh said.

Charles hadn't said another word, but she saw his throat work as he swallowed. She wished she could see what was in his eyes, but from this angle it was impossible. She didn't want to move, for while she started to feel her world spin with Charles's proximity to her, she wanted to ride the sensation for as long as she could before she was lost. She wanted to test Hugh's theory. Perhaps she could build up a tolerance to him. She closed her eyes. Him with the episodes and damage, and her with the walls and tolerance. This wasn't going well.

"Amelia." She looked at Hugh when he spoke. "We're here to help you. You wish to marry Charles, to be his wife and his duchess, to carry his name and title, to be responsible for his household…his nursery." Hugh paused, and her mind churned through the words.

Wife.

Duchess.

Nursery.

"We're here to see to that." This, this deep gruff voice, belonged to Charles, and she felt it reverberate against her back as much as she heard it against her shoulder. "Whatever it takes."

She caught Hugh's gaze as he was in front of her, then his gaze drifted past her, and she knew he and Charles were silently considering the moment.

"What does that mean?" she asked.

"Amelia, Charles and I are going to show you what passion is. We're going to bring you to a crisis. We're going to drive you beyond every emotion you've ever had, to bring this part of you forth that you're so very afraid of. We're going to do this here, in the safety of the Cliff House, because this *is* where you feel safest. I'm going to be with you the whole time, because—" Hugh swept a hand down her chin. "I know…I know, Amelia."

She dropped her mouth to speak, but he waved her off…knowing she was going to attempt to avoid this. "And I know we'll not be disturbed because your staff doesn't come here unless requested of them. We are safe here."

With that, he shattered every objection she could have possibly had. Every objection any reasonable person could have had.

"I would never ask this of you," she said quietly.

"You never have to," Hugh said.

Silence. There was so much silence. This was what she wanted. They wished to help her. She wanted to marry Charles, and this was a way to get past…whatever it was she needed to get past.

"What…exactly does that mean?" The words were nearly a breath instead of a statement. A voice rumbled behind her, and her heart kicked against her breast.

"We're going to touch you," Charles said. "Intimately."

The word was deep and moved through her blood like laudanum.

"Our hands, our mouths, our tongues…your body. We'll come to know each other as God intended…with nothing between us."

Her mind raced.

Our.

"Our?" Her voice was breathless.

"Like we did at Hugh's house, Amelia, only…more." As Charles said it, his chin brushed her temple, his whiskers like sweet sandpaper against her skin.

More.

Maypole.

Her favourite quarters…

All my animal spirits…

That tender part of me…

Lay in ruin…

Lay in ruin…

Lay in ruin.

Amelia closed her eyes and attempted to quiet her mind, but Charles's heat was sinking into her, carrying the words from his tongue.

We are going to touch you.

Our hands, our mouths, our tongues…your body.

"I don't know what to do," she said quietly.

"You can do anything you wish, touch anything you want, and we'll help you. There are no rules here. We will not judge you," Charles said.

She was truly dizzy at that, and her knees weakened.

Hugh stepped closer, crowding her infinitely, and the pace of her heart reacted. It calmed as they paused there, as if waiting for her acquiescence. If they gave her too long, though, her mind would have off with her and…her hands tightened on Hugh's lapels and pulled him forward. Hugh's gaze snapped back to hers before her lips took his.

This.

Charles's hold tightened on her waist as though to pull her away, but instead his heat sank through her wet clothes as he gathered himself forward, nudging her books aside with the toes of his boot. She kissed and kissed and kissed and lost herself to the feelings. Hugh's mouth was warm and wet, familiar, and the hands on her waist were warm in equal measure and, surprisingly, familiar.

Her hands grasped Hugh's shirt and waistcoat, popping the buttons and laying waste to his fashion, then they traversed the hot countryside of his chest as she had explored Charles's in the gardens. The hills and valleys that made up Hugh's own personal landscape. She could do this with him. In some fashion, she'd always wanted to touch Hugh, to explore his man's body, but she'd always held back. That wasn't something for friends.

Forbidden.

The word came to her unbidden, and she paused, saw the edges of her vision fade only slightly, and she forced it back, shook it off.

There are no rules here.

She concentrated on Hugh. He vibrated under her touch, the groans adding more to his movements. She affected him. That simple knowledge spurred her on. She wrapped her hands around Hugh then

and let the vibration sink into her chest, her nipples hard as pebbles, her corset scraping his chest. His arms moved, his hands coming up to frame her face, then…

Blue serpentines of its veins…

She had to see. She had to know. And here Amelia was caught between…between…*a steel rod and a maypole.*

She giggled against Hugh. She simply couldn't help herself. Then the chests, both of them, loosed around her, and the heady, unsure laughter of all three of them once again filled the meadows.

Amelia watched as Hugh removed his coat, then rolled his sleeves. She turned within the warm circle of arms, and a shiver rushed her spine from the wet frock starting to chill her skin. Once she was against Charles's chest, she tilted her chin up and up until she placed a kiss in the hollow of his jaw, just under his chin, unsure. Her hands followed, scraping across his unkempt face, and she smiled. Then there was tugging at her back, and she looked over her shoulder to find Hugh undoing the laces of her simple gown.

Charles moved his hands to her wrists when her hands tensed on his jaw, nearly giving him eight tiny gashes from her fingernails. He pulled them together then down between them, kissing her fingertips as they passed his mouth, drawing her attention. He placed her hands on his chest and set them to fidgeting with the length of his unbound cravat to give them something to do.

Charles looked into her face, her expression wary, concerned, and with every bit of himself, he wanted to allay her fears.

"I want this," he whispered.

Amelia's eyes widened, and her mouth dropped open.

He took her face in his hands and kissed her. Gently. He needed to do as Ender had instructed, to keep part of her mind busy with trivial things when perceptibly difficult things were happening—such as the removal of her clothing. Charles had never attempted a conversation at such a time, and his mind panicked to find a topic.

Then he closed his eyes and breathed of her, of the fresh air of the moors, the salt tang of the ocean beyond the cliffs, the lemon that had somehow accompanied her last meal, and the lilac that was always so prevalent with her.

It seemed stronger today, the lilac, and Charles looked around at the yards of fabric.

"Soap," Charles said quizzically.

"Soap?" she questioned. "Really, Charles, cryptic one-word statements are my foible. You should find your own oddity with which to annoy society."

He couldn't help but smile and laugh. "You always smell of lilac," he said as he drew her closer. "It's in the soap. I only just realized."

"Yes, the laundress makes the laundry soap by hand because my skin is sensitive." Her voice was unsteady as Hugh pulled on her trappings. "She uses only natural cleansers and adds the lilac. It's quite prevalent here at Pembroke. The lilac is."

"It's wonderful." Charles held her gaze as her dress and corset slipped between them, then unable to *not* look, as he was a man—a man quite in want of *this* woman—and he knew, *he knew*, her breasts were just *there*. He skimmed his hands down to her shoulders and looked.

The taste of her came back to him in a rush of sensation, but he stayed his impulse and caressed her arms as the dress slid, the heavy corset fell, and with great difficulty he looked back to her eyes.

Charles could see her concern. As perhaps they all should have been. But…*whatever happens…happens.*

Charles realized that he wanted to be first in all things. As an explorer sets his flag in uncharted territory, it was his flag he wanted to plant on all aspects of her introduction to passion. He felt that realization in the tension that had begun to wring his muscles, and he fought momentarily to stay it, locking his gaze with hers as the two of them swayed in whatever it was Ender was doing with her skirts. Charles dared not consider it.

"You are so lovely," Charles whispered. "So very lovely."

The smile she bestowed him would be forever burned in his memories of this place. With that in his heart, he believed himself strong enough to check Ender's progress. Speedy, this one. Her chemise rode low across her shoulders, her soft breasts peeking out over the neckline. Her dress was nearly gone, as were the petticoats that supported it. She was down to her underthings and this brilliant smile that truly covered her in ways no clothing ever could.

Her eyes closed, and she shivered.

"Don't...Amelia, open your eyes and look on me."

She did, and her shivers stilled.

Charles ran his thumbs over her eyebrows, then pushed his fingers into her hair and kissed her once again.

Her legs bent as Ender nudged them so he could remove her boots and her skirts could fall away. But they also hesitated of their own volition, pushing against his hard thighs, as if finding a place of their own to be soothed.

Charles wanted to touch her everywhere, to wrap her up in himself and keep every inch of her body in a soothing and safe place.

He pulled his hands down her back, then wrapped them about her waist, picking her up and carrying her toward the laundry tub. "Step in," Charles said quietly.

He placed one hand on her thigh, easing her leg up. It slid against his trouser-clad leg, then slipped into the warm water, a small sigh escaping her mouth against his. Once steady, the other moved. Charles saw Ender's hand on her, guiding her in. Charles held her steady against the slippery water of the wash tub, as Ender took up covering her with sheets of water, which splashed back to the tub, to the ground, to his very person.

Amelia held on to Charles as the sensations from Ender's actions rippled over all of them, then Hugh stilled at his masterpiece. The fabric of her shift and drawers slicked tightly to her figure, the water rushing down her form to spill again around them all. The fabric was thicker at her hips, from the dual layers of her drawers and chemise, but thin, and inviting, down the middle, where the separation of her underthings left a void Hugh quite wished to explore. He knelt beside the tub and slid his hands up her ankles, then looked up at Charles.

"You have her?" Hugh asked quietly.

"I have her," Charles responded.

Hugh turned back to his work, sliding his hands farther up her soft legs, beneath the chemise, gathering the sodden fabric on his forearms as he moved up and up. When he reached her buttocks, his hands paused, then slowly, carefully, his thumbs skated over the bare flesh of each of them, sending a shiver to course her spine.

I have her.

The words stole into his head, and Hugh closed his eyes. *Anything for Amelia. Anything,* he thought.

She responded to his touch, and then his movements as Charles held her tighter in his arms. Hugh nudged one of Charles's hands, the one low on her waist that covered the back of her drawers, and Charles moved his hand slowly away, granting him access.

Hugh reached around her waist, insinuating his hands between them to grasp the ties of the drawers. As he did so, layered so closely between the two of them, his knuckles brushed the evidence of Charles's arousal, and he paused, catching Charles's gaze over her shoulder.

They silently exchanged apologies and understanding in that glance. They *knew* this would happen, had discussed it at length in the carriage on the trip to Pembroke. They'd come to a clear understanding, which required a great measure of trust on both their parts. They had to brush aside the discomfort to prevent Amelia feeling any from them. If this was to happen. If this was to work.

This was truly the point of no return, and while the touch he bestowed Charles was entirely incidental, without purpose, and unavoidable…it *was* contact. Hugh's knuckles bent, pressing against Charles's cock and abdomen, as he grasped the ties and pulled the bow loose, sliding his hands from between the two of them, then returning to finally untie the knot.

It seemed as though it took forever, when in reality the time he'd been between them had to have been mere seconds. Charles's hips

pressed into Amelia as soon as Hugh's hands were free, and Hugh rested his hands momentarily on her hips, taking a single, strengthening breath before his hands moved the fabric of each leg of her drawers, and he smoothed them down her hips, bringing them off. He urged her to step out of them, finding her legs rather more pliable then expected and realized Charles truly *did* have her, supporting all of her weight on him.

"Charles."

Had the breeze moved another direction, he may not have heard her quiet plea to the other man, or the answer that followed.

"Amelia, I have you, we have you. Don't think, just feel. We have you," Charles said quietly.

Hugh watched for a moment as Charles nipped, licked, pressed and tasted her. It shook Hugh to his core.

Anything for her.

Hugh stood and smoothed the arms of her chemise down, as Charles moved his arms to allow his access. Hugh's hands skimmed the smooth skin over her rib cage, paused at the nip of her waist and then, with another deep breath, he pushed the chemise down to her hips, leaving her upper body fully unclothed but for the drops of water on her skin and the other man wrapped around her.

Hugh stood momentarily, just taking her in, this woman who'd grown from the girl of his best friend. He took up a serviette from the basket and wetted it, then wrung it out on her back, following the water that coursed her spine. He knelt again, and dropping the napkin in the tub, he ran his hands up one smooth leg, playing at the edge of her stocking, feeling the difference between the silk of the stocking and the silk of her skin.

He loosed the tiny bow and slid the stocking down, only to repeat the maneuver with her other leg. This time, as his hand slid up her inner thigh, drawn to the heat of her very core, his hand swept gently across the smooth pink lips he could see peeking out. He saw her hips push back at him to allow more access and knew then she wasn't steeling her control, but allowing her body's response for the moment. That response was magical, it was wondrous, and he had never felt more accomplished in the entirety of his life.

He was overwhelmed by the moment, the reality, something he'd never thought to witness. And witness he did Charles's hand, slipping down her back to cup one of the sweet globes of her bottom, pulling her closer to him possessively. Hugh's breath halted. He nearly choked on it, and Charles's gaze moved to him.

FOURTEEN

Amelia felt. Simply felt. It was the simplest explanation, really. She did nothing else. Her back curved, her hands held gently against Charles's warm chest. She was naked as the day she stood in. Well, nearly.

She kept her eyes closed.

Her heart was full.

There were hands on her seemingly everywhere. There was a slight breeze, but the bright of the sun cut the chill of it, warming her skin even as the goose bumps rioted against it.

Charles held her, supported her with one strong, solid arm around her waist, his fingers spread against her side, lifting her up. His other hand…his other hand was warm on the round of her bottom. Squeezing and stroking.

Charles's hand is on my bottom. On my bottom. I can feel his hand on me…on me. Hugh's as well, though Hugh's was of less concern to her, except that his hand was there at the same time as Charles's, or perhaps it was there…because of Charles's.

Charles's hand shifted slightly, and she panicked. *Charles…is touching me. Charles is touching me. Charles…*

Amelia's mind swirled, and she tensed, attempting to ward off the coming deluge of emotion. She knew where that feeling led. She always knew where it led. That feeling, that swirl, always led to the same place.

The same damned place.

The loss of control, the darkness that spreads, the complete failure of her mind—

"Amelia."

She felt more hands moving on her, up her back, but not Charles's hands. His hands still held her to him.

Hugh.

She breathed deeply and opened her eyes. These were Hugh's hands, and they calmed her, as they always did. She was grateful.

"Stay with me, Amelia. Stay with us. We're here. We're not going anywhere. I have you... *We* have you," Charles said.

Amelia shook her head and closed her eyes again. Charles couldn't be witness to this...this. Charles had never been a true witness to what happened once her tethers broke loose and she lost her mind to the dark. That cold, shuddering place that wrapped itself around her and wouldn't let go. A deep, swirling terror, nothing to hold on to, no anchor to the world. The fall from herself...

"Hugh." Her voice broke on his name. She heard it. She knew how her voice sounded and expected Charles to back away again, like he had before. Speaking his name put Hugh between them, like in the gardens. He would always be between them. The pain of it manifested behind her breastbone, spread like a flood to her bones.

"Amelia, he's here, he's with us. Hugh isn't going anywhere, and... neither am I. Look at me, Amelia. Open your eyes," Charles said.

She didn't...instead, she tightened her hands on his lapels. If Charles saw the crazy in her eyes right now, he'd leave, and she'd be truly lost. She wished for Hugh, and as an answer to that whispered prayer, she felt the full warmth of his body against her back. Warming her soul. Hugh's mouth against her ear stilled her heart's raucous cadence.

"Amelia mine, I'm here. *Feel me.* I'm here. Open your eyes."

Amelia did, and Charles's beautiful eyes were there like a stormy day bearing down on her. That incessant strength that oozed from his very pores attempted to saturate her very being. She heard the sob more than anything. It rent the air like a crack of thunder, and her skin answered in an electric jolt of response shuddering between them.

Charles held her gaze, refused to let her look away, spoke softly as Hugh breathed against her neck, his hands warming her arms, willing her body to relax into him with his very presence. Hugh took her hands, *willed* them to relax into his, massaged the stiff tension from them, and removed them from Charles's lapels.

Their fingers entangled, Hugh pressed her hands up Charles's chest, against his neck, then brought them to Charles's face, cradling his chin.

"Kiss him, Amelia," Hugh said.

Charles leaned toward her, his eyes dropping to her mouth. "Here," he said, then touched his mouth to the edge of hers and ran his tongue the length of her lower lip as she gasped and watched his eyes sear her flesh, igniting her nerves, pulling her toward him like static.

Then Hugh's mouth was on her neck, wet, open kisses running up her nape.

"Here," Charles said again. "Stay here, Amelia. Stay with us."

Charles's tongue touched the very center of her upper lip, drawing it out, before he kissed it back. "Here," Charles said so quietly it might have been the breeze. Then he pressed his mouth to hers.

Hugh's fingers separated from hers, and she held on to Charles, though she felt the loss of that contact in every part of her through the shudder that racked her physically.

"Hugh," she cried.

"Here," Hugh replied. "I'm still here." His words warmed her neck. Then his hands alighted on her hips. "I'm here," Hugh said as he pulled her bottom against him, his hands heavy and demanding. "Here," Hugh said, the heavy, thick evidence of his cock resting against her backside. "Here," Hugh whispered gruffly as the wet fabric of her chemise rose against her leg, his hand gathering it from where it rested against her hips, the fingers moving so slowly. Then his hand smoothed around her thigh, his fingertips cupping her bottom, teasing the crease there, that sensitive flesh where her backside ended and her leg began.

"Hugh," she breathed and knew the word found its home between Charles's lips.

"Yes," Charles breathed back. "Stay with us, Amelia. Stay here."

She looked at him again in a fascinated way. Charles had seen into her eyes while her mind had tried to hide. She'd said Hugh's name into their kiss, and he was *still here*.

"I'm here, Amelia. Look at me," Charles said.

She couldn't take her eyes from his for anything. The pull of his gaze was a tangible thing, the strength in his eyes big enough for both of them, for all of them. "Charles," she whispered against his lips, and she saw an answering spark when the black of his eyes widened, overtaking the gray of the storm. His eyes darkened, and they held her, mesmerized.

Charles knew she saw it, knew by the way her mouth dropped open that she recognized the passion in him. The pure *want*. Charles pulled her tighter against him and was reminded of Hugh by the feel of his hand on her hip, pushing against parts of Charles that were no longer soft. But it had been *Charles's own name* on her lips. It had been *Charles's own name* she'd last breathed against him as he looked into her eyes. She was here, and she was with him. She blinked, and the tenuous connection faltered.

"Amelia, stay with me," Charles said quietly, then Hugh's hand shifted, coming between he and Amelia, pushing against the very core of her womanhood, stroking Charles as Hugh stroked her.

Her eyes widened, and her breath caught.

"Feel, Amelia, feel. Everything is right, this is right, this here— with us, this is right. Just stay with me, just feel."

Charles saw the slight nod. Her hands slid to his shoulders as she held on to him, and her mouth dropped open so he could see the sweet pink of her tongue, and Charles groaned. The sound resonated between the three of them. Hugh's hand delved between her thighs, his hold on her tightening as did his own.

The puffs of her breath against Charles's mouth sped, her hands clenching on his shoulders, digging into his muscles through the layers of fabric, and he desperately wished to be rid of his clothes, to give up the blood from his very body to her hands if that would help her find release from this tension. Then her tongue darted out between them, licking his upper lip. Charles tensed, bringing them all closer together.

Charles slid the hand on her bottom, his knuckles grazing Hugh's cock through the fabric of his trousers until Charles's finger traced the crease of her thigh, leading him to her center—and Charles had found home. The breath left him in a heady rush at the discovery of her warmth. And he rested there, his hand between her thighs, his fingertips teasing the softest of her lips until they met Hugh's own fingertips, there in the middle, their fingers touching at the confluence of her very being.

"Charles, I—"

"Stay with me, Amelia." Charles heard the roughness of his own voice, the want in it. Knew he needed to rein his passion. This was her moment, this was all for her. This was her awakening, and that he was here for it, that she was with him, *truly with him,* touched him soul deep.

"Amelia," Charles whispered against her mouth.

Her eyelashes fluttered shut against her cheek as he took her mouth in a searing kiss, Charles's tongue sliding against hers, sweeping, tasting, tickling, willing her to open to him in every way.

Warmth suffused her core, and Charles knew Hugh felt it as well, his movement against her picking up, the steady roll of his fingers sliding through her wet folds, teasing her core, certainly circling that nub of pleasure. That Charles could feel Hugh stroking her in the answering strokes against his own erection, and against his own fingertips, only drove him further into his want of her.

Her mouth fell open, her head fell back against Hugh's shoulder and her breath turned to veritable pants as she held fast to the remaining binds.

Charles moved toward her, his lips against her ear. "Let go, Amelia. You're safe," he said. His warm breath collected in the shell of her ear, and she cried, her tears joining his breath there. "Let go, Amelia, we have you."

Her hands clenched on his shoulders, and the whole of her tensed as his arms took all of her weight onto his frame, his hand sliding from her warm heat and pulling her leg up against him as she broke—and he merely held on.

It was the most beautiful moment Charles had ever been witness to. He looked down, caught her gaze, saw her focus soften on him as she bit her lip, then dropped her jaw in a scream. He didn't know whose name had been carried away on the wind, but he chose to hear his own.

Beautiful. There was no other word for it. Simply beautiful.

Amelia had shattered, her back against Hugh, her head leaning on his shoulder, her warm, wet quim in his hand. He and Charles had done something for her seemingly so simple. But, in reality, what they'd done was truly monumental.

Hugh saw one of her hands relax on Charles's shoulder then move, almost float across the great expanse between them to rest on his jaw. She was with them.

Hugh closed his eyes, feeling the burn of tears in the strength of that reality. He hadn't realized until that moment that his true fear was that this was not possible for her.

"Ah, Amelia, I…Amelia." Hugh found he had no words for the reality of the moment, so far from anything he had ever considered. So far from any reality he'd ever believed possible. This was so much more than anything he'd ever done or hoped to do with her—for her. This was something he'd never allowed himself to consider.

Hugh opened his eyes and caught Charles's gaze, and it was genuine. Charles knew as well as he did how much this meant to him, to all of them. There was no judgment, no censure, no annoyance or anything beyond the love for Amelia in his eyes. Hugh could see it, could feel it, knew it to his bones that this was right, as Charles had said over and over again to her.

Charles shifted, pulled her legs up, since she wasn't truly using them, and handed her to Hugh. Though Charles's hands never left her body in the movement, or the placement, the moment her full weight was in Hugh's arms, it seemed to him he held the very world, and every second of his life had been so carefully scripted for this one singular moment.

Hugh had not known.

Hugh glanced around the clearing.

"We should go inside," Charles said quietly.

It wasn't what Hugh had expected, and yet it was. At times he'd felt an intruder in this…that his attendance was merely at the behest of Charles, that he didn't fully belong here. Yet in everything that had come before, there had been no verbal acknowledgment of what *was* to pass. What had just happened…had simply happened. It was truth.

But those simple words, no assumptions, no corrections, no condemnations…Hugh nodded, then Charles yanked a dry linen sheet from the line and wrapped it around her as best he could. This was much easier than Hugh had imagined, being with her *and* Charles. She flowed easily between them as if choreographed, as though this was perfectly acceptable, normal, expected.

"There are no sheets on the bed. If you wish to put me there, you must make the bed first." Her voice was small, yet calm, almost sleepy.

Her sudden speech made Hugh smile, and he kissed her nose. "Oh, we intend to put you there, we do."

Her hands escaped the linen and snaked up around his neck, the cool fingertips sending a spark down his spine that he would forever swear went straight to his cock—the hardest it had ever been.

Hugh lost a bit of control then, his groan quite heavy in his chest. Charles turned and checked for the driest of the linens, pulling them from the lines and hauling the armload to the Cliff House as Hugh followed.

A

How had it come to this? Amelia thought.

Her best friend held her. The man she was supposed to marry led them. They were headed into the Cliff House with the intention of… well, she wasn't entirely sure what their full intentions were, and she was oddly okay with whatever they decided. She'd understood they meant to show her pleasure, to allay her fears, and *that* they'd accomplished. Beyond doubt.

That crazy, loose, searching feeling she always felt with Charles wasn't quite the same as when she lost herself, and she knew, now, that there would never have been any words that could have done what they'd done in showing her. For now she knew—*she knew*—beyond doubt that the path with Charles did not lead to certain ruin, it led to this…this jelly-like softness that overtook her limbs in a way she'd never, in her life, felt before.

She wasn't sure how far they intended to go now. Did they mean to lay waste her maidenhead?

Maypole.

Goodness. Her mind needed to still itself.

Maypole.

She tensed, and her mind began to swirl around the word, and she wondered how she'd held herself together for this long. The water had been soothing. Hugh washing her had been soothing. Charles holding her had been…surprisingly soothing. She looked up to the man who carried her over the threshold. Was that as monumental an action as it was meant to be?

Her husband was meant to carry her across the threshold of her home, and this, the Cliff House, was the closest thing to home and comfort she'd ever known. Hugh held her when they crossed it. Not Charles. She tensed, latched on to him and tried her level best to still her mind as he stopped, knowing something was wrong.

It means nothing.

It meant everything.

Hugh stood there, holding her in the doorway as Charles came back to them. She caught his gaze, seeing something of the same disappointment in his eyes that it wasn't him to carry her at that moment. She reached out to him, and Charles moved closer, behind Hugh, and let her hand slip down his roughened chin. Charles moved closer still as she pulled him to her, and their lips met, the two of them wrapped around her best friend's hard biceps, which flexed into her ribs as they kissed.

They moved again, the light dimming as they ventured into the house, then she slid down the front of Hugh as he released her legs, setting her on her feet but not letting go. Hugh held her body, and Charles held her eyes, and she'd never felt more safe than in this moment. Charles skimmed a finger from her ear to the tip of her chin, then smiled, and looked around the room.

After a moment, surely to familiarize himself with the layout, he moved toward the bed at the side of the room, for it was one simple room. Bed, table, chairs, fireplace. Only the necessities.

She swayed dreamily in Hugh's arms, reveled in the feel of his hands sweeping up and down her back, across her hips, up into the hair at her nape, but watched Charles as he billowed one sheet and tucked it tightly around the heavy featherbed. She watched the flex and release of Charles's muscles, visible even through his jacket. Then as Charles turned and removed his jacket and waistcoat, the muscles of his abdomen became brilliant in relief with his wet shirt plastered to them.

Charles was beautiful. So incredibly beautiful and so incredibly different from her. Different from Hugh. She looked back at Hugh.

You can do anything you wish, touch anything you want, and we will help you.

We will not judge you.

There are no rules here.

Amelia carefully reached out and traced a hand up Hugh's abdomen as she turned and watched Charles work, feeling Hugh's muscles bunch and shift under her hand as she watched Charles make the bed. She focused back on Hugh, counted the mounds and valleys she found against her hand, and those of Charles before her eyes, though Charles's shirt moved and wrinkled, impeding her visual progress.

Her hand met Hugh's chest, and it tensed, so impossibly hard, then she waited to see the action in one of Charles's movements. She felt then, at the very center of her palm, Hugh's nipple harden and press into her. She gasped and pushed away from him, her eyes on his chest.

Hugh was watching her curiously, but his eyes were dark, even more so than the room would cause, and she looked back to his chest, one hand holding the sheet around her body.

Touch anything you want...

She moved her other hand across his chest from the one nipple to the other, and that nipple peaked against her palm, and she giggled. She loved that her touch had such a visual effect on his body. She wanted to see that visual effect on Charles as well and looked to find him watching them, his head canted to the side.

You can do anything you wish...

She crooked a finger at him, and he moved closer while she pushed at Hugh's rent clothes, and he pulled them from his shoulders. She looked up to him. "Sorry about that."

"Not to worry, Amelia, I have many shirts and waistcoats with which to replace them. They are of little consequence—"

While his arms were trapped behind his back in the act of taking his clothes from his body, she pulled his head down and kissed him.

Brave. She was so very brave. *And where had that come from?* she thought.

Charles made himself known in the warmth against her side, and she released Hugh, fumbling for Charles. She met the hard wall of his chest, realizing that he'd removed his shirt at some point while he'd moved toward her. She skimmed the surface, measuring the muscles as she had with Hugh, until she met a nipple and gave it a gentle tweak.

Charles groaned, and she felt accomplished, puffing her chest out, causing her breasts to collide with Hugh.

When had the kissing stopped?

Amelia opened her eyes and looked on them both, standing shirtless before her. *Breathe,* she thought. *Where has my bravery gone off to?*

We will not judge you.

She closed her eyes, considered that she needed both of her hands for what she wanted to do next, and steeled herself. Then with a deep breath she let go of the blanket, feeling it sweep a good-bye swiftly down her body to pool on the floor around her feet. One hand already on Charles's chest, she lifted the other and blindly placed it on Hugh, and when she reopened her eyes, she left her vision to the distant wall, somewhere beyond the two of them, unfocused.

Amelia caressed them until she had her hands in mirrored positions on their chests, then moved across them, in unison, as though to learn their differences, as though to know their similarities. When her elbows bent more, she knew they'd both taken another step toward her, and when the hot breath came on her shoulders, she knew they leaned in, allowing access to their sides, their backs... Her hands came to rest again on their stiff nipples, the feel of them pebbles in her palms.

"There are more parts of us that will change with your sweet, blessed touch."

She concentrated to discern who had spoken but couldn't by the sound alone, the voice so gruff it sounded nothing like those she'd become so familiar with.

More parts of us. Amelia's breath caught.

The most striking assemblage of figure and colours in nature.

It could not have been Charles. He would never be so coarse. And yet…he knew what to say to spark her curiosity. She looked at Charles, then a shiver ran her spine, settling at its base. Hugh moved close behind her as she gazed at Charles.

The rending of her chemise was something she would remember for quite some time, the sound like the whisper of a tear, not loud enough to be satisfactory, but just enough that she knew it could never be worn again.

She sank into Hugh, letting the warmth soothe her, allowing it to traverse her skin, loosen her nerves. She nodded slowly, then watched as Charles moved to the bed. He took up at the head of the bed, his back against the wall, his legs spread before him.

"What are we...I thought that—"

"We have more to show you," Hugh said.

"More?" She was jelly again, and Hugh lifted her from her feet, moving toward the bed. He laid her out like a banquet, first arranging her bottom between Charles's legs. Charles took her head onto his chest, removing pins and spreading her loose hair across him, making sure none was caught.

Amelia looked at her tiny form surrounded by this man, the man who should be her husband. Charles had not run yet. Hugh had not sent him away. She had come apart in Charles's arms and remembered every soul-shattering second of it. She tilted her head back to find him looking down at her, patiently, then his warm arms closed in, surrounding her rib cage, his hands settling on her breasts, his fingers swirling the small buds.

Amelia closed her eyes and sank into the sensations, willing the shadows he brought with him to recede.

What's it feel like? she thought. It was rather like the ripple in a pond, him tossing stone after stone, and she the water at his command. And the ripples, oh, the ripples.

It was then that she did scream. Charles's name perhaps, or just the possibility of it, she wasn't sure of it's coherency. But he stilled, so she was quite certain it was aloud. *Please don't stop,* she thought.

She opened her eyes on Hugh, and her world centered. Hugh stood at the foot of the bed, watching, his eyes so dark, his chest bare and moving steadily up and down. She watched it move, then saw the rapid flutter at the crest and reached up to Charles behind her. She put her hand on his neck, feeling the beat of his heart as she watched Hugh's. Hugh. She concentrated on Hugh, and her breathing steadied, the shadows receded, the fear subsided, her bravery returned.

"I'm not sure what your intention is here. I realize you meant to…to introduce me to this, to make me…" She closed her eyes, then shook her head to clear her thoughts. "We are not done?" she choked out finally. She opened her eyes and tried to focus on something.

The ceiling needs dusting.

"Amelia." The vibration against her back told her Charles had spoken before she heard her name. She smoothed her thumb across his shoulder to let him know she'd heard him, because words were beyond her at the moment. "We are far from done with you. Can you feel my heart race? This is what you do to me. To both of us." The words were warm air across the crest of her ear.

Her eyes closed against the spin behind her eyes, the falling, then Hugh lightly touched her feet, ran his thumbs over their bridges in tandem, squeezed them gently.

"Come back, Amelia," Hugh said, and she did.

Charles's hands resumed their work on her breasts, and she arched into them.

"But I'm not ready. I'm not yet married, and my husband should—"

Charles's hands stilled, and his arms wrapped about her carefully. She was more at ease with her breasts covered and attempted to forget that her nether bits were still out for perusal, as it were.

"I'm not yet married," she whispered.

Hugh spoke then. "Our intention today is not to ruin you, but to do nothing more"—the bed dipped as his knee came up and his full weight was placed between her legs—"than to introduce you"—he pushed her legs up and open, resting them against Charles's own knees—"to passion."

Hugh's hands skimmed up her thighs, and he lowered to the bed before her, his dark curls sinking between her legs. He said one last thing that she thought would send her over the brink. "Oh, Amelia, but you are the most beautiful thing I've ever seen." And he wasn't looking at her face when he said it. The heat of a blush raced her skin. Hugh's hand skimmed down her folds. "Soft as petals and pink as the blush on a rose." Hugh's fingers played, and she pushed back, her heels digging into the bed, pushing her into Charles's chest.

"Oh, no no no, I can't, I—"

"Hush, dear sweet Amelia. Remember, I have you," Charles said.

We will help you. We will not judge you.

"Charles?" She was worried and clenched her eyes, the image of Hugh between her legs more than she could bear. She felt Charles's hands on her thighs just as she tensed, and they nearly snapped shut on Hugh's head. Charles massaged her thighs. Then his legs lowered to the bed, and he moved hers over them, resting her legs across his knees, spreading her even wider, keeping her open. Then Charles wrapped his arms around her torso again.

Amelia was naked, and they still had their shoes on.

Their shoes. On the bed. With her...naked. On the bed. They were all on the bed. The three of them. At least my breasts are covered.

"Amelia." The voice rumbled through her as Hugh dipped, and his tongue ran the length of her most intimate parts.

Amelia opened her lungs, and she screamed.

So inappropriate. Hugh's mouth was on her...on me. This was beyond the pale...surely unacceptable. Surely. Surely not something proper gentlemen would do. Surely not something a proper wife would allow.

Hugh looked up to her. "You taste so good, like lilac, honey, and woman," Hugh said, before bowing his head once again.

I don't even know what that means. What does that mean?

Charles's hands came back to her breasts, and she screamed again, arching away from him even as he held on to her, massaging, teasing, holding and caressing her heated flesh.

Her hand flung out, tangling in Hugh's thick hair, but he was too far away for her to push, so she simply held on as Charles spoke. "Let it out, Amelia. Give it to the world. Nobody can hear you out here at the ends of the earth but us, and we're here with you. We want to hear you, every bit of the passion you have, whatever you say, however it comes. Give it to us. Don't hold back. Give us everything you have, my brave Amelia."

Brave.

Her foot twitched, and Charles lifted his leg, no doubt to prevent Hugh from being kicked in the head.

"Talk to me, Amelia, talk to us. Seeing you laid out here before me, as Hugh gives you pleasure, is one of the most erotic things I've ever been witness to. Tell me what you feel. Tell me what you like."

"I…I like…"

We will not judge you.

She closed her eyes to concentrate. "I like the feel of…of his tongue."

She felt something. What did she feel? She concentrated, looked down at Hugh and realized what it was. She felt him smile against her. *There.* She felt Hugh smile against her most intimate parts. It was the oddest sensation.

She'd felt him smile against her neck, against her mouth. Perhaps that's why this was so familiar—yet so *not*. Then his tongue flicked out and delved between her lips, and she simply lost her train of thought.

"Oh God oh God oh God, I can't—" She twisted, and Charles's arms roved. He tucked his head to the crook of her neck and sucked at her, kissed, bit her flesh then soothed it with the sweep of his tongue.

Hugh blew a breath over her. "Amelia, there are no words for the beauty that is you. This—" He circled and licked the little crux at the top of her quim, and she shuddered against his mouth. Hugh moaned.

Our hands, our mouths, our tongues…your body.

Her other hand flew to Hugh's head, as though she attempted to push him off again, but she found herself holding on tighter, not wanting him to leave.

Our hands, our mouths, our tongues…your body.

Nothing between us.

She spun. Like a sudden drop, then complete darkness. She could hear muffled words, as though someone spoke on the other side of a linen closet.

Amelia concentrated.

Amelia, stay with me, darling.

Amelia concentrated, but knew it was too late. Amelia succumbed to the darkness as the wet warmth left her to the cool air of the Cliff House.

Charles knew the second she was gone. Her body swayed and released, but not in the way they'd wished. Charles had never held her, been close to her, at the point at which her episodes took away with her completely. He saw her hands fall away from Hugh, and he lifted, shook his head, her arousal clear on his face. "It was so sudden. There was no—"

"Just…give me a moment," Hugh said.

He smoothed his hands down her chest and abdomen, then back up. "Speak softly to her," Hugh said.

Charles brought one of his hands to rest just above her heart. Then, because he simply couldn't help himself, he leaned in and licked her ear before he whispered, "Amelia, my darling, my life, my love. Come back to me. Come back to us. Hugh is here. We're both here. We haven't gone anywhere."

Hugh's hands continued to minister to her, running across the landscape of her body, and he smiled up at Charles, calming him, as Charles continued to speak. "Amelia, you haven't gone anywhere. You're here with us, in the Cliff House. There's no judgment here. There's no pain. Only joy, only happiness, only love. Come back to us. We're waiting for you." Charles's voice broke on the last words, and he saw her skin react to Hugh's touch, the blush chasing the movement of his hands.

Hugh knelt and moved closer to them, his hands lighting on her torso again, and Amelia's chest heaved under his hands, as though her breath was the first of her to return.

"You're safe. You're with us," Hugh whispered.

Amelia took another breath, and Charles felt his life was returned with the words that followed.

"Why did you stop?" She said the words so quietly Charles thought Hugh could not possibly have heard. But her answer came in the return of Hugh's mouth, his tongue, and the scream that rent the peace of the moors in two.

Amelia's hands returned to Hugh's dark curls between her legs, as though nothing had happened, as though she'd never left them. Her nipple peaked beneath Charles's hand, and he stayed the desperate need to hold her tightly against him and never let loose.

Amelia screamed again and again, indecipherable words that included both of their names in innumerable ways, woven tightly with *God* and *please* and *more*. Charles was overwhelmed, overwrought, absolutely spent in the most wonderful and joyous way imaginable.

Charles saw Hugh's hand smooth down her thigh, below his mouth and knew when she surged forward on yet another scream that he'd breeched her, and she was spent. The racking sobs shook her body and his soul, as Hugh rode the wave of her body to the shore, then soothed her aching muscles as she relaxed across Charles's chest.

Hugh reached up and massaged her hands until they released his hair, then laid them on her chest. Hugh leaned back on his knees and scrubbed his hands across his scalp. Charles shifted with her, bringing her in front of him on his side. He motioned to Hugh, who crawled up the bed, pulling a sheet with him.

They tucked her between them and let her sleep.

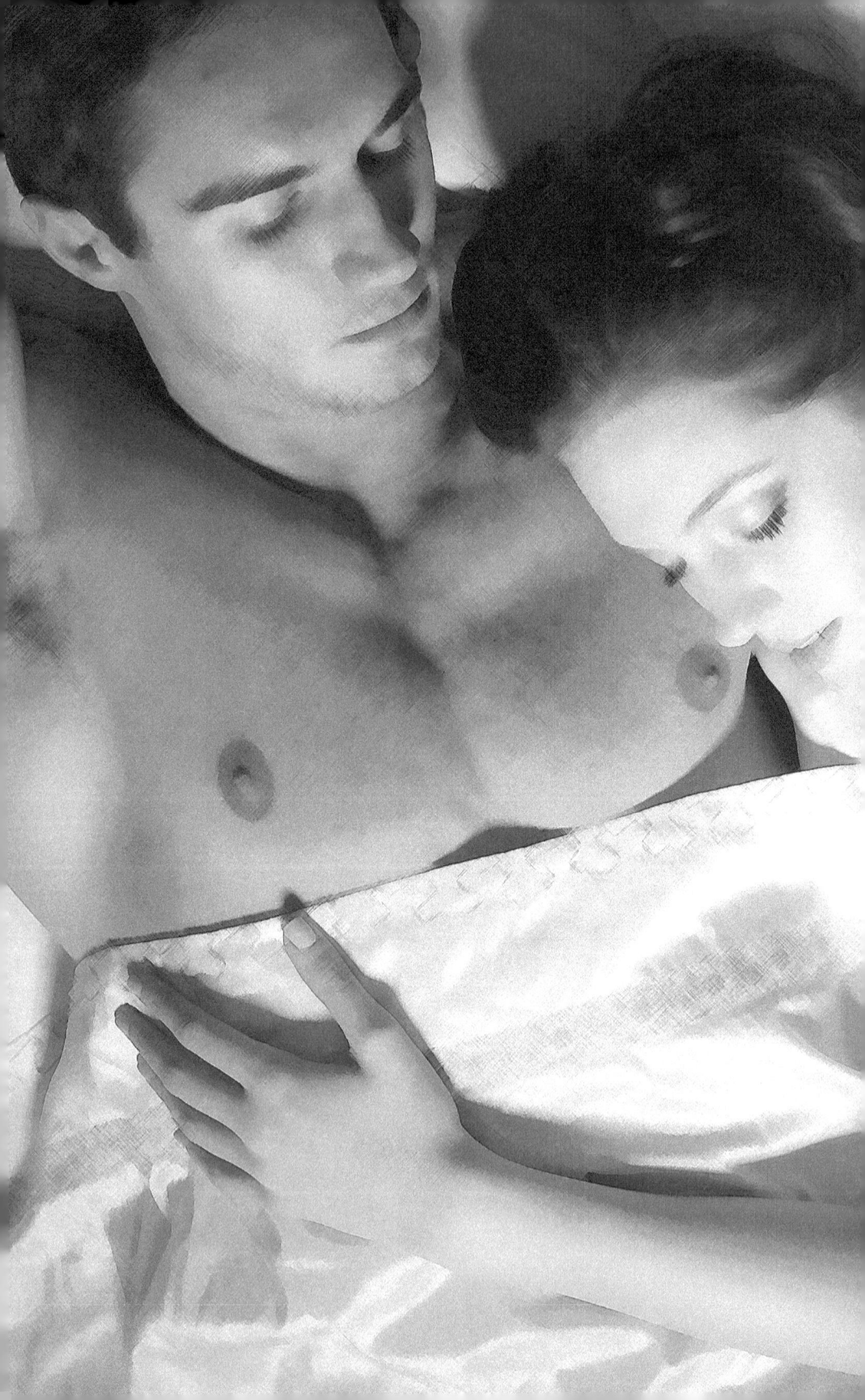

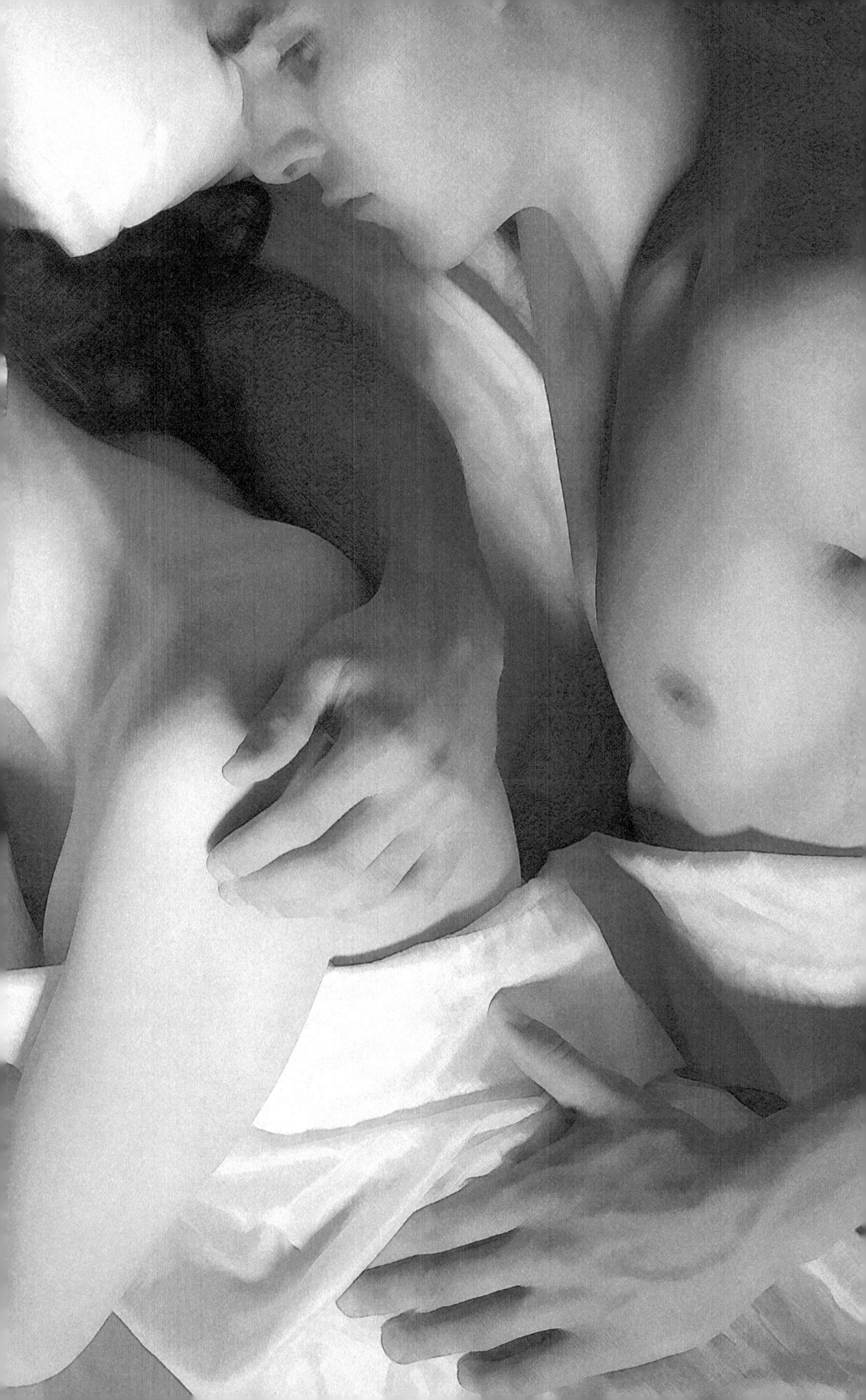

FIFTEEN

"That was…" Charles's voice was gruff, breaking at the edges.

"Yes," Hugh said quietly.

Hugh faced Amelia on the bed as she curved into Charles's strong frame behind her. Charles had his head propped up in his hand and was staring down at her with a wondrous look on his face.

"I wasn't sure I could do this," Charles said.

"You mean watch another man pleasure her?" Hugh asked.

Charles nodded.

"More than that," Charles said. "I could see her connection to you, and what's more, I could feel that connection through her. I—"

"I don't understand," Hugh said.

"I mean that…I could feel her calm come from you." Charles closed his eyes and breathed slowly. "She truly needs you, Hugh."

"Soon she will be with only you, as it should be," Hugh said.

"No, I don't think so," Charles said.

Hugh stopped the hand that was caressing hers gently as she slept. Stared at it. "Charles…we did all of this so she could be with you. I don't understand."

"Neither did I…I can't begin to explain to you the feeling. I don't even know how to put this into words. I could *feel* her physical reaction to your proximity. When you moved away, she tensed. When you drew near, she relaxed. When you spoke, she nearly melted into me. It was a tangible thing. It was a physical reaction. She needs you," Charles said.

"Are you attempting to cry off?" Hugh was confused. He didn't understand what Charles was trying to say in explaining this to him. Further, he wasn't entirely sure Charles wasn't simply looking for excuses to be done with this situation. Perhaps he couldn't manage the three of them, but it was a temporary arrangement. They both knew that.

Charles's eyes clenched, and his hands drew to the bridge of his nose and pinched as his hand shook. His entire arm shook. As Hugh concentrated on the slight movement, he realized the *whole* of Charles shook, as did the bed they all lay upon.

Hugh wasn't sure what to do.

Charles still hadn't answered him.

"Charles," Hugh said again quietly. Charles didn't respond. "Charles, you must marry Amelia. It's what she desires above all else. But more than that. She belongs with you…Charles." Hugh reached out over Amelia, placed his hand on Charles's forearm, not gently—because that would have been awkward—but not so strong that he would jostle Amelia between them. "Charles."

Charles's hand dropped to her shoulder then swept down her arm and rested around her waist, his hand taking the sheet and fisting it. Charles dropped his face to the crook of her neck and seemed to just breathe of her. Hugh's hand found her hip, below Charles's, and he waited for Charles to speak.

"She belongs with me," Charles said finally. "But she belongs *to* you. I…you belong with her. You should always be at her side. I cannot come between you. I *will not* come between you."

"Charles, we've only just begun to settle this whole matter. We cannot possibly go back again, change everything we agreed on…"

"Then find another solution." Charles paused. "There isn't one, is there?" he asked, full well knowing the answer would be no.

"Her father will not allow me to marry her. He'll not allow us to be together," Hugh said, then shook his head. "Regardless of my position in her life…she's meant for you." Hugh attempted to control the timbre of his voice so as not to disturb Amelia, but the control was becoming more difficult.

"If I step aside, if I cry off—" Charles tried, but Hugh cut him off.

"You will *ruin* her! None of this will have mattered!" Hugh tensed, attempted to rein his anger again.

Charles shook his head. "Then help me figure this out. I will never be for her what *you* are for her. And I won't...I can't...take that away from her. It's part of what makes her whole," Charles said as he leaned into her, pulled her close. "I don't want pieces of this woman. I want all of this woman. Without you..." Hugh watched as Charles breathed deep of her, seemed to hold on as if to the last thread of his lifeline. Charles looked as though he was saying good-bye, and an answering pain sounded somewhere in the vicinity of Hugh's heart.

If ever Hugh had a doubt about the honor of this man, he repented for that now. Hugh would see Charles and Amelia married if it was the last thing he ever did. Amelia deserved this man. She deserved this unwavering strength. She deserved to be loved, the way Hugh could plainly see that Charles loved her—whether Charles was aware of it or not. Hugh knew that this was what Amelia wanted for herself. She wanted to be with Charles. More than anything else, she wanted to be Charles's wife. Knowing how difficult her illness was for her, how much she would face and need to overcome, Hugh knew, more so than any person in the world, how powerful her need of this man was. To face these difficulties, she needed Charles's strength.

This was her choice. Charles was *her* choice, and Hugh would see it done. There was no other solution to this.

"Charles, I need you to keep the faith. We are not yet at the point at which either of us can leave her. We both knew this would not be easy. The truth of it, the physicality of it, is obviously more difficult than I believe either of us expected. But we've begun this. Have some faith, for her sake. Please give this a chance. Please let us finish what we've started."

Amelia heard their words penetrating her dream, ever so slowly.

I cannot come between you.

It was disturbing at first, since she was dreaming of the two of them to begin with…but not quite in the way they were discussing here in bed. Well, they were in bed as well, but not—

She twitched. Just a quick shake of her head to move the thoughts along, to stop the circling. She opened her eyes slowly to find Hugh watching her, silently smiling. After a time, he spoke to her.

"You were dreaming," Hugh said.

She brought her hand to her cheek to wipe some wetness away. Had she cried? She watched Hugh's expression sadden, and she closed her eyes to concentrate on the words that had seeped through her semiconscious state.

None of this will have mattered.

I will never be for her what you *are for her.*

I can't…take that away from her.

It's part of what makes her whole.

I will not come between you.

Her eyes popped open and found Hugh's. She knew why Hugh was sad. "Where is he?"

"I'm here," Charles said quietly, from just behind her.

Funny, that. He was right there. She was burrowed into the lee of his form, and she was so comfortable there that she hadn't even realized he was a separate person. Her heart picked up a beat to know it. Would that she could make this comfort with Charles happen at will. She wiggled into him, feeling the solid warmth of his chest behind her, his legs cradling hers, her head pillowed on his arm. She reached out to Hugh and pulled him close as well, his body curving around hers, his head resting against her chest.

Her fingers played in Hugh's curls as she thought about the words they'd spoken around her, then her mind shifted to her tombstone. What would it say?

Here lies Amelia, between two mostly naked men.

An improper young lady.

A disappointment to her mother, and London in general.

And she realized…she simply could not be bothered to care.

"Can I tell you what I want?" She spoke to both of them as she stared at the ceiling.

Hugh nodded against her chest, as Charles's deep voice acquiesced.

We will not judge you. They'd said that earlier, and she hoped it still applied.

"I want for you to touch me. Again," she said.

"Amelia, I shouldn't—" Her hand reached up and covered Charles's mouth, stopping his words. She knew he was attempting to distance himself because he believed she should be with Hugh…or something like that. But she refused to hear it. Right now, right here, they were together, and she'd never had this full peace, this whole self, this completeness.

While she'd always been safe with Hugh, there had always been part of her in want of Charles, and this was like the missing piece of her puzzle. Right now, right here, she had all her pieces come together, slide into place. Amelia wanted to hold on to that for just a while longer. And then they would face reality, difficulty…pain—undoubtedly—and the future. She realized she'd merely thought all these words and wished she'd actually voiced them. She tried to force them from her lips, to explain to these men, but couldn't.

"Please just…touch me. That's what I want," she whispered. "For the moment, leave tomorrow for another day."

Hugh moved first, pulling the sheet down her chest as he lowered his mouth to one nipple, ministered to it, swirled his tongue and gently drew on that nipple, and from there her world exploded. She could never get enough of how their hands worked in tandem, how they were everywhere at once, how they never collided or overlapped, but instead moved as if choreographed perfectly, covering the expanse of her skin with lightning speed, igniting her blood within. The sheer improperness of the situation once again attempted to sway her, but she locked the thought away, took her own request, and left tomorrow for another day. Doing that was easier at the moment, because she'd already suffered severely today. It would take longer to wind her up again. She had some time, and she meant to use it.

Charles's hand slipped from her waist, pulling the sheet farther down her figure, then the bare skin of his fingers skated across her abdomen until his hand cupped her quim, the heel pressing just at the crest where she wanted his touch most. Charles wasn't going to wait for another invitation, it seemed.

Thank God for that, she thought.

Amelia arched against him, her hips pushing back into his, her breasts pushing against Hugh, who seemed perfectly happy to be drowning in her soft flesh.

Her hands moved down the ridges and valleys of Hugh's chest, then curled around the waistband of his trousers and held on. He froze as if cold water had been thrown on him, his hands covering hers, and she looked at his face.

"Is this not…is this not part of what you intended to show me?" Amelia asked quietly. She could feel the hard ridge of Charles's arousal

cradled by her bottom, the tip of Hugh's erection just under her thumb beneath the fall of the fabric she held on to. She ran a thumb over Hugh's erection, and he tensed, groaned. He sounded pained, and she was suddenly more concerned than upset by his change in demeanor.

"Amelia, we hadn't intended to—"

She swept her thumb across his hardness again, and a stiff groan cut across his words.

"I want to see what passion looks like in you—and in Charles," she said. "I believe that only fair."

The heel of Charles's hand pushed into her, and her breath caught. "Don't—" She closed her eyes and concentrated. "Don't you dare try to distract me, Charles," she finished. Charles smiled against the back of her neck, and she looked up to the ceiling. "I…I find myself quite curious."

"As you please," Charles said. "Since Hugh seems to be in a convenient position…"

She clenched her eyes.

"Oh, thank you *very much*, Charles," Hugh said, his voice strained and breaking across the words. Hugh didn't seem to be happy about this turn, and she was confused. Then she felt his hardness wane.

"I don't understand. I enjoyed very much what happened, and from what I know…neither of you were brought to that same enjoyment. *Before.*" Amelia knew her speech was halted and difficult.

"No, that we did not…we…honestly, we didn't think that far ahead…or perhaps we thought that part would not be necessary," Hugh said breathlessly.

"So you discussed it?" she asked.

"We discussed *your* passion, Amelia," Charles said. "We did determine that it may be difficult for either of us to *come off* with another man in attendance and never quite reconciled that," Charles finished simply.

"To…*come off,*" Amelia said. She had *come,* and they had not, and she felt terribly selfish in that knowledge, regardless, she realized, that that had been their intention. "I see." She thought for a moment. She could wait, but she didn't want to. She wanted to know what passion looked like on them. She believed being a witness to passion an integral part of the process, in fact. She swept her thumb across the front of Hugh's trousers again, and his size bloomed beneath it.

"Please," she whispered. She looked to Hugh, caught his dark gaze, pleaded with him with her eyes. She saw a stiff nod, and she moved her hands to the buttons that kept him from her. He lay still beneath her hands, save that one spot that grew again—slowly—as his breath stilled.

Six buttons. That's all that lay between her and him. Amelia's gaze moved to her hands, and she concentrated. She loosed the first button, then stilled. *Charles.* "Charles, is this—"

"Carry on." Charles's voice was gruff against her ear as his fingers began again to do amazing things to her.

"As a lamb to slaughter," Hugh grumbled. "I cannot believe it. We were to work together, and *you* have effectively thrown me under the carriage wheels, the sacrificial son."

"You're mixing your metaphors, Hugh," Charles said quietly, and she shivered against his hot breath on her shoulder.

"Damn you," Hugh whispered as the third button slipped free. He flung his head back against the pillow. "I can't watch this."

I can, she thought. *I most certainly*—the sixth button slid free, and the fall of his trousers was loose—*can.*

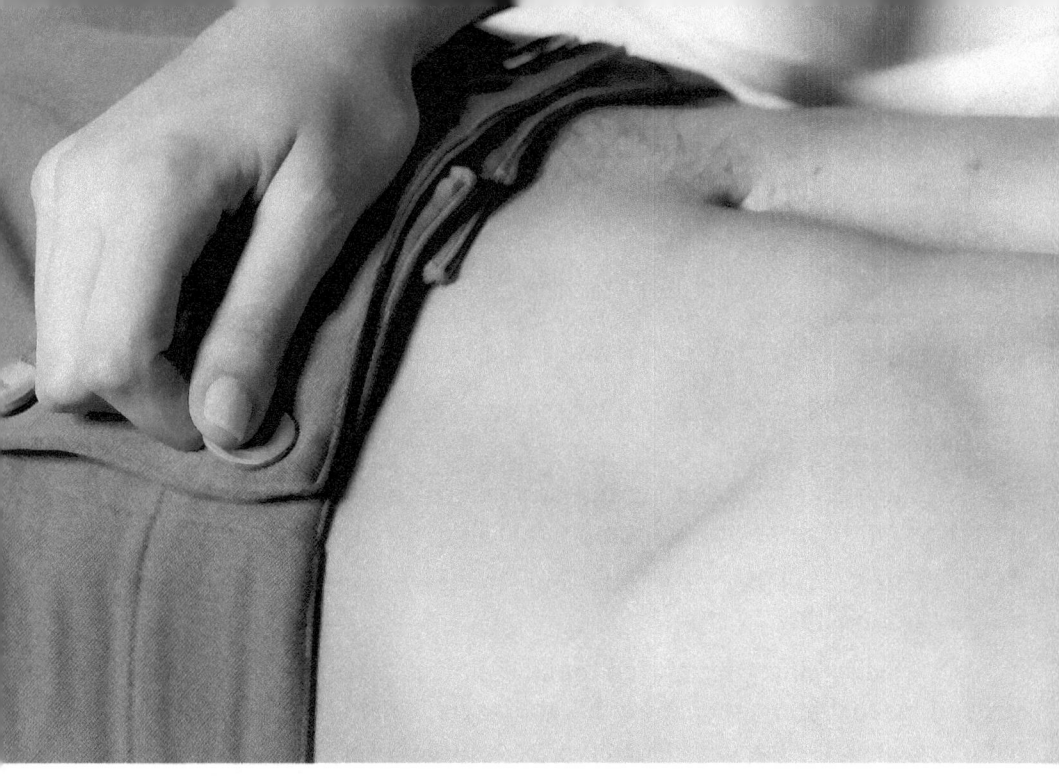

She brought her hands to her mouth as she chewed on her lower lip, deep in thought. Charles had moved a hand to her breast and was doing something incredible her nipple, making it quite difficult for her to concentrate.

She saw Hugh move his gaze from the ceiling to the contact between Charles's hand and her breast, and as her gaze shifted back to the fall of his trousers, he grew. She saw his hardness expand, the fabric of his drawers pulling tight across his...*maypole.* She shook her head. *Penis. It's a penis,* Amelia thought. At least, she *thought* she thought it. But perhaps she hadn't, because Charles smiled and laughed against her shoulder blade, and Hugh...

"Dear God!" Hugh exclaimed.

She reached for it. With her right hand. She kept her left hand at her mouth to attempt to contain any further inappropriate words that may escape. She watched as her fingers undid the top button of his drawers, and she could see the skin pulled tight around the appendage, like a sleeve. She ran a finger across the very edge of that overskin, felt the wetness it held back, and heard a string of curses the likes of which she'd never—not ever, not even on his worst day—heard from Hugh.

Charles's arms tightened around her, holding her together in a miraculous way, one hand still at her breast, the other returning to her nethers.

She loosed the last button. She'd been wrong—there were eight buttons, the six of his trousers and the two of his drawers—but she couldn't have known this until now, obviously, because—

"Ahhhh…Amelia. For fuck's sake, you're killing me," Hugh groaned.

She reached out, but her bravado faltered, and her hand stopped just there, within a breath of his manhood. "I don't know what—"

Charles cut her off. "Take him in hand, Amelia. Wrap your fingers around him."

Amelia's fingertips grazed the silky skin as they passed, reaching around his shaft, then meeting at his abdomen. It was…like a steel pipe, wrapped in skin—no, not just skin—the softest, most supple skin she'd ever felt, like the skin of her lips, or her nipples. She moved her other hand to one breast and slid a finger around her nipple in a circle. His skin was not like the peak of her nipples, mind, but just around it. She smiled at the thought, then grew serious to her task once again.

"Now what?" she whispered.

"Whatever you wish," Charles groaned.

She slid her hand gently up, toward that opening of flesh. The very end of his penis was round, and it was softer there, more pliant, and wet, almost as though it cried for her. Drops of moisture slicked her thumb as she ran it across the tip.

Charles groaned again, against her back. She could feel his nose on her spine as he looked away, and she wasn't sure he looked away because he was upset to see her touching another man or—

He can't become hard when upset.

She remembered that. So she pushed her hips back into his and felt his hardness. She knew he was aroused, and the knowledge shot straight to the point where his hand connected with her quim. Earlier, Hugh had gotten aroused watching Charles's hand on her breast. Yet they'd both been concerned about being able to *come* in the other's presence.

They liked what they saw.

"Oh God," she whispered. This was so…*something*. She couldn't take her eyes from that part of Hugh.

Hugh grumbled unintelligible words, and Charles's hips pressed hard against her backside as Charles spoke. "Move your hand slowly, up and down the length of him," he commanded, and she did.

"Hugh, I'm not…can you please help me?"

Hugh moved slowly, his muscles jerking. His hand wrapped around hers, skimming it up and down his hardness, then he held her tighter around him than she would have done and repeated the motion. The skin slid along his length below their joined hands. She pulled her eyes away for a moment to look on Hugh's face. He looked pained.

She looked back to where Hugh worked her hand, and Charles slipped a finger between her legs. Charles moved between her slick folds in an identical rhythm to her hand on Hugh—and she knew he was watching. Charles's hips moved against her in the same rhythm as well, and she pushed back, caught the rhythm set by Hugh, and held on.

Charles's breath was heavy on her neck, Hugh's chest heaved as his hand moved with hers, his strokes becoming faster, and her breath stilled. Hugh bucked, and Charles's mouth opened on her back. Hugh leaned up, his abdomen tensing and folding in on itself, then he stretched out and thrust into her hand. At the same moment, Charles pushed one long finger into her tight wetness and closed his teeth gently on the skin between her shoulder blades.

She screamed and held on to Hugh as the crisis coursed her spine, rested in her womb, then sent the shocks outward, her vagina clenching around Charles's finger as white jets streamed from Hugh, landing on his belly.

Hugh held on to her, she held on to Hugh, Charles held on to her…they were all together.

The first thing Hugh perceived—after a time of simply lying in the bed with his eyes closed, trying to regain his breath—was her fingers on his belly, slipping through his seed. Amelia was so curious. His cock twitched yet again at the thought of her sweet innocence, and he groaned.

Her head shifted on the bed, her face turning up to him. "That was quite beautiful," she said.

Beautiful. She'd called this beautiful. The mess of him on his belly. *Beautiful.* She was truly, madly, deeply…incredible.

Hugh let out a breath, wondered how Charles had fared, but was simply thankful that he hadn't noticed much of Charles during the whole…*beauty* of it.

"This…is the seed you plant in me. This is what makes a babe," she said quietly as she swirled her fingers through it.

Amazing, Hugh thought. *A true innocent.* He'd always coveted that innocence, and this was most likely the reason he'd treated Charles so badly, saw the worst in him. Hugh should have been more wary of that particular commandment.

If anyone knew how innocent she truly was, it was Hugh, for he knew her better than anyone. He looked down at her hand, watched her—here, she was an explorer. And that did make sense, because she'd always been overly curious. Yet even the most curious of women were shy of his mettle if ever they saw it, and here, *she* thought his seed beautiful. Discussion-worthy even. He saw his cock twitch in the distance and laid his head back to the pillow to concentrate on…not twitching. He smiled, the realization that she was so familiar with that particular want coming across him.

The bed shifted, and Hugh knew Charles stood, so Hugh followed suit to break the moment, perhaps to attempt to regain his composure, certainly to prevent himself from *rising* once again. Hugh grabbed his ruined shirt from the floor and wiped himself clean before replacing the fall of his trousers. He turned to find Charles pacing, stiffly. Charles was yet the only one of them without release to this point.

Serves him right, let his bollocks twist a bit, Hugh thought. *Tossing me in front of a moving train like that. As it happens, I can come in the presence of another man.*

Hugh looked on Amelia, who studied her hand. Her brows were drawn together in confusion, but she'd never looked more beautiful than at this moment in her flushed, mussed state. *He loved her.* Truly.

Hugh stood, looking on her, and the realization that this was far from friendship hit him like waves on the shore, each one breaking across him larger and harder than the last until he knew he stood there aghast, arms akimbo, his fall buttoned crookedly, his jaw hanging open like a child's.

He'd always known he loved her, but he'd never allowed himself to accept it. *Crash.* To truly feel it. *Crash.* He loved his best friend. *Crash.* He had to let her go. *Crash.*

Hugh may have whimpered then.

He turned to Charles, who was watching him. "You understand now," Charles said.

Hugh felt his head shake, *more* than he felt that he'd caused it to do so.

Charles nodded in response.

Amelia watched them both carefully, pulled herself to sitting, curled up in the sheet against the head of the bed.

Charles turned and paced again. "I should go. I should let the two of you…do what it is you will do. I need to go," Charles said as he looked around the small cabin, most likely for his clothes.

"You're not leaving her," Hugh said as he turned on Charles.

"We discussed this," Charles said. "She needs you."

"She needs you as well! You're not thinking straight because your bollocks are in a bind!" Hugh yelled. The windows shook at the force of his voice, and Charles turned the full height of himself on Hugh, who drew himself up as well as they faced off. Charles lowered his chin as Hugh went on, "You cannot do this to her. If you wish the very best for her…that's you. I should be the one to go."

SIXTEEN

They were fighting about who was to leave her. Good Lord, had it truly come to this? A complete turnabout? The tension in the Cliff House soared, and Amelia wasn't going to sit by and listen to them discuss her, yet again.

Charles shook his head. "I'm leaving."

Hugh moved closer to him. "If you go, I go. If you stay, I stay." The statement sounded like a threat but that the last of it Hugh said quietly.

Amelia wasn't entirely sure of the silent message that passed between them, but could feel that they were communicating beyond words in the way they stared at each other.

Charles looked at Hugh then, more silence passing between them. Was she going to be required to get used to this? This silent intercourse? As if the communication they had about her, around her, wasn't bad enough, they managed to communicate without her even when she *was* present.

"Listen, you both need to stop this pointed staring. You're unnerving me," Amelia said.

They both looked to her, and she shrank. That wasn't exactly what she'd had in mind.

"Perhaps some tea?" she said quietly.

Hugh turned to Charles. "Have faith," Hugh said, practically begged, then he rested his hand on Charles's shoulder and held it for a moment before he turned to the kettle. Hugh moved the kettle over the grate, stoked what was left of the fire from earlier in the day and stood.

"I need to get some more firewood," Hugh said. "I trust you'll both be here when I return. The woodpile is just behind the house, after all." He seemed to be attempting to break the mood with idle chatter. He put his hands on his hips when no one responded, shook his head, then turned to the door and walked out.

Amelia looked at Charles then. He was staring at the door, and his intensity served to unnerve her further. "Charles." She said his name quietly, tightened her grasp on the blanket she held to her chest. "I… want to be frank with you, but I'm frightened."

Charles turned to her, appeared to consider something, then pulled up a chair and sat. She relaxed a bit as his large frame melted into the chair, his presence much less overpowering to her.

Charles looked at her as though to tell her to continue. He seemed frustrated with her, and she thought she understood why. "I know this is all very…difficult," she said.

Charles nodded but said nothing.

"I believe, in my heart, that if you learn the things that Hugh knows, that I could be the duchess you need."

Charles didn't move.

"I think, at this point, Hugh believes the same. If he didn't, he wouldn't be helping you…helping us."

"I understand that…now. I believe I understand more of the issues at hand, having been witness to them…finally," Charles said, and Amelia nodded.

She knew that her mother had kept this a secret from him as much as possible out of the fear he would not take her to wife if Charles knew the truth. Amelia realized, by his tenor, that he was frustrated at having been kept away.

Charles continued. "I don't necessarily believe that what you have with him will transfer to me…that what he does can be learned. Amelia, the only happiness I remember as a child was the time I spent at Pembroke-by-the-Sea. You know my life has been one of discord, difficulty, but I don't think you realize the level of joy I gained from simply *seeing* joy in you. I did not know how to be happy, and I believed that I could learn joy from you because it came to you so naturally. I was always told to ignore my feelings, to learn outwardly, not inwardly. So I thought to learn to be happy by watching you. Even if I couldn't learn...I wished to bask in the glory of your happiness, because it was so freely given."

Amelia stilled, she'd known his childhood wasn't the happiest. Charles wasn't raised by his parents as much as by the servants of his household. His father was distant, and then he was dead, and his mother was emotionally unavailable. How must it have been, as a young boy, to have nobody? She'd had Hugh, and without him—her heart knocked against her ribs in violent retaliation on the thought, then her vision narrowed, the edges darkening. If she'd never had Hugh...

No, not now, please not now...

Amelia closed her eyes and took a stilling breath. Hugh was close by, just outside. She lifted a hand toward the back of the house as though to feel his presence. Then she looked on Charles. He was here as well and wanted nothing more than to be with her. She breathed. Sank into the blankets and pillows on the bed.

Hugh...if there'd never been Hugh, she would have been forever lost.

She would have had nobody. She would have been so very alone.

Like Charles had been alone, completely alone.

Alone alone alone.

And he had been so small. He'd reached out to her...and been denied. If Hugh had denied her at such a moment—

But. He. Never. Had.

The spin and the dark of her illness began to crash in on her.

"Amelia—"

She realized she hadn't said anything, Charles had just laid his soul bare before her, and she had closed herself off. What must he think of her now? She had to at least say something.

Say something!

Her eyes popped open. "I believe I understand what that kind of loneliness would feel like. If I had not had Hugh—" Her voice broke and swayed. She should not have voiced this, but she considered this much too late. Her head spun. She didn't want to think on this. She'd had Hugh. She still had Hugh. She wasn't rewriting history merely by speaking about this. "If I had not—"

This feeling isn't real. I have Hugh. I've always had Hugh.

Her arm flung to the side, meeting the bed, to steady herself.

Charles moved toward her, wrapped his big arms around her, lending her his strength. She sank into him but knew it was too late.

"Amelia, don't think on it. I should never have—"

"No! You should have. You most definitely should have. You should have. Most definitely. These are the discussions you spoke of, these are the things I wish to know of you, I want to know you. I do want to know you."

Please don't think I don't wish to know. I do...I wish to know. I wish to know everything, as if you'd been there, as if I'd lived it myself.

"I wish you'd not been so very alone." Her arms wrapped around his and held on. "I want to know you, I do. Please don't think that you can't speak on difficult things. Please don't think you must tiptoe around me. I simply need an anchor. I—" She was spinning then, truly spinning. Her mind had latched on to the loss of Hugh and made that loss a tangible thing to her.

Amelia's eyes closed, and her head fell back against the heavy wall of his chest...

You were so very alone.

So very alone.

Alone...

"Hugh!" His worried yell was the last thing she heard for a while, because when the darkness came that time, she was truly bereft of all safety. In her mind, Hugh was gone—as if he'd never been. The feeling of loss was complete, and she was met with a bleak emptiness.

SEVENTEEN

"Amelia, sweet, sweet Amelia." Amelia heard the heaviness of Charles's boots on the floor, like the beat of her heart, and his pacing steadied her. Hugh held her as Charles walked. They didn't speak to each other. Perhaps they'd learned how much it unnerved her. Perhaps they were following her wishes.

"Charles." Hugh said his name quietly, then the bed swayed beneath her, and he was there, she between them again—the warmth, the safety, the strength enveloping her.

"Amelia, I—" Charles stopped himself. He didn't want to say something again that would have that effect on her, no doubt. He'd said so much, and what he'd said had opened her eyes, while closing them. She'd felt his pain, *literally* felt his pain as her own. She took that pain into herself and couldn't stop it. She allowed the tears to run her cheeks, hot, wet streams of that sadness pouring from her soul.

Amelia reached out to Charles, took his hands and brought them to her chest, close to her heart. "You were so very alone, and we…we were not friends to you. We should have been friends to you. You should not have been left so alone," Amelia said.

Hugh's hold tightened on her waist, his arms like a steel vice around her.

Charles released one of her hands and swept the tears from her cheek. "Amelia, open your eyes." His breath was soft against her chin, close, warm, comforting. She did as he asked.

"I find it simply amazing and beautiful that you're so powerful, that you could feel my pain so many years later. I find it to be wondrous and incredible that you have a heart big enough to encompass not merely yourself, but all those around you. You are a miracle to me."

It wasn't nearly what she'd expected to hear from him.

She gazed into his eyes as they came closer, then his lips met hers, and the kiss was warm and strong, and in it the loneliness receded and vanished like smoke. Something that was never tangible to begin with was gone in a simple breath. Charles spoke without separating their lips.

"You are the strongest person I know, to be able to do this," Charles said as his mouth moved over hers. "Please know that I'm here to share this with you. You never have to face that kind of pain alone. Hugh is here to share this with us as well. You never have to feel that kind of loneliness. That kind of loneliness is behind us. The pain is behind all of us, because we have each other. We will always have each other."

She wrapped an arm around him, pulled him closer, closed her eyes, and fell into an exhausted sleep in the safest place she knew, between her men.

When next she woke, the sun was peeking in through the back windows, and Charles was holding her, his hands languidly roaming the curves of her backside, while his mouth languidly roamed the curves of her front side. She smiled against his crown, and he pulled back to look at her. "Good morning, beautiful," Charles whispered, then he kissed her. "Hugh is just outside. He believed we needed yet more wood and perhaps more blankets and sheets." The door opened.

"As well, a basket with eggs, bread, cheese, biscuits, fruits, a…few other things," Hugh said as he returned, closing the door behind him.

"Is that so?" Charles asked.

"Louisa would have brought me a basket this morning. She—" Amelia looked at Hugh. "Does she know you're here?"

Hugh nodded. "Someone needed to. Otherwise, it wouldn't have been safe. Servants orders or no."

Amelia nodded against Charles's chest.

"There's tooth powder, towels, and warm water just outside," Hugh said.

Amelia looked up at Charles. "Go on, you first," he said.

Charles sat up and pulled his shirt from the chair it was flung across. "Here, put this on," Charles said as he pulled her up before him, still warm in the sheet. Charles wrapped his shirt around her, letting the sheet fall from beneath the hem as he buttoned the neck, pulled her close for another warm kiss, and steered her toward the doorway.

Amelia pulled the door closed behind her and moved toward the little space Hugh had made for them outside on the table. So much

had happened yesterday. *So very much.* Her eyes had been opened to pleasure, and she wanted to feel that again at the hands of these men.

So many hands.

She washed her face and used the tooth powder on her finger to clean her teeth.

She used the cup and rinsed her mouth, then took up one of the small towels and doused it, unbuttoning the shirt that Charles had only just buttoned. She washed herself with the warm water, realized she was listening for their voices. When she heard the rumble of them, she gathered closer to the window and concentrated. They spoke of breakfast, eggs, coffee, tea—warm things that sounded so good to her at the moment. Her belly rumbled, and she realized just how hungry she was. They hadn't eaten any supper last night before they'd slept.

Amelia knew it was too much to ask that they not consider the future. Everything they did here was in preparation for that future, and if they didn't know what it was…well, what were they doing? She knew Charles was her future in the same way she knew her corset was worn over a chemise. It required very little thought. It merely was. It was the question of Hugh that sent her into a panic. She did not know how to live without him.

She would have Louisa, and Hugh had taught Louisa well, as he was now showing Charles. Yet it still wasn't the same. Though she wished it to be, there was something in her that settled with Hugh's very presence, a bone-deep knowing that everything was okay as long as Hugh was there. She wasn't sure how long it would take to feel that with Charles, and in the meantime…

Amelia looked out over the moors, let the soft breeze wash over her damp skin. Here she was, so very improper, standing at the edge of England with only the great sea as a witness, nothing on but the scent of Charles in his shirt. *This is all so very inappropriate.*

She grinned then turned to the house for breakfast. She was determined to embrace this…this impropriety. Because, for as long as she'd been concerned with being proper, it had done her no good.

Hugh slid the iron skillet over the grate, the eggs nearly done as Charles watched helplessly.

"Nothing?" Hugh said.

Charles shook his head. "No. I wasn't allowed to even wipe my own arse, much less touch something that could injure me," Charles said.

"Fire cannot injure you unless you fall upon it, and this one is contained below a grate, for the skillet, so even more safe than an open fire," Hugh said.

"Even still," Charles said quietly. "It got rather tiring watching my servants play with my wooden soldiers for me."

Hugh turned on him, though crouched as he was before the fire, the move was more of a swivel. "What the bloody hell were you going to injure with wooden soldiers?" Hugh asked.

"Put an eye out on a bayonet, I imagine," Charles grumbled.

Hugh laughed, then raised a hand apologetically, "Pardon, Charles, it's only laughable as it's so unbelievable and there's nothing to be done about your childhood at this point. However, as I remember, you had a governess who followed you around everywhere…"

Charles grinned down on him. "We aren't going to speak on my governess, and the rest is of no issue. It's long past at this point, and I agree, there's nothing to be done about that past." Besides, that past no longer bothered him. Charles wasn't that small, lonely child any longer. He had grown not merely in stature, but in the security of who he was. Still, he wasn't keen on taking a ribbing from anyone about it. And Charles made sure Hugh understood that fact well in the delivery of his decree.

Hugh stood and scraped eggs onto the plates. He put the skillet at the edge of the hearthstone, then pulled the kettle from the fire. "Coffee or tea?" he asked.

Charles looked at the coffee biggin and the teapot, then back to Hugh. "I'll take coffee…if you know how to prepare it well."

Hugh smiled and poured water into the teapot then set the kettle on an iron pot holder. He handed Charles a small tin cup, then pointed at the grinder on the wall next to the hearth. "Hold the cup below the spout and turn the handle."

Charles turned and looked at the contraption suspiciously. The grinder was a can with a lid and a big spindle crank on the front. Charles put the cup under the spout and turned the crank, quickly filling the cup with coffee grounds. Charles inhaled deeply. "Oh, now that is wonderful," he said. He turned to Hugh, quite proud of his accomplishment.

Hugh laughed. "Now place the grounds in the top half of the biggin. There's a linen pouch hanging in there."

Charles did as instructed, then watched as Hugh poured the hot water over the coffee grounds and placed a metal plate over them. "Now we wait."

Hugh closed the lid and patted Charles on the shoulder as he stared at the coffeepot. The hot coffee grounds smelled delicious.

Charles startled a bit when the door opened, and Amelia walked back in.

"There are such lovely scents pouring out from in here, my belly was complaining," Amelia said as she closed the front door.

Charles turned to her and froze. He'd expected to see her in clothes, for some incomprehensible reason, and he was struck once again by her mien in naught but his shirt. Amelia stood there in the morning light from the window across the room, her body outlined in his large white shirt. Charles ran a hand down his naked chest as if in response to that vision, as though he could feel her inside his shirt where *his* chest should be. Charles watched as her nipples peaked and realized from that that he was regarding her rather thoroughly.

Amelia brought her arms up, covering her chest from his view. Charles was hard as rock once again. That he'd not reached any sort of release the previous night didn't help. Charles's hands stirred, as if to move the hem of his shirt over the evidence of his arousal, but his hem was before him, not on him, and he was terribly exposed.

"Charles!" He realized Hugh had been attempting to get his attention. Apparently, he hadn't heard him the first time he'd called his name. Charles turned on him. "Your turn for the privy and wash," Hugh said with a grin. "Though I must agree with your assessment of the… situation."

"Yes, I…well." Charles smiled at Amelia, crossed his arms in front of his waist to attempt to hide his erection, then took one of her hands and kissed the back of it. He moved past her, closing the door solidly behind him. *Then* he breathed. And adjusted himself.

Good God, he needed to piss, and it was going to shoot like a fountain across the woods.

A

"Don't mind him. His mettle's backed up. Come, sit," Hugh said with a smile. He pulled a chair out and put a blanket over it, then helped her sit and pushed her forward. Hugh moved a plate in front of her piled with eggs, sliced tomatoes, bacon, and toast. "The coffee will be ready after Charles returns, or the tea should be ready now," Hugh said quietly. "Alternately, we do have a bit of chocolate. If you'd like to wait a moment, I could prepare that for you."

"No, thank you. I think tea will suit me just fine. Thank you," Amelia said.

Hugh smiled at her repetition and took the seat next to her.

"Are you well?" Hugh asked.

She nodded. "Last night was…well, yesterday was—" She shook her head. "This was an interesting idea, Hugh."

"Are you enjoying the lesson?" Hugh asked.

She was staring at his mouth…and nodded. Hugh reached out and swept his hand down her chin. "You are terribly beautiful in this mussed state. I find I could become quite used to seeing you like this." And Hugh knew he spoke the truth, even though him seeing her in this unkempt state very often wasn't bound to happen.

"Please, can we forget all the expectations?" she asked. "Expectation simply adds a level of discomfort that rather sends my head to spinning. I'm having a difficult enough time holding on as it is. I know you understand…"

"I do, and so I shall refrain from speaking of the future while we're here."

The door opened, and Charles walked in. "Damn, that coffee smells good. Is it ready yet?" he asked.

Hugh laughed again. He couldn't seem to help it this morning. "Yes, come on, finish what you started."

Charles approached him, and Hugh pointed. "Turn those two screws in tandem. It presses the plate, crushes the grounds, and releases the coffee."

Charles did as he was told, and the smell of fresh-brewed coffee intensified around them. Hugh loved the excited look on Charles's face. Truly, it was a little ridiculous how excited this man was about making coffee. "Right. Now, lift the top off the pot, put the lid on it, and pour yourself some coffee," Hugh said.

Charles did so, added a lump of sugar, then took a sip. Hugh thought Charles's eyes might roll back in his head. "That's…this is simply incredible. Why doesn't my coffee taste like this every day?" Charles asked.

"Well, most likely your servants steep the coffee once a week. Then the coffee probably tastes burnt, or old, because it is. They're just warming it up, or possibly burning it, in the same pot daily. For coffee to be good, it must be fresh. You need to try a cup with fresh roasted beans, that's something truly amazing. This is nothing. This is just coffee," Hugh said.

Charles shook his head. "It's coffee. It certainly isn't nothing. It's life, pure and simple." Charles looked at the table and took the chair across from Amelia. Hugh pushed a plate to Charles, and they ate.

Breakfast was incredibly good, but Hugh imagined that had much to do with the company and the fact that they hadn't eaten supper the previous night. It had been a long day, an incredible day. He could still taste her on his tongue. All he need do was close his eyes and think on it. Hugh wanted to be between her thighs again.

"Amelia, what do you wish to do today? Given why we're here, you should make some choices of your own," Hugh said.

Hugh watched the blush rise from the neck of Charles's shirt, then she looked at Hugh. "We should do some laundry. The two of you have no extra clothing, and you'll have need of it," she said quietly.

Silence. Then…

"Laundry," Hugh said, quietly nodding. Two men at her disposal, and she thought of laundry. Yet Hugh knew he needed to orchestrate ways for Charles and Amelia to be together alone, because the goal of this outing was just…for them to be alone together. Laundry, as it happened, was a perfect distraction.

A

"I will happily do laundry every day for the remainder of my life if it's anything like the laundry we did yesterday," Charles said, knowing what he said was the truth. Charles looked to Amelia. "You truly are beautiful today," he said.

She smiled genially as she smoothed her hair back and twisted it down over her shoulder. "So I've been told."

"Well, then you know it must be true," Charles replied. He shifted again in his seat as she watched. Her mouth dropped open slowly, and she looked as though she were considering something important. For his part, he couldn't wait to learn what it was.

"Is there anything I can do for you?" she asked quietly.

Charles looked at her, surprise surely plain on his face. He realized he was staring at her mouth, and his bollocks tightened further. He looked away. He shifted in the chair again uncomfortably. Then he looked back up to her eyes. She was pure innocence. She'd no idea the power she held, or the visions she created in his mind with her simple words.

The idea of her innocence was like a bucket of ice water to his groin, and he groaned with the sheer force of it, looking to the floor to attempt to gather his composure. Charles really was in a deal of pain. The pressure in his bollocks was becoming close to unbearable. He knew then, that when he finally did come, it would not merely be a force…but almost sheer pain. The erection he'd posted earlier could have buckled his knees had he not been a strong man, but he was thankful that, at the moment, he sat.

"No, Amelia." Was that his voice? It sounded so feral to his ears. Charles would deal with his bollocks later on his own, if need be, and the need *would* be, no doubt. Until then, he would simply deal with this pain.

"Is there something wrong?" she asked sweetly.

As she spoke, another sharp spear rent his spine and landed in his cods.

She seemed to be taking stock of him. Looking for damage somewhere that perhaps she could fix. If any other woman had said that to him in that tone, he would have thought her evil…but he knew Amelia to be honest.

Charles shook his head. "Nothing of immediate consequence. Nothing to bother yourself with." Charles attempted to smile then but knew his smile looked strained. From the corner of his eye, he could see Hugh was enjoying this a bit too much. Hugh's elbow rested on the table, his hand covering his mouth, his eyes wide, as he also watched Amelia. Charles attempted to ignore him.

Amelia's eyes widened, and her hands fell to her lap. Charles knew she was about to say something improper, because her eyes were darting about the room, as if to work up a bit of nerve. Charles watched as her mouth dropped open. "Hugh mentioned an issue…with your mettle."

He heard Hugh cough, choke on the bite of eggs he had in his mouth, hoped that the eggs went down the wrong pipe. Charles's throat tightened, and he nearly spit his coffee out, which would have been a great travesty, as good as the coffee was. "That isn't something we're going to discuss," Charles choked out.

"There seems to be quite a bit you don't wish to discuss *with* me. I grow weary of the things you don't wish to discuss *with* me," Amelia said, and Charles felt like an ass.

Hugh cleared his throat and stood, gathering their used plates. "Well, on that note I'm going to take these dishes out to wash, and see how much damage we did to the tub yesterday."

Charles shifted in his seat. They were silent as they watched Hugh walk from the Cliff House, and the door clicked shut quietly. They both stared at the closed door for a moment, then Charles turned to her. She seemed to be deciding on something, so he started. "I…well, Amelia, it's a bit discomfiting. You're an innocent, regardless of what's passed here already. You're innocent. I wouldn't wish to ruin you, and this process…" Charles took a deep breath to stop the maundering, pinched the bridge of his nose. "I'm frightened of a great many things—as well," Charles said, attempting to control the timbre of his voice. It only came out stiff and uncomfortable, and he hoped she wasn't put off by it. Charles needed to think on something else. "Hugh loves you."

"I'm aware," she whispered.

"I wasn't," Charles answered plainly. "He's explained as much… but the reality of it—" Charles shook his head. "This has all become incredibly complicated."

EIGHTEEN

"Yes, it has become incredibly complicated. Can you do something for me?" Amelia asked quietly.

"Whatever you wish." Charles looked into her eyes, and his attention was entirely palpable. She felt his look as she'd felt his hands yesterday, on her breast and her quim, his breath on her neck, his teeth and tongue on her back. She felt him everywhere, as though he'd marked her, and one simple glance was all it would take to recall that branding of her flesh. Amelia knew then, regardless of the physical status of her maidenhead, she was already ruined. She struggled to continue.

"I understand there's much to discuss. I understand we've a great deal of questions, all needing answers..." She paused and drew a breath, her skin tightening as his shirt rubbed all the wrong places on her. Charles was still watching her, and his gaze was unnerving. Amelia held on to his shirt, as though the fabric held her to the moment, which seemed to extend for a very long time. As it happened, intimacy was much more powerful than she'd ever expected. These men weren't merely in her mind but her body, and the farther they got into her body, the further they went into her mind.

She was virtually stripped and laid bare. Like they were standing over the ruins of her, examining in stark detail everything that made her who she was, all of her secrets. She pictured herself naked on the bed, Hugh and Charles with magnifying lenses, examining every detail and discussing their predicament logically over her—with no emotion.

"Amelia—"

She looked up to find Charles...the same look on his face that he'd just had in her daydream, the one that was attempting to figure out some puzzle.

"Where's Hugh?" she asked, as though she'd been sitting in thought for hours.

"He's still outside," Charles said quietly. The funny thing was, it didn't seem to bother him that she'd asked about the other man, and it had always bothered him to speak of Hugh before now. It seemed to her that they were taking all these giant strides, when in reality they were small steps.

"Lie with me?" she asked quietly.

Charles shifted, as though his body was so willing it nearly overpowered his conscious mind, then he stood slowly, his eyes never leaving her.

"Hugh is nearby, somewhere. There's nothing to fear," she said, considering what his hesitation may involve.

"It isn't merely that I worry about the effect I have on you, Amelia," Charles said quietly.

"I understand that you think I should be with him alone at this point because he can control me. Has it ever occurred to you that what you do to me…that the feelings I have with you are just as important? Even as uncontrollable as they seem to you?"

Charles shook his head as he pulled her from her chair, led her to the bed, and laid her down. Then he leaned in, one hand pushing into the bed beside her. Then one knee. He lay next to her, his shirt and trousers between them, even as they were, him with his trousers, she with his shirt.

"Tell me, then, about these feelings," he said.

Amelia closed her eyes and concentrated on him. "I feel your breath against my shoulder. I know what you're looking at even when my eyes are closed, because I can feel you breathe. My body…my body reacts to every breath. My heart…it's as though my heart knows you and wishes to leave my body to get to you," she said.

"What am I looking at now?" he asked.

Her breath left her in a rush. "My temple," she said.

Charles tugged the buttons loose from the shirt, then pulled the neck of the shirt slowly open across her chest. Her nipples raised and tightened, her body's applause, its acquiescence to his ministrations. The sensations were twofold, because as he separated the neck of the shirt, the bottom rose from where the hem had covered her, and a chill raced the skin over her abdomen. The mattress dipped and swayed around her as he shifted his very heavy body over her, yet not touching her with anything more than his breath.

"And now?" Charles asked.

She shuddered in response, trying to discern where his body was. Where his hands were, his legs, the rest of him, but all she could feel was his breath.

"Amelia, what am I looking at now?" Charles groaned.

"My…my breasts." Her voice wavered as if she wasn't too sure, but it was his proximity that had her confused. The bed shifted around her again, and she heard fabric tearing, then his shirt was open all the way to the hem, leaving her practically bare for him, a mere few remaining threads holding it together. She pulled her knees up, but they didn't move far, meeting with his rear end as he hovered above her, straddling her. *So that's where he is.* She let her knees fall to the side.

"What am I looking at now, Amelia?" Charles's voice was dark. Every inch of her skin reacted to it, but her mind stilled as she concentrated on what he was asking instead of what he was doing.

"My belly."

His hand eased her legs straight then, beneath him, and her heart sped.

"Amelia." The sound was low, physically, audibly, against her most intimate parts. Charles's breath and the ghost of a kiss coasted across one hip and then the other. Then he placed a kiss there, at the crux of her thighs, where Hugh had kissed her so intimately yesterday, and her mind swirled, began that march to spinning, and she did her level best to make the spinning stop.

"Charles," she said quietly, reaching for him.

Charles moved up the bed next to her, stretching out against her frame, his warm skin against hers.

"Amelia, do you realize that's the first time you've ever called for *me* when you…"

She opened her eyes, startled by his realization, and Charles was right there, looking into her face, watching.

"You knew. You could tell?"

He nodded.

"Charles." She reached for him then, turned toward him because she had to feel him under her hand. She held her hand between their chests first, the fingers gently curled, as though her hand waited for direction. Her eyes left his and stared at her hand, deciding what instructions to give. Then her hand flattened against his chest, her thumb smoothing the dark hair, and she looked back up into his gaze. Charles's eyes weren't focused, and she let her gaze travel over his features. Charles didn't touch her.

She pushed at his chest, and his back met the bed. Then her hand skimmed down that warm chest, swirling here and there around a mound of hard muscle, watching that muscle dance beneath his skin, shudder against her fingers.

Her thumb found the edge of Charles's trousers first, and he shifted, groaned, sounded quite concerned as the whole of him tensed.

"I just want to…" She saw his head shake.

"I'm at your mercy…but, please, I'm not entirely sure I can survive—"

She cut him off, smoothing her hand down his length, and he nearly doubled in half.

"Is this painful?" she asked.

Charles looked at her and nodded, his hand pulling hers away from his manhood.

"Why is this painful? I would think if there was pain men, wouldn't—"

Charles's face was strained, and for a moment, she didn't think he would answer her.

"Amelia, I am…stalled. I've been in want of you…in that very specific way, for quite some time. As a result, I—"

"Your mettle is backed up," she said the words plainly when they popped into her head. That's what Hugh had said. She watched as he closed his eyes and breathed very slowly. "Is there something I can do to help? I don't like to see you in pain." Charles's eyes opened on her, and she knew he would refuse to allow her this service of him. "Hugh allowed me to—"

"Amelia…the more we discuss my issue, the worse it becomes… please—" He still held her wrist, preventing her touching him.

"I happen to know that feeling." She pushed up from the bed and straddled him. As she sank down, her naked quim rubbing against the fall of his trousers, she could feel, for the first time, the true size of him cradled just where it was meant to be, before he grabbed her hips and lifted her slightly.

"Maypole."

A

What now? Charles thought. Amelia had both of her hands covering her mouth, her eyes terrified at the word that had spilled forth. He had no idea why.

"May...pole?" Charles repeated. His fingers were digging into her hips, the muscles of his arms vibrating as he held her above him to keep her from sinking down fully on his painful cock and bollocks. If he'd been anywhere but here, he would have alleviated the problem himself at some point...but here he hadn't had an opportune moment to get himself off.

Amelia's eyes widened, and her fingers paled in their tension against her mouth. "Amelia, I don't understand what—"

Hugh re-entered the Cliff House then, a bundle of laundry in his arms. "Maypole," Hugh said with a grin. "She's sitting on yours." His head tilted, "Well, she's attempting to, at any rate."

God's blood. Must Hugh bring his mind back to the pained ache in his belly like that? Charles was beginning to think Hugh's comments intentional. Certainly they were.

Charles watched as Hugh placed the laundry on the table without another word as Charles looked up to Amelia, who was incredibly pale. She looked terrified, and he needed to protect her. Charles pulled her forward to her knees, then brought the edges of his shirt closed across her chest. He then gathered her up against himself and held her, still attempting to keep her from brushing the painful cockstand in his trousers.

"Hugh?" Charles questioned.

"Tea," Hugh replied. Apparently they weren't to discuss this at the moment.

Charles sat up, shifted Amelia, then stood and carried her to the chairs before the fireplace. He sat and brought her with him to his lap, not quite ready to let her go in this moment. Charles could feel the slight tremors, but they also eased as he neared Hugh. It surprised him that the realization didn't bother him, when yesterday he'd been willing to let her go because of it. It was as though she were hiding in plain sight, perfectly quiet and still, avoiding eye contact. Charles wasn't entirely sure how to reassure her that he wasn't bothered by what she'd done, whatever she might have meant by it.

"A maypole is it then?" Charles asked finally, smoothing the hair from her face. "I'm…flattered."

She closed her eyes and hid her face in his neck, and he looked at Hugh for direction.

"A maypole. Our dearest Amelia has a copy of *Fanny Hill*. I believe that's what she was reading when we arrived yesterday," Hugh said.

She shook against Charles's lap, which wasn't exactly helping his issue, but she didn't open her eyes or look on him.

"Well, how on earth did you manage to find yourself a copy of *that* book. It's…not merely illicit, it's banned," Charles said. He smiled but knew the tension in his voice from his cods colored his emotions.

Hugh spoke. "I read *Fanny Hill* when I was quite young. I happen to have a couple copies, in fact. You could have asked me, Amelia. I'm glad you managed to find it, but I find myself curious as to how you did so as well." Hugh's voice was so light and gentle.

Charles tried to calm his nerves so he could match it. At least his erection was waning, receding back to the dull ache centered in his bollocks.

Hugh stirred a cup of tea, blew across the top of the tea and brought the cup to her mouth as Charles nudged her with his shoulder so she would see it. Charles watched as she sipped, her mouth cautious on the lip of the tea cup. Hugh's hands were careful as they tipped the cup toward her. Charles suddenly realized that he loved watching this interaction between her and Hugh. Charles loved being a part of it. Perhaps he could learn this intimacy from being close to them, as he'd learned about happiness so long ago. Being included was something he'd never been when they were children. When they were younger Charles had always been an interloper, a watcher, never invited, just…there.

Now…they were wrapped around him. Hugh had one hand on the back of the chair Charles sat in, steadying himself as he leaned in, tipping that delicate cup to her to drink from. Charles saw the steam from the tea drift toward him as he took a sudden breath on the realization

of their complicity. Charles couldn't leave her, no matter if he loved her. Charles wanted and needed her in his life. More than desperately. It was quite selfish of him.

Charles closed his eyes and thought back to yesterday, when they'd all been together. There'd been nothing disturbing about what they'd done. They'd worked in tandem for her. Could they continue this way? Charles needed a duchess who was to be the figurehead of his household. Charles couldn't share her with another man. There was no way for them to be together like this beyond today, tomorrow, the next day—whenever this lingering here at the Cliff House ended—and that thought saddened him.

Charles leaned into her neck, breathed of her as the tendons of her throat moved as she swallowed the tea. He concentrated on being here. Now. If they only had these moments together, Charles wanted to feel them, to be here with both of them, to feel her peace in the way he knew he would never feel with her when they were alone—because he knew that Hugh was an integral part of her peace. Because he knew he didn't love Amelia in the same way Hugh did, though he believed this burgeoning care he had for her might be some semblance of love, whereas before it had been merely the want of her.

Charles understood now just *how* integral Hugh truly was. Charles also understood why he'd been turned away when he'd begun to court her in earnest. Why, after they'd gone off to school and returned only on breaks, Hugh was allowed to stay while Charles was sent away. Now that he'd seen this, this powerful part of her, had seen how the episode had begun, how it progressed, how it felt to his hands and even his heart, Charles understood that he'd been turned away every time she'd become distressed because her mother hadn't wanted him to bear witness. Her mother had treated her issue like a dirty inconvenience. The truth was, her mind was one of the most beautiful things about her.

Her mother. *What a—*

Amelia needed Hugh because her own mother wasn't the least bit understanding of her illness. Hugh was the only person in her life she trusted, save Louisa, because Hugh had always been there, had never turned her away, was a rock of permanence in her twisting sea of emotion. Charles understood now, that for him to gain her trust, he had to do the same, and it could take years. After all, how long had Hugh been this for her? Charles *would* be this for her as well. Someday. It didn't change the fact that Hugh already was this person, and surprisingly, Charles didn't begrudge Hugh that anymore. But Charles knew without a doubt that to gain her trust, he could never remove Hugh from her life.

In fact, Charles had to find a way for Hugh to be part of their life, and Charles had to be sure she understood that Charles would never come between the two of them. In the mean, Charles understood what Hugh had tried to explain before, something Charles simply couldn't understand at the time. That this thing between Hugh and Amelia really wasn't something to be learned.

Charles still hoped that someday he might learn what it meant, how it felt, to be that close to another soul. Then, and only then, Charles might gain enough trust to be a part of her future. The man who could accomplish this truly did deserve her, and Charles meant to become that man.

NINETEEN

ugh could feel the tension in Charles next to him. Knew Charles was thinking their situation through and thought for certain that Charles would come to the proper determination. That Charles could not leave her, Charles could never leave her, Charles was her future and their life together was all entirely possible.

Hugh smiled. He couldn't help it. Amelia finally opened her eyes over the rim of the tea cup and looked at him, then at Charles and leaned against Charles's shoulder. Hugh downed the rest of her tea, then shuddered.

"Good God, woman, how do you drink this? It's sweeter than maple candies." This brought a smile, and Hugh felt the reward of it. Hugh looked at Charles and could see that he was relaxing some. Hugh knew he must be in a deal of pain and was impressed by his ability to put that aside. *Again*, he was impressed with this man. *Again and again and again.* Hugh shook his head and moved to another chair before the fire.

"So…" Hugh let the word drift off a bit. He wasn't entirely sure how to proceed at the moment, then his eye caught on the book he'd brought in with the laundry. He stood and retrieved it, then returned to the chair. Perhaps he could help Charles for once. The book fell open, and he read…

"Not the weapon of a man, but a Maypole, of so enormous a standard, that had proportions been observed, it must have belonged to a young giant. Yet I could not, without pleasure, behold, and even venture to feel, such a length, such a breadth of animated ivory! Perfectly well turned and fashioned, the proud stiffness of which distented its skin, whose smooth polish and velvet softness might vie with the most delicate of our sex, and whose exquisite whiteness was not a little set off by a sprout of black curling hair round the root…"

Hugh looked up to find them both staring at him. He grinned. "Well, the mystery of the *maypole* has been solved. One of them anyway." Hugh stood. Their eyes followed his every move. He leaned to Amelia, bussed her cheek, then slapped Charles on the shoulder. "I found the wash tub in perfect working order. So I've started a fire in the outside grate. I'm warming kettles of water, and I'll be doing some laundry. As best I can, at any rate." Hugh wandered the Cliff House, collecting random bits of linen, a sheet, his waistcoat, his shirt, then he turned back to Amelia.

"I need this as well." Hugh reached for the placket of Charles's shirt, his fingertips skimming the blushing flesh as he uncovered her chest further, then carefully, as she wiggled to help him, pulled the tail of the shirt from under her bum and pulled it over her head.

Amelia's hair fell to her shoulders in a shower of brilliant color. Her breasts bounced against her chest as her arms fell back to her lap, and if Charles had ever once thought he could never be harder, he'd been wrong every damned time. He heard the door to the Cliff House close, but he couldn't take his eyes from Amelia. "This is going to be painful," Charles said in that voice that he didn't recognize as his own.

Amelia's eyes widened, and her hands trembled. Charles shook his head slowly to and fro. "I was referring to myself."

Amelia's lips dropped into an O, and he caught sight of that perfect pink tongue, homed in on it, took her face in his hands as gently as his overwrought countenance would allow and brought her mouth to his. Charles sucked that pink from her mouth into his and held on for all his life, attempting to control his want…for he did not wish to give her any pain.

As well, Charles did not wish to ruin her just yet. Beyond that, it was not his choice that he should be the doing of it. It was hers. She may yet want Hugh to be the one to breach her maidenhead. It seemed all too likely, even as much as this one action yet rankled with him, but Charles would allow it.

Allow. That wasn't the right word, for it wasn't up to him to allow. That was to be her decision, and one Charles would not take from her lightly, because he wanted it—her maidenhead. Charles wanted it badly. That pure male part of him wanted to be the first to traverse her sweetness, be streaked with her virgin blood, to claim her in the most primal and official of ways. But his feelings for her allowed that this illness of hers may not allow for that.

Pure want had been bred into him. To relinquish that which he wanted was not a natural thing. It was difficult.

Charles pulled back and looked into her glassy eyes as a stray thought occurred to him. Could he raise Hugh's child as his own? He watched her face as though for the answer, even as he knew she'd no idea the question. Yet something more they would need to discuss, regardless that Hugh had no notion that these thoughts were in his head…and his head churned like a meat grinder on all of them. The thoughts, the considerations, the complications. This is what he did, and well.

Charles was trained to see all facets of a situation and find the most efficient, effective and prosperous path. That was of little help to him here. Charles needed to shift his paradigm. He needed the best possible outcome for Amelia. It was that simple…so not at all simple, really.

Charles smoothed a thumb over her cheek and thought he understood a little how her mind had off with her. If he couldn't control his runaway thoughts, if he were so passionate as to be unable to stop their flow, their power… He knew she had that in her without doubt, because he knew she understood to her very core his own loneliness. A loneliness Charles himself hadn't felt in years.

Amelia's hands came to his chest. Her thumbs teased his nipples, as her eyes dropped to his mouth.

"Amelia, I—"

She shook her head, then bravely stood from the chair, fully naked before him and not the least bit bashful in this moment. She was stunning, and Charles was floored. His breath stopped as his eyes feasted. He was pained, so very pained, but he watched her and knew he had to hold himself longer. Charles could see thoughts cross her face. Confusion, contentment, love perhaps, pain. He watched as all the evidence of her musings was clear in the emotion on her face. Charles stilled, waited for her determination. There was nothing about her that said her mind was having off with her, and until there was…he would give her all the time she needed.

"There is something…" She paused as she considered more. "I don't think I can live without Hugh."

"I've also made this determination, and I intend to see to it that he agrees to be a part of our life together," Charles said quietly.

Her chest hitched in a sudden breath, and he knew she was caught off guard. "How will this affect your position?" she asked.

"It won't. I'll not allow it. Somehow…we'll figure this out. I'm not sure what this will look like, as I only just determined it necessary. While I hope that someday you trust me—"

"I do trust you," she said, cutting him off.

"I understand that what you have with him is deeper than that, and for lack of a better word, trust is the one we'll use. Thank you, though, for trusting me," he said.

"I do. I merely have to convince my mind of that fact and—"

"And there's no telling how long that would take. Years perhaps… perhaps never. Hugh has been part of your life since you were very young. You truly love him, and he you. I've considered it entirely possible that this is what binds him to you, and there's no way to sever that. No way to imitate it as well. Beyond that, I could never in good conscience destroy something so…incredible." Charles's calm talk on the subject impressed even himself. "Hugh will need convincing. He believes that he'll throw us together and move on with his life, but I can see in him that moving on isn't possible. I saw the realization in him earlier, but he's refusing to accept it." Charles took her hands in his, smoothed his thumbs over them, then looked back up to her. "I don't think this conversation is what Hugh expected when he read from *Fanny Hill* and removed your shirt."

Amelia laughed, and he basked in the glory of it, allowed his pure enjoyment to show on his face, then pulled her to him and wrapped his arms around her and held on. Her hands tangled in his hair, and her breath quickened in the movement of her belly against his cheek. Then Charles felt a tremor, and he looked up to her.

"I need…we need Hugh."

Charles stood as his hands skimmed up the length of her, then he kissed her quickly and went to the door without a single complaint or question. He opened the door and paused there. Charles was strong, efficient, reasonable—all things she never felt in herself. Amelia moved to the bed, pulled a sheet from it, and wrapped herself up. She turned to see them both watching her, then he shut the door and waited.

She clasped her hands on the sheet, in front of her breasts.

Her aching breasts.

She knew what she wanted. Amelia now understood what Charles meant by *want*. Charles was always talking about his *want*, and until yesterday she'd not understood. She wanted for Charles. She had this incredible want of him, to have him inside her physically as he was already in her blood and her mind. The problem was that every time she was close to him, she lost herself, so concentrated was she on him that her mind would spin, she forgot to feel, and then—without Hugh—she was gone.

She took a deep, steadying breath and was thankful for the sheet—more due to fear than modesty—because she wanted to hide.

"I believe we've come to the point at which we need to make some very specific decisions," Amelia said.

Hugh and Charles exchanged a glance, then looked back to her.

"Charles, I've always expected to marry you. It was a foregone conclusion in my mind. I was told you could protect me and that you were necessary to my future, and I've believed that wholeheartedly. What I wish for you to know is that in the interim years between our ridiculous childhood and the moment you began to court me in earnest, my opinion of you changed.

"It wasn't merely that you grew into a man, but that you're growing into your heart, and I can plainly see myself in there through all the confusion."

Charles swallowed hard, looked away, pinched the bridge of his nose, then looked back to her and nodded. She wasn't sure whether she expected him to say something, but it wasn't necessary.

Amelia turned to Hugh. "Hugh, you've always been." She shrugged. It was that simple. "That, my dearest friend, is the crux of it. You're a requirement in this life even though I cannot see a solution. I love you now more than I ever have before, because I've seen a possibility in you that I never knew existed." Amelia saw Hugh's eyes widen, then they darted to Charles and back to her.

"That is…the simple of it," she said quietly.

The room was silent, and Amelia looked at Charles, who turned to Hugh.

"She'll not give you up." Charles paused, taking stock of Hugh, who seemed to be very concerned with his shoes. "And…neither will I. You're a requirement to what makes this work. I know not how this will happen. I only know that it will, and the sooner you come to terms with that fact, the sooner we'll all be able to live."

Amelia watched as Hugh shifted uncomfortably, and it seemed an age before he spoke. "I came here…I brought Charles here…for you, Amelia." Hugh looked up and caught her eyes and refused to look away, would not allow her to shy. She was caught. "From the moment we arrived, I've wondered how I would be able to walk away from you after this. The easiest of all scenarios was to toss myself from these cliffs, because there would be no return, no feeling, no life to argue afterward." Hugh's voice quavered.

Amelia could see in his gaze nothing but the reality of this statement, that death would be the easiest way to walk away from her. "I knew this would happen," she said. "I knew you could not be pulled into this without damage to yourself, and I warned you. Hugh, I…know that feeling well, but cannot allow for that to happen."

"You misunderstand me. I would never, not ever, take the easy way out where you're concerned, Amelia. Were I that kind of man, I wouldn't be worthy of you." Hugh stilled. Waited. She was sure none of them knew *what* they waited for. Hugh looked peaceful, as though he'd been holding this back.

Charles, on the other hand, looked much more…aggrieved and pained. She wished to alleviate this, at least the physical aspect of it.

So very much.

"Charles?" she said quietly.

"It seems we are at an impasse," Hugh said.

Charles tensed. Looked rather angry.

Amelia closed her eyes and willed her mind to the point at hand. She looked at Charles, who stood not far from the bed, his jaw tight as he took her in. "I want—" She cleared her throat…the spin, the spin, she knew an episode was coming. She forced her mind to embrace it, but she needed to get through this next bit for her plan to work. She knew Charles was at a tipping point. In all she'd learned from *Fanny Hill*, in everything Hugh and Charles had said, in everything she'd seen in Charles's very actions, she knew Charles could not hold off if pushed. As for Hugh…she closed her eyes and hoped.

Please, God, let me say my piece, she thought as she allowed the swirl to gain.

She opened her eyes. Her heartbeat raced.

Keep it short and sweet.

She looked directly at Charles. "I demand that you take me to wife, Charles." Her chest heaved beneath her hands.

Silence.

Her demand was met with silence.

"Th-this is what I want. If you truly are both here to see to my happiness, and nothing more, then marry me. Be done with this waffling and take me to wife, Charles. Do it now."

"What did you say?" Charles ground out as he shifted his stance.

She truly had taken him off guard.

Charles looked rather terrifying at the moment. Perhaps… perhaps she should have thought this through.

"I said…I wish for you to…I would like very much if you—"

"No, Amelia, what *exactly* did you say?" Charles's voice dropped. It was almost feral.

A shudder coursed her spine then seemed to settle near her womb, warming her from the inside out.

"I said…" She sank to the bed, before her knees gave up completely. Closing her eyes to steel herself, she raised her hand to stay him then took a deep breath and opened her eyes. "I demanded that you marry me, Charles. I asked that you take me to wife."

"You want me to take you to wife?" His voice was harsh, sharp at the edges.

She nodded. That nod was all she could effort in response, and she was grateful for it.

"What…here? Now?" Charles asked stiffly.

"Yes. Here and now," Amelia said.

Hugh spoke up then, seemed to be jarred from his silence. "Amelia, that isn't within the realm of—"

Charles stalked toward the end of the bed, cutting off Hugh's thought. Then something broke in Charles's eyes as she watched. "Let me say this so that you understand that I mean it." Charles took her shoulders. Pulled her to her feet. He surely marked her skin with his fingers. "I marry you, Amelia. Here and now. I marry you with your best friend as a witness. I marry you before God and my parents in heaven. I marry you, Amelia. I will take you to wife."

Amelia's breath stopped, and Charles lifted her farther, letting the sheet slip away as he pulled her flush against him. He breathed against her jaw, and her whole body shook. "You amaze me," Charles said softly, and she *knew* that Charles understood she'd done this intentionally. She'd meant to call this reaction forth in herself. The darkness came at the very edges of her periphery, and she was only happy she'd managed to say her piece first. She'd held out through so very much, and now she was thoroughly taxed. She collapsed into his arms.

"Hugh," was all Charles said and that she felt more than heard, until Hugh was behind her, his hands on her shoulders, smoothing down her arms. She knew there'd been no way Hugh would abandon her when she needed him in this way.

Charles watched her closely. It took some time, but once her heart steadied and her vision cleared on him, Charles spoke again.

"You have a choice, Amelia, and I want to hear this from you. I want you to truly consider this choice. I would like to give you as much time as you need, but you must understand at this moment, I have very little—"

"You, Charles, I want it to be you."

A crash. His mouth possessed hers in such a way she truly believed the world would be able to see that claiming whenever they looked on her from here on out—and perhaps they would. Her hands flew back and latched on to Hugh behind her, held him.

This, she thought. *This. I've waited the whole of my life to feel this and not be terrified.*

The absolute surrender.

Charles still supported her, which was a good thing when her knees did decide to quit. Amelia's hands moved to his bare shoulders and scored his flesh. She marked Charles for her own, and it seemed to spur him on. She shivered when more hands landed on her, and she knew Hugh was with them, that her actions had efforted to keep him here, with Charles. In her complete surrender to this, she'd managed to have all the control.

Amelia felt as though she were floating then descending, the soft feather tick mattress meeting her back and Hugh with her. She knew it was his hands spreading her hair across the bed, holding her hands and soothing her. Hugh kissed her forehead, smoothed her hair aside and brought her full attention back to the moment.

"Amelia, we don't have to do this." Hugh pleaded, truly pleaded, in a tone she'd never heard from him.

"Yes. We do," she said, and her tone brooked no arguments. This was their moment.

Charles stood at her feet. Amelia watched as he pulled his boots off one at a time and threw them to the floor. Charles reached for the buttons on his trousers, and he caught her gaze.

"Amelia, you've made your choice, and in it our fate is sealed. Tonight, I've made you my wife in word, I consider you my wife in thought, and I will make you my wife in deed." Charles paused after he released the buttons and stood before her.

The reckoning.

The words came back to her in that moment as she looked on Charles's tall, strong frame, as she took in the power and truth in his eyes. She pulled her own strength from Hugh, tightened her hands on

his, and nodded. "Yes, Charles. My husband. Tonight I consider you my husband in thought, I make you my husband in word, and you will make me your wife in deed."

The smile that broke across his face lit the room like nothing ever could, as the light changed from the harsh light of day to the warm glow of early evening. Her skin flushed—toes to nose—as he looked on her. She felt the blush rise, every single bit of her wanting to be in contact with every bit of him. She heard herself whimper, was separate from it, tightened her grip on Hugh.

Charles hooked his thumbs in the waist of his trousers then bent as he pushed them off. When he stood, it was like a golden god had made himself manifest in the Cliff House. The brilliant light through the window warmed his entire being, and his manhood rose to welcome as she watched. Charles took himself in hand, adjusted his bollocks, then smoothed a hand up and back down the length of his—

Maypole.

This she could believe, as he stood there before her. *This* she could believe. She was to be rent in her softest of places. Amelia panicked and clenched her thighs together as she pushed back from Charles, but she felt Hugh wrap his arms with hers, kissing her all over her face. "Shhhh, sweet Amelia," Hugh said. His tears were on her face, and she looked to his eyes.

"I love you."

The bed swayed beneath Charles when he mounted it, as if in deference to the strength and reality of this man. Just as she was sure she would sway beneath him in deference to that strength and reality.

"Amelia," Charles said gruffly. "Be with me." Charles lowered his body to hers.

"I'm with you, Charles." She reached for him. "I'm here with you."

TWENTY

Hugh thought that if Charles could hold this woman and watch as Amelia brought him off, certainly Hugh could be next to her, with her, hold her, as Charles ruined her. Amelia had arranged for this, after all. She'd pushed Charles to the tipping point, frightened herself in the doing of it, and made it impossible for Hugh to leave. God, she was incredible.

Amazing.

Brilliant.

Truth be told, Hugh thought his part in this would be easier... perhaps if he didn't consider the reality of what they were about. Just as he'd done when Amelia had wrapped her small fingers around his cock and stroked him until he came across her hand—and Charles had been watching and directing her. That cock stirred in his trousers now at the sight of Amelia stretched out before him. Hugh couldn't help it. The sight of her—Jackson in his periphery or no—was terribly erotic. Possibly more so, considering some of the hands on her were not his own.

Hugh leaned up from his precarious position on the floor, grabbed a pillow to shove beneath his knees on the hard wood, then gazed on her. She was a veritable masterpiece. Her hair was spread about her in a tangled web of silk, her lips swollen from the crushing kiss Charles had only just bestowed on her. Her eyes were lit from within, the reflection of the coming sunset over the cliffs filling them to glowing as she looked at her husband, and Charles *was* her husband. Hugh had been witness. Certainly there would be an official ceremony, but today, here in the Cliff House, was their wedding day.

Charles shifted, and Amelia's head fell back into Hugh's hands as Charles kissed his way down her long, graceful neck. Hugh spread his hands beneath her, cradling her head, then kissed her as her lips came closer to him. Her fingers came up to tangle in his hair, and somewhere above his head—for he was positioned upside down in relation to the two of them—Hugh saw a rosy nipple disappear into Charles's mouth, and he tensed. Yet it wasn't the tension of jealousy or discomfort. It was an altogether different kind of tension.

Amelia's hands tightened in Hugh's hair as Charles took her in his mouth. Hugh could almost feel that very touch on her as that pressure translated through her body to her hands, then to him. In turn, Hugh had to touch her. His big hands slid beneath her, then opened around her like wings across her back, his thumbs skimming the very edges of her breasts. Her hands tightened further in his hair, and she gasped against his mouth.

Perfect, Hugh thought.

She writhed beneath them, her flesh pinked with the blood of passion, and Hugh was made whole in the moment. This moment was the beginning of her forever, and he was grateful to be part of it, because it was something he'd never thought to be. In this moment, he found possibility…even as he knew that possibility could destroy him.

Mine.

It was the only thought in Charles's mind for quite some time, though upon a bit of reflection, it could have been mere moments. Part of him wanted to pull her away from Hugh. To claim her fully without him while other parts of him reminded Charles how important it was that Hugh be here. How much a part of *this* Hugh was. How much Amelia deserved what Charles could never give her. What Charles had never known and thus could never bestow. *True, uncompromising love.*

Charles was all hard want and possession, and Hugh was all soft need and love, and Charles knew it. Hugh was necessary, but Charles wasn't, not really. Charles knew she could disappear with Hugh, never to be heard from again, and all fear of being taken away and committed would vanish. Part of him allowed them to believe in her ruination so Charles could remain part of this. Charles could protect Amelia, whether he married her or not, but his want had kept him here.

Charles paused for a moment, wishing he could feel for her the way Hugh did—to have that connection with her. Charles had thought, at one point, that he might become that, learn it, replace Hugh—until they'd arrived here and realization had hit him like so many explosions lighting the darkness. Charles could never be for Amelia what Hugh was for her.

What's more, Charles hadn't believed in love until he saw them together. How could he destroy something so precious? Charles would never feel that, but he was caring enough to understand that something so beautiful shouldn't be destroyed. In that realization, Charles found a new hope. That she would come to love Charles for who he was, this hard difficult shell of a man. That her heart was big enough to hold both he and Hugh. Equally, yet differently. Charles knew she was just that incredible, Charles knew that it was possible, and Charles found strength in all that possibility.

So here they were, and all Hugh had to do was continue kissing her, holding her steady. Charles had momentary thoughts of discord, but he pushed them aside. This was going to work. Somehow, this was all going to work. Tonight, Charles had a bride to please, a wife to make.

Charles kissed his way down the center of her rib cage from her collarbone, then across the sweet underside of one breast before licking his way straight back up the center of her chest to where he'd begun— and a heavy shudder that racked her. Charles drew against her throat with his mouth.

"Ahh, Charles—" The sound was muffled by Hugh's mouth, but Charles's name had never sounded more beautiful to him.

Charles moved down again, kissed straight down her center, until he knelt on the floor, placing her feet on his shoulders. Charles had wanted this in a terrifying way from the moment Hugh's lips had first met Amelia's yesterday. Interestingly, Charles wasn't jealous of Hugh having tasted her first, because Charles had been as much a part of the moment as Hugh had.

Charles groaned at the thought, his exhaled breath ruffling the curls at her very center. Charles could see the slick wet of her arousal already and inhaled her heady scent. He wrapped his hands around her hips and licked. Sucked. Delved between those honeyed sweet lips—tasted.

Amelia had a musky sweetness he'd never had the likeness of, and her honey was like champagne straight to Charles's head. He couldn't wait. Charles wanted to slow time. He wanted to draw her out, to prolong this moment for as long as he possibly could …but he knew he'd already met his threshold.

The longer Charles waited, the more painful he knew his orgasm would be. Charles already knew this coming would be the most painful—the most powerful—of his life, and that was as it should be. They would share in the pain of it, he and Amelia, but they would also share in the glory of it. If Charles waited much longer, he wouldn't be able to contain the force with which he took her, and this alone frightened him. Not the other man at her shoulder, not the will of her mind, not the future that they couldn't yet see clearly.

Charles wanted, quite desperately, to ensure he was gentle in this. Charles knew these moments would color her future, that every time she lay with him, she would remember this first coming together—the three of them—and he didn't want it to be violent. So Charles slowed down as much as he could, savored her flavor, took her scent into his soul, treasured the toes curled against his shoulders, and the gooseflesh under his fingers.

Hugh's thumbs skimmed the edges of her breasts as his hands seemed to span the entirety of her back. His mouth was melding with hers. And Charles…oh, dear Charles, he was the magic between her legs at the moment. Amelia held as still as she possibly could against their mouths, just absorbing the sensations they had zinging to her center. She let go of Hugh with one hand and reached for Charles, tangled that hand in his hair.

Hugh was calm and so very gentle moving across her skin. It didn't feel different from the way Charles touched her until she concentrated on their hands and felt the tremors in Charles's like Braille against her skin. She knew then Charles was so very restrained, while Hugh was allowing everything, feeling everything.

Hugh pressed into her skin, swept across it, felt the texture and made it change against his fingertips like an erotic painter. Charles was all superficial touches and restrained pressure. She knew Charles was holding himself in check, as though he might somehow hurt or damage her physically. She shook with the knowledge of it, but she wanted his bruises, she wanted all of him. Every bit of emotion Charles had to give, she wanted to take it all into herself and feel it. Amelia knew, *she knew,* how different Charles was from Hugh, how trained he was in restraining all feeling.

She wanted him to let go.

She wanted him to feel.

Tonight of all nights, she wanted this of Charles, for her body to be the vessel of his passion, the doorway to his revelations of love. Amelia wanted to carry the evidence of it beyond the blood on her sheets. She knew she could make him feel but was afraid at how her body and her mind would react. Her greatest fear was that she would lose herself in the doing of it, that she would frighten him away. All this was so new to Charles, he was quite fragile in it no matter how strong he seemed.

Amelia closed her eyes and abandoned herself to sensation. She believed every word Charles had said, and thus, she was a married woman.

In bed with two men.

At the behest of her husband.

Nothing a husband wished of her was improper.

He, her lord and master.

Don't break him.

Stop. Thinking.

Charles sucked, and a shudder racked her body, forcing a low guttural yell from her throat that Hugh answered with his own. Hugh moved then, kissed her eyelids, her temple, her nose and chin as he shifted and leaned over her. Then Hugh took one of her nipples into his mouth, and the sensation of his tongue on her matched with Charles's tongue on her was almost too much. Her body bucked as if to throw them both from their seats.

"More." Amelia hoped that was audible. She hoped they'd heard her. She waited for the evidence of it, then tightened her hands on both of them. "More," she said louder.

She hoped she wasn't pulling hair from their scalps.

Charles's hands moved then, smoothing up her sides, still quite restrained. Charles's hands met with Hugh's, and their fingertips intertwined momentarily until Hugh retreated easily, his hands and mouth coming back to pay homage to her neck and lips. It felt like a beautiful dance across her flesh, and Amelia reveled in it.

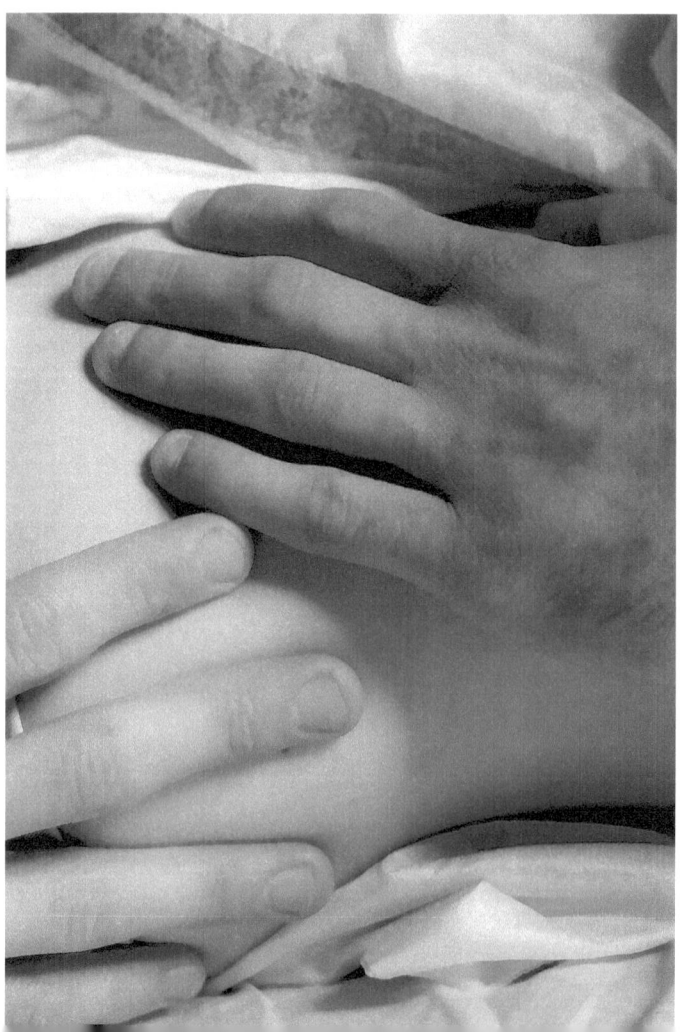

She felt Hugh shift, her head coming to rest on his shoulder as he held her. Her breasts weren't bereft for long as Charles's warmth moved over her, pulling her legs around his waist, his hands tilting and shifting and adjusting as he moved above her.

Charles was bringing himself to her.

OhGodOhGodOhGod.

This was to be it.

Already?

She'd thought she had more time, more time to...more time to what, exactly?

What time do I need? To effect what? This is the time, right here, right now, this man is to breech me...in the most intimate of ways. Perhaps not the most intimate, as the mind may well be more intimate. And she wanted him there as well, in her mind. She wanted him to have that complete understanding.

Charles did, to some extent. She knew he understood a bit about what it was to live inside her brain.

But that's not what I mean. I want him inside my mind while I'm there, with me present, the three of us.

The three of us.

There are three of us...

What a beautiful dance.

"Amelia," Charles said as he licked and nibbled his way between her breasts, then up the sharp edge of her chin.

They were both there. Charles and Hugh. She opened her mouth to take in as much air as she could as Charles kissed one side of her mouth and Hugh the other.

She stared up at the ceiling, concentrating on the hands, the tongues, the forms shifting in and out of her field of vision. She was married, wedded to Charles, and he was set to take her maidenhead, and it would be done.

Final.

Forever.

She'd always thought she was caught between her friend and forever. And now she truly was.

Wedged, as it were.

But friend was no longer the right word for Hugh.

Another shudder coursed her body, and she sucked in a deep breath, forcing her chest up into Charles's.

"Amelia mine," Charles said as he wrapped his arms around her and held tight to the entirety of her. "Amelia… our Amelia," he corrected.

She was surrounded in every way. Head to toe, covered in man. Amelia was so warm—then one of them would kiss her, and the air would catch the moisture and sweep it away, sending a chill through her skin, rushing her veins, pinging some very deep spot, which then sent out a million smaller signals to the far reaches of her soul.

One of Charles's hands smoothed between her legs, his fingers teasing between her folds, circling her entrance, and she felt the maypole that would rend her, and she tensed anew.

Hugh lifted from her a bit, kissed her eyes and whispered, "Sweet Amelia, stay with us."

"I'm with you, I'm with you, I promise I'm with you, please feel me, make me feel. I want you to feel, Charles, feel." She took his eyes with hers as she watched the edges fade.

She let go of Charles's hair and reached between them, skimming the reality of him all the way to his cock, and he tensed at that touch, even gentle as it was, letting out a deeply pained and powerful noise that filled his chest then saturated the air around them.

"It truly is painful?" she asked, feeling that incredible hardness, wanting to experience it but afraid at his reaction.

Charles looked in her eyes and nodded stiffly. "Yes, Amelia, it's quite painful. But we shall remedy that together, and in future, neither of us will be rent with pain from the act of it."

The meaning of his words sank in, and she looked back up to the ceiling, willing the fade to recede as she felt Hugh nudge her ear with his nose. Skimming her hand up Charles's abdomen, across his chest, up his neck and to his face, her hand rested momentarily as Charles turned his head into her palm and kissed her.

"Amelia?" Charles groaned, and she flicked her eyes to his, then closed them, nodding her head in acquiescence.

Then, "Yes." She breathed it, and felt the air come back to descend warmly across her face.

"Look on us," Charles said as he leaned into her, whispering. "Hugh…"

"I'm here," Hugh responded. "Are you ready, my darling? We're here, stay with us." Hugh breathed against her neck.

Amelia opened her eyes and concentrated on the ceiling for another moment. She was here, and as it happened, so were they all. Hugh held her, grounded her as he did, while Charles was everywhere—certainly between her legs—but surrounding her in the most powerful way above her, whispering precious words in her ear.

"Amelia, sweet Amelia, my wife."

She looked at him then, saw so very much in his eyes—the emotions difficult for her to discern, but *they were there*. She felt them in her bones. That was what she'd hoped for, wished for, wanted so very desperately that she felt it in her toes. Then she saw Hugh, like a halo of safety holding her, supporting her, mirroring Charles from above.

There is no judgment here.

Stay with us.

Look on us.

She relaxed. Her mouth fell open on a breath, and they both raised above her, into her field of vision, with nothing but their warmth surrounding her, nothing but safety, nothing but strength. "I marry you. Charles, I marry you. Hugh, I marry you…I marry you…I marry you," Amelia chanted.

The length of Charles's body tensed against her. The head of his cock slid past her folds, rocked there for what seemed the longest moment of her life, like the last vestige of her grip off the beautiful cliffs before she would fall, and then, "Amelia."

Charles groaned, and the moment her eyes met his, he pushed into her with a primal growl, and she let go—and she fell.

Amelia arched against the pain in the rending, but the weight of him held her steady as his arms around her kept her together. Her eyes flitted to Hugh then back to Charles, and Charles kissed her.

She closed her eyes then and fell, fell, fell. She felt so many things whizzing past—hands, tongues, arms, fingers, and she searched for that repetitive motion against her that would signal her crisis. She'd come but twice in her lifetime, and already she craved for more. She shifted her hips, and Charles filled her further with another pained groan.

Charles had said this would be painful...for both of them, and she knew in the sounds he made against her that it was. Charles's every muscle tensed like a massive steel cage slowly closing in...but the tightness comforted. She was contained in it, secured by it, and she relaxed into his hold as he flexed more, even as she thought calming impossible.

The falling, oh, the falling...

His cock reached for the very mouth of her womb, the touch sending a shock through her system and lighting in every limb, every fingertip, the nape of her neck, the tips of her ears, and the tip of her tongue.

"Amelia, are you—"

"Yes, Charles, yes. Don't hold back. Please don't hold back."

She ran her tongue over her lip as though to feel the bit of current that coursed her system but was shocked when Charles sucked her tongue into his mouth, sending shudders through her muscles. He took her, with his hands, with his mouth, with his teeth, with his cock. He took and took, and Amelia gave everything, following him blindly.

Amelia's hands released both of them then. She hadn't even realized she still held them, her arms had been so pliable as they moved. Amelia wrapped her arms around Charles's shoulders, crossed her ankles behind his hips, and held on as he pushed and pushed, stronger and harder. The rending subsided to a dull sting with echoes of something trailing behind it, and she trained her mind on that.

Charles's teeth closed gently on her shoulder, and she pushed against him, wanting more of that burn. He obliged, and she knew he marked her, was inordinately pleased by it, and she turned toward Hugh at her other shoulder. Hugh kissed her, so soft, so sweet. The kiss sank through her, opened her up, and settled her in. She lay in that embrace, feeling that kiss as it traced all the different paths to her toes.

"Oh God, Amelia, you are so warm, so wonderful, so tight." Charles slowed, his action more determined, as though he searched for something more…and she followed in the search. She concentrated on the contact deep inside, as if he attempted to strike a flint against her core. Charles loosened on her, lifted above her, and like a magnet, her eyes were drawn to him.

"Amelia—" Charles's voice sounded so pained, and she smoothed her hands up his shoulders and held his face.

"Charles. I love you."

"Amelia," Charles ground out, and the reverberation against her sent shivers across her flesh. "Amelia."

Her vision narrowed on him, and she stilled, unsure whether this tunnel was the moment or the darkness, and was momentarily afraid of both. Hugh's arms came around her, shadowed her own arms, smoothed over her wrists so his hands caressed hers, even as she held on to Charles. His breath was hot on her shoulder.

Hot.

So very hot.

The heat of it.

"Slowly, Charles, slowly," Hugh said, and Charles responded to Hugh's direction, and the spark fired almost instantly against some secret part of her, pulling a scream from her lungs and racking her body in such a great shudder she thought she'd unravel through the bars of her muscled cage.

Charles's lips met hers again, and her hands slid around his neck and tangled in his hair as she held on through the spasms, her womb kissing his cock, her body like a fist clenching around him.

She reveled in Charles's pained groans against her mouth until he seemed to break, pistoned into her like a steam train, then with a single final thrust, Charles pushed, harder and deeper than she'd ever thought possible. It felt as though he crawled across the bed into her, pushing her deeper into Hugh's embrace. Then Charles held against her there, his warmth, his mettle, that warm, white, life-bearing seed, flooding her as his own scream rent the air, cracked like thunder above her. And the last thing she knew—*she knew*—was that his crisis was as painful as he had said it would be.

A

Charles's release was a strike of lightning, the flash blinding and the sound of blood rushing his veins deafening, as sheer pain coursed his system and found the outlet in his ears—as though his bollocks had been squeezed in the metal jaw of a vice and become so overburdened that the metal snapped and his seed flowed freely. But the mettle didn't merely flow at that. His seed exploded from him, ricocheted within the constraints of his cock's tight, warm sanctuary, until it saturated every nook and cranny and flooded back toward him.

The pain...*dear God, the pain,* like a rending, yet satisfying. The most pleasurable pain one can know, truly. Funny, that, as he considered what they'd just done—what he'd just done. He'd torn asunder the most delicate part of her. Claimed her maidenhead for his own—and he basked momentarily in that pure male triumph, that *knowing* beyond singular doubt that no man had trespassed here before.

Charles lay still upon her as Amelia trembled when he lifted too far from her bodily. She seemed to enjoy the pressure of him, the pure restraint of his heavy bones upon hers, and he was happy to stay. His bollocks ached like nothing had in all his life. This had been a much more extended delay of gratification. Nothing he'd experienced before and hoped never to again.

Blessed as it was.

Charles wasn't truly sure how soon the ache at his bollocks would dissipate, and even though his slow stroking yet inside her was preventing his cockstand from receding completely, he wasn't sure how soon he would, or could, rise again. Charles hoped that this one painful orgasm would satiate him for a time—because soon they would leave the Cliff House, and it would be at least a fortnight before they could be together again.

Charles's hands traveled her body, occasionally avoiding Hugh's. Charles watched Hugh's hands for a time, dancing across her skin, before looking up to her other man. Hugh's smile was one of pure devotion as he watched Amelia drift. Charles hoped she merely slept, that they'd laid waste only to her energy and not something deeper. Hugh looked at him, gave a quick nod, and Charles knew she was safe.

Charles rolled to his side and pulled her with him, then reached over to Hugh's arm and tugged until Hugh rose and slid into the bed behind her, pulling a heavy counterpane with him from a nearby chair. Hugh returned the pressure along her back that had been lost when Charles had shifted them. She settled between them once again, her arms wrapped around Charles, their legs tangled together, Hugh keeping her safe in the lee of Charles's strength.

Charles was certain they could make this work. Charles knew he and Amelia would be wed in the official manner and that they would live as husband and wife—Hugh with them. Charles felt an incomparable care for this man, something he'd never felt for another man—another person, even. It was different from his care for Amelia, but that of a brother perhaps, or stronger even, as the regard wasn't a requirement of blood. Charles wanted to ensure his future with them, that Hugh and Amelia would be safe to be friends…or more, as it seemed to him they were most definitely more than friends now.

He understood that Hugh wasn't entirely set upon the idea of them being together, but he knew in what Amelia had done tonight that she showed him that she needed him yet. She showed Hugh that he could not yet abandon her, and she refused to let Hugh be martyr to her future. Hugh was very much a part of her future. In fact, Hugh was just as much a part of her future as Charles was, albeit one that the public wouldn't know the truth of.

And what of him? Charles had not expected some of what happened tonight. It wasn't the three of them nor the situation of it all, but something more. Something had slipped inside of him when he'd pressed into her. Something had shifted, opening a fissure that had allowed in just a bit of light and from it, warmth. He wasn't sure what it was even as it bloomed when he looked on her. He'd thought perhaps it had something to do with his, now resolved, predicament, but he was much too exhausted to consider it at the moment.

A

Hugh watched Amelia's steady breathing. Hugh had not taken any joy in the pain Charles had endured in the ruination of his best friend, now lover, and that troubled him. Because what Hugh had taken from it was the feeling of sheer love, a complete joy, he'd never felt with anyone until now. As though this moment, here, was exactly where he was supposed to be. It was unfortunate he couldn't stay with them in the future. It was obvious to Hugh that at some point Amelia would trust in Charles—her body, her soul, whatever piece of her had latched on to Hugh and decided he was her sanctuary—that part of her would accept Charles as well, and Hugh would absolutely be superfluous. Regardless how much they loved each other.

Hugh owed Charles a great debt, not only for Hugh's mishandling of their friendship as children, but for Charles's care of Amelia now and in the future. Hugh wanted to stay with them, but his fear of being cast aside eventually…it was too great. The longer Hugh stayed within this warm haven, the more painful, the more difficult, it would be to be forced from it. Hugh wasn't sure he would survive it now, but he would find a pliable virgin to take to wife and settle in the seat of the barony, his holdings secured by the funds settled on that marriage.

If Hugh stayed with Charles and Amelia, he would lose everything but his title. Baronies very rarely had entailments, and his certainly didn't. And his parents…well, they thought they were doing him a service by requiring a marriage to receive his limited fortunes— that in itself was a tragedy.

Hugh could give it all up to live with Charles and Amelia. He could walk away from everything he was and allow himself to be a kept man. But what then? What of when they turned him out? Hugh would be ruined. No holdings, no money, no anything to live in, or off of, or on.

Not a damned thing.

Hugh would then marry a suitable girl, but she would have nothing but money. Hugh could buy properties…he could…he needed to silence his mind for the time being. To enjoy his last moments holding his beloved Amelia in his arms. He swept her hair aside and curled into her form, his forehead pressed into the curve of her neck, his arms wrapped around her, his legs like shadows of her own.

It wasn't so terrible. Certainly Charles would honorably settle some money on him. Like a mistress released from her protector. Hugh shivered against Amelia at the thought, and he suddenly knew he would never survive this as he attempted to drift off to sleep.

TWENTY ONE

Amelia tried to take a deep breath only to realize her chest was compressed by the rather large arm swept across it. And it was naked. Her chest, not the arm. Well, the arm as well, of course, but—she clenched her eyes and let out a breath as steady as possible.

"I know you're awake," Charles said.

"Well, then, if you don't mind, would you please move your arm so I can breathe?"

Charles shifted. His arm went to her waist, and she took a deep breath, then realized his hand was on her buttock. Kneading it. Like bread dough. Pulling her forward, toward him and—oh my. Were they to do it again?

"Where's Hugh?" she asked.

"He just stepped outside. Amelia?"

"Yes, my...yes..." She paused. What did she call him now? Was it still Charles? Did she decide on some term of endearment? He was calling her Amelia. Obviously, that was acceptable under the circumstance, but she wasn't entirely sure of the circumstance, of course, because she'd not done this before and—

"Charles," he said.

"I'm Amelia," she said distractedly.

"I'm aware that you're Amelia. I'm also aware that you're deciding how to address me. You use my name, as you did several hours ago. It's not a great debate. Charles. Use it." His morning voice was low and rough from disuse, and the reverberation of his proximity sent sparks across her skin.

"Oh," she sighed.

"Amelia."

"Yes?"

"Say my name."

"Oh, you meant now?"

"Amelia," Charles said again, and she marveled at the many ways he could say her name. Calming, driving, exciting, warning, arousing… at the moment, it seemed deep and threatening.

She cleared her throat. What a bit of nonsense! It was like stage fright. She couldn't get her throat to work. "Ch—" She cleared her throat again. "Charrr—I…Charrrllles," she slurred carefully, as his hands continued to loosen her muscles while having the most amazing effect of tightening other parts of her that he wasn't even near to touching.

"Again. It appears you need some practice." Charles's breath blew across the skin between her shoulder and her neck, and her nipples peaked.

"I'm a bit shaken up…Charles," she said achingly slowly.

"Again." Now his breath hit her chest and curved up her throat to her chin, while her skin shuddered at the back of her neck.

"Charles." Her voice was gruff and low, possibly from that bit of screaming from…before.

"Again," he said, his voice gravelly. He seemed to have the same issue. Charles rolled over her, his hands each on their very own cheek of her bottom and his face buried in her neck. "Again."

Her toes tingled.

Her toes!

"Chaaaaarless."

"Again." His hands swept down her thighs, spreading her beneath him as she felt his hardness slide between her legs.

She squeaked.

He looked up, seemed to be considering her, waiting.

"Charles," she whispered. She meant it as an invitation, even as it terrified her.

Charles took her mouth, spoke with his lips pressed against hers. "Don't stop, Amelia. Never stop."

Amelia repeated his name, over and over, until it was like breath for her, an incantation. Every sigh, every gasp carried those seven letters upon it as Charles's tempo rose and fell with his urgency. She ignored the fading. She ignored the warnings.

When Amelia opened her eyes to look on him and his eyes crinkled at the edges with a smile of brilliant happiness, she thought she might be lost forever in their depths. As though he was exactly where he'd always wanted to be, and she belonged there as well.

She felt Charles inside her as he thrust slowly, building, watching her watching him. She continued her incantation as she took him in, every minute detail, attempting to ward off the shadows at her periphery. Charles's dark hair appeared burnished by the sun from the window. His eyes were dark and deep from the shadows. She touched Charles then, his name an echo of her hands on his skin.

The cords of his neck…she traced them, her hands moving slowly to his shoulders, and what shoulders they were. The roping muscles stood out. She'd never realized how detailed a man's body was until now, and she watched as the muscles of his shoulders moved with them, shifting, bunching and relaxing under his skin. They looked like they were braided, so intricately woven they were.

"Charles."

She smoothed her hands over them and closed her eyes, feeling the movement and comparing it to the steady thrust of his hips, that part of him moving inside her, so very well choreographed, his body like a well-planned ballet—the muscles of the dancers, each carefully following a set rhythm and pattern, each quite specific in their movement, with the rushing of her blood the music that set the tempo for their dance.

"Charles."

She could hear the music then, lilting yet quickening, the thrusts picking up tempo, the dancers following suit. Her hands shifted down to his arms, where the large muscles would tighten like stone, then relax. Her hands fell to his ribs, and he jerked, a staccato rhythm in her internal symphony.

"Charles."

She fit her hands to that weave of muscles on his sides, her fingers resting in the valleys between his ribs as she concentrated on the sweep and the pull of these muscles, so different from the bunching of his arms and the shifting of his shoulders.

"Charles."

She was taken away with how miraculous his body was, how absolutely amazing the movement within, that without thought so many things came together in the most perfect way, only to bring about the crescendo which was upon her.

"Charles."

"Amelia."

She snapped back to awareness and arched into him as she moved her hands to his back and pulled him to her as hard as her small arms would allow for, felt his powerful thrust upon her, shocked she did not split right in two like a log prepared for a fire.

Amelia felt carried away on Charles's name, on his tide, in his arms. They undulated as though one, like ripples in her pond, the tide on the shore. She could hear the waves crashing, and she breathed with them, spoke with them. Charles picked up the cadence, and they writhed together with the sea and his name on her breath until her world came apart in his arms, and she screamed—much too late—her arms flailing, searching for purchase as she fell, fell, fell past the cliffs and into the sea with only Charles to buoy her—

He's not enough.

Amelia was blinded by the thought, her mind a brilliant light. The only thing she knew was his name on her lips, the warmth of his seed against her womb, and the sound of their voices on the wind.

A

"Amelia." Charles breathed heavily.

Waited.

"Amelia."

He'd thought she was with him. Miraculously, he'd thought she was still with him. He'd been wrong. Every muscle in him tensed, and she seemed to melt within the confines of his structure.

Charles held her face in his hand, kissed it, attempted to steady his heart. "Amelia, please." His voice sounded rough, breathless, breaking across the words. How could he have been such an ass? He knew better. He knew she couldn't be close to him like this. He knew she needed Hugh. It had been too much to hope for. Charles was too much for her. There it was, just a small bit of that jealousy he'd thought had been dismissed. He shook it off.

"Hugh!" he yelled, and the door swept open.

Hugh didn't look very happy as he approached them on the bed, and that look from Hugh wasn't helpful as Charles felt his stomach drop. "I was...we were...it all just happened, and it felt right. I thought she was here...and then...she was gone." Charles started to move away, shame gripping his spine like a bony fist, but Hugh grabbed his arm and shook his head.

Charles knew it had been a mistake. He knew he wasn't worthy.

Hugh knelt by the bed next to Amelia as Charles swept the sheet up over them, their nakedness now a testament to his improper behavior. Charles felt as a child in need of a scolding, even though Hugh was far from berating him. Charles rolled to her side as Hugh spoke quietly, gently. This was disheartening, and Charles stilled, watched, simply worked on learning all the small movements, the calming sounds, the soothing words, that would bring her back.

Charles felt her awareness returning slowly. First in her hands, tensing on his arm, his side. Then her toes curling against his calf. He watched as Amelia slowly smiled and reached up to his chin. "Hugh?"

Charles froze, then moved suddenly, rising from the bed and yanking his trousers on. Charles heard Hugh call his name in warning and knew it wasn't a good idea, knew he should take more care with her, but he'd been frightened. So very frightened. If Hugh hadn't been here... Charles shook the thought off. He had to step away from her, from them.

"Charles." Hugh called to him as he followed him over to the fireplace. "Breathe, Charles. Everything's okay. I understand—"

Charles turned on him. "You understand what, exactly? How weak I truly am? How unmatched for her? How unequal to the task? How ignorant?" He berated himself, hearing his father's voice the whole time.

Hugh grabbed his arm. "Charles, stop!" Hugh was shaking his head. "I understand that you were frightened. But you did nothing wrong."

Frightened.

Yes, he had been, and Hugh could clearly see it. Charles was angry with himself for feeling so helpless, so frightened. This woman

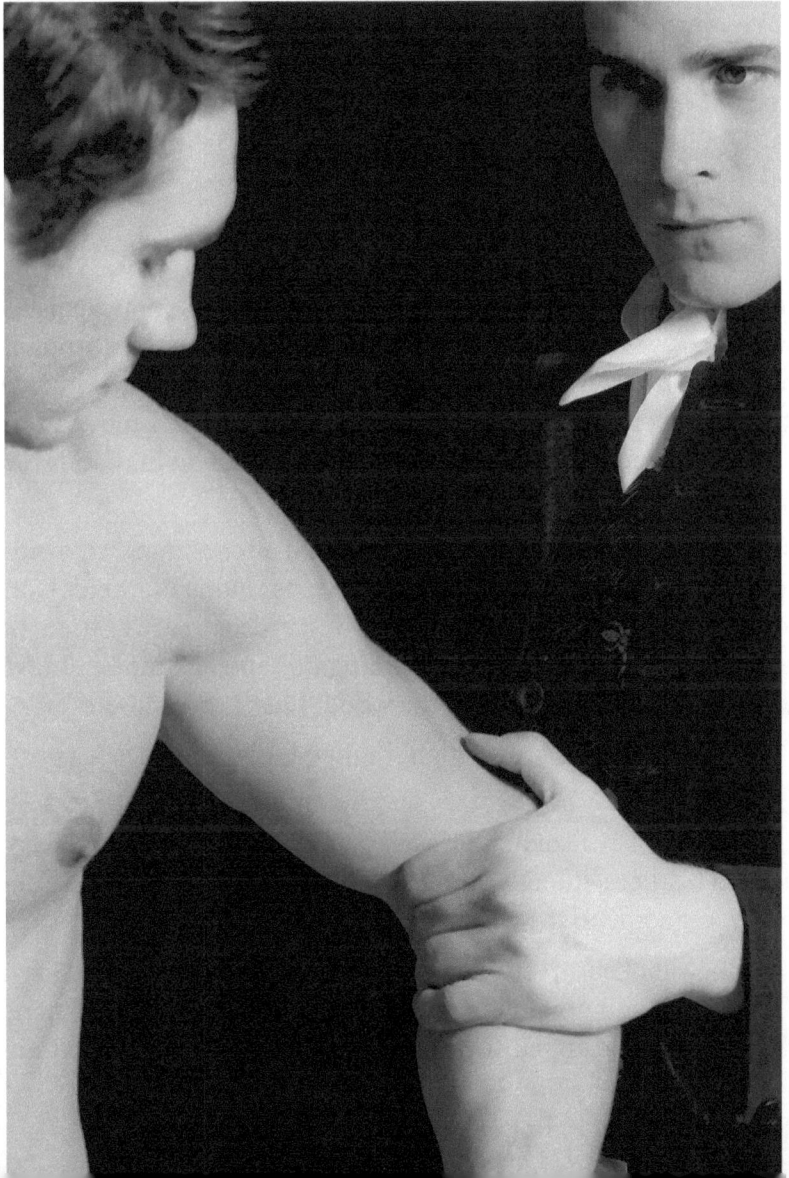

made him feel so many things he was unaccustomed to feeling. Charles stopped trying to pull away from Hugh and turned, meeting his eyes. Daring him to point out again how weak he was as a man.

Hugh straightened, cleared his throat, and Charles saw fear in his eyes as well, knew it, because he now understood it.

Hugh spoke. "The first time—"

Hugh let go of Charles's arm, tapped him once on his shoulder then turned to look at Amelia and sank into one of the chairs by the fire. Hugh let out a heavy breath, then started again.

"The first time it happened was the day I told her I was off to Eton. We were walking out here, away from everyone, just as...just as it usually was. I was leaving in two months' time. She should have known I was to go, I don't...it shouldn't have been such a surprise." Hugh leaned forward on his knees, and Charles moved to the chair across from him, not taking his eyes from Hugh's face as he continued.

Hugh's words were stilted, slow. "I told her I was leaving. I thought nothing of it. She went pale. Her eyes...the color was gone. Her hands fell to her sides. I mean, *every part of her* seemed to simply vanish with the wind across the moors. It was like the breeze had come through and simply swept her soul away with it. I didn't understand. I didn't realize what was happening. She hit the ground before I even moved to help her." Hugh's fingers weaved together, and the tension in his hands turned his knuckles white.

"I didn't know what to do," Hugh said after a time. "I considered running for help, but I didn't want to leave her alone out here. I simply stood there for the longest time." His voice dropped. "I stood there, staring at her, as though I were imagining this and any moment I would awaken to see her running from the wood. I just...*stood* there."

Charles watched as Hugh bumped his knuckles against his forehead before he went on.

"Finally, I realized she wasn't getting up, so I knelt, picked her up, carried her here, though I thought my legs would explode in flame... we'd only just come to the clearing..."

Hugh looked up suddenly and caught Charles's eyes. "Charles. That terror"—Hugh pointed to Amelia, then himself—"I understand it." Hugh held his hands open toward Charles. "Our Amelia wasn't always this way…or perhaps she was of a fashion, but not the same as it is now. She was always safe as a child. There was no cause for it. She and I, we were inseparable…this you know."

Charles nodded, leaned back in the chair to attempt to dissipate some of the heat of the tension coursing his muscles. Charles closed his eyes and listened intently to Hugh's story.

"I believe it was that I was leaving, and she feared being alone, though she wasn't aware of it. We had this way about us, you see. We had these games. *Damn me* and such. I believe we controlled her issue, without even knowing what we did. Children are brilliant like that. Making up languages, devising games…"

Hugh went silent for a while, and Charles listened for her breathing across the room, steady and quiet. Charles turned and watched the sheet rise and fall, her tiny movements as she shifted.

"I laid her here, on the bed, talked to her the entire time, smoothed her hair back, massaged her muscles, certainly annoyed the hell out of her with my tending. But she came back to me. It seemed to take forever…and maybe back then, it did take longer. We didn't understand. We were unpracticed—unlike now. She's learned the signs. She's become adept at slowing the process, sometimes even stopping the advance altogether. She knows when the panic sets in. I've become adept as well, as will you…"

Charles turned his head to find Hugh looking directly at him. "You will. You won't need me. You won't. You must understand this. Just remember: She always comes back," Hugh said quietly. Charles started to shake his head, but Hugh waved it off. "Listen, please. Louisa…I chose her for Amelia. I taught her everything I know, and she's learned to care for her as I do. She has more to lose than any of us, and her love of Amelia was born of that dedication. She may even be more adept at handling Amelia's episodes than I am at this point." Hugh was speaking very softly, and Charles knew he didn't want Amelia to hear what he was saying.

"You're attempting to back away," Charles said, and then Charles actually looked at Hugh, took him in, realized Hugh was fully dressed… boots, jacket, waistcoat, etc., and Charles was angry. "You were leaving!"

He practically launched himself from the chair, and Hugh stood as well in defense. Charles cut a glance to Amelia and attempted to control his anger, yet he seethed with it. "After all that's happened between us this weekend, you yet attempt to walk away." It was more accusation than question.

Hugh looked at Amelia then. "My staying by her side would only call attention to her. The very attention we've been trying so hard to avoid. The attention she doesn't need. Married to you…she'll be safe. No one would dare go against you and take her against your will. My very existence in her life is a danger to her. I cannot protect her. She could be too easily taken from me, and I have not the means to protect her." He held his hands up in front of him, begging Charles to stay himself.

"Coward," Charles seethed.

"And perhaps I am, but in this world, what kind of *goddamned choice* do I have?" Hugh threw back at him, his hands fisting.

"But I'm incapable of love," Charles said quietly.

Hugh stared at him, and Charles supposed the statement was a bit odd. Then Hugh spoke. "Ridiculous. You simply don't know what it means. You simply don't understand, because you've never been loved, but you'll understand. You'll learn."

"No…I *do* understand," Charles said. "When I see the two of you, I do understand. I can see it so easily in between you, and I don't begrudge you that, amazingly, I don't. I…I *was* jealous of you until I found I couldn't be jealous of something I find simply incomprehensible."

Hugh shook his head. "She'll be furious."

"*I am furious,* if you hadn't noticed." Charles stepped forward and leaned toward Hugh then pointed at himself. Charles knew his lip was curled, tried to sway the conversation before something happened he would regret. "We shouldn't be talking about her again."

"But it's the nature of three," Hugh said. "It's an impossibility to always converse with all three of us, by the nature of it. As she would need to get used to the two of us chatting, you and I would need to get used to the same treatment as well. I couldn't possibly expect that whenever you were alone with her that I would not come up in discussion. You see? An impossibility. Are you prepared for a relationship of so broad a structure? So open a discussion?"

Charles couldn't say he'd even considered it, and certainly a part of him shied from that. "We said we would do whatever it took. To see her happy…*we* would do whatever needed be done."

Don't beg, Charles thought.

Begging is beneath you. Convince him. You're a duke. You have that power. Make this happen.

These were his father's words. His father's voice in his head.

Hugh spoke, breaking through his thoughts. "We did, yes. But can't you see now that it will be possible for the two of you to carry on without me?" Hugh sounded pained, his voice strained and hurt, and Charles knew it, because he knew that pain.

"No," Charles replied quietly, restrained as best he could. "I *don't* agree. You *don't* seem to understand...she will *never* be whole without you." Charles pointed at her, then pointed at Hugh as he took a step toward him. "Just as *you* said, you've been part of each other's lives for so long that you are two halves of the same coin. One side is only good *with* the other."

"Charles?"

Charles hardly heard her and refused to look toward the shuffling noises. Charles shook his head, then collapsed back into the chair and waited. What the bloody hell was he to do? Now he was angry again, and not with her, but with Hugh...and himself, if he were being honest. Mostly with himself, truthfully. Charles knew he could convince Hugh. It wouldn't take much, he imagined. If Charles had felt that way for someone, he could never leave them, no matter the circumstance. At least he believed such.

Charles couldn't let her know that Hugh intended to leave her. To leave them. Charles still had to convince him, and he could. At any rate, Hugh couldn't just leave now without telling her. Hugh was a better man than that.

Charles glanced up to see she was fiddling with the throw that was once again wrapped around her shoulders. He let out a breath at the sight of her, knowing she was truly okay.

"You frightened me," Charles blurted out, then shook his head, knowing that wasn't what he should have said, knowing that showed his weakness too blatantly and, as well, it placed the blame on her, not where it belonged—on his own shoulders. "You don't need...you love him." Charles pointed at Hugh and knew he wasn't making sense.

"Of course I love Hugh," she said, confused. "I've known him the whole of my life. I've always loved him." She looked back to Charles, and he knew she felt the need to defend herself. "He's been everything to me when I had nothing—no one. Out here—"

Charles cut her off. "Yes, out here at the ends of the earth, the friends we have are those born to us. I quite remember what you said that day. Trust me, I remember everything you say with crystal clarity. It seems to be rather a nuisance at this particular juncture." Charles closed his eyes and rubbed his temples. He wasn't doing better. His frustration was with himself, his reaction to her episode, with Hugh as well...but Charles was acting like this was her fault. He needed to just stop talking. He looked to Hugh for help.

"Amelia," Hugh started slowly, and Charles realized he didn't like the tone of his voice and feared what he was to say next. "It's time I quit Pembroke for London. I've been away for too long. I'd considered leaving while you slept, but...I didn't want to startle you. But now, as we're all awake, and well...you understand I should depart. We can't all three of us be missing after the incident at the Row."

Damn him, Charles thought. Hugh intended to abandon her yet and leave her without disclosing his intentions. Leave her pain for Charles to deal with.

Charles's opinions of Hugh shattered in that instant. What a great deal of work it would take to repair Hugh's good name in Charles's eyes...if ever. As far as Charles was concerned, he would ruin Hugh in every possible way. And he had that power. It was something that was born to him, belonged to him, something that he was. *The reckoning.* Charles hadn't truly lived up to that moniker...yet.

Charles bit his thumb as he stared daggers at Hugh, who was spinning a beautiful tale of wanting to cover for their escapade, to get back to the *ton,* to make some excuses, to be seen where he should be seen, etc. It was only so much buzzing in Charles's ears now, fodder from a liar.

Charles cut him off. "Are you sure, Hugh, that this is how you mean to move forward? I wish you to be quite certain that *this* is how you intend to go on from here," Charles ground out, trying to get his intention across in the simplest, most direct way he possibly could, without openly threatening Hugh in front of Amelia. Everything he did to Hugh from here on out would be kept from her.

Hugh seemed to contemplate Charles's words, and Charles saw Hugh's understanding in the widening of his eyes. Hugh nodded, took Amelia in his arms and kissed her cheek, said something Charles was sure comforted her. Probably along the lines of: *Don't let him touch you, and you'll be fine. Or, just remember me whenever he's close.* Perhaps even something such as, *I'll see you soon.*

LIAR.

Amelia patted Hugh's shoulder as he released her and smiled. Then Hugh turned to Charles, as he must, as the past days had dictated he absolutely must, and Charles waited to see if he had the bollocks to pull this off. Hugh's hand jerked as though he meant to reach for Charles to say his good-byes, but Charles didn't move. He refused to dishonor his wife by playing into the farce.

His wife.

Charles's eyes flitted to Amelia, then looked on Hugh, and Charles knew Hugh understood the depth of his anger in that moment as Hugh took an involuntary step back.

Hugh meant to leave the explanation to Charles. Hugh meant to leave him with a woman who couldn't, without Hugh nearby, bear his company, his words, or his touch. Hugh was so terrified of the future that he was going to abandon Amelia to whatever fate was to come.

The woman he said he loved.

Hugh turned away and nearly ran from the house as Charles watched Amelia's confused gaze follow.

TWENTY TWO

ugh stumbled blindly across the green expanse of the moors. This pain, this rending, this wresting of her from his soul was like an evisceration. Parts of him never seen, meant to be hidden and kept safe, were laid bare and spread across the countryside. He would never again be whole.

Damn me...forever.

Hugh stopped halfway to the forest and turned toward the cliffs and considered. How much of a coward was he? For Charles had him there. He *was* a coward, a spineless, timorous coward. He was *beyond* cowardly. Hugh was not even fit to be considered a martyr for this, because what he did now wasn't truly for Amelia, but for himself. Hugh simply couldn't conceive of a solution in which he was not the one on his own in the end. So why not effect that end now? Shouldn't that be easier?

If Hugh could not manage an ending of any kind in which he wasn't the one bereft of her...why see it through? Hugh looked up to realize he was walking back toward the Cliff House and fell to his knees to stop his advance. Thrust his hands into the soft, unmanageable dirt of the rolling hills. Pulled and dug and felt the rocks tear at his flesh.

Coward.

Hugh punched the ground.

Worthless.

Punched it again.

Nothing.

Again.

He felt the pain lance through his hand and up his arm to his shoulder like an arrow. He stood and turned, staggering away from the Cliff House once again. He shook his left hand and felt a rill of blood trickle from a cut, spiraling his fourth finger, then dripping toward the earth. It served him right. Because even if he did return…Hugh no longer deserved her.

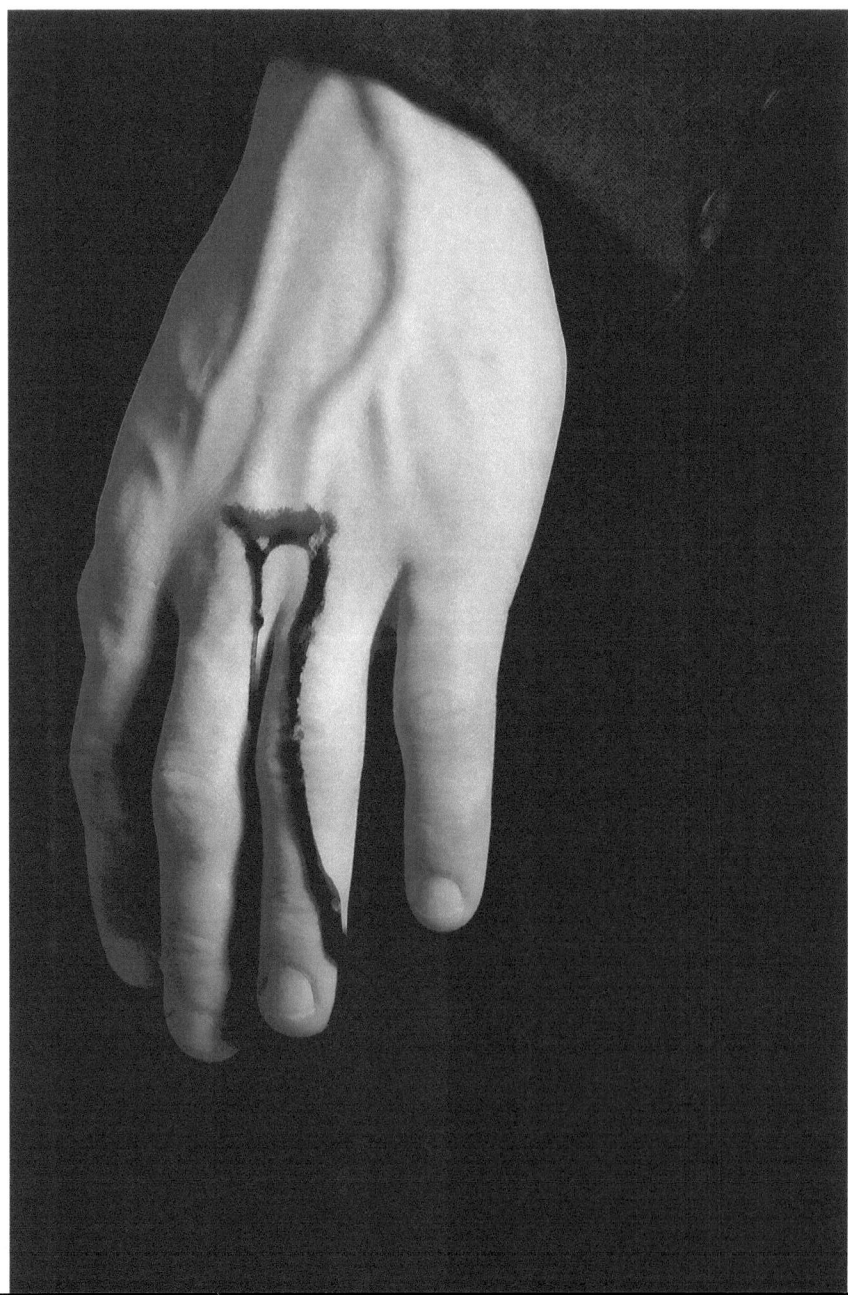

A

Amelia knew.

In the way Hugh made too many excuses.

In the way Charles didn't move.

In the way Hugh practically ran from the Cliff House.

In the way Charles had been silent.

In the way she now felt Charles's presence, his anger, emanating from him like a great furnace behind her.

She couldn't pull her eyes from the door.

She couldn't move her feet.

She couldn't turn around.

Amelia stood.

She simply stood.

She did nothing else.

Her back straight, her hands held gently—not too tight—on the throw around her shoulders.

Hugh.

Hugh left.

He left.

Hugh was gone.

He went through that door and let it close behind him—without me.

Hugh left me.

She breathed, felt her heart stop in her chest, then sucked in more air—forcing her heart to beat again. She wondered how exactly to alleviate the pain. It would stop when her heart did. Yet, that wasn't a possibility now, was it?

He'd left her.

He left me, she thought. At least, she thought she'd thought it. Apparently not, however, because Charles caused the air in the Cliff

House to shift around her, the floor to sway beneath her, then her very skin to shiver as he spoke over her shoulder.

"But that's *not* what I'm going to do." Charles's words behind her were hard, stern.

Very sure. Very specific. Very certain.

Yet he didn't touch her, and she was thankful. She was fairly certain if he touched her, she would spin, fall apart, rage, destroy, hurt.

What was it she did now if not hurt?

She took a deep breath and hoped, *hoped,* that in that breath, in the expansion of her chest, that Charles would be close enough behind her that she would collide with him, melt into him, possibly disappear into him, to allow him to feel this for her.

Shock. This is shock, she thought.

Hugh left me.

...

...

...

...

That's not *what I'm going to do.*

She efforted to turn, but it really just ended up being a twitchy dance of muscles as her body fought to stay where she was in the hope that the door would open and Hugh would be there.

The darkness came for her, as it always did, from the corners of her vision at first, a simple threat, a crawl, a snail's pace. Just a warning, this…this beginning of it. Though most of the time she missed this very beginning because she was preoccupied with other things. Whatever it was in the world that was causing her to panic—things, so many irrelevant things, simple and mundane things. Comparatively speaking.

Yet here, now, as she stood and did nothing else, she saw it clear as day as it closed in. Faded the corners, softened the center, loomed like a great winged bird over prey, the shadow chasing until there was nothing but the blackness.

This time, though, felt different. Because she wasn't the only one here. There was someone else with her, as though he waited in the darkness for her to arrive.

That's not what I'm going to do.

Charles didn't touch her with anything more than his breath across her shoulder and the heat of his hands close to her waist...it was not enough.

That's not what I'm going to do.

That small, gentle, quiet reminder that she was not alone. That no matter what happened, he was here with her and he would care for her, and as the final darkness came for her, she allowed it, she sank, and as she did, he spoke, the words on his breath settling on her soul as they chased across her skin.

"That's not what I'm going to do."

Charles's hands were on her before her head fell back, before her eyelids drooped, before her hands had released the blanket around her. He caught her long before she collapsed. Charles had been prepared for it. Knew he couldn't yet touch her as she would spin away from him, possibly hurt herself in some terrible way if he startled her enough at the beginning of her crisis. He wasn't sure how he knew this...but he did.

Charles just stood with her, comforted her as much as he could with only his presence, hoped that he could prevent any damage that might be caused by the fall.

Charles knew one thing...he could do this. He could be here for her. Charles could give her whatever strength he had, be her consciousness, her safety, her eyes and ears while she was away.

She always comes back.

Hugh's words in his head rankled.

Charles wrapped the blanket around her and moved toward the hearth. He kicked the rod that sat by the fire, knocking it down, then kicked the sharp end of it into the embers, and with his foot on the handle, he stirred the embers enough to let them reach new wood.

Then he turned to the big, overstuffed chair he'd recently vacated. Charles lowered himself, bringing her to his lap, letting her legs curl across his thighs, tucking her toes into the throw so they wouldn't grow cold.

Charles held on to her, rubbed her back, kissed her temple, whispered at her ear.

"That's not what I'm going to do. I'm not going to leave. I'm here for you, Amelia, I'm right here. I'm not going anywhere."

Come back to me.

"I'm waiting."

I'll wait for as long as you need.

Charles had never been so gentle, not in all his life. He'd never believed himself capable of this level of caution, care, as though his hands were not his own. It took all of his concentration to do this, to effort this kind of care, but he did it, thinking it was what she needed because it was what Hugh had always given her.

Charles listened to her breathing, watched for the changes. He knew she would be exhausted and wasn't certain whether she would actually wake this time or simply sleep. She'd done both in the past, depending on just how powerful her episode had been. Charles closed his eyes and held on.

How was this supposed to work without Hugh? Hugh anchored her, brought her back from the edge so easily. Hugh never panicked. He could see the episodes coming, knew what to do.

Charles couldn't yet do this. Perhaps this was more important, being here while she was gone. Perhaps he was concentrating too much on preventing the episodes, when what he should have been concentrating on was somehow lessening them.

Amelia didn't move. She didn't soften, and it frightened him. Charles wished to keep her as close as he could and threw aside what Hugh did for her, taking her into his form. Charles's arms wrapped about her like a vice, held her everywhere, caged her in and held her as tight as he could to his chest. Charles leaned his head in to surround her completely. He tightened every muscle he had mastery over. Charles held on—even as his muscles complained and started to vibrate—Charles refused to release his hold.

Finally, Charles felt her hand tighten on the blanket at his chest, and he opened his eyes. Her breathing was slow and deep, and she nestled into him, curling her toes against his thigh. She'd moved to sleep. It seemed to him that it had taken much longer than usual, but here it was. The change happened as he'd held on to her as though he'd never release her. Charles finally breathed, kept her close, and closed his eyes, letting his head fall back against the chair.

Every single one of his muscles complained. Charles was spent, beyond measure, as he'd never been in all his life. Sleep would do no harm at the moment, since there wasn't much else to be done, so he allowed it to take him.

TWENTY THREE

harles watched his wife sleep, the waning light from the sea shattering the darkness in the Cliff House with brilliant light. Charles had moved them both to the bed at some point in the afternoon, when his legs started to cramp, and he knew she wasn't going to awaken soon. He looked around them at the quiet of the Cliff House and understood what she loved about it, the simplicity. It was so easy to be here. One room for everything, instead of one room for each thing.

Perhaps he could disassemble the house and have it moved to the grounds at Castleberry Keep. There they could live happily in the tiny one-room home, undisturbed until they were both safe and sated. Charles didn't believe that time would come soon for either of them. Particularly since he was terrified of intimacy with her at the moment. Charles had no idea how he was to manage this.

Charles could see her mind working. It never seemed to quiet even as she slept, and he was mesmerized by it. The ideas that flitted across her features…if he could only hear but one. Perhaps one day she would share with him.

Charles moved a strand of her iridescent hair from her face, and she shook her head. "Shhh," was all he said as he tightened his muscles around her, and she settled back into his arms quietly. He was concerned, because she had been sleeping for hours. He knew she was exhausted after—everything—but he'd honestly thought she would have been lucid by now.

"Charles."

It was a whisper of a breath, but it meant the entire world to him to hear his name from her. Charles didn't mind at all being a pillow for this woman. He didn't mind at all that her hands were still clenched upon his sides, as though they belonged there.

He did mind when she then called *his* name.

"Hugh."

Charles tensed.

Her eyes snapped open, and she drew in a sudden breath.

"Is it not who you expected?" Charles said quietly.

"No, I...it's not the who but the what. Well, it is the who, as well as the what, is what I should say. I mean—"

"Amelia."

Her eyes caught his, and she smiled so brightly it stole his breath and took it straight out the window to set with the sun.

"I was dreaming of Hugh. He was quite angry with me," she said with a frown that Charles wanted desperately to kiss into oblivion.

"Why was Hugh angry with you?" Charles asked, restraining his own displeasure with Hugh. It wasn't for her, after all.

"Because I married without letting him know. You," she said quietly. "I married you, and he was not there as a witness."

"Truly?" Charles asked. She seemed so sweet, so young suddenly. It was disconcerting.

She shook her head. "Hugh should be a witness."

"Amelia, he was a witness," Charles said carefully.

She watched him, and then as if their entire stay was replayed in her mind, he watched as her features went from happy, to frightened, to sad, with nearly every other emotion in between. Then he watched as she clutched the blanket against her chest, closed herself off to him.

"Hugh is gone," she said finally, and the weight settled on them, reality back from wherever it had been while they'd slept.

Charles closed his eyes and rolled to his back. "Amelia, believe me when I say I would chase the man to the ends of the earth and drag him back screaming if it was what you wanted of me. But I fear it is not what he wants."

"I know."

"Amelia, when are you expected back at Pembroke?"

She shook her head, considered. "Sunday afternoon."

"Tomorrow?" Charles asked.

"Unless you must return, we have the night," she said.

Charles was concerned with this statement. Much could happen in one night. "Are you sure this is a good idea?"

"We—" She stopped abruptly, didn't finish the sentence, though from watching her he was fairly certain she'd finished her thought. "No time like the present. I'm sure they've brought some dinner. It's most likely outside in the box."

"I imagine we must be together, alone, at some point. However, today has been rather…difficult. I wouldn't wish to tax you."

Charles was already concerned. She wasn't acting herself. She'd just gone from childlike confusion to not caring that Hugh had abandoned her. Perhaps her mind had broken. Perhaps this reality was one she simply couldn't manage.

"Charles, we do this or we don't. There's no more Hugh. We have no options. It's us or nothing, and we both know what nothing means for me, so I'm quite well determined to see to this. You brought me back, Charles. You did. In fact, in what was possibly one of the most painful experiences of my lifetime, you were there for me and did exactly as you should have. It doesn't look as though I've damaged anything here."

And now she was perfectly lucid, reasonable. Not at all his Amelia. "No, you did not. You merely collapsed. I didn't touch you…I waited for it, for your mind to fade or…something else. I didn't want to startle you. I only wanted to reassure you."

Her eyes seemed to look past him out the window. "That's not what I'm going to do," she said quietly, and Charles knew. She looked back to him, and Charles felt a pain in his chest as though his heart had tripped on a stone and attempted to right itself. He truly wished to not speak of Hugh for a while.

"Amelia, you're truly brilliant. I still wish to know everything you're thinking…"

"I wish for that as well. I mean, when one thinks, often it's quite possible that everything will be thought of at some point. Though I do wish at times that thinking would cease, particularly when I'm tired. I do grow tired, and it would be so wonderful if my mind would cooperate and be quiet for me."

"You mean to say your mind never stills? Not ever?" Charles remembered this Amelia, the one who rambled. She had done this when they were younger. She would go on and on about something, and the subject would change as rapidly as the words flowed. It had been mesmerizing, and he realized he'd missed this side of her. She must have trained it out of herself to prepare for the *ton*. He looked back to her and concentrated on her words again.

"No, I don't believe it does. I believe my mind goes about its business regardless of the situation. It's quite distracting, really. I would so like to be at rest. I mean, not asleep but just...content. It seems like it would be such a nice thing to be content."

"Well, if that's what you wish, then we'll find a way for you to be content," he said simply.

She looked up at him then. "Well, St. George, I thought I'd not see you again so soon," she said with a smile. "I'm afraid I've no reticule for you to battle, though tossing one into the waves of the ocean from the cliff might well be dramatic enough. No geese to frighten, however, I'm afraid..."

Charles cleared his throat. "There are teachings in other cultures that promote inner thought and the control of it. Perhaps we could start there?"

She nodded, and her hands grasped his sides rather suddenly, making him jump.

"I'm sorry," she said.

"No, Amelia, I'm simply a bit sensitive where you're holding my ribs."

"You're ticklish?" she asked. Her eyes sparkled in the late afternoon light.

"Now, I didn't say that, exactly," Charles replied nervously.

Her eyes went round as the setting sun just over the horizon, and he felt her fingers vibrating with the urge to test her newfound knowledge.

"Amelia," Charles warned stoutly as his arms moved to hers.

Her fingers relaxed, then brushed his sides, and he jumped again.

"Amelia!" Charles shouted as he grasped both of her arms awkwardly and attempted to fend off her attack.

"You are ticklish!" she shouted as she pushed him over and straddled his thighs.

Charles bucked beneath her, trying to throw her off, but the strokes of her hands coupled with the tensing of his muscles hindered his movements terribly. He let go of her arms and grasped her hips then, truly attempting to arrest her movements. The sun shifted outside, and a beam of light caught across her eyes, and she ducked, stilling.

"Hugh left me," she said quietly, her eyes in the distance.

"Yes, but that's not what I'm going to do," Charles replied, pulling her down to his chest, stroking her hair back from her forehead.

She looked up to him, and her eyes cleared.

"Do you have clothes?" he asked. "Something not destroyed? I would like to take a walk on the moors."

She nodded and smiled, but it wasn't the brilliant one he'd hoped for. It was a start, however.

Hugh threw his head back against the tree and closed his eyes toward the sun, breathing deeply as he took in the moment of solitude in one of the most glorious places on earth. Hugh would never feel the same about this place. He would never feel the same about anything. He resolved to never return.

Hugh had fallen asleep leaning against the tree as he'd waited to make sure Amelia was okay. As much of a coward as he was, he could yet abandon her without knowing she would be well. But his exhaustion from the sleepless night and this morning caught up to him as he rested in the warmth of the day.

He dared not approach the Cliff House, but assumed they were doing well, since he'd not heard anything, and neither Charles nor Amelia had left. Perhaps he was lying to himself, perhaps he was still here because he needed to see her again, one last time.

He realized that seeing her after what he'd done may be his true end. He stood and turned to leave. When Hugh heard the laugh, he startled, tripping as he turned back toward the Cliff House and scrambled behind the tree to hide. He scanned the expanse of the moors.

The crimson slash was like blood through the trees, her thin shawl carried away on the breeze. Charles started to move toward it, running to catch it before it was carried out to sea.

Amelia's laugh carried on that breeze toward Hugh, taunting, calling to every nerve in his battered soul, and he leaned into the tree, his fingers digging at the bark as though to stay himself.

Charles caught the sash, then turned and ran back to her. Charles lifted the fabric and wrapped it around her shoulders, then rubbed softly, possibly to lessen the goose bumps that had no doubt formed on her arms from the chill breeze.

So she was well.

Charles stepped away from her, and she stilled, looking off over the cliffs. Hugh could feel the tension from even this distance. They pulled at him, Charles and Amelia, as though he were fettered to the both of them, some invisible rein that refused to break and would not allow him to simply leave.

But leave he must. Hugh pounded his forehead against the stiff bark of the tree. He must leave. He could not go back. He knew the next time he saw Charles the man was likely to destroy him physically, as much as he was already destroyed emotionally.

Hugh had had his chance. He'd tasted his future, but all he had seen was that it would lead to his pain, and he was too much the coward to see it through. This had been coming for years, even if he had refused to accept it.

Hugh turned, leaned against the tree for another moment, listened to the sound of her on the wind, the sound of Charles. The small banter.

Amelia will be fine. She will be fine. Hugh chanted it in his head, because he had to convince himself of this. *Amelia will be fine.* Even as all indications—everything he knew of her, all of their past together—told him something different.

Hugh had to return to London, do all the things that he said he was going to London to do. At least keep that much of his word. He wanted to return and hold her until she forgot what he had done.

Hugh pushed himself away from the tree and disappeared into the forest.

A

"I've never felt this...I don't know what to call it. I've always believed that I loved you, or at least, I convinced myself of it because it was necessary. But, this...when you touch me it...it awakens me...places in me I never knew were sleeping. That sounds a bit trite, does it not?" Amelia said as Charles wrapped her scarf around her shoulders. "Thank you for chasing it."

"You're welcome. I would hate to lose it. It's a perfect color on you. Particularly when you laugh and your cheeks go all rosy. Like this." Charles reached out to caress her cheek, then drew his hand back and left it suspended between them for what seemed, to her, forever. His fingers curled in on his palm, and he waited.

Amelia turned to the cliffs and watched the distant waves for a time. She loved this. Had always loved this, but now it felt, somehow, different. Why should it feel different? This had always been hers It would always be hers... *But Hugh had always been a part of it as well.*

"Amelia?"

"Charles, I want for you to touch me. Please."

She turned to find Charles had moved away—she hadn't realized. But he turned and gazed at her. It was not quite what she was expecting after saying something like that to a man, but that's what he did. He watched. So she smiled, and she waited. "Charles, I—"

"No, Amelia, don't—" Charles took a step back toward her and lifted his hand again, cupped her cheek. She felt the warmth of that hand to her toes and closed her eyes as his thumb traced the ridge of her cheek just below her eye. She breathed deeply of the forest and fields. She felt him move, and her mind stilled.

"Mon Dieu," Charles whispered.

Her lips parted, and Charles's hand at her back drew her in to meet him, the kiss more sweet than sensual, more staid than passionate.

She opened her eyes and gazed up at him as he kissed her, his hand moving to the back of her neck, his mouth on her mouth, *his mouth*. That thought made her twitch, and his eyes snapped open as he drew back.

"Amelia. This is well outside the range of possibility, I fear. We shouldn't," Charles said.

"I want..." She drew her eyebrows together, let the tension rest there in her forehead, sink into her mind, and start a whirlwind of sensation. "Charles, I...I'm nervous, but I trust you."

He frowned.

"Charles, kiss me again, please."

Charles seemed to recognize something in her eyes, then his chest quickly inflated and deflated against her. He shook his head, "I just...I need to wait a bit longer. I need to get my bearings. Today has been a bit much for us. I need to be sure..."

She wrapped her hands around his forearms, leaned into his chest. "I understand. What Hugh did...he hurt us both." Then she turned and pulled him toward the cliffs, watching the sun as it sank against the ocean.

"It's truly beautiful out here," Charles said.

She knew he was avoiding discussion. They walked the path at the edge of the cliff, far enough back that they were safe, but could still hear the ocean throwing itself at the base.

Amelia shivered and moved closer to Charles. Shivers meant so many things, and she wasn't sure what this one lauded. Fear? A chill?

Charles wrapped his arm around her shoulders, and she sank into him. They walked quietly along the cliffs for a while, and when the light changed, they turned back for the house.

"You must be starving. It's been a long day, and you've eaten nothing since yesterday," Charles said as he rubbed circles into her back.

"I very much doubt my stomach could handle food…" Her voice faded, and she shook her head, and he watched as her gaze drifted once again.

"Amelia, my love, come back to me," Charles said quietly.

He saw the blush spread like a slow tide moving just below the surface of the sand, growing and retreating incrementally.

The sound of her stomach growling broke his concentration.

"Oh, I beg your pardon. I…well. I suppose perhaps I could eat."

"Very well then," Charles said. He put her hand on his arm, and they moved toward the house.

Charles washed his hands under the pump, then splashed water on his face, noting that it had a slight salty tang to it because they were so close to the sea.

He pulled a basket from the stone box by the door used to protect deliveries from the elements and scavengers. Charles took it inside and found Amelia wrapped up in that throw, sitting in the chair by the fire. He put the basket on the table, then went and knelt before her.

Charles was afraid to touch her—but simply could not resist. His knees were on both sides of her feet, and he put his hands on her ankles, slowly stroking the soft skin just above her boots.

"Amelia, sweet," Charles said quietly.

She turned from the darkened embers and looked at him, her eyes nearly vacant she was so lost in thought.

"Hugh—" She stopped, and he waited patiently. "He's hurting."

This was something Charles had not considered. "That does not excuse his choice today," Charles whispered, desperately checking his temper.

"You don't know him as I do," she said.

Charles was still very concerned about pushing her, but she wished to talk, and so talk they would, for as long as she seemed able.

"I don't know him like you, this is true, but I do know what we decided. I do know that he said he would do whatever you needed of him. I do know that he made certain promises, not only to you…but to me. I do know he went back on all of those things."

"Pain…fear…these are the greatest of motivators. Hugh will never be bound to us in the way we will be bound to each other. There would be nothing for him if something happened between the three of us. He would be ruined. In every way. His inheritance requires marriage of him." She looked to Charles.

"I had not thought…we hadn't even discussed that far. I assumed we would…instead, he walked away without so much as a word. I trusted—" Charles stopped the thought. This pain wasn't for him. He was here for Amelia. What Hugh had done, he'd done to her.

She looked at him carefully, then continued. "As well, while you could protect *me* from rumors, you would be powerless to protect him. What could you say?" she whispered.

She was absolutely right, but, again, these things needed to be dealt with, not run from. "Are you wishing for me to forgive him?" Charles asked, shaking his head. Forgiveness wasn't in him. Forgiveness required something of him that simply wasn't there, hadn't been there. Had it? He and Hugh…they were just acquaintances. Weren't they? Two men with a common goal. That's it. Charles wanted to know why she was defending Hugh after what he'd done.

"I—" She looked him in the eye then. "I don't know what I wish for. But what happened here today was very unlike him."

Charles leaned forward, resting his forehead against her knees, and felt her hand tangle in his hair. It had seemed to him that this was not at all the Hugh he'd come to know in the past few days either, but the cold, heartless part? He'd known that Hugh before. He'd met with him often when they were younger. Part of Charles had expected this from Hugh, even as he had trusted him implicitly. He couldn't lie about this, not to himself. Certainly, he'd trusted Hugh with all his heart.

Charles and Amelia stayed like that for a time, his forehead on her knees, his hands traveling up her calves from her ankles, then back down. Then she tugged, and he lifted his head. She cupped his chin.

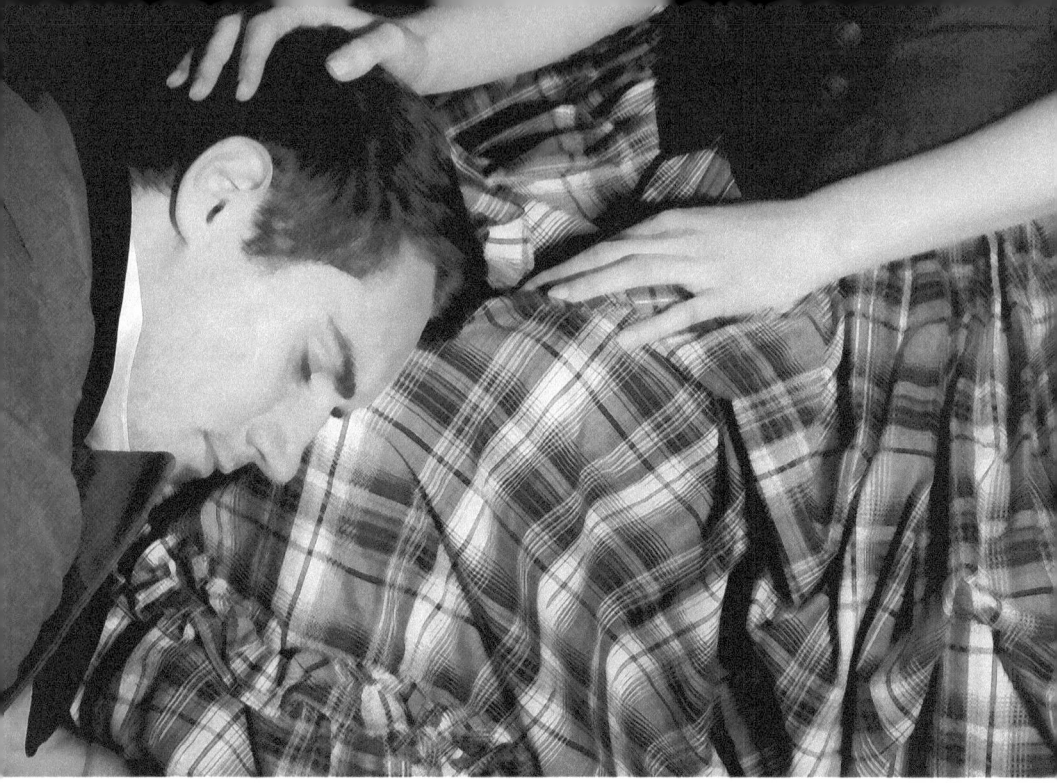

"I know this is difficult for you. I know…forgiveness is often dependent on love, and that's something you're unfamiliar with."

Charles drew a slow breath. *Love.* He didn't know what love was, did he? He didn't love Hugh, certainly. Perhaps he cared deeply for Amelia, but for Hugh? No, but he would allow Amelia some leeway in this discussion.

"And I know, Amelia, that of all people in this world you trusted him more than anyone. Hugh should not have broken that trust," Charles replied. He didn't like this. He felt very uncomfortable with all this talk of feelings. At some point, that raw new edge of his that had only just begun to open had closed again, seared with anger. It was the moment Hugh left.

"No." She let her hands fall to her lap, and Charles shook his head. It was as though the light had left her eyes, and he wasn't sure how to return it.

Charles considered all that she'd said. He wanted to destroy Hugh, pull him limb from limb, physically, mentally. In every way a man could be crucified, Charles wished to see it done. Not merely destroyed on this earth, but everywhere. Could Charles forgive him? But this assumed he cared for him, something Charles wasn't sure he could admit to. He knew that Amelia wanted Charles to simply leave Hugh be, or find some semblance of forgiveness for his actions, but Charles intended to destroy Hugh and never speak on it. Charles groaned against the thought. He was suddenly unsure whether he could do that to Hugh or to Amelia—and what did that mean for him?

Charles concentrated on the feel of her hand, which had returned to tangle in his hair. He closed his eyes. This felt like…falling. Charles felt unconstrained, at the world's end, unable to stay his advance regardless of the terror he felt at the fall. Like walking straight for the cliffs outside without a pause, just as she had described to him, except he knew she was waiting at the bottom to catch him. Amelia always felt as though her fall was never-ending.

Charles suddenly wanted the fall…that rift opened back up, and that's when he knew.

Charles stood abruptly and waked to the table. He pulled the basket of food toward him and unpacked it. Some ham, a block of cheese, some fruits, and a large loaf of crusty bread. There had also been a cast iron pot next to the basket with a lid on it. Charles shuffled around as he considered all the facts, everything that had happened.

He removed the lid to find some sort of stew, so he pulled one of the arms from the fire, hung the cast iron pot on it like Hugh had done and swung it back over to start the simmer. Then Charles added a bit of wood and stoked the fire back up.

Charles filled the kettle from the other arm with fresh water and pushed it back over the fireplace next to the stew and broke off a couple pieces of cheese, poured a glass of water and took them to her. Amelia still stared into the fire. Charles sat next to her, placing the water and cheese in her fingers.

Charles knew from his travels that there were practices in Asia meant to open your mind, to make you more accepting of the world. At the time he'd learned of them, he'd thought them hogwash, as he was perfectly able to still his mind wherever he was. There was no need for him to concentrate in order to be silent and accepting of his surroundings or situation.

She, apparently, could not. Charles thought perhaps she could learn to do this. That practicing some sort of concentration would help her to quiet her busy head. Of course, he wasn't entirely sure he wanted it quiet. Charles loved the way her expression flitted from idea to idea, even though she could rarely tell him what it was that was flitting around in there. As for the occasional words that escaped without her permission? They were like small gifts, though he knew she hated them. Perhaps this concentration would help her to explain these things as well?

He breathed deeply as the scent of the stew assaulted him, clenching his hungry belly as he groaned.

"Lamb, I reckon," Charles said quietly as he stood and went to stir the pot. "Oh…yes." He took a small taste from the spoon then stirred some more as his stomach lurched and rolled, fighting its way toward the succulent brew.

The sudden feel of her hands on his sides startled him at first. Then Charles leaned back toward her warmth, and leaving the pot to simmer with the spoon handle sticking out, he turned and wrapped her up in him.

"Amelia, I do believe…I'm quite desperately in love with you."

Amelia stared at his neck, that small divot that held the very taste of him. His chin, rough with whiskers. His mouth…her heart kicked like a mule. She shouldn't look at his lips, so she moved to his stormy eyes. It felt like he looked straight into the depths of her soul. Charles was not looking at the girl on the outside…she could feel him within her. Moving around there, looking at her memories, examining the very fiber of her being, refusing to leave.

"I—"

Charles did not allow her to finish but closed the distance between their mouths and kissed her with all the sincerity and passion of a man in love. He was…in love with her, and Hugh wasn't here. She needed to push Hugh from her thoughts because this…this was a massive revelation for this man, and she truly needed to be here for him. Now. There were no two ways about it—his realization changed everything. Her mind shifted like tumbled locks.

She moved her hands to his arms as Charles held her face, his hands tangled in her hair. She felt the tears on her cheeks, but dared not move to wipe them away. They gathered there above his hands, little pools of saltwater in the crooks of his thumbs that she could see the room reflected in. She started to fade and knew she had to change tack before she lost it. Because Hugh was gone, and Charles was here, and he had just conceded a great thing.

She opened her eyes to find him looking down at her, his thumbs stroking the paths of her tears, cleansing her cheeks and letting them be on their way.

"Amelia?"

"I love…"

"Pudding?" he asked with a smile when she didn't complete the thought.

She tried to smile but knew it hadn't happened. "There is something I must say. Perhaps we should sit down."

Charles nodded and released her, then turned for the stew. "First, you must eat. I know you're famished, as am I. Please, let me serve you." Perhaps he understood that they needed to slow the pace of this conversation.

Amelia dropped the throw to the chair, then walked to the little table in the center of the room and sat. Charles placed a steaming bowl of Cook's lamb stew in front of her. She'd always hated the idea of the stew, had had terrible nightmares about it as a child. She was forever attempting to rescue the poor little things from the hatchet.

Her father had scolded her when she'd named the animals that were to be used for food, but she couldn't help it. She believed they deserved to be remembered in some small way for their sacrifice.

"Amelia." She looked up to find him across the table. "I must say, if you learn to quiet your mind, I will be greatly disappointed if you do it so often that I'm not allowed to see your thoughts painted across your face."

She smiled.

"What were you thinking?"

"Of the lambs."

"I thought that was what this was. Was it a favorite?"

"Of mine? No. Well, yes. And no. The stew, of course, is wonderful, but I always felt for the lambs, you see."

Charles nodded.

"Do you? See, I mean?" She believed he might—or at least that he was beginning to. He was starting to understand the circles her mind traveled in, and she marveled at that for a moment.

"I do." He paused. "I was once whipped for setting free a pig that was to be roasted for a dinner with Her Royal Highness."

Amelia gaped. She knew she did. She felt the weight of her jaw as it hung there in shock. "You did not!" She snapped it shut.

"Oh, but I did. In fact, when I was presented at court to receive my title, she mentioned it. Her Majesty has a brilliant memory. She said she'd eagerly awaited the day I would come before her, only so that she could tell me—"

"What? What did she tell you?"

"She told me that she hated pork and was glad to see it run the land outside the Keep," Charles said with a smile.

Amelia's jaw dropped again. Then they laughed together. "I don't believe you."

"Oh, my dear, whether you believe me or not, I've no doubt it will be mentioned when we go to court."

She frowned.

"Amelia, I'm aware you don't appreciate the *ton*. In fact, I have little patience for society as it is. However, you do understand that I must present my bride at court for the queen."

"Oh yes, I do. I was only...well. I thought that you were supposed to do that before the marriage?"

"There are ways around that. Her Majesty is aware of our pending nuptials, of course. I spoke with her before I quit London. As is absolutely required of me."

Amelia nodded. "Of course. Far be it from me to assume you'd not done something so bold as to speak with the queen before even securing my hand," she said distractedly. "Charles, I need to say something."

"Eat first, please."

Charles moved a laden spoon to his mouth and blew across it to cool the stew before leaning across the small table and touching it to her lip. She acquiesced readily as the aroma rose to her, and she was overcome by the heady scent of Cook's famous dish.

The spicy sweet tang of the sauce and the light buttery flavor of the lamb filled her senses, and she melted into her chair, taking up her spoon and, rather unseemly, shoving stew into her mouth. When she was finished, she looked up to see him transfixed on her mouth. "I... pardon. I suppose that was rather indecent of me."

"Not at all. In fact, if you'd been delicate, I would have thought I'd not properly exhausted you, which might have damaged my male pride," Charles teased.

Male. Charles was male, and she female, and, by God, hadn't they proved to the heavens they knew just what to do about that? She blushed. Charles cocked his head...just a touch.

"Please eat, you must be just as famished as I am," she said.

He took a bite, and after a long moment she said, "Now if I might say what it is I wish to say?"

He pushed the stew around in his bowl. "Ender."

"Yes, I—" She narrowed her eyes. He hadn't called him that since they'd been here at the Cliff House. "I want to say something about... Hugh. Before, when you said you loved me, I only just realized—"

"What I said was, 'I do believe I'm quite desperately in love with you," he corrected.

"Yes," she replied.

"Just so you have it correct," he said over a large bit of lamb.

She smiled. "Yes. You said you're quite desperately in love with me." She felt breathless.

Not now not now not now...

She concentrated on where she was, kept her eyes on him.

He nodded once and smiled, and she felt she could go on.

"I love Hugh."

A

Charles put the spoon down and leaned back in his chair, studying her.

"You're mine," he said quietly.

She twitched, and he winced.

"Charles, please…"

He waited…he thought for a decent amount of time. "Please what, Amelia?" It seemed every muscle he'd had tightened on his bones, attempting to break them.

"Please. Let me finish."

Charles winced again at her tone. He rested his elbow on the table, then his head upon his fist to prevent the shaking he felt from rage, or sorrow, or pain—he wasn't quite sure just yet. Whatever it was, it was powerful, and he fought to prevent it overtaking him.

"I love Hugh," she repeated slowly. "But it's not what I feel for you. I've known all my life, really, that I love him. I've felt it in my bones, as though always a piece of me. I cannot now decide that I do not, because I do. I always have." She stood and walked around the table in front of Charles. "But what I feel for you is so very much…*more*."

Charles kept his chin on his fist.

"I've handled this bit terribly," she said. "I see that, and here's the rub. Generally speaking, I figure things out in my head long before they come out of my mouth. I have learned to do this. It prevents terrible pickles the likes of which can be so very destructive. You understand?"

Charles nodded again stiffly but did not yet move. *I love Hugh* continued to whisper just at the edge of his thoughts.

"The issue I see," she went on, "is that you have me speaking my mind. Screaming it at times, in fact. I…I simply do not have control of all my well-learned faculties at present, and for that I beg your pardon."

I love Hugh.

Charles narrowed his eyes and turned to face her as she sank onto her knees, and her hands came up to his thighs. Bother, that, regardless of the state of his mind, his libido was most definitely on full steam ahead. Her hands started to move lightly across the flesh of his thighs, and his mind tilted. Charles tried to concentrate. Charles knew she'd no idea what she was doing to him with her hands.

"What I feel for Hugh is so much more profound than simply love. I not only feel him in my bones, but deeper. I feel him in my soul. His is a calm love, while yours—" She closed her eyes and concentrated. "Yours is overwhelming, so powerful it is, so full, so…wild and unconstrained." She shook her head and looked at him.

"I think what I should have started out with, instead of *I love Hugh,* is that you…Charles, we have yet to truly know each other and even so…when you look at me, I can hear you speaking to my heart, even when you have not yet uttered a word. You simply take my breath away. This is something I've never felt in all my life, and it truly does affect me in ways beyond my control. A control which Hugh has always held for me. Knows better than I do. A control that is severely lacking where you're concerned, but I wish for you to have."

Charles brought his hands down over hers, pressing them lightly to still the incessant tingling that followed her fingers so he could concentrate on what he wanted to say. "And what I feel for you is so much more, so much stronger, than anything I've ever felt for anyone. At this point, I cannot imagine my life without you a part of it. And I do love you. Though this is all very new to me." Charles tried to smile then but felt the tension in his jaw waver, and he looked down.

"Charles."

He clenched his eyes then looked back up to her. Charles raised his hand to her face and shook his head. This sort of vulnerability was not familiar to him, and it made his skin crawl.

"Charles, I'm sorry to have distressed you. I'm so…I am so terribly sorry. I want you to understand this facet of love. You cannot love someone without the capacity to forgive them. You cannot. By that same tenet, you cannot forgive someone unless you hold a bit of them close to you. Otherwise, there is no need for forgiveness. When I speak of Hugh—and let me be clear—I may not yet have forgiven him for what he's done to you, but I will. I know I will because I love him, and

I trust him, completely. This is a misunderstanding. There is no other explanation."

Charles felt truly inconsolable. He'd heard what she said. He felt the truth of it to his marrow. But the pain he'd felt mere moments before was taking its time in dissipating. Possibly because he was still reeling from Hugh's departure. *Hugh's departure.*

It was a very real thing, that fear coupled with the thought of losing Hugh. Like a heavy blanket on his shoulders. And not merely because Hugh helped Amelia, but because Charles felt a kinship with him. He realized then that she was right. He'd never had need to forgive anyone in his lifetime. He'd never loved anyone to where that heaviness of hurt hindered him.

Charles had never forgiven his father for his callus mistreatment of him, because there had been nothing to forgive. He'd never loved his father as a son should. The relationship he'd had with his father on face was the relationship they'd had in truth. He'd simply been a man who trained him up to be who he was today. Charles hadn't understood then, but he did now.

To rid himself of this grief, he would have to forgive Hugh, for what Hugh had done to Amelia and for what he'd done to Charles as well. Charles was hurt by it, because he cared for Hugh. There was no other explanation. Though Charles had a feeling that destroying Hugh may give him the same satisfaction as forgiveness and was quite a bit simpler…

Charles nodded again, then patted her hands and stood. He grabbed the heavy counterpane from the end of the bed and took her hand as he passed by, waiting for her to stand and follow.

Charles stoked the fire one last time, then turned her, loosening her dress, letting it fall, then kneeling and removing her boots. He then sat back in the overstuffed chair by the fire, pulling her with him and wrapping them both securely in the counterpane.

Charles didn't want to speak. He was not yet ready, and he did not trust the words that would come. He did, however, want her to know she was cared for, and so very precious, and that what had happened, though it had torn him asunder, would be forgotten.

Hopefully soon. Perhaps after some rest.

Charles put his feet up on the small foot stool by the other chair and silently rocked them, staring into the flames as he caressed her back and felt her grow heavier and heavier, until she was full asleep.

TWENTY FOUR

"Jacks," Amelia said quietly, concentrating on the finger that circled her breast so carefully. The room was bathed in darkness, the moon cutting shafts of light wherever the breaks in the Cliff House allowed for it.

"Oh no," Charles replied.

"What?"

"Well, you've called me Jacks. That must mean I've gone and done something terribly wrong."

"Oh no…not terribly. Not at all, really." She paused, concentrating on the circles of his hand. "Charles?"

"Yes, Amelia?"

"I cannot seem to sleep with that…what you're doing there. It's a bit…distracting."

"My apologies, I didn't mean to wake you," Charles whispered. "I suppose more sleep might be healthy, but I find myself so terribly mesmerized by this soft bit of flesh here, and the way the moonlight from that window causes it to glow. Quite beautiful, really."

She leaned up to look, effectively moving the glowing bosom that had him mesmerized, bringing her mouth into the shaft of light. "Well, that's not quite the thing, is it?" she said.

"What?" Charles asked.

"I cannot see what you're talking about because I must shift to see it, but by doing so I move myself from the spot I was in, which is what had you so terribly mesmerized to begin with…you see?"

A

Charles was now staring at her mouth.

In the moonlight.

"Charles?" she whispered again.

"Shhh…" he replied. He leaned to her sweet, pink mouth and captured the next words with his tongue, not allowing her a breath as he pulled her toward him and the beam of moonlight emptied, leaving the room effectively barren.

"Charles?"

His head spun in the passion of her mouth on his. He knew he should stop.

"Yes, Amelia?" Charles grumbled against her mouth.

"Was that the solution to your predicament?" she asked sweetly from the darkened spot on the bed.

"Oh yes, quite," Charles said. "For now you are here in the dark with me, and my eyes can shut without fear they would miss something important."

"Oh, I see…Charles?"

He mumbled.

"Am I forgiven?" she asked quietly.

He shifted, and she tensed. "What need have I to forgive you?" If anyone should beg forgiveness, it was him. He'd caused her so much pain.

"I rather forced the issue with you and Hugh. I felt that—"

He pulled her tighter against his chest. "Amelia, you were forgiven the moment I laid eyes upon you. There is no chance I could hold any regrets against you. Yes, Amelia, you are forgiven."

"And…and you still love me?"

Charles stilled. Was love often so easily bestowed then taken away? "Yes, Amelia, I still love you—truly, madly, deeply. I'm in love with you. I always will be. You will always be forgiven." He wrapped his heavy arms tight around her and pulled her in as she melted against him. Settled. It occurred to him then that what he'd said then was exactly as she'd spoken of Hugh. In love, forgiveness was a foregone conclusion.

"Thank you." She seemed to tense as though to say more, but she didn't, and he let it go with the moonlight. Some discussions should be left to the darkness. Some discussions were better for the full light of day. This discussion, the one pertaining to he and Hugh, would possibly never reach breath in either.

He had a decision to make about the future. And he needed to do it soon.

Charles had visited Amelia daily since the return to London. His concern for her grew with each visit, as she seemed to be further and further away, constantly caught up in her thoughts.

He looked to Louisa. "You're concerned as well." he said simply.

She nodded. "I am, Your Grace."

"Has Hugh been to see her yet?" he asked.

"No, my lord, he has not. It's not like him at all."

"She isn't even aware of us at the moment, though her eyes are open and her mind is quite obviously working."

"She needs him," Louisa said quietly.

"I know she does, though I don't understand it. I thought we'd become closer, and yet here we are."

Louisa nodded. "I could never replace Hugh either, Your Grace, even as he taught me everything he does. I'm only able to help her to… manage her episodes."

"You'll be coming with her to Castleberry," he said it stiffly, not at all a question, even though he knew it should have been. He was just so…worried and frustrated as of late.

"Of course I will. I go where she goes. I always will."

"I'm grateful." He looked at Amelia again, her full attention out the window, at least it seemed. He knew her attention was actually somewhere inside her mind. "Has she ever been like this?" he asked quietly.

Louisa shook her head, then took Amelia's hand. "No, never. She comes and goes, but she's still here. We would not be having this conversation like this before." Louisa squeezed her hand, and Charles wished it was him touching her. They had been so distant since the return to London, as was proper. They couldn't possibly be anything more than absolutely proper at the moment.

"Amelia," Louisa whispered. "Amelia?"

Amelia turned her head, stared at the hand in Louisa's but was still silent.

"Amelia," Charles started. "I must speak with your father again." He wished to take her up, to hold her, to try to suffuse her with his strength, his warmth, to melt the freeze that held her.

"Charles." She looked up. "Charles, but you've only just arrived," she said with a smile.

He looked to Louisa then back to Amelia. "I'm afraid a short visit today. I have so many arrangements to make before the wedding and such." He stood, and Amelia and Louisa followed. "I will see you tomorrow," he said as he tried to smile. He took her hand, turned it over and placed a kiss in her palm. "Louisa, you should begin to prepare her things for the move," he said quietly then he nodded. "If you need me."

"Your Grace," she replied. Amelia took Louisa's hand and turned back for the window.

Charles was led to the duke's study to sign the marriage contracts that should have been drawn up for him. He wished he could find Ender. He had so very much to say to him. Truth be told, he couldn't manage to stay with Amelia for long, because when he saw Amelia, his anger toward Hugh tended to spiral beyond control. He needed to go over the contracts and quit this house to find him.

"Ah, Castleberry. Welcome," Pembroke said.

"Your Grace. I assume you have the final contracts prepared?" Charles asked.

"I do. I'm happy to forward them to your solicitor, if that would be amenable to you."

"There's no need. I'm here. I can look them over," Charles replied as he took the chair across the desk.

"I assume you saw my daughter first?" Pembroke asked.

"Yes, I quite look forward to the marriage. She will be a splendid duchess," Charles said carefully.

Pembroke watched him as though looking for some sign of discord. "As I have always said, she has been raised to be such. Though, lately I have some concerns—"

"Do you?" Charles asked. "I don't." He wondered if he should push Pembroke when they were so close to being done with this. He took the offered papers and started to read them. The usual clauses were in place, the transfer of her holdings in her dowry, all of her property, everything she owned listed as though she were naught but property. Perhaps that was all she was to this man.

"Castleberry, I look forward to a strong partnership with you in the House," Pembroke said.

Charles looked up from the papers. "As ever," he replied. "This looks to be in order, except for the Cliff House. It's my understanding that property, which borders mine, is part of her dowry."

"I had planned to give it to her as a wedding gift," Pembroke replied.

"No, include it here, and then I will sign the contract. She already expects the property. There's no point in playing at a surprise gift," Charles said frankly.

"Of course, Your Grace. I had only…well, I hadn't considered that, I suppose. I will have it added to the marriage contracts." Charles knew he wasn't happy.

"Well, bar that, I will request an audience with the archbishop and obtain the license." Pembroke didn't say anything, and Charles stood. "We have an agreement."

Pembroke held his hand out across the desk, but did not look all too happy. "Castleberry, until then."

Charles shook his hand, then turned and left. He still had a man to find.

TWENTY FIVE

Hugh had no idea what he was to do next. He'd gone to White's, made a circuitous appearance, a few well-placed nods, then left. Hugh wasn't in the mood for talk, bets, seeing or being seen. But at least he'd been and done his duty. For, what was he now if he didn't keep his word?

Now he sat at a table in the back of the Iron Duke, a pint warming between his hands.

Hiding.

At the bottom of a glass.

Coward. Coward. Coward.

The word bounced and echoed in his head. He heard the chair next to him slide as someone took a seat, but he didn't lift his gaze from the deep amber liquid.

"You've finally turned Amelia over to her future husband then?" It was Perry's voice beside him. Hugh was at least thankful for that. Perry was Lord Peregrine Trumbull, the Viscount Roxleigh, brother to one of the most powerful dukes in the UK and recently married to someone quite beneath him. If anyone knew of scandal, and the quashing of such, it was this man. In fact, if anyone were familiar with mental illness, this man was. His mother had been committed to Bedlam when he was young, and his brother's wife nearly had been as well. Perhaps—but, no, there was no help for him anymore.

"Husband," Hugh grunted out.

"Is that so? I hadn't heard—"

Hugh cut Perry off with a wave. "It's not yet official, but she's truly his wife. There's no going back on it at this point." Hugh didn't mind alluding to what he was with Perry, because he knew Perry would never speak of this with anyone, as he was happily married and had no need to impress anyone in the *ton* and, truthfully, never had attempted to anyway. Perry was safe.

"I see, and what of you then, Hugh? We always thought her father would give up on his sights for the Castleberry, or that she would wait him out and marry you to spite him," Perry said.

Hugh shook his head slowly. "I would never have been able to protect her. You know more than most. You know how the *ton* treats women. She would have been ruined, could possibly have been committed once Pembroke died—or if she were disagreeable, possibly before then. You understand."

Hugh saw Perry nod. "I do understand that particular difficulty, but happen to believe, as my brother does, that doctors, conventions, opinions, are not always correct. You have to listen to your heart. If you believe this woman to be sound, or at least sound enough to be a wife, then why wouldn't you pursue and protect her to the best of your ability regardless of the *ton* and her father?"

"I do believe this, with all my heart, it only…the situation is so difficult. She thinks…and now Castleberry believes…that she needs me in her life."

"Perhaps she does. You may know her better than most at this point. What do you believe?"

"That I was meant for her."

"Then what's the issue exactly?"

"Her father won't allow us to marry. She's promised, and now, well…"

"Married but not married?" Perry asked.

"Yes. Married but not. I believe Jacks will learn to handle her, and they will suit. I believe this."

"Does he love her as well?"

"I believe he does, though he has yet to acknowledge the fact."

"So it isn't merely a cockfight, but that you both love and care for this woman, who loves, cares and needs the both of you, albeit for different reasons. And, finally, the problem, that she cannot have you both. Is this correct?"

"That is…the simple of it, I suppose," Hugh said.

"So what of you, then?" Perry asked again, a bit more somberly.

Hugh shivered. "What of me? Does it matter? I'll find some woman who wants to bear me children and leave me be. Perhaps that Rigsby girl. I know she would be amenable to that."

"You're an ass," Perry said after a moment of silence.

Hugh looked at him then.

Perry continued. "Who do you find yourself talking to? You truly believe this kind of martyr speech will set well with me? Try again, and this time attempt to avoid speaking like a buffoon. If you wish for the world to treat women better, then you, yourself, must do the same. Don't pretend to throw yourself away on some 'chit' in the *ton*. We shall cease being friends."

Hugh blinked down at his ale, then looked back to Perry, who continued to stare at him in challenge. "We were together, the three of us, and it was one of the happiest moments of my life. One that can never be repeated. A situation that would never suffice. I—" Hugh shook his head, quite unbelieving that he'd even spoken of what had happened in the Cliff House.

"Well, why is it you cannot be together? The three of you? I understand Castleberry's land is far from London, rather out in the wilds on the coast. Unless you invite people there—"

Hugh shook his head, momentarily shocked by Perry's easy acceptance. "And what happens to me when they don't need me anymore?"

"Oh, so that wasn't the simple of it. I see."

Hugh felt like he was shrinking into the background. Where once he'd been the single most important person to Amelia, now he was one of two. If he continued on this path, he would mean nothing to her. That was something he couldn't stomach. "I am too much the coward," he said quietly.

"That much is blatantly obvious. Love requires bravery, my friend. You cannot be shy. You cannot be lax. You must stand for something, be someone. Amelia needs for you to be something, and you've taken that away. In her state, what do you think that's done to her?"

"I haven't seen her. I left her at the Cliff House with Castleberry. Alone." He knew he was becoming agitated. He should have been watching his words more carefully.

Perry looked around, then grabbed his arm. "Let's go before you damage the lot of you. Come, I've a sudden need to kiss my lovely wife, regardless," Perry said.

Hugh grunted as Perry pulled him up and shook him off, holding on until Hugh got his legs beneath him. How many pints had he managed?

A

Amelia dug through the boxes in her sitting room, wondering what she was to do with all of it. It seemed she'd managed to keep so much from her past that her future was to be burdened by it. Trinkets, clothing, even natural artifacts like rocks and leaves. She was overwhelmed both by the thought of moving it and of disposing of it all—for she remembered every single moment attached to every single piece. That was what mattered to her. She had a room like this in both houses, here in London as well as at Pembroke-by-the-Sea. Some of the most important of the boxes traveled with her.

Each little thing took her back, immediately, to the time and

place from whence it came, and it calmed her to revisit these things, because they were all joyous memories. That was all she kept in these boxes, the hopeful memories, not the bad, never the dark. She visited the dark enough as it was. There was no use in her keeping remembrances of it. So here she sat in a dim room next to her own bedchamber, full to brimming with boxes of things from the past. And what did it all mean to her future?

She wished she had the reticule, the one Charles had thrown in the pond. But she didn't, and of course she didn't. That reticule was at the bottom of a pond. She regretted that, even that in the keeping of the reticule, the moment that had made it important would never have happened. She considered it, remembered that day so very clearly. The moment he'd picked it up and weighed it in his hand to determine the strength with which to toss it. The reticule taking flight, the sun glinting off of it as it sailed through the open air. The beating of the wings from the startled geese as they took flight when the reticule-bomb hit the water amongst them and exploded in a shimmer of water.

She didn't need the actual reticule to remember these things, and she suddenly realized her memory of that moment might be stronger for it. Because, while in some of these things she remembered the moments surrounding them, some of them she remembered more for the keeping of them. The why she remembered, of course, but the moments, the feelings, the exhalation and reasoning behind the wish to keep? Not as much.

She could live a second lifetime in this room just remembering… or she could go out in the world and create new memories with Charles and Hugh.

Hugh.

Amelia pulled a familiar box toward her. The box held some rocks from trips to the stream and a snubbed candle she'd used to sneak out of her rooms to meet Hugh at the back of the house, after which they ran to the Cliff House and lay gazing up at the stars as they fell from the sky. It contained the linen sheet they'd lain upon…well, what was left of it, as it had become so weary-worn with time that it was no longer truly a single piece. Louisa had tried to persuade her to keep just a square of it, but Amelia hadn't been able to part with any bit of it. This box also contained pressed, dried flowers that Hugh had given her that night.

Louisa. Amelia looked about the room, wondering where she'd gone off to. "Louisa?"

"Here, my lady!" Her voice was muffled, and Amelia heard shuffling and scratching, as though a large rodent was coming through the stored boxes to find her. Amelia stiffened, though she knew it was merely Louisa, and waited patiently for her to emerge.

Louisa's hair was a nest of curls on her head. Her mobcap had slipped off at some point and was stuck in her apron pocket. She had smudges across her cheeks, and her nails were rather grubby. Amelia smiled.

"This room is not nearly that filthy is it?" Amelia asked.

Louisa's eyes widened, "Oh, no, my lady, no. It's only that I tripped and fell into a rather dark corner and had to fight my way out beyond the old holly brambles and evergreen chains."

"Ah, yes, well, those were from the last Christmas Hugh was with us, before he was off to Eton. That made it special. Greens filled the town house with such a lovely scent—though now they're rather dry." She knew every single piece, and where it was in this room.

"Yes, dry and brittle and a bit dangerous, like tiny knives they are! At any rate, perhaps we save just a bit of it now? After all, he had yet to tell you of his departure when you saved these greens, milady," Louisa begged quietly.

"Yes, of course," Amelia said as she turned back to the box in front of her. Louisa was right. She saved too much, out of fear of losing so many memories. She'd had no idea when she'd saved the greens that they would become special in that way. That was the crux of it. She kept things with the distinct fear of losing something she did not yet have, or even know of. "Louisa, I really think I should lessen the load for the carts. I see no need to take all of this with me…and I wish to make new memories. I wish to…move forward."

She looked up to Louisa and could see the surprise and concern in her features. Was this choice truly that monumental? These were only things. *Things.* Yet, they'd meant everything to her at different points in her life. But now…

Now.

Now she wished to throw off the constraints of her life and move forward. *None of these things matter.* Amelia's hands tightened on the box before her, and she amended the thought. They mattered in their own ways…but they were small, and she wished to spend her time with the people in her life, not the things of her past.

"Amelia, I can't—"

"No, no, Louisa, I'll go through these. I'll choose. But they don't need to be packed up just yet. Let's work on my wardrobe and other things first, shall we? I'll definitely need clothes." Amelia took Louisa's hand and pulled her through the door to the hall. "Now, all the winter clothes are already packed up and ready—"

"What of Ender?" Louisa cut in.

Amelia turned to her. "What of…pardon?"

"Forgive me, my lady, but Lord Endsleigh? What of him? You haven't mentioned him since you returned, and I thought…well…"

Amelia shivered, then sat in her overstuffed chair. She didn't know the answer to Louisa's question. She'd no idea what would come of Hugh. Charles had said to leave him be and to trust him, that if Hugh were of a mind, he'd return to her. But Amelia wasn't so sure. After what Hugh had done at the Cliff House, Amelia knew that he thought his reputation with Charles, and certainly with her as well, was irreparably damaged. Amelia wasn't sure that Charles would allow himself to forgive Hugh either. That concerned her above all. It was something she knew Charles could do…but something he'd never had need to do.

Growing up in a household where love wasn't necessary and the by-products of love were absent created a man who was so entirely sure of himself…Amelia wasn't sure how he was going to handle the changes. In a mere few days, Charles's life had been upended. A man who didn't believe in love, had no idea what it meant or what it felt like, had discovered it. Not merely in her, but in a friend. For that friend, for Hugh, to then upend all the strides Charles had made—and she knew it had not been easy for Charles—it could be devastating. Yet there was nothing for her to do. Charles had to face this on his own, and Amelia had the feeling that Charles was going to hunt Hugh down once he arrived in London, after he settled everything with her father.

Amelia felt Louisa take her hand. "Amelia?"

Amelia shook her head. "Sorry, Louisa, I was…I don't really

know."

"I'm sorry, my lady, I just…I knew he was at the Cliff House with both of you, and he left before you. I thought as he'd reconciled with the two of you and…"

Amelia was sure Louisa wasn't quite sure how to ask what she wanted to ask, and Amelia, upon returning from the Cliff House, had not shared anything with her beyond that she was to remove to Castleberry Keep at the behest of her future husband. Amelia knew Louisa had expected more from her, for Amelia always told Louisa everything, until now. Everything that had happened at the Cliff House she'd kept to herself, closely guarded. She didn't want to damage Hugh in anyone's eyes. It was going to be difficult enough for him to recover with Charles. If Hugh had to fight everyone else in her life as well…she simply couldn't do that to him.

Amelia turned her head to the window, letting the warmth of the sun soak into her eyelids. She missed him like…the flowers must miss the sun at night. She felt closed, quiet, somehow shadowed, and she knew the minute Hugh came back to her, she would open to him as she always had. She would feel free, basking in the warmth of his love, and Charles's. Charles hadn't been the same since Hugh had left either.

Something had happened between the two men, she felt it. Amelia didn't think Charles had ever trusted another man, not truthfully. Charles was ever wary of all people, but men in particular. A boy raised merely for the purpose of command had no idea what it meant to love or trust in another man. He only knew what it meant to rule and to be ruled. People were merely his wooden soldiers. Trust was not a requirement, because he was taught to trust no one but himself. He must be solid in his beliefs, that he knew what was best in any situation. He must not second-guess himself, and he needed nobody to tell him what needed to be done. If he couldn't figure that out for himself, he wasn't truly worthy.

Amelia and Charles had talked a bit about how he'd been raised, the cold truth of it. The analytical, perfectionist control of it. Lacking of anything requiring trust, love, care, kindness…all the things that meant the utmost to her in her life, he'd been raised to ignore, trained to avoid, and had learned to cut emotion from his dealings.

Amelia believed Hugh had gotten to Charles, and Charles had conceded some level of trust, certainly, but possibly more than that.

So when Hugh had left, though she was wholly caught up in her own emotional turmoil, she'd felt through Charles such a great discord that it frightened her. To the point that she'd made Charles promise, on his honor, that he would do nothing to damage Hugh.

"Amelia?" Louisa's voice was quiet, and Amelia turned to her. She'd knelt beside her and placed one hand on her knee. "Is aught amiss?"

"No, I…yes, Louisa. I should tell you. Charles told me to trust in him…but I fear, I fear that what Hugh has done has put him in grave danger. I fear Hugh has gone much too far this time…and though Charles attempted to convince me that everything would work out in the end—because it must—I'm simply not convinced of that."

Louisa ran her hand down Amelia's leg through her heavy skirts, then back up again, a soothing, calming gesture. "Well, my lady, tell me what's happened and let me see if I can help at all."

Amelia turned to her. Louisa had been friends with Hugh before she'd come to work as her lady's maid, and she'd always seemed to have a sort of insight into his behavior. She thought perhaps Louisa had come from London originally, but she hadn't really asked, as Hugh had told her that Louisa's past was painful and irrelevant. She watched the concerned face of someone she actually considered more a friend than a servant, though, of course, she was the latter.

*The point was…*Amelia trusted her. Even so, Amelia wasn't sure she should tell Louisa what Hugh had done. Of course, Louisa had never judged anything in her life, so perhaps she could hear this and not cast Hugh aside or treat him differently. Further, how would Louisa react to Amelia having been with both of them? How was she to explain this?

Trust. Everything in Amelia demanded that she trust. Charles had asked her to trust him, and Louisa, she'd never done anything that would hurt Amelia. So Amelia would tell Louisa everything, and she hoped, *hoped*, that of everything she had done in her life, it wouldn't be this latest action that Louisa determined to judge.

"Amelia?"

Amelia heard the concern in Louisa's voice and turned to her.

"Where do you keep going off too, milady?"

"I...didn't realize." How long had she been contemplating? She felt like she kept drifting away...long enough to draw attention and concern from Louisa. "I have to tell you something, Louisa. Please sit with me."

A

"You're an ass," Perry said easily.

"I believe we already covered that topic, Perry. Perhaps we could move on?" Hugh asked as he stared down the too delicate tea cup in his hand. After all, if anyone knew what kind of jackass he was, it was he.

Hugh shook his head. He should never have come here after all. What the hell was Perry going to do for him? "Can't we have a bit of whiskey? This is—"

"I believe you've imbibed enough drink for the moment. I need to get you clear on a few things, and I need to be certain you're hearing me. Down it and be done with it." Perry watched him, rubbing his thumb along his jawline.

"You're not having tea." Hugh knew he sounded like a child.

"I'm not behaving like an ass. Wait, let me quantify that," he said when Hugh opened his mouth to argue. "Previously, I had only assumed you were a jackass based on a few random statements you said in a pub. But now having the story in its entirety, I have the proof needed to determine the actual level of jackassery you've attained, and let me just tell you, sir, it's astounding. Drink the tea," Perry said stiffly. He obviously wasn't being sarcastic.

Hugh drank, then placed the cup on a side table before his tension broke it. It was desperately delicate, and when Lady Trumbull had handed it to him, the pride had shown through her eyes. He was terrified of breaking that cup. To see her disappointment when she returned to shards of china would have certainly shattered his already ruffled composure. He leaned forward on his knees, and his head fell forward into his hands. He knew he was lost.

"Do you love her?" Perry asked.

"Ye—I…it's so much more complicated than that," Hugh said.

"What's your plan?" Perry asked simply.

"Plan?" Hugh looked up at him. "What plan? I've effectively declared war with the Duke of Castleberry. I may as well have done so with your brother, for all the power that man wields. If I thought I'd be ruined by being with them…I expect to be dead within a fortnight. I have no need of plans," Hugh said as Perry studied him. Perry was so disarming, just his gaze felt like a fillet knife peeling back layers of his skin.

"Well, if you're resigned to such a fate, so be it. But I believe Amelia expects quite a bit more of you," Perry said quietly.

Perry stared at him, waiting for his reaction and response, and Hugh knew he was being tested. Hugh was exhausted. What was it with all these peers pushing his buttons to see how he would dance? It was a constant test of his dedication, courage.

Courage.

Well, he was a coward, so there was no courage here. Hugh turned away. "I should not have come here. I—"

"Ah, I see," Perry said.

"What?" Hugh said a bit too loud and much too short. "What is it you see?"

"Well, that you merely came here to wallow. You didn't, in fact, come here for aid or solutions. But, Hugh, you should know by now if you're simply looking to wallow you needn't take up my time. You merely needed to pay someone to pretend to listen to you. A whore, for example, or a bartender. Unfortunately, you found me, and as I was actually *listening* to you, I now require something from you in return," Perry said easily.

Hugh shook his head. Perry was correct, but was it possible? Did Hugh think there was a way to repair what he'd done? No...not possible. He'd broken with Amelia in the worst possible way, and not just that, but he'd effectively broken with Charles as well. In fact, at this moment, Hugh believed what he'd done to Charles much more grievous than anything he'd done to Amelia. Hugh said, "I...I don't...I can't...I just can't begin to fathom..."

"Exactly, *you* can't, which is what brought you here," Perry said. "The fact is, when you're in the middle of the tempest, you can't easily see the cause, or the solution."

"Do you...do you have difficulty with the *ton*?" Hugh asked, nearly *sotto voce*. He knew he didn't need to explain himself. Perry had married a milkmaid from Kelso. A viscount from one of the oldest and most esteemed families in the United Kingdom had married a milkmaid.

Perry shook his head. "The problem, as I see it, is you're actually concerned with what the *ton* thinks. That's something you need to rectify immediately. Once they discover you've little care for what they think... well, they'll move on to someone who does care. It makes the entire situation much more entertaining when the victim cares.

"I would think you'd learned to play this game already. I brook no arguments. I give no quarter. We've an understanding, the matrons of the *ton* and I: They leave my family alone, and we leave them well enough alone. Nobody needs an enemy in the Duke of Roxleigh, to be sure. As for the gentlemen...well, not a single one of them need Roxleigh as an enemy in the House. That makes it all very simple."

"You make it all sound so easy when we will be labeled as sodomites!" Hugh yelled.

"Are you? Sodomites, I mean. I'd assumed that it was only Amelia that you—"

"Yes, it is. Jackson and I do not...we don't even care for each other. So you see it isn't that simple."

"Isn't it?" Perry asked. "I much prefer simple to complicated. You seem to enjoy making everything much *more* complicated than it need be." Perry held up a hand and ticked off his fingers. "Protect the women, stand for something, work. What more do you need in life? Amelia was given to you to protect. What are you doing at the moment to ensure that protection?" Perry asked.

"I have given her over to Castleberry," Hugh replied.

"Not good enough. That protection was given you by her father. *Her father*! Did he give you leave to pass it off on another man? Did Amelia?" Perry asked.

"No…but he made it clear when he accepted Castleberry's suit that—"

"I see…No, I don't. *Do you love her?*" Perry enunciated each word as he leaned toward Hugh.

"Yes." It was so unquestioned in Hugh's mind that the answer was nearly a knee-jerk reaction.

"For fuck's sake! Getting you to admit that was as difficult as getting my brother to realize the same. If you love her, then what the bloody hell are you waiting for?"

"I don't know. I thought—"

"You're thinking too damned much, Hugh. If you love her, nothing else matters."

Hugh watched Perry for a moment as he let the words sink in, then his head fell to his hands. "What am I doing? What have I done?" He looked up to his friend. "Thank you."

Perry flicked his fingers as if to send him on his way, and Hugh couldn't help but grin. "Thank you," he repeated, then turned and left.

TWENTY SIX

Charles threw his hat and coat toward his butler as he stormed through the grand entrance of his town home. "Bloody fucking hell!" He'd been in London for only a few days, and he'd already had enough of society. And Hugh—*goddamned bastard*—where the hell was he?

"Your Grace."

Hugh was never home when Charles had gone to his rooms. At least, that's what he'd been told. He certainly hadn't forced his way into the man's home. He'd promised Amelia.

"Your Grace."

Charles never should have made that promise. Tracking down Hugh had been impossible. He supposed a rat that wanted to hide was about as difficult to find as…as…well, a rat that wanted to hide.

"Your Grace."

Charles stormed through the entry toward his study, his mind flaring on Hugh. Charles missed Amelia with a soul-deep, gut-wrenching power. Yes, he'd seen her, but it hadn't been her. She'd changed. She was different. He wanted to return to the Keep. Charles didn't want to be here chasing down a man who had no wish to be found, but Charles needed him. Amelia needed him. This was a right damned turn. Charles wanted to break things.

He threw open the door of his study, but the crash wasn't satisfying enough. He turned to grab the door and slam it against the wall a second time, but stopped when he considered that even should the wood splinter and crack, he wouldn't find enough satisfaction in it.

"Your Grace!"

Charles finally realized his butler had been attempting to get his attention this whole time. He stopped in the doorway, disbelief washing over him.

"Your Grace, you have a guest," the butler said quietly, a bit out of breath from chasing him through the entry.

But Charles was busy assessing the scene before him. The guest stood and turned. Charles took two steps toward him.

"That will be all," Charles said to the butler.

Charles waited to hear his butler's footsteps recede, then he took the door he'd failed to damage and swung it shut as hard as he could, his eyes never leaving the man before him.

"Hugh."

$\mathcal{A}$

"My lady, are you sure 'tis all right if I leave?" Louisa asked quietly. She was concerned with leaving Amelia alone, considering the way she was behaving lately. Amelia seemed so very lost.

"Go, Louisa. I'm simply packing things, so you go see your beau. I'll be fine here, working on this."

Louisa ruffled a bit at the mention of her beau. She wasn't truly sure how Amelia would react when she discovered the truth of it, but she knew the deception to be necessary at the moment. This secret of hers could be her lady's salvation. As well, it could be Louisa's swift end—quite literally. It terrified Louisa, but she had to take this chance for Amelia after all she had done for Louisa.

Amelia seemed happy to stay at the town house, collecting her things and readying them for their own journey to her new London residence, and Louisa was glad they were here in London so she could track down Endsleigh. She had to figure out what he was doing. He had to know that Amelia was not well, and Louisa knew he couldn't abandon Amelia, though by all indications that's exactly what he'd done.

Louisa considered going to Castleberry as well, but they weren't familiar enough, as she was a lowly servant. She simply could find no situation in which that would be considered acceptable. She stopped as suddenly as the thought had occurred to her, almost tripping over the sway of her own skirts. There was one situation in which a lowly servant could pay a visit to a duke. Now she needed only to determine whether to see Ender first or go straight to the source.

This was a right bosh of a mess. The fault lay squarely on Ender's shoulders for it as well, from how it sounded. Ender must be so desperately hurt, but the only way to fix this…well, she wasn't sure *any* of her efforts could fix this if the duke was set to destroy Ender, and that's exactly what she figured he was planning to do, no matter what Amelia said.

What a mess. Louisa straightened her back, determined to do what she must. She stopped again. She was leaving the house under the pretense of visiting her beloved and wouldn't her acquiescence be required for this idea to work? Perhaps she should go there first. But Louisa could never go there. That would have been entirely too dangerous for both of them.

Louisa's head spun. So many factors. She'd no idea where to start. Louisa drew a deep breath and headed outside and down the walk. Since one of the destinations was walking distance from where she was, she decided to let fate have it, and that's where she headed.

A

When the door to the study slammed open, it sounded as though a freight train had crashed into the room—and perhaps it had. Hugh could very nearly see steam rising from Charles's head, the anger roiling from him like a tangible force, so palpable the very air grew heavy around him, weighted his shoulders, attempted to push Hugh to his knees.

Amelia is not here to protect you, he thought.

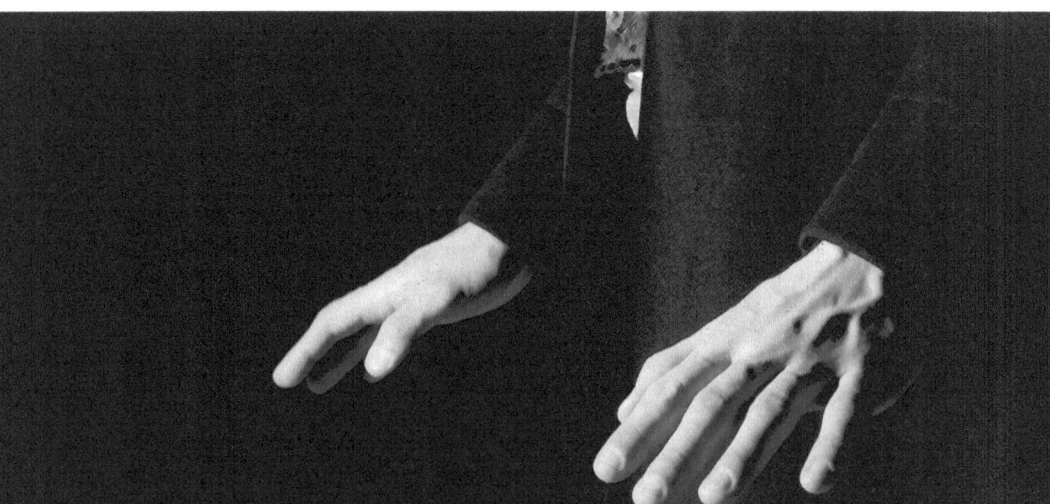

Hugh fought his own body's response to kneel, though he did want to fall to his knees now. He wanted to beg, he wanted to plead, he wanted to explain, but Hugh knew that whatever happened next was entirely up to the angry duke who stood at the entry and stared at him as though he'd just found the one thing he'd been looking for…only to ensure that *thing* would never be heard from again.

"You." Charles's voice was deep, rough, broken, and quite honestly the most terrifying thing Hugh had ever heard. Hugh wasn't entirely sure what Charles had said, be it his name or the simple word, but Hugh could not effort to respond, frozen in place as he was.

The door slammed shut behind Charles, and the sound was twice that of when he'd slammed it open. Hugh realized then, as his brain caught up with the last few moments, that Charles hadn't known Hugh was in here until after he'd entered. So he'd been angry before he'd arrived—and wasn't that the damned luckiest timing ever?

Charles stalked toward him, and Hugh straightened, as you did when a predator approached, in an attempt to make yourself seem bigger than you were, prepare for battle, puff up your wings, attempt bravery in countenance if not mind.

Don't move, don't move, he told his feet. *Stand your ground.*

Hugh wasn't sure whether he dared speak, then Charles stopped, just out of range of touch, but not out of range should he lunge at Hugh to, say, rip his throat out.

Hugh finally found his voice. "Charles, I—"

"I've never given you leave to call me that."

"Your Grace…" *Is that my voice?* Hugh cleared his throat.

"We were more *familiar* than that, now, weren't we?" Charles said with a sickening smile. The words stalked from him as he'd stalked Hugh moments ago.

God help me, I don't know where to go from here, Hugh thought.

"Jackson, I beg you—"

"Don't beg. It's unbecoming a gentleman, even one of your station."

Dear God, Charles was good at the cut. "Please, please let me—"

"I said, *no begging.*"

"I'm not—"

"Are you now attempting to make excuses? *I* am not interested in those either," Charles said.

"Jackson." Hugh cleared his throat again.

"I'm waiting," Charles said so very patiently it chilled Hugh straight through. Charles had waylaid every attempt he'd given to grovel, so Hugh wasn't sure where to go from here, but he stood his ground. Somehow, Hugh stood his ground.

Truth, simple truth, Hugh thought. *Then let the rest come as it may.*

He took a strengthening breath. "I was…am frightened." Seriously, this voice couldn't be his. He sounded weak, inept, lost to his own ears. "I accept everything you've to give me. I deserve it…and more."

"And what if I've nothing left to give?" Charles asked quietly.

Hugh trembled, because now he was truly scared. "I have no right to be here. I've no right to ask anything of you. I'd earned your trust. At least, I believed I'd earned it—" Hugh stopped and looked at him then, but Charles gave no indication of agreement, so Hugh continued. "I handled the situation badly, worse than badly. There are no words for what I've done. There are simply no words for it."

"I agree. So why are you here?"

"Because I have to try." Hugh looked up.

"It's a bit late, don't you think?"

"Yes, it is late in coming. I should have trusted you." Hugh closed his eyes and turned his head. Then he repeated himself, speaking more to himself than Charles. "I should have trusted."

Charles crossed his arms over his chest. "Here I was, operating under the belief that we were both working toward the same goal, a common goal. That whatever happened between us, between *all* of us, it was acceptable, and that no matter what that was, we would work together to make sure Amelia was safe, happy even. Here I was…*trusting* you."

"It wasn't misplaced," Hugh replied, knowing that's exactly what Charles was now thinking. "It wasn't. I swear it wasn't."

"How am I to believe you?" Charles asked quietly.

"I don't know. I understand that I've destroyed that trust. I also understand that I've destroyed what possibilities we had."

"I don't believe you do understand," Charles said. His hands came up slowly as if to prevent Hugh from startling, then Charles took the last step toward him and grabbed his lapels pulling him in close. Ever so slowly. "You have shattered everything we worked toward. Amelia is in some…some *state* I can't even describe to you. She's here but not. And when she is lucid, which is not often, she's in some sort of denial. She goes on as if nothing has happened. As if you are still with us. As if you did not abandon her without a single word. Like a child. Like she feels *nothing*."

"Jacks, I—"

Charles shook him, hard. "Stop, just stop. Why are you here?"

There it was. The one question Hugh had no answer to. It was so simple, yet he had no response. Hugh lifted his hands and placed them on Charles's shoulders. "Jacks…Charles—" He waited a moment, attempting to read the unreadable—Charles's expression. "I am truly sorry for hurting you."

"I'm not the one you should be apologizing to. You—"

"No, I will see to Amelia. I'll apologize to her as well, and I've no doubt it will be…much worse than this, if you can believe it. But right here, right now, I'm apologizing to you. You, Charles. I owe you a debt. I hurt you."

"That you hurt me implies that I cared enough to be hurt. That I was weak enough to allow for it," Charles said, a warning tone to his voice.

"That I hurt you merely implies that we were close. It does not imply weakness. In fact, I believe it implies a great strength to let another person into your heart."

"And when did we begin speaking of hearts? Don't be so damned maudlin. You assume too much."

"Yet you did trust me, and I damaged that, destroyed it possibly, though I hope one day—"

"Gaining my trust again won't be so simple next time," Charles replied.

Hugh paused at that, tightened his grip on Charles's shoulders, watched his eyes as they bored into him, straight through, as if they could see every bit that made him who he was. "Next time?" Hugh said the words quietly, almost timidly, terrified he would startle Charles into realizing he'd given him a toehold.

"Next time. Next time you attempt to gain my trust, it will not come so easy to you," Charles repeated, as he loosened his grip on Hugh. And, of course, that phrase had not been accidental.

"Are you saying the first time was easy?" Hugh asked hopefully.

Charles narrowed his eyes on him, and Hugh stiffened. *Too soon*, Hugh thought. Damn, and he'd almost survived the night. Hugh hoped Charles would tell Amelia he loved her after Charles killed him.

Hugh felt the tension in Charles's fingers return, ever so slightly, then slip away.

"I've no idea where to go from here," Charles said. "Your forgiveness, apparently, is a foregone conclusion in Amelia's mind. What you did…it was more between you and Amelia than you and I. I've no right to interfere in that."

"Charles, like I said before, I understand that I hurt Amelia, but my transgression didn't end there. I understand how difficult it was for you to trust in me, given your history. I am truly sorry for that."

"My only concern is for Amelia. As it has been," Charles replied.

"I understand that as well, but mine is for the both of you. It wasn't merely her that I hurt. I don't expect you to forgive me, but I do need to apologize." Hugh waited a moment then said, "I should go."

"What happens next?" Charles asked.

"I've no idea. After this…I'd only hoped to make amends. I've no doubt that you and Amelia will continue without me. She'll learn, I've no doubt of it. You're becoming more confident. She's trusted in you more. Not that I presume to take credit, but perhaps my leaving has helped in that regard, even a small amount—"

"I'm not so sure of that, since she isn't herself at the moment. You see, there's this disconnect, as though she's paused all emotion until…

until what, I don't know. Until you return? She just stops, and stares… and there's…nothing. It's beyond disconcerting. She and I haven't been alone together. I mean, Louisa isn't an intrusion…but she is."

"Is she in London as well?"

"Yes, she is, and my immediate concern is that her behavior will be discovered. I've no power over her yet, Hugh. Do you understand?"

Hugh understood. While Charles had every intention of taking her to wife, he wasn't yet in control of her future. If someone called attention to her, if her mother discovered the issue, or her father. Hugh thought certainly it wouldn't get to that point…certainly. Certainly, her mother would continue to protect her daughter from that possibility, from a future in Bedlam, or worse.

"I am sorry, Charles." This time the statement was met with a steely gaze and suffocating silence, and Hugh took that as an improvement. He was determined to repeat those words until Charles understood what he meant by them.

"Look, Hugh, I cannot pretend to be something I'm not. I've never had it in me to love, but what I feel for her is more than what I've ever felt for anything. I believe I love her. I don't understand it, but I wish to. While I should be thinking of my responsibility to the crown, I'm not. I'm thinking solely of my responsibility to her. I believe it has become quite painfully obvious that she may not be up to the task of duchess, and I don't rightly give a damn. When, exactly, this change occurred, I'm unaware. But it has, and I've yet to feel regretful. I will see to her, regardless of my station. If Her Royal Highness chooses to reprimand me somehow, so be it. I can care for myself. I'm not fully entailed."

The ensuing silence shimmered with possibility, and Hugh latched on to that possibility with both hands. "You would allow yourself to be ruined in the eyes of respectable society for her? In the eyes of the crown?" But Hugh's question went deeper than this, and he steeled himself for the response. He continued nearly without breath. "You would allow yourself to be ruined…for me?"

Charles paused, and Hugh knew then, and appreciated, that Charles wasn't taking this question lightly.

"I would…I thought that obvious already. Amelia means everything at this moment, and that includes you. Again, I don't know what that looks like, but somehow we will muddle through." Charles's gaze rose to Hugh's again. "I cannot do this alone. This, her condition, is entirely too much for one person. She needs both of us. At some point you're going to understand that fully. I just hope that understanding comes much sooner rather than later."

Charles realized in that moment, in the speaking of it, that the reason for his own anger wasn't that Hugh had left him, or Amelia. It was that Hugh belonged with them and refused to accept it. That Hugh cared for him, just as he cared for Hugh. Hugh spoke of forgiveness and apologies being tied to care, to love, but had yet to acknowledge that he cared for Charles. Hugh truly didn't understand that, even as he said the words. This realization took Charles a bit by surprise. As well, he understood in Hugh's question where his true fear was rooted, and the rest of Charles's anger fell away on the realization that Amelia had been correct.

"I forgive you."

Hugh's eyes widened somewhat.

"I forgive you for leaving. I forgive the decision. I forgive the moment. I do not yet forgive you for abandoning us, the three of us. Because I now understand what you did, but you do not understand why. When you do understand why, I'll forgive that as well."

Hugh didn't blink, and Charles waited. Hugh paled a bit, and Charles was afraid his words had knocked the breath from Hugh. Charles moved to shake him, but Hugh took a step back before speaking.

"No…I, please don't. You've given too much. It will just take a moment…or two."

Charles waited, and finally, Hugh said, "I never expected this much from you. I suppose part of me still believed you to be that stiff, immovable force of a man you grew up to be. I will give a great deal of consideration to what you've said, and I'll have an answer for your unposed question soon. I believe I should speak with Amelia first. Before we move forward."

Charles nodded, temporarily appeased, then Hugh continued on, a bit dazed. "Well, I want to thank you, for your time. I apologize for disturbing you this night. I promise to see Amelia as soon as possible. I've no doubt I would be turned away by her family, so it may take some maneuvering to get to her. Though I imagine Louisa would allow me to pass," Hugh said a bit distractedly.

Charles held his hand out, and Hugh took it, much like a drowning man, and perhaps he was, of a fashion. So Charles did what moments ago had been entirely inconceivable to him. He pulled Hugh toward him, wrapped his arms around him and lent him his strength.

TWENTY SEVEN

Amelia knelt in her spare room amidst the boxes of memories, attempting to imagine all of it gone. She supposed part of why she held on to so much was because she never truly believed she would have a future to look forward to. Some part of her had always believed Charles would find her lacking, or Hugh would move on with his life without her, and she would be left with nothing but her memories. She liked to have something tangible. With her mind always questioned, she loved that she had things she could touch that reminded her where she'd been.

However, now that her future was a possibility, she was having difficulty ridding herself of the pieces of her past.

It should have been so simple.

But what of Hugh?

What if he never returned? What if she never saw him again? What if she tossed away so many years of her memories with him, and then had nothing of him to remember—past or future?

What if what if what if?

She felt stuck in the moment. Unable to move forward, not wanting to look back.

Amelia…

She heard Hugh's voice in her head and twitched, the sound merely a precursor to an episode. The corners of her vision wavered, and she knew this would be a difficult night. She suddenly wished Louisa hadn't left her.

Amelia?

Her hands tightened on her skirts at her knees as she attempted to fend off the coming darkness. She wished her mind would stop calling her name. She should go to her room, wrap up in her counterpane, and try to calm herself, try to sleep.

"Hugh," she said to no one.

He left me.

…

That's not what I'm going to do.

Amelia closed her eyes and let the swirl pull her mind from the corners and into the dance. She was resigned to let it come, to allow it to sweep her away, off to the other place.

"Amelia."

She glanced to the doorway, where her mother looked down on her as she sat in the middle of the floor.

"Amelia, what are you doing down there? Where's Louisa? Supper will be soon. You should be getting ready."

"Mother, not tonight. I fear…I'm much too much exhausted," Amelia managed. She knew this was not going to end well.

"Amelia, you've returned to London. Castleberry has spoken with your father. There's nothing more to fear. You should be celebrating."

As if now that she was spoken for, her illness would simply disappear.

Amelia stood too quickly, and her hand shot out to the doorway to steady herself. "Mother, please." She couldn't be bothered at the moment. She didn't want to be concerned with the future at the moment, this moment, the moment she was in.

She could only hope to last long enough to make it to her room.

"Amelia Marie, you must come down to supper. Your father—"

"Mother…" She looked up, knew she was pleading with her eyes, knew she wasn't going to last long. The floor lurched, and Amelia held on to the doorway with both hands. "Mama—" Amelia watched as her mother's gaze shifted, and she paled.

A large shadow moved slowly across her, as though Helios's chariot was chased from the room, bringing night, and Amelia collapsed to the floor.

A

Hugh knocked at Pembroke Town House, hoping to be allowed entry. When the door opened, the butler's eyes widened, then shifted away and back again.

"Is she home?" Hugh asked.

Smythe paused, the hand at his side fidgeting in an unseemly manner. Hugh looked past him but saw no one else in the entry.

"Amelia. Is she home?" he asked again.

"Sir, I'm to turn you away, should you come," Smythe said quietly, but he didn't shut the door.

"Smythe, is Amelia well?" Hugh asked.

Smythe merely stared at him, his eyes pleading. Hugh looked past him again and concentrated on the sounds of the house. The scream, when it came, was much louder than it should have been, considering how far her room was from the entry.

"Send for Castleberry. Now, Smythe. Now!" Hugh yelled as he pushed past the butler and took the stairs three at a time, running for her rooms.

Hugh heard the gruff voice as he rounded the corner toward her suite. "That is it! This is the last time! I'll not be made a mockery of. She'll be taken to Bedlam. I'll not be ruined by this. You had your chance, woman. You failed." The strong, deep voice rang through the hallways toward him, and Hugh knew.

They had just run out of time.

A

The water swept over Amelia in a rush, cleansing her soul along with her body. She allowed the hands, all of the hands, to roam where they might—skimming, soothing, pushing, pulling. Her head snapped to the side, and she tried to push the hands away, the pulling shifting her off-balance.

Amelia.

Amelia flung her hands out at the clothesline as the sun sank—much too fast, entirely too fast, much faster than fast, as though it had been chased from the sky—beyond the cliffs.

One breath in, one breath out.

She looked down at the hands, so many hands, more than four to be sure—so many she simply couldn't count them. So many. She heard the fabric of her dress give, the popping of the stitches at the side, and she fisted it, held it together, as she attempted to scream.

Amelia.

She let go and turned, stumbled, thought she would fall, and she put her hands out before her to catch herself. When she looked down, she was alone. No hands, no bodies—save her own. She was alone, so very alone. The world darkened around her—funny, that, since she'd watched the sun set only moments ago, not so very long ago, but long enough ago that the world should have already been dark.

She closed her eyes and scrubbed her hands across her face.

Amelia.

What is this devilry?

Amelia dropped her hands—she stood in the dark, alone. She was surrounded by the boxes. Boxes upon boxes upon boxes. Boxes of memories reaching as high as she could see, in all colors…and they were beautiful, so very beautiful in their satins and brocades, tied with bright ribbons and bows. The one she wanted—the green brocade with the linens and the candle wax—it was all the way up at the top, and she began to climb. The stacks were impossibly high, and it took forever. She reached and reached, but the box grew farther and farther away. The towers got to be so tall that they started to tilt from the weight of her—closing in. She realized—too late—that they were coming down. Amelia fell back to the floor, crouched when she landed, then covered her head as she attempted a scream that never came, and the floor beneath her fell away as she dropped through.

Amelia?

She concentrated on the voice in the darkness. The voice she knew as well as she knew her own. Hugh. She felt her descent slow as the floor came to her chest, and she lay upon it, the solid reality embracing her. Hugh was here in this darkness with her, and she took a deep breath that truly felt like the first breath of civilization, the sky warming around her, the lids of her eyes turning orange and red and pink as she stared and tried to see him.

"Amelia mine?"

She opened her eyes to find Hugh lying on the floor before her, his hand holding hers between them. Why was he on the floor? That was terribly inappropriate of him. He shouldn't be on the floor…why… wait, what was she doing on the floor? She closed her eyes slowly, concentrating on the feel of his fingers on hers.

"One breath in, one breath out. That's all you need concern yourself with at the moment, Amelia. One breath in, one breath out. Amelia, I'm here. I'll not leave you," Hugh whispered.

She shook her head. But he *had* left her.

He left me.

That's not what I'm going to do.

Amelia stole another deep breath. "I need Charles, because, you did—you did leave me. You're not here. You cannot be here. I've finally lost my mind, haven't I? This is what it looks like. It could be worse, I suppose. I suppose I won't be alone now. Wherever I am, you'll be with me. I do wish Charles would be here with us as well. Wherever here is. I would feel ever so much better if Charles were here as well."

A great sob rent her as she realized she'd spoken aloud, and she suddenly had the fear that giving voice to the words would send his spirit away. "Please, please don't leave."

"Amelia." Hugh's voice was different. It seemed damaged, older, and she opened her eyes on him, gazed into those eyes that were so familiar to her. "Never. Again."

The moments that passed following those words seemed insurmountable.

"Charles will be here soon. Only give him a moment."

"You left me. Hugh, you…left me."

"I'm here now, Amelia. I'm here. There's no apology great enough for what I did. There are no words that would suffice, my darling Amelia. Would that I could take it all back…"

"You left." She searched his face. "Charles was there."

"He was, wasn't he? And it was glorious, was it not? He loves you, Amelia. He truly loves you. He can care for you. He can help you. He's more than the man I believed him to be, and he's yours, all yours."

"But I'm not all his. I never can be."

Her head spun.

He left me.

That's not what I'm going to do.

"You. *Left*. Me." She closed her eyes tightly, forcing the darkness away.

He left, Hugh left, he left me. He left me, and I was…I was gone. I fell down…down…down…and I haven't been back since.

Amelia realized she wasn't speaking as she reached out and curled her fingers into the top of his waistcoat. His hand skimmed the length of her arm, then cupped her elbow. What happened? Only moments before, she'd wanted Hugh with her. She'd mourned the loss of him. Only moments ago, he had been naught but the memories in the boxes that surrounded them now.

She opened her eyes. Not now. Now he was here, lying beside her amidst her memories of him. The true man, flesh and bone. "You're here."

"I am. I'll not leave you again. I promise you this. I'll never willingly leave you again. I'll come to you whenever you need me. I'll be with you no matter how difficult. I'll follow wherever you may go. I'll not abandon you. I promise you."

Never. Again. She took those words and let them repeat in her mind.

She closed her eyes again and took an inner stock of her physical form. She was sprawled on her belly, her legs tangled in her skirts. She couldn't begin to imagine what her mother might think of this. She stretched her legs, kicking her skirts loose and felt Hugh jump to his feet. He stepped over her, then reached beneath her body, rolling her into his arms and lifting her to his chest. She kept her eyes closed and simply felt.

The light shifted in the doorway, and she concentrated on the heat of Hugh, the strength of him, and her hands tangled in the fabric of his jacket as she held on tight.

"Charles." Hugh's voice rumbled through Charles and crept into her soul as the light dimmed further, and she felt the heat of another body beside her.

"Let me stand." Amelia felt her legs slip, as Hugh bent his knees and brought her feet to the floor. Then he held her as he straightened, and she felt Charles's hands on her shoulders behind her. She took a deep breath and looked up at Hugh, half of his face blocked from the light by Charles's shadow. She stood there, for a time, between them. Just allowing them to be. Then she let go and moved away from them, into the room.

"Look…this is my life, in all these boxes. This is the entirety of me, where all of my memories reside. I feared disposing of anything because I believed it was the only place in my life that you would reside in my future. I believed, only moments ago, that I would never see Hugh again."

"I—"

"No, no. *NO!*" Amelia screamed. She let loose her faculties, threw propriety to the wayside and filled her lungs with as much air as she possibly could as she railed. She took up one of the boxes, held it to her chest, then threw it across the room to shatter against the wall. "This, this is what I relegated myself to, without you. I was going to live forever in these boxes, amongst my memories. Forever bereft of human touch. I was gone, *GONE!* How could you? How? You always said you loved me!"

"I do love you, Amelia!" Hugh argued, and she picked up another box and threw it at him. He was showered with buttons as the top came off and the contents bounced off of his chest. "Amelia, I was frightened, so very—"

"You, Hubert Garrison, know nothing of fear. *NOTHING! Why?* Why did you leave me?"

"I was a coward. I am a coward. I couldn't see past my fear to what could be, what Charles would do…I…I'm truly sorry, Amelia. So very sorry. Please—"

"I don't know, Hugh, I—"

Hugh took a step toward her, and she put her hand up. "No!"

He stopped.

Charles spoke then, and Amelia turned, seemed to sway in his direction. "Amelia, you were right. About everything, about love, about forgiveness, about everything."

"What…what do you mean?" she asked.

"You were right." Charles walked toward her slowly. "When you care deeply for someone…you forgive them. As I have done."

She watched him carefully as he approached, and they stood there, within arm's reach, as she tried to figure out what he was on about. Who had he forgiven? He had forgiven her back at the Cliff House, but that wasn't—

"He forgave me, Amelia. Charles forgave *me*," Hugh said, and she looked to him. Hugh seemed to be considering something, looking from her to Charles. "We belong together. The three of us. We were created for each other." Hugh turned to Charles then, "I understand what you meant. I gave up. It wasn't about either of you. It was about me. I left because of my fear…and that wasn't fair to either of you."

Charles turned as Amelia watched. Part of her thought that he would shred Hugh now, and her brain tried its level best to understand how Charles and Hugh were in the same room and both breathing. It was impossible. Hugh said Charles had forgiven him. She stared at Charles then, watched his features. He wasn't angry—and she had seen him angry.

Charles looked…he looked…peaceful. He moved toward Hugh, and she felt her muscles relax, then tension flowed from her body like a cleansing. She felt clean. Charles took Hugh's shoulders, leaned in, waited for Hugh to meet his gaze. "I forgive you," Charles said.

Amelia felt those words like a corset. She couldn't breathe. She wrapped her arms around her middle, attempting to hold herself together as she watched them embrace, Hugh's tense hands on Charles's jacket as though they wrapped around her heart—and she felt it skip.

Charles straightened and looked at her, and she shivered. "Come, Amelia, there is no us without Hugh."

"What now?" she asked.

"There is no *us* without *you*," Charles repeated. "Come here."

She shook her head, then took two steps, coming up next to them. Hugh and Charles both reached for her.

"Please, wait," she said. She turned and brought her hand up to let it rest on Hugh's waistcoat, just below his cravat.

His cravat.

His very rumpled cravat. Ruined, really, this cravat.

There isn't even a semblance of a knot remaining—he should see to that.

She put her hand to it, pushed it back, tucked the edges into his waistcoat, then tucked her fingers into the top of his waistcoat and held on. His heart beat against her fingers, and she concentrated on the feel of it. Willed herself to stay here, now.

"You left me." Her voice was so quiet she almost didn't hear it herself. "I never thought you would do that to me, and in that belief, I found strength. You shattered the very foundation of who I believed myself to be. For better or worse? I've no idea. I understand that I need to find that strength in myself, but at times…at times, I simply can't, and at those times I always looked to you. I don't know why."

A realization came over her suddenly, instead of in stages, as though an idea simply hardened and crystallized in her mind without force. When before she'd believed that in the right situation she would be perfectly fine, she now realized…she never would be. This is who she was, for whatever that meant. Knowing this gave her strength. Knowing that she was to live this way forever gave her a certain power over whatever it was that did this to her. It was finally okay to be who she was. To not fear her reactions, to simply *be*, and to deal with whatever came.

Amelia lifted her other hand, tucked it into Charles's waistcoat, beneath a perfectly placed cravat—and of course it was. She smiled. These men couldn't change her. They couldn't heal whatever was wrong with her, but they were willing to stand by her side as she lived with it.

"You men. I'm blessed. Well and truly blessed. I understand I'll never change. There are certain things about me that simply are. You both continue to believe that I'll change, and to continue on that way may be our undoing. I will *never* change. I can't make excuses for myself hoping that neither of you see through me to the truth of it. This is me.

I will not change. I understand that now. Perhaps there's a place for me in this world, perhaps I belong somewhere where I can't hurt myself, or others."

"Amelia, you'll not be better off anywhere but with us," Charles said, and she looked up at him.

"Us?"

"Amelia, whatever the future holds, we will see to it, together," Charles replied.

She looked at Hugh, who smiled. "Hugh, you stand here next to Charles, alive and well. That surprises me a bit, even though I did ask that he not damage you."

Charles smiled, and Hugh laughed. "Yes, I'm alive and well and here, with you, the both of you, and it has never felt more right. Amelia, I believe you, but I also believe that there's better, there's more. I believe that you will be healthier when you feel safe. I believe these things with my whole heart. Will you change? No, not at your heart. You'll always be my Amelia, our Amelia, whatever comes our way."

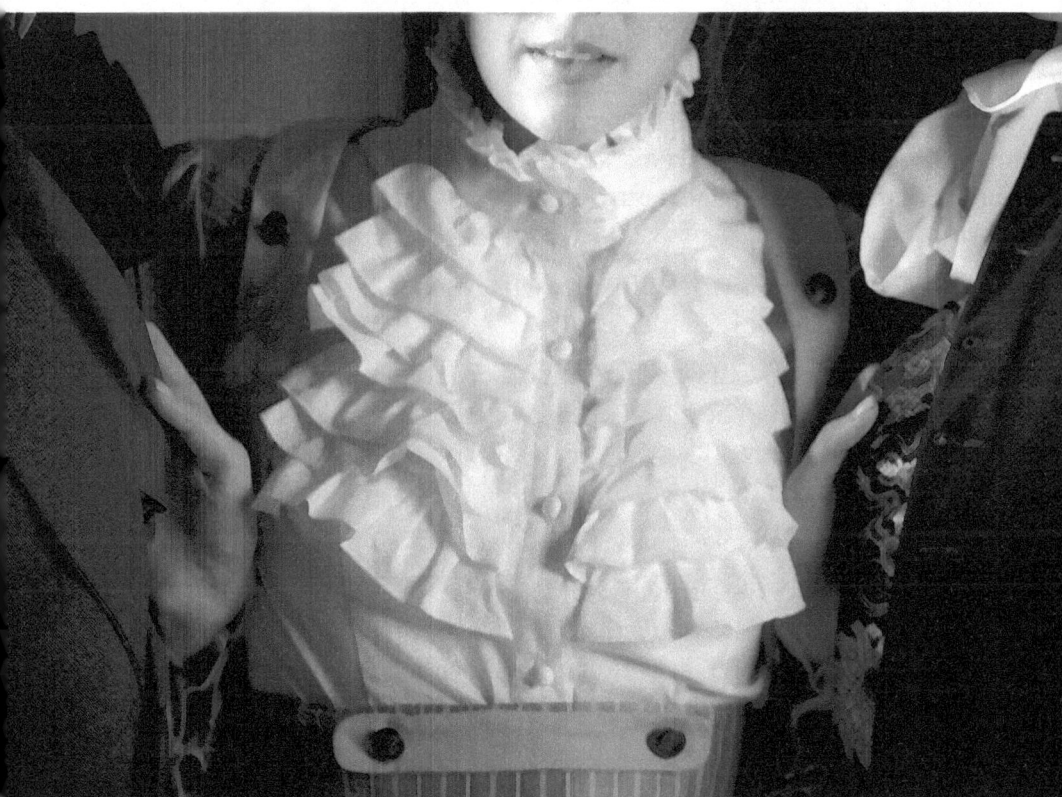

A

Charles put his hand over hers. He had to touch her, though he knew he couldn't do anything drastic, not yet. "Amelia, I…my mind is full of all the things that would need to be dealt with before we can marry. The how of it is at the foremost of my mind, of course, but then what follows…children, for one." He looked at Hugh then back to her. "Beds, for another. It just seems that everything, *every small thing*, must be taken into consideration in ways we'd never thought before. Previously, these were things that were simple. We marry and carry on, but now—" Charles stopped and looked at her.

"It's insurmountable," she whispered.

"No." This came from Hugh, but Charles shook his head in agreement immediately. "It's merely something to be dealt with. The most important thing is your marriage to Charles. Once that's done with, the *ton* will look the other way for a while, because you'll then be uninteresting. We only have to ensure their interest is not piqued again. Somehow. It will take some time. There are other factors that…well, we can deal with this later."

"I grow tired of being a slave to society. First for the protection of my family, now for the protection of Charles's position to the crown." She said it offhandedly. She hadn't thought it through before, as she did most things.

"My position with the crown is irrelevant. I'll give it all up and be done with it if need be," Charles said.

"That wasn't at all what I meant, Charles. I…you misunderstand. It was merely a wish to be left to ourselves, that if we didn't have this—" She released Charles and waved her hand about her head. "Please do not…not on my account."

She saw Hugh take Charles by the arm, give him a shake.

"I'm just not in the right mind at the moment," Charles replied, then he did reach for her, pulled her into his arms to soothe her, and himself. "I promise you, I'll not do anything without us all coming to an agreement first. I promise."

The memory of what had happened before her episode came back suddenly, as it always did, and she tensed. Hugh stepped closer when her hand tightened on his clothing. "My father?"

Hugh looked away, and Charles spoke as he set her back so she could see him. "When Smythe came for me, all I knew was that the need was dire. When I got here, you were already…on the floor. It was the most disturbing sight of my life. While Hugh attempted to get to you, your mother cowered and your father railed at Hugh. He was determined to have you taken away."

Charles fell silent, and Amelia considered his words, allowed them to sink into her. "He is not as weak as he pretends to be," Charles said.

"He is quite done with me," she whispered finally.

"Which is of little consequence, as you are no longer his concern. Amelia, we are to remove you to my town house immediately. Whatever happens from there is with his *outward* blessing." Ever concerned of the opinions of the *ton*, her father.

"And my mother?" she asked.

"She's chosen to remain with your father, as is her place. Her words, not mine," Charles answered quietly.

"What will they think?" she asked. "I shouldn't go to your house, not before we are wed. There will be talk."

"Their talk is irrelevant to me. We'll be married as soon as we have the license."

"And Hugh?"

Before he could answer, Louisa burst into the room.

"Oh, bless your heart, Amelia! What the devil happened?"

Charles and Hugh both swayed away from her instinctively.

"The servants are all in a bind. I could't find Lord Endsleigh or His Grace—and here you all are." Louisa threw her arms in the air in exasperation. "Apparently, I should have stayed in tonight. I'm so terribly sorry."

Amelia released her men and turned to sink into a warm hug from her maid. "Pack your bags Louisa."

TWENTY EIGHT

"My lord, if I may have a word."

Louisa stopped Hugh as he walked for the entry of Charles's town home. Amelia was finally settled, and Hugh was headed for his own town house and some much-needed sleep. They'd considered him staying, but he wasn't but a five-minute ride away. Close enough, being as the situation was precarious as it was. It would have to do.

"Is something wrong?" he asked.

"My lord, I wanted to speak with you about this predicament we find ourselves in," Louisa said.

"Which…predicament is that?" Hugh asked carefully.

"The predicament of you, living with them as a family…for lack of a better term. You can't possibly live with them at Castleberry and not raise some sort of suspicions. You do realize."

Hugh took her arm and led her into the parlor, away from any remaining servants. They walked to the settee, then he sat next to her, heavily. Hugh wasn't sure he was prepared for what she had to say. It would be the first of many *how inappropriate!* discussions to be had with the people who were closest to them.

"My lord, I may have a solution."

Hugh froze. This was unexpected. Louisa had always been a cunning sort, but this…

Hugh was willing to listen, however, and hope that she truly had a way to manage the mess they found themselves in.

"Go on," Hugh said.

In the end, Louisa saved them all, but watching Hugh marry another woman was the single-most-heartbreaking moment of Amelia's life. She held on to Charles's hand as though he were the only thing left in the world, and in some respects, he was. Hugh was standing before God and country—marrying another woman.

Hugh can't marry me. He simply cannot. He can't. It simply isn't a possibility in any fashion. This, this is for the best. Because he must marry. Hugh must marry.

Amelia hadn't expected it to hurt so very badly. She hadn't expected so many of the feelings she was having lately, but this…

When she truly considered what was happening—right before her very eyes—Amelia had to stop and force herself to breathe, because Hugh's one request was that she be here, that she sit behind Miss Rigsby and be present throughout the ceremony.

Hugh could have asked her to fly, and it would have been easier.

Charles's hand swept warm circles into her back, across her spine, helping her breathe. What Amelia wanted to do was scream. To fill the rafters of this church with the air from her lungs and frighten all the doves from the tower. Or perhaps curl into herself and disappear into the darkness for a while. Would that she could command it as such. Amelia closed her eyes, then opened them and watched. Breathed. Held on.

Hoped.

Amelia allowed the words to flow over her. So many words. Words to consider, fear, love, and look forward to upholding.

The officiant spoke of the purpose of marriage.

"First, it was ordained for the procreation of children."

No problem there. They intended to make children. For all of them, as many as was practical, as often as they wished. They'd decided that any of Amelia's children would be raised as Charles's heirs, as it should be. Then, of course, Maitland wanted children as well, and of course she did. And, of course, Hugh would need an heir. And, of course, they would see to that.

Of course they would.

Of course.

"Secondly, it was ordained for a remedy against sin, and to avoid fornication."

Well, this could get interesting.

"Thirdly, it was ordained for the mutual society, help, and comfort, that the one ought to have of the other, both in prosperity and adversity."

Yes, they all needed each other. They all intended to support each other. They all purposed themselves with being the strength for one another, whenever one was needful. They would be a society unto themselves. Amelia knew in her bones that she was the most needful of them all. She felt somewhat guilty about that, regardless that none of them ever gave her cause to—she did.

Amelia watched as Hugh looked to Maitland, who smiled up at him. Practically beamed. The joy in her eyes was nearly blinding, and

Amelia's heart kicked its revolt. *It has nothing to do with him,* Amelia told herself. Yet it did have *something* to do with him. Hugh saved Maitland, after all.

But Maitland saved us all. Remember that. Maitland and Louisa saved us all.

"Wilt thou have this woman to thy wedded wife, to live together after God's ordinance in the holy estate of matrimony? Wilt thou love her, comfort her, honor and keep her in sickness and in health; and, forsaking all other, keep thee only unto her, so long as ye both shall live?"

Hugh said, "I will." Then he looked to Amelia, held her gaze, and spoke to her very soul. "I will," Hugh repeated, his voice deeper, thicker, somehow heavier as it settled across her senses like a warm, soothing, blanket. Amelia felt her breath stop then, and Charles raised Amelia's hand to his lips, placing a kiss upon her knuckles, which were white with tension.

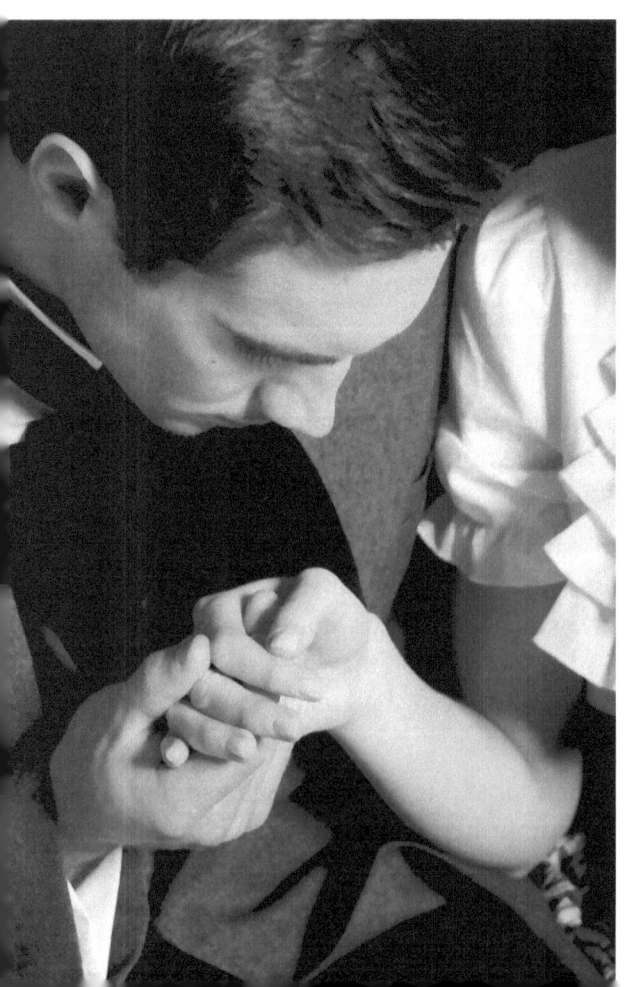

Amelia tried to loosen her fingers to no avail, and Charles swept his hand across them, back and forth, until she felt the blood rush her digits, the stinging numbness slow to recede.

"Wilt thou have this man to thy wedded husband, to live together after God's ordinance in the holy estate of matrimony? Wilt thou obey him, and serve him, love, honor, and keep him in sickness and in health; and, forsaking all other, keep thee only unto him, so long as ye both shall live?"

Amelia didn't realize she was nodding until she felt Charles's hand steady her. He pulled her closer, tilting her chin up so he could place a kiss on her cheek. Amelia opened her eyes and looked back toward the ceremony as Maitland closed her eyes and said, "I will."

In that moment, Hugh turned to Amelia, expectant, and Amelia's cheeks were wet with tears as she said those very same words to him, *sotto voce*. "*I will.*"

Then it was time for Hugh to repeat the officiant's words: "With this ring I thee wed, with my body I thee worship, and with all my worldly goods I thee endow. In the name of the Father, and of the Son, and of the Holy Ghost. Amen." Amelia watched as Hugh closed his eyes, knew he spoke to all of them, knew he was pledging himself to their care and safety.

The rest of the ceremony fluttered by in words like heartbeats.

Pledge, declare.

Safety.

Protection.

Gracious and fruitful.

Consecrate.

Loving.

Cherishing.

Faithful and obedient.

Peace.

Husbands, love your wives.

Husbands.

Wives.

Husbands.

Wives.

The phrase rolled in her head like stones in a tumbler, slowly polishing to a perfect shine.

Husbands, love your wives.

Amelia was quite certain they had not meant it, the way it sounded to her. She smiled.

A

"Louisa, you're no longer my lady's maid. Please stop, sit, have some tea with me," Amelia said as she listened to Louisa fidget in the other room with the dresses in her wardrobe.

"Well, your new girl has packed your summer dresses in with the winter, instead of moving the winter dresses to the other wardrobe! You'll be a…a… fright of wrinkles," Louisa said in her typical worry pitch, her voice carrying from Amelia's bedroom.

"Louisa, she's young, she's lovely, and who's to know if I'm a bit wrinkled anyhow?" Amelia said with a giggle.

Louisa stepped through the doorway, her hands fisted on her hips, head cocked to the side.

Amelia sobered, but only for a moment.

"Oh, dear Amelia, have you annoyed my Louisa?" Maitland came through the entry to Amelia's sitting room with a tray of tea and small cakes.

"I'm sorry, yes, I have," Amelia said. "You'll need to calm her nerves a bit, I'm afraid. She's much too concerned of the wrinkles in my wardrobe at the moment, wrinkles not a soul will see."

"*I* will see them!" Louisa screeched as Maitland took her hand and pulled her into the sitting room.

"Look now, I brought some biscuits and tea cakes. Come sit with me," Maitland said quietly as she turned to Amelia. "She's concerned for us, but has no way to put that to words, so the wrinkles will take the brunt of her consternation. For now, however, my Louisa, tea."

Louisa's face instantly softened, and she allowed herself to be led. Amelia smiled and squeezed her arms about her waist, watching Louisa and Maitland together.

Maitland's quiet meekness and reason were the perfect balance to Louisa's sometimes overwrought concern, and Amelia had never seen Louisa relax as much as she had since they'd all removed to Castleberry Keep.

Relax.

Perhaps relax wasn't quite the proper word.

Calm? Perhaps that was better.

No…she wasn't calm. In fact, her stress seemed higher, or possibly lower, or perhaps there was a different balance?

Amelia thought about Louisa's behavior over the past weeks.

Amelia, Charles and Hugh, and Louisa and Maitland as well, all went day-by-day, figuring out who of the house staff could truly be trusted and who needed to be pensioned or removed to another property. Charles was adamant they find positions for each of the staff who could not remain at the Keep, and she felt blessed that the majority of the staff was to remain with them, though they were still a bit shy of the full staff required of such a grand property.

They all still tiptoed a bit in the house, wary for the time being, but they were all quite concerned about the future. And to ensure they'd survive a lifetime together, they were happy to be overly cautious for the time being.

Amelia saw the same thing with Louisa. She wasn't more relaxed. It was merely that the periods between her being high-strung and—*whatever it should be called*—were further between. In fact…she looked at Louisa sitting next to Maitland, cozy and…calm.

Yes, calm. She was calm.

While at her parents, Louisa had been ever wary. So it was better, it truly was. It was merely that the difference between a calm Louisa and an overwrought Louisa was much more defined.

Amelia smiled at having figured this out. She considered the past few weeks again. She and Charles had been married, officially, as soon as they'd returned to Castleberry Keep with the help of another license from the archbishop, and this time Louisa and Maitland were both in attendance, standing for her as Hugh stood for Charles. The ceremony had taken on more meaning than anyone else present knew.

Of course, her mother was annoyed that someone so new to her had stood with her—*You have only just met this Maitland girl!*—and her maid—*her maid!* It was simply unheard of. But Amelia had insisted. Even her father had been there, something she'd not truly expected. Charles held her father's secret closely. He decided knowing her father wasn't quite the invalid he had always professed would come in handy at some point, say, when they needed another ally.

Amelia was still settling into her suite of rooms, adjoining Charles's and across the hall from Hugh's. As for Hugh, his rooms were next to Maitland's, of course, and Louisa happily set up her things in a nursery adjoining Maitland's room.

Charles had started renovations in a closed wing of the Keep. He said he had some master plan for the older section at the back of the main castle. He wouldn't share his plans, insisted it was all to be a surprise. Charles had also secured the town home in London adjacent to his. Amelia thought anyone would believe this odd, but Charles insisted, "*They wouldn't, because there was nothing to be concerned of.*" Or, alternately—when he was of a mood—that he simply, "*Did not give a damn for their opinions.*"

Charles was truly seeing to everything he said he would. Straightforward, one step at a time, with great care and regard or, at times, simply will and want. The caution they held helped Amelia, because she was frightened to be with them again.

The fact was, they hadn't yet had a wedding night. The last time they were all together…well. As well, she had yet to be with Hugh, which tore at her heart a little. She avoided contemplation for the most part, and Charles and Hugh accepted her distance as her need to be familiar with her surroundings, to recover from the chaos, to settle into her new life—

"What a beautiful sight."

Amelia's skin tightened, and she turned to see Charles standing in the doorway to her sitting room. "Three lovely ladies enjoying an afternoon tea."

Amelia felt heat suffuse her skin and rush her face, and she closed her eyes to steady her racing heart. Just because in her mind she was being careful did not mean her body had agreed to follow suit.

Amelia lifted one hand and steadied when he caught it, drawing it to his lips as he lowered himself next to her on the settee. After a time of nothing but feeling his hands on her, his lips on her, his body crowding her, she opened her eyes to take in the sight of Charles—just in time to see him lean toward her, his hand wrapping around her neck and drawing her mouth toward his.

Amelia stood suddenly, her gaze sweeping the room, and Charles followed. "They took their leave…something about knitting," Charles said.

The pretense of knitting was becoming all too much. At some point, they would need to buy some yarn and needles. *Certainly.*

Amelia shook her head and turned back toward him, but he was closer than she'd thought. Charles pressed along her side. Every bit of her length, from the floor to her shoulder, was in contact with a bit of him. When she turned, she bumped straight into his chest. His large, warm, solid chest. One she'd seen naked. Touched naked. Felt rub against her as he…she nearly choked.

"Amelia, we've been waiting…" Charles let the words drift away as his hand came up, his thumb softly caressing her chin. She closed her eyes and nodded as he turned her toward him, framing her face in his palms.

"As have I. I realize…oh, I do realize. But then I think of Hugh and what he—"

"I know you're frightened," Charles said.

It was lovely to hear the words of her mind spoken by someone else. It was pure magic that she no longer had to explain herself. To anyone. She simply was, and that in itself was the greatest gift of all.

Amelia caught Charles's gaze then, wrapped her hands around his wrists and squeezed. "Please believe my hesitation has naught to do with you, or with Hugh even. Merely that the situation itself—"

"I understand, Amelia, I do. One man and one woman, so simple, and look what we've done. You couldn't even take something as simple as marriage. You had to even turn that on its ear."

Amelia shuddered, and his hands slid around her, holding her face to his, their foreheads resting together. He was close, so close, so very, *very* close. He whispered until she felt his breath across her skin, and it settled her nerves.

"I also understand how difficult it is for you to simply live, without considering, deconstructing, investigating, and piecing every little thing that happens. I just want for you to know"—his thumbs smoothed across her eyebrows in unison—"that when you're ready—"

I'm ready I'm ready I'm ready, she thought as he placed a kiss at the edge of her mouth.

"When you have at last pieced this one final thing"—Charles drew back until she could see into his eyes—"I'm here for you. Until then…would you like to go for a ride? I thought perhaps we could head to the Cliff House for a day."

Wait…what?

Charles let go and took one hand as if to lead her away.

Charles's bright smile caught her off guard and released the bobbin of tension that was winding through her heart. She wanted to be with Charles again, and with Hugh—she truly did. She wanted to make love with Hugh as she had Charles. But all the silly details…Charles had said it best. He understood, as did Hugh. It was in that understanding that she found a measure of peace and perhaps a place to momentarily hide.

"Come, let's be off," Charles said. "I left Hugh a note to meet us there when he returns from his manor."

TWENTY NINE

Amelia hung the sheet on the line, per the ritual. The first thing she did when she arrived at the Cliff House was the laundry. Regardless of whether it needed to be done or not. Charles had gone into the house. He said he was going to straighten a bit, make some tea. Charles knew she needed a little time to herself, to reconcile how she felt. She hadn't been back to the Cliff House since Hugh had left them here. Left her here.

Hugh left me.

She tried to shake the thought off.

Hugh left me.

That's not what I'm going to.

Her hands released the sheet on the line, then as she reached for a dry sheet to wash, she shuddered. She felt the vibration keenly, through her fingers, up her arms, down her spine—all the way to her toes.

One breath in.

One breath out.

That's all you need concern yourself with.

One breath in.

One breath out.

Amelia pulled the sheet to herself and inhaled the salt tang of the sea as her muscles tightened. The skin of her fingers paled as they clenched on the fabric. This place had always been her haven, but at the moment all she felt was the cavern of her chest, her heart lost inside, because Hugh had abandoned her here.

Maybe she was wrong to think this a good idea. Maybe it was too soon. Perhaps she would never be able to return here and not feel this. What if…what if she'd been robbed of all her memories of this place because of one day? One day, and one night, without him.

Amelia pushed her face into the loose fabric and wiped away the tears. She didn't want Charles to worry, and while he knew how to help her, the episodes still made him quite nervous. She took the corners of the sheet and flung it out before her to release the wrinkles. The fabric sailed to the ground, and she smiled—just a little. She snapped it back up, then snapped it in midair, but it didn't float to the ground this time.

"Hugh."

He caught the opposite edge and held it. "Amelia."

"You're here?"

"Of course I'm here. I—" Hugh's face fell a little, and she was taken momentarily guilty by the words. "I'm here," he said finally.

"I'm glad of it," she returned. "I've missed you terribly."

"We've all been quite busy, as of late," Hugh said.

"Yes. We have…" Amelia froze, trying to effort her mouth to speak the words her heart held. "Why is the world so different out here? Out here—" She stopped herself. "I was frightened. I never thought we'd be the same."

"I had that same fear, Amelia, after what I did."

"I thought perhaps that my feelings about the Cliff House would change as well." She watched as his hands tightened, then Hugh started to draw her toward him, his fingers wrapping up in the linen of the sheet.

"And?" he asked.

She allowed him to pull her. "And what?"

"Have your feelings changed?" Hugh took another fistful of fabric.

"I…am unsure, only that I realize just how strong they are."

"I've been looking forward to seeing you again, for quite some time. Oh my love, my love—" Hugh's voice was low, gritty.

It caused a ping of electricity to shoot her spine, and she felt the small hairs on the back of her neck stand at attention. "I—" Well. She'd thought she'd more to say than that.

Hugh narrowed the gap between them.

This sheet is entirely too large, she thought, but then he yanked, and she fell, and he caught her up mid-stride, his hands holding her ribs as his mouth came down on hers so very hot and wanting.

Hugh lifted, and she wrapped her legs around him. It was like coming home, and she finally breathed. No…no, she didn't merely breathe. This was the first breath after a long absence of pure air. It was the first step after being released from a prison. It was the first drop of rain after a drought.

"I have hungered for you, Amelia. I've been desolate without your touch. I need your love, Amelia. I need you. Touch me, please, feel how I tremble inside, for you. Oh God, Amelia, I need for you to touch me."

"Hugh," was all she could manage as she put her hands to his chest and tore at his clothing, sending the buttons flying in all directions. She sank her hands in, around him, and held on.

"I need you, Amelia. I'm so sorry for my betrayal. You're everything to me. Forgive me. I love you."

"Yes. Yes." She felt his arms wrap around her like a vice and welcomed it. Then he moved, swiftly, toward the Cliff House.

"Charles!" Hugh yelled, but it wasn't concerned. It was a greeting.

Amelia couldn't be bothered to care. Hugh was here. He was here with her, and she wanted nothing more than to have him inside her, finally. The last piece to the puzzle. She could not get close enough to him. She held on to Hugh, the last vestiges of her sadness evaporating as he stormed toward the Cliff House.

She could hear him whispering in her ear, surely attempting to soothe her. It wasn't working. She could feel a void, deep and insistent, and she needed it filled. By Hugh. They rushed through the entry and straight for the far wall, without so much as a pause.

She felt the hard surface of the wall against her back as he pressed her up against it, his hands roaming, and Amelia set to her task of getting this man naked. More buttons—gone. Cravat—gone. Jacket…stuck.

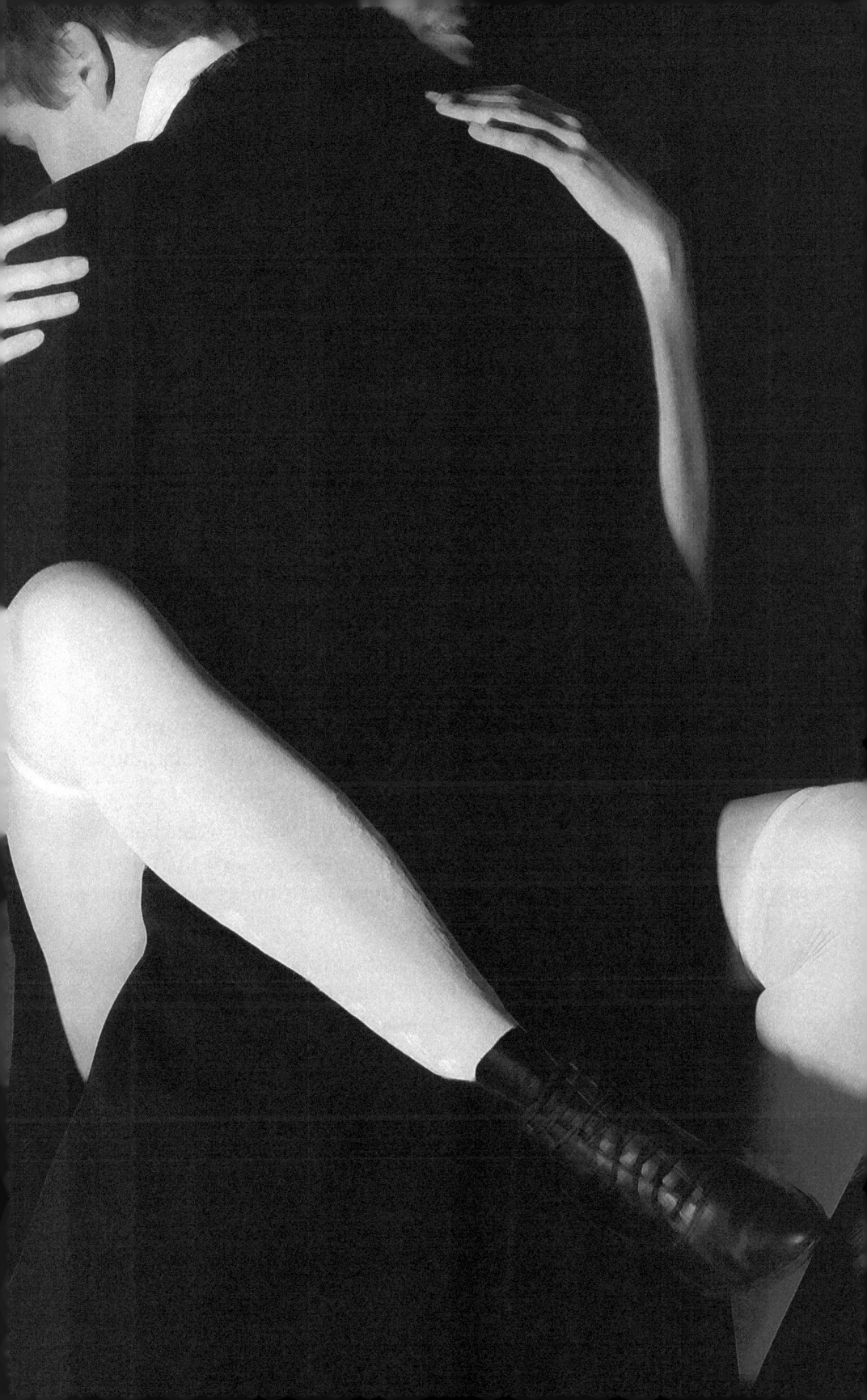

"Amelia, pull it back on. Just leave it. I need to be able to touch you. I need...I need to kiss you. I need so much." Hugh's arms, stuck as they were at his sides, still held her waist, balancing her as he pressed her against the wall, doing exactly what he said he'd wanted to do, parting her lips with his own, and with more of a demand than a request, he sucked her tongue into his mouth and proceeded to undo the fall of his trousers.

Amelia wrapped her legs about his waist again as he shifted her skirts. She felt his hands test her, and she was wet. She'd felt it before he had. He thrust into her, and she broke away from him, her head falling back against the wood panels of the wall.

"OhGodOhGodOhGod!" she screamed as she held on to his shoulders for dear life. This felt like a reclamation.

"Oh my love, my love, my love. Amelia," Hugh breathed against her chest.

She felt the wall shudder and shake behind her, the glasses neatly sorted on a shelf next to her shoulder vibrating closer to the edge, and certain disaster, with each thrust.

Her tension from the impending crash heightened her sensitivity, and as her arm flew out to push the glasses back, her passion broke, and she cleared the shelf with the jerks and shudders of her climax.

Hugh followed quickly, leaning into her, the weight of his body pinning her to the wall, holding her there. His arms steadied them for a moment, then he flattened his hands on the wood panels behind her. Just breathing of her.

A few minutes of heavy breathing and reassuring words later, he moved his hands beneath her thighs. Hugh looked up at her, and his face seemed to open, alight on her gaze. "Amelia, you're...*with* me," Hugh said.

A slow smile broke across her face, and she wrapped her arms around his neck. "Of course I am, Hugh. I'm right here with you, just as it should be."

Hugh looked down at the mess of broken glass about their feet and tightened her legs about his waist, then held on to her and straightened. He pushed the shards about with the toes of his boots as he turned and walked carefully to the center of the room.

"Well, hello to you as well," Charles said.

Amelia flushed, and Hugh blanched as they swung toward him as one.

"Hello," she said.

Charles came over and hugged Hugh with one arm and drew her into a kiss with the other, wrapping it around her waist.

"I apologize for being a fly on the wall, but you gave me little warning," Charles said with a smile.

"No, I don't suppose we did," Amelia replied.

Hugh laughed. "I, uh…" He placed Amelia carefully on her feet, adjusting her skirts. She watched as Hugh tucked himself away, buttoned his trousers and turned with a grin. "Apologies. That must have felt awkward for you," Hugh said, a question in his voice.

"Surprisingly, no," Charles replied. "Though perhaps a bit of jealousy, excitement and a touch of arousal may have crossed my mind… and my trousers."

Amelia was shocked by his words as she gazed on him, her hands reaching. Reaching. She was more than happy to help him with that.

EPILOGUE

Five years later...

Amelia waited nervously on the bank of the pond, Tristan cuddled in her lap and Andrew by her side on the bench. She remembered the day she and Charles had first come here, their first outing. In some respects, it seemed only yesterday. While in others, it was so very long ago.

Not far away, Louisa and Maitland were chasing Kathryn, Gabriel, and Alice along the banks. The children's laughter never failed in calming her nerves, even as she worried about what *could* happen. Amelia had been working with, in her estimation, a brilliant psychologist by the name of Clarke. He'd helped her so very much in the past few years, and her attacks, as they'd decided to call them, because that was how she felt at the time, had lessened for the most part. She still did have them. She still very much needed Hugh and Charles to help her at times, but for the most part she felt so much more whole than she ever had. As well, Dr. Clarke had helped to rid her of most of the need to collect things, which was an incredible relief to her.

Amelia took a few deep breaths to rest her mind—*the children are perfectly safe*—then looked back to the water. *Has it been too long? Should someone see to them? It seems that it has been entirely too*—a whoosh of water and splashing stopped her internal maundering, and she stood, Andrew taking her skirts with his little fists and holding on. Tristan snuggled deeper against her chest as though nothing had happened.

"I am the champion!" Charles yelled.

Amelia smiled, watching as her men splashed as they moved toward her. She could hardly believe they'd found the thing.

"I call foul!" Hugh shouted in disagreement.

"You may have spotted the blasted thing, but I did the actual rescuing of it," Charles said.

"You never would have if I hadn't seen it, as covered in muck as it was," Hugh replied.

"Ah, yes, Hugh you always were better at locating frogs than I was!" Charles shoved him playfully, and Hugh launched back, the both of them disappearing momentarily in the waist-deep water before erupting once again.

"Now you've gone and lost it once more. Well done," Charles grumbled as he turned in the water, searching the bottom of the pond at his feet.

Hugh dove in, then launched from the surface with a great shout. "Now *I* am champion!"

Not for long, however, because Charles deftly tackled him back to the water.

This is going to take awhile, Amelia thought. She sat back on the bench and curled her fingers through Andrew's curly hair as he wrapped his arm around her leg, through her skirts, then stuck a thumb in his mouth, watching as his fathers tossed about in the water.

"Aren't they silly, Andrew?"

"Papa," he replied, pointing at the tussle before them.

"Yes. Papa," she replied with a smile.

He looked up at her then and smiled back as he popped his thumb in his mouth again.

"Mama," he said quietly.

The word tugged so hard, her heart knocked in her rib cage in revolt. He was such an incredibly dear boy. Amelia leaned over and kissed his forehead.

"Yes, my sweetling, I'm your mama."

He giggled in response, then turned to the shouting and playing that grew suddenly louder. Tristan stirred against her breast, his little mouth opening and closing like a fish against her blouse, searching, and she knew they were running out of time.

"Charles…Hugh…I must be returning home!" she shouted, hoping they would hear her over the ruckus they created. Good thing this had been an early trip to the park. Certainly they would have gathered crowds at this point with the melee.

"Charles?"

He stopped and turned to her, and his face lit up. Then Charles ran as best he could through the water toward her, water splaying from his careening body like the wings of a bird.

Charles fell to one knee in the grass at her feet, his hands raised before him, a soggy, moss-covered lump of…something across his palms. She watched it carefully as though it may flop, proving he had not, in fact, found her reticule but possibly a rather perturbed fish.

"My lady," Charles said with all the knightly bearing he could pull from his soggy boots.

"My prize was stolen!" Hugh yelled as he approached, falling to his knees beside Charles, his hands crossed over his heart. "My lady, don't believe a word he says, as it was I who found your misplaced reticule, not this thieving brute!"

Charles laughed and elbowed Hugh in the ribs, causing him to flop over to the grass from a mock wound.

Hugh let out a great roar of defeat, and Andrew let go of Amelia's knee and threw himself on top of Hugh—obviously today's true champion.

Amelia laughed then turned back to Charles, who raised his palms higher and ducked his head in deference.

"I beg your pardon," Amelia started, "but *that* cannot be *my* reticule. My reticule was quite lovely, and cheerful and intricately beaded. Pink, in fact. My reticule would catch the light and toss it about like so many ice crystals dancing on a lake. This…thing you have here is quite obviously"—she thought hard for a moment—"green, for one. As well, it's slimy. More like a toad than a reticule." She poked it with one finger, and Charles looked at it.

Charles flicked a few strands of moss from the side, then attempted to polish it on his sleeve. It didn't work very well, leaving a green streak up his sleeve as he laughed. "It simply needs a bit of…cleaning. The handle could use a bit of polish and some, er, fresher water."

"Perhaps…though I think it may need a bit *more* than that," Amelia said.

Charles perked up, his smile returning. "Actually, if it weren't for the large silver handle, we wouldn't have found it. So have I pleasured my lady?" he asked.

"Pleasure?" Hugh said suddenly from the grass next to them, where he had Andrew rolling in a fit of giggles.

Amelia knew her cheeks pinked. Hugh stood and tossed Andrew in the air. "Did someone say pleasure?" he boomed. "This is certainly something I would happily search the muck for." He grinned at her, putting the laughing, wiggling boy under his arm. "Again, and again, and again." Hugh very nearly growled the words.

Charles stood and held his hand out to pull her to her feet. She shifted Tristan to her other arm, and he shook the water off his cleaner hand, then skimmed it across Tristan's tiny bald head. "He's going to need to nurse soon," she said quietly.

Charles nodded and waved to his men, who jumped to the carriage, driving it closer to them then cleaning up the picnic rugs and leavings from their dinner. Charles lifted his hand and looked at the reticule, and Hugh's gaze followed, as did Amelia's. They stood there for a moment, contemplating the now-twice-offending bag.

"It's going to start to smell bad," Hugh said.

"Don't be sore because I brought the prize to our princess," Charles replied.

Amelia had to laugh at that. She looked at the reticule she'd spent years wishing she still had—if only to help her remember the moment she'd lost it—and she realized that it wasn't the reticule that she wanted to keep close to her heart. She looked at the men, who stared at her bag. She no longer had need of so many things when she had so much love.

"Actually," Amelia said with a sniff, "I believe it already might smell." She looked at Charles apologetically. "I believe, St. George, that we should return this dragon to the depths from whence it came."

"Truly?" Charles asked.

"Yes, truly. I believe our dragon would be much happier if left to its natural habitat."

Charles shrugged then turned. He tossed the bag in his palm once, to measure its…current buoyancy, then drew his arm back, took a step and let the reticule take flight…right back to the spot where they'd so recently discovered it.

"Well done, sir," Hugh said with a broad grin.

Charles turned to Amelia and gave her his cheek. "I believe I've earned a kiss from my lady?" he said, pointing to his cheek.

Amelia took his chin with her free hand and lifted up on her toes, being careful not to touch any part of his wet self. She sniffed his cheek, then brought her lips to his ear. "Perhaps…after a bath."

THE *end*

"And what is the use of a book,"
thought Alice,
"without pictures or conversations?"

Alice's Adventures in Wonderland
-Lewis Carroll

find me:

If you loved this book you can join my newsletter to be notified of releases before they come out, and to participate in fun giveaways.

JennLeBlanc.com
@JennLeBlanc
IllustratedRomance.com
Facebook.com/IllustratedRomance